Princes in Exile

by

Richard Denning

Princes in Exile
Written by Richard Denning
Copyright 2013 Richard Denning.
First Published 2013.
ISBN: 978–0–9568103–8–0
Published by Mercia Books

A catalogue record for this book is available from the British Library

Book Jacket design and layout by Cathy Helms
www.avalongraphics.org

Copy-editing and proofreading by Jo Field.

Author website:
www.richarddenning.co.uk
Publisher website:
www.merciabooks.co.uk

**In fond memory of my grandfather
Louis Henry Smalley**

'Turn your wishing into working and gain what you will..'

The Author

Richard Denning was born in Ilkeston in Derbyshire and lives in Sutton Coldfield in the West Midlands, where he works as a General Practitioner.

He is married and has two children. He has always been fascinated by historical settings as well as horror and fantasy. Other than writing, his main interests are games of all types. He is the designer of a board game based on the Great Fire of London.

Author website:
http://www.richarddenning.co.uk

Also by the author

Northern Crown Series
(Historical fiction)
1.The Amber Treasure
2.Child of Loki
3. Princes in Exile

Hourglass Institute Series
(Young Adult Science Fiction)
1.Tomorrow's Guardian
2. Yesterday's Treasures

The Praesidium Series
(Historical Fantasy)
The Last Seal

The Nine Worlds Series
(Children's Historical Fantasy)
1.Shield Maiden

Northern Britain 603 A.D.

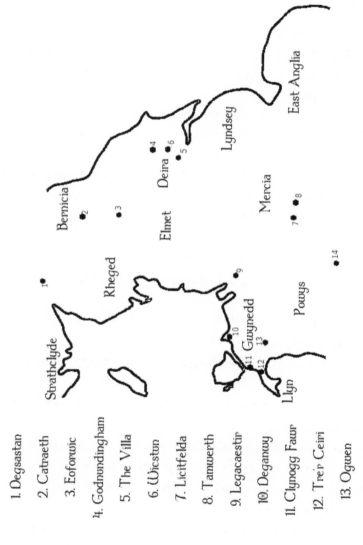

East Anglia

Lyndsey

Bernicia

Deira

Mercia

Elmet

Rheged

Strathclyde

Gwynedd

Powys

Llyn

1. Degsastan
2. Catraeth
3. Eoforwic
4. Godnundingham
5. The Villa
6. Wicstun
7. Licitfelda
8. Tamworth
9. Legacaestir
10. Deganwy
11. Clynogg Fawr
12. Tre'r Ceiri
13. Oguen
14. Augustine's Oak

Names of nations, cities and towns

Here is a glossary of the main locations referred to in Princes in Exile and what they are called today.

Augustine's Oak – Possibly the village of Rock near Kidderminster.

Bernicia – Anglo-Saxon kingdom in Northumbria.

'The Villa'/'The Village' – Cerdic's home at Cerdham - modern Holme-on-Spalding-Moor.

Catraeth – Catterick.

Clynnog Fawr – Village of the same name in Llyn.

Dál-Riata – Kingdom of the Irish Scots from Ulster in what is now Kintyre, Argyle and Butte.

Deganwy – Ancient hill fort in the modern town of the same name near Conwy and Llandudno.

Degsastan – Battlefield in 603. Uncertain location. Possibly Dawstone in Liddesdale.

Deira – Anglo-Saxon kingdom north of the Humber.

Din Eidyn – Ancient capital of Manau Goddodin - modern Edinburgh.

Dunadd – Ancient capital of Dál-Riata. A hill fort near Kilmartin, Argyll and Butte.

Elmet – Welsh/British kingdom around the modern day city of Leeds.

Godnundingham – Site of Deiran Royal Palace. Possibly modern day Pocklington.

Gwynedd – Ancient Kingdom of North Wales, covering what is today the counties of Conwy, Denbighshire, Flintshire, Gwynedd and the Isle of Anglesey and possible parts of Cheshire

Legacaestir – Chester

Manau Goddodin – Welsh/British kingdom around what is

now Edinburgh.

Ogwen – Valley in southern Gwynedd – in this book location of a hunting lodge.

Powys - Ancient Kingdom of Central-East Wales, covering what is today the modern county of Powys but also at times Shropshire and Cheshire and Flintshire.

Rheged – Welsh/British kingdom in what is now Cumbria.

Tamwerth – Capital of Mercia, modern day Tamworth

Tre'r Ceiri – Iron age hill fort near Nefyn, Llyn.

Wicstun – Market Weighton.

List of named characters
* Denotes historical figure

Acha* – Sister of Edwin and Princess of Deira.

Aedann – Once Cerdic's family slave but now his companion.

Áedán mac Gabráin* – King of the Dál-Riata Scots.

Aelle* – Former King of Deira.

Aethelberht* – King of Kent, Bretwalda

Aethelfrith* – King of Bernicia.

Aethelric* – Late King of Deira.

Aidith – Cerdic's wife.

Aneirin* – Welsh Bard and Poet

Augustine* – The first Archbishop of Canterbury

Bartholomew – One of Augustine's priests.

Bebba* – Queen of Bernicia and first wife of Aethelfrith.

Belyn (of Llyn)* – advisor and steward to Iago. Has lands in Llyn.

Cadfan* – Son of Iago, Prince of Gwynedd

Cadwallon* – Grandson to Iago, Cadfan's son.

Cenred – Father to Cerdic. Lord of Wicstun and Earl of the

Southern Marches.

Coerl* – Lord in Mercia and one day king

Cerdic – Main character, Lord of the Villa and son of Cenred.

Cuthbert – childhood friend of Cerdic.

Cuthwine – Cerdic's older brother, died in 597, also the name Cerdic gives his own son.

Edwin* – Younger son of Aelle.

Eduard – Childhood friend of Cerdic.

Felnius – Captain of the Scots.

Frithwulf – Son of Guthred.

Garrett – King of the Llynii

Grettir – Cerdic's family retainer.

Guthred – Lord of Bursea to the south of The Villa.

Gwen – Aedann's mother.

Harald – Earl of Eoforwic.

Hereric* – Son of Aethelric, Grandson of Aelle.

Hussa – Cerdic's half-brother.

Iago* – King of Gwynedd

Lilla – Bard and friend of Cerdic's family.

Mildrith – Cerdic's younger sister.

Osric* – Son of Aelle's younger brother.

Pybba* – King in Mercia

Rhun* – Bishop of Gwynedd and Powys, one time King of Rheged.

Sabert – Earl of the Eastern Marches.

Taliesen* – Welsh Bard and Poet

Chapter One
Which Path to Follow?

The flames of our campfire danced higher, the flickering light illuminating the ruined old Roman temple we were sheltering in. Then they died back and as the light retreated the night's shadows crept once more into the corners of the ancient place. It seemed to me at that moment as if the encroaching darkness mirrored the gloom in our hearts.

"Enough!" Edwin barked out and in a sign of his frustration he threw a branch into the fire. Embers, sparks and ash flew skywards.

"Enough running!" he continued, "Let us return this very summer and attack Aethelfrith!" In the firelight his eyes glittered with a sudden passion. Around him the twenty warriors of our little band were silent, wary to speak out in front of the young eighteen-year-old prince, the sole remaining son of the great King Aelle, who had ruled our land, Deira, for fifty years and carved out a nation for our people. Yet Edwin's older brother, Aethelric, had proved a weak successor to Aelle and had lost Deira to the Bernician king Aethelfrith, just two weeks before. Edwin and Hereric, his nephew, had been forced to flee with a handful of warriors including me, as well as the women folk and children from the village where I, Cerdic, was once thegn. We made a pitiful, vagabond force and were certainly far too weak to face the might of Aethelfrith, who could summon a thousand and more spears to his banner.

"We at least should go back and find my cousin, Osric." Edwin persisted. He had felt this way on the night Deira had fallen and Osric had been captured, but we had persuaded him then of the futility of facing the Bernician king with our tiny force. I thought he had seen reason at that moment. Since then we had plodded on into Mercia, hiding in hills and forests and avoiding settlements where possible for fear that the inhabitants might report our passage to Hussa, my treacherous half-brother and Aethelfrith's lieutenant, who we all feared was close behind us on the road and who, when we fled my village, I had fought and almost killed. Yet he had survived and I knew he would not give up the hunt. To say we hated one another does not say it strongly enough, and yet it is complicated. Were it not, I would have killed him years ago when I had the opportunity.

Each day took our little band deeper into foreign lands and further from our homes and a possible confrontation with Aethelfrith. As the days passed Edwin grew more irritable and more frustrated so that now, almost nightly in fact, the prince returned to his original idea of confronting Aethelfrith.

"We have been through this before, Edwin," Hereric retorted. He was also a prince: the son of the late King Aethelric, and usually dull-witted and less able than his uncle Edwin. Yet right now his arguments made sense. Mind you, I suppose that is an advantage of having a limited imagination: Hereric simply latched on to one idea and repeated it whenever Edwin raised the subject, as now. "We cannot do this alone. We do not have enough men."

Edwin glared at him, "If we can surprise him and kill him, then maybe the Witan and the people will support us. Surely Acha would not abandon us?"

Sabert, Earl of the Moors and Wolds, was shaking his head. The oldest member of the company, he had once advised Aethelric and also – for many years – Aelle before him. Earl

Sabert sometimes had little patience for young men's ideas – a fact I knew full well from the time when he and my seventeen-year-old self had argued bitterly. But I was twenty-three now, a man full-grown with a wife and son of my own. Sabert and I had long since become friends and allies. Indeed, he was the one man present whose wisdom I trusted above all others.

"Why are you shaking your head Sabert?" Edwin snapped irritably.

"Your sister will choose her own son's future over that of you and Prince Hereric," the grey-haired Earl replied. "And besides which, if Aethelfrith dies, Eanfrith would take over his father's throne and would have the support of the Bernician lords and their huscarls. No, we cannot go back now. Not yet."

He was right on both counts. Acha was Edwin's sister and Hereric's aunt, but had married Aethelfrith in the days when our nations were friends. Indeed, it was not that long ago and it had seemed to us all at the time that our brother English lands were coming together. Yet if we were brothers then one brother had betrayed the other. For Aethelfrith had turned on us, killed Aethelric and forced Edwin and Hereric to flee. Now the two lands were but one nation ruled by Aethelfrith and his Queen. Not long ago Acha had produced a son, Oswald, and Hereric was right – his aunt would do anything to ensure her child sat on the throne of a united Northumbria. As for Eanfrith, he was Aethelfrith's son, the sole child from his first marriage to Bebba, who had died some years before of the plague. I remembered with sadness that the same plague had also killed my father and almost lost me my wife and son. Thank the gods they had survived. I glanced across to the side of the temple where, snuggled up inside my cloak and now fast asleep, my boy, four-year-old Cuthwine, was lying beside the remains of a stone pillar. Close by the lad, my wife Aidith was warming her hands over another, smaller fire then helping Mildrith, my sister, to hang fish over the flames. She saw me looking and smiled at me. Returning to her work her smile faded and I saw fatigue replace it. She was tired. We all were. Small wonder for we had been running from the pursuit we feared was close behind us for two weeks now and we were all very dirty and exhausted.

My beautiful Aidith was the daughter of one of the villagers, yet although her father had been neither thegn nor earl, she had taken to the role of my wife and become mistress of our little valley with ease, as if authority were her birth right. Alas, when our home, the Villa, had gone up in smoke, her world had turned upside down. She had never really been part of this world of kings and princes that we now inhabited – this other part of my life that had sometimes taken me away from home. Now here she was, fleeing from one king in the company of all that was left of Deira's royal line and it was obvious she was not taking well to the change in our circumstances. I could not blame her. Seeing her exhaustion I knew we could not run forever, but what could we do?

"What we need is an ally!" I exclaimed. I had not realised, until I saw heads turn to look at me, that I had spoken the thought out loud. I shrugged and repeated, "We need an ally, Highnesses. A friendly king who will support your claim."

"I agree with Earl Cerdic," a gruff voice spoke. I glanced at its owner in surprise. This was Guthred, Lord of estates that lay to the south of my own. He had harboured a grudge against me ever since I prevented his son's marriage to Mildrith in favour of my childhood companion, Cuthbert, whom she loved. I glanced across at her and saw that Cuthbert had now joined her by the pillar and was grinning, holding up a brace of pigeons

4

he had shot. Cuth, as we called him, was the best archer in our company. All his arrows had been lost in the fight against Hussa at the Villa, but he had managed to acquire a dozen more from a village we passed through a couple of days ago and our cook pots had benefitted from his skills these last few nights.

I turned back to Guthred, who must have seen me looking at Mildrith and Cuthbert because his face now grew dark as he regarded the cause of his humiliation. I spoke swiftly to distract him. "You agree with *me*?" I asked in disbelief.

"Yes... on this occasion," Guthred said, with another sour look at Cuthbert. "We cannot fight alone. If Prince Edwin is to reclaim the throne in Deira we need a sponsor, someone who will provide troops and support."

"Well yes, but who?" Edwin asked, picking up another branch and this time poking the fire with it.

"The obvious choice is Kent. Let us seek aid from the Bretwalda."

I shook my head in disagreement. "Kent is a long way from here and a long way from Northumbria as well. Why should Aethelberht of Kent concern himself with affairs north of the Humber when he is master south of it?"

"Perhaps he would be master of all - a true Bretwalda mayhap? Or maybe he would fear Aethelfrith challenging for it?"

He had a point. Bretwalda - Lord of Britain - was the title that was given to the king who held the greatest authority over the English kingdoms. Other kingdoms, though self-ruling, granted the Bretwalda respect and would be swayed to follow his policies. For years it was Kent - the first and oldest Saxon kingdom - and its king who held that power. Yet up till now it had not much concerned us Angles north of the river Humber. We had our own troubles - our own struggles for power to contend with. Now though, we were south of the Humber and Aethelfrith, now the master north of it, was surely a threat to the power of any king in the land, even the Bretwalda. Maybe Guthred was right and we should seek Aethelberht's aid.

Sabert, was looking at me and shaking his head again. "We need to seek more local aid, and from those who have more immediate reasons to fear Aethelfrith," he said. "As Cerdic says, Aethelberht is too far away and we cannot go on as we are for much longer."

"Who then?" Edwin asked, nodding his thanks to Aidith who was handing him a hunk of bread and a piece of fish. She came round and gave me my portion and I hungrily wolfed it down, thankful for it. Food was scarce and we had eaten little for two days. Today we had managed to buy some bread in a village we passed as well as catch a half dozen eels in a river not far from the temple.

After only a few mouthfuls of the fish I began to feel a little stronger, but as Aidith turned away I noticed how weak she looked. Had she been starving herself to give me food? I pulled her back and gave her the remains of my portion of bread and she took it without much resistance. I knew then that Sabert was right – we could not go on much longer scavenging an existence in this way. We needed shelter, but where?

"Mercia is the answer,' Sabert answered my unspoken question. 'I am acquainted with one of the king's earls and his kin – Ceorl is his name. He is a cunning man who would need a reason to help us, but I think I might be able to give him one. The present king's court is at Tamwerth, barely two days from here—"

"You mean King Pybba?" interrupted Lilla. The bard was cleaning mud out of his little bone flute. "I have met Ceorl, he is a decent fellow, but I am less sure of Pybba." Lilla had fallen over in a stream earlier in the day, as had I, but whilst I was still caked in mud he, as always, looked clean and tidy with only his flute the worse for wear. How did the man manage to always look so good? I supposed it was all part of his act.

"Why are you unsure of Pybba?" I asked him.

Lilla sniffed. "He did not like my singing last time I was there."

Edwin turned and looked at me, his expression quizzical. "Well, Cerdic. What do you think?" There was an edge of challenge in his voice. Was I being tested?

It still took some getting used to, the prince asking my opinion. It was not long ago that he had dismissed me, insulting me by saying I was nothing more than a farmer, but since then we had fought together side by side at Degsastan and Godnundingham and reached something of an accommodation. Not only that, but I had got him and his nephew away from Deira unscathed. Then again, the princes had precisely three lords left – myself, Sabert and Guthred – to ask for an opinion. Sabert was the more senior, but I realised it was not yet clear in whom these young princes would put their trust. Guthred had been a member of the Witan almost as long as he had been a thegn and had his own opinions, which often conflicted with my own and Sabert's.

"Well, Cerdic?" Guthred chimed.

There was no disguising the taunt in his voice. I was experienced in war, but not in statecraft and politics. I knew little of affairs south of the Humber and he knew it. 'Stick to your sword and axe, boy,' is what he was implying, 'and leave politics to those of us with more winters behind us.'

Ignoring his tone, I replied, "I would agree with Sabert." I knew it sounded weak even as I said it. There was a snort of derision from Frithwulf, Guthred's son – the one who would have married my sister Millie were it not for my cancelling the betrothal my father had arranged before he died. Needless to say, there was no love lost between us.

"Lapdog!" Frithwulf whispered, loud enough for only me and his father to hear. Guthred smiled at the insult. 'Sabert's loyal lapdog,' is what they were calling me. My hand went instinctively to Catraeth, the old Roman short sword I had carried since I took it off the first man I ever killed when defending my village against raiders from Elmet. I had killed a lot more since then!

I shook my head and got up from the log I was sitting on. He was not worth the fight and in any event we could not afford bloodshed amongst us. We were so few I could not pick a battle with one of only twenty-five men the princes had at their disposal.

"With your permission, Highnesses, I will check the guard," I muttered and moved away towards the entrance of the temple. Aedann and Eduard were standing there, looking out into the darkness. As I walked across to them Cuthbert joined us. The half-light of the moon illuminated the empty hillside upon which the temple stood, as well as the dense woods all around.

"You are going to have to deal with those two before long," Cuthbert grunted, tilting his head towards the fires. I looked at him sharply and then laughed. My keen-eyed friend did not miss much.

"Causing you trouble are they, mate?" Eduard asked. "Want me to sort young Frithwulf out for you?" He offered this in an ominous tone, gripping his axe tightly and tensing his bulging arm muscles. I shook my head and with a sigh, Eduard slid his axe back into his belt.

"No my friend," I smiled. "We can't afford to squabble. He still holds a grudge and I can understand that, but he and his father chose to come with us when they could have stayed behind or turned us over to Hussa. They are loyal to Aelle's line and however much we don't get on we must co-operate if we are to get the princes home one day. Trouble is, we don't know how to go about achieving that."

I glanced at Aedann, my other companion. The dark–haired Welshman was watching the edge of the woods and did not seem interested in the discussion. I patted him on the shoulder and walked back across the temple, past the fires to the rear door. This was narrower – probably the priest's personal entrance. Maybe his own house had once stood nearby. I passed through the doorway. Out here the hillside dropped down into a marsh. The woods on either side petered out into scrub and bush and then faded away entirely. A stream meandered through the meadow between the woods, which as a result was boggy and marshy, but was penetrated by a faint track running across a patch of dry ground. We had scouted it briefly earlier. It would take us further south and west, so we had decided that was the way we would go in the morning.

Leaning on a spear near the rear entrance, the grizzled old veteran Grettir was studying me in silence. I frowned at him.

"So, you have been listening to the discussion too have you? Do you have something to say, Grettir? Something I am missing?"

Grettir had been a warrior since before I was born. He had stood back-to-back with my uncle on the battlefield and seen him killed. Later he had trained me and my friends, as well as fighting beside us at Catraeth. I trusted his wisdom in war just as I did that of Sabert in statecraft.

9

He gazed at me, "It is not my place to comment on the discussions of lords and princes, my lord."

"Ah, so you *do* have something to say. Go on then: do you know about Kent and Mercia?"

He shook his head. "Not much and still less about kings and courts, my lord, but I know about armies. Armies need hope and we have little. They need to believe that their lords have a plan and we have none. Our army may be tiny, but it will not be long before there is no army left if the men lose heart."

I stared at him, knowing he was right. "Then we must decide tonight what to do," I said, turning back to the fire.

I sat down and looked around at the others. "For my part, I say we go to Tamwerth. Not just because Sabert said it," I added with a sharp glance at Guthred, "but because it is common sense. We are starving and have no land, no crown, little money and no plan. Tamwerth is close and I say try there."

Edwin opened his mouth to speak, but before he could Aedann was kneeling between us. "My apologies Highness – but come quickly Cerdic, Cuth thinks he has seen something in the woods."

I got up and moved hastily to the doorway, Edwin on my heels. "What is it Cuth?" I asked.

Sharp-eyed, Cuthbert was a natural scout and he was studying the dark shapes of the trees down the hillside. "Something is moving down there, Cerdic, I am sure of it."

There was silence as everyone strained his eyes to pick out any detail, but I could see nothing unusual. "Check the south door," I instructed Aedann.

He nodded and scuttled away, past the main fire to the other side of the temple where the small door led out of the rear of the structure. For a moment he scanned the woods on that side and then turned to shake his head at me.

Above us, through the caved-in roof, I could see the moon on its descent towards the horizon. We had not stopped our march today until just after nightfall when we had found the abandoned temple. It was now the middle of the night and there were still a few hours before dawn. I was tired so maybe Cuthbert was too. He had been out hunting for several hours on his own after all.

"Cuth... I don't see anything. Are you sure?"

He spun round to face me, his eyes wide. I thought he was angry and about to strike me, but instead he seized me by the shoulder and tugged me over to one side. We fell in a heap at the top of the slope. Above me an arrow sped through the space I had occupied only moments before.

"Thanks," I gasped, breathing heavily. I lifted my head to look. "Where did it come from?"

Another arrow zipped past my head and I ducked again.

"There!" he pointed to a large oak tree. At its base I could now see a smaller shadow, it was an archer loading his bow.

"Come on!" I shouted, pulling Cuth up the hill behind me.

A moment later there was a shout at the bottom of the hill and glancing back I could make out other shadows joining the first. A dozen now. No – more than that. There could be two dozen maybe. The shadows moved forward and broke into the moonlight and I could make them out now. Around twenty warriors, fully armed and armoured, emerging from the woods and coming up the hill towards us, sword and axe blades glittering silver in their hands.

We had reached the doorway. Eduard pulled us back inside even as he was tugging his own axe from his belt and reaching for his shield from where it was propped against the wall to the side of the door. Then he turned and bellowed out a warning to

11

the rest of the company.

"To arms! To arms! We are under attack!"

"Is it Aethelfrith?" Edwin asked as he peered around the doorway. Another arrow leapt out of the darkness toward us and smashed into the lintel above our heads.

"Highness, get inside the temple!" I shouted. Edwin looked reluctant, but I turned to glare at him and he moved away. Grettir, who had come running over from the rear door, thrust my shield at me and then moved past me to block the doorway. With a clatter of wood, Eduard locked shields with him, the two of them standing side by side. Now more men had joined us at the entrance. I glanced towards the rear door and saw that Aedann was dragging others into formation over there, including Frithwulf. Over at the cook fire, Mildrith and Aidith were herding the village children and women folk into whatever shelter they could find amongst the rubble of the temple interior. Cuthwine tried to scamper past them to join me, his little wooden sword in his hand, but Aidith latched onto his tunic and with a squeak of protest he was tugged back into the relative safety afforded by the pillars.

At the main fire, Edwin and Hereric were buckling on swords and finding their helmets. The younger prince started towards the door but Lilla and Sabert were now with him – telling him to stay out of harm's way.

I returned my attention to the front and chanced a glance over Eduard's shoulder. There was enough light from the moon and our fire to distinguish about thirty men at the base of the hill. They were forming up into a shield wall, spears held in readiness. Behind them, still half hidden by the trees, was a figure on horseback. He shouted out an order and the shield wall began rolling up the hill towards us.

12

An arrow sped downhill towards them, caught one man in the shoulder and he fell back into the bushes. Above me, having found a way up to the ruined roof, Cuthbert gave a shout of triumph and notched another arrow. A couple of sling shots were fired back at him in answer, but Cuthbert was moving into cover behind an intact part of the roof and the missiles ricocheted harmlessly off the stonework. My friend grinned down at me and then moved to pass across above the lintel to another gap in the roof. As he did there was a sudden crack and Cuthbert gave a cry of alarm as the lintel and a chunk of roof teetered sideways. Chips of stone rained down upon us and I moved my hand to cover my head realising I was not wearing my helmet. I held my breath, half expecting the entire structure to come tumbling down upon us. Yet, after a few moments, Cuthbert managed to manoeuvre himself away from the unstable part of the roof and had soon found a more solid section off to my left.

There was a tap on my shoulder. It was Aidith thrusting my helmet at me with an expression on her face a little like my mother used to wear if I went out in the sun without a tunic on when I was just a young lad. "Thank you lass," I smiled. "Now get you back in cover. Where is Cuthwine?" I asked then relaxed as I saw my little boy holding Millie's hand over near the fire, his expression both excited and frightened at the same time. What was he now? Going on five years? He was still holding the little wooden sword I had carved for him. I sighed, thinking about how the plots and arguments of kings had dragged my son and indeed my whole family into the fury and horror of war. I wished I could protect him – indeed I wished I could protect them all from this.

"Cerdic here they come!" Eduard shouted.

Pushing my thoughts behind me I turned my attention back

to the imminent battle.

Chapter Two
Moonlight Battle

As the warband passed from under the trees and out into the moonlight we could make out more details. I saw chain shirts, sharp spear points reflecting the moon's glow with flashes of silver, great axes and long swords. Above them a banner flew but I could not make out the design.

"Maybe they are Mercians and think we are bandits?" Eduard suggested.

I grunted – he had a point. Just because Aethelfrith might want us dead did not mean these men had to be Bernician.

"Hello!" I shouted, "Are you from King Pybba? Are you from Tamwerth?"

They did not answer. The warband had not halted and still plodded up the hillside towards us. I tried again, cupping my hands around my mouth and bellowing the words.

"We are not bandits! We are Deiran. Are you Mercian? Can we talk to you?"

A pair of arrows shot out of the gloom and buried themselves in Eduard's shield.

"That would be a no then!" Eduard grunted.

I nodded then gasped. The arrows were evidence enough of this band's warlike intent, but I now spotted the horseman who had ridden out from the shadows under the trees. He turned his head to look up at us and seemed to be searching the hilltop. Then his eyes flashed, catching the moonlight as they found the doorway and I recognised Hussa, my bastard half-brother, traitor to Deira. He had once allied with the British against his homeland and then later betrayed us to the Bernicians – an action which had led directly to the fall of the kingdom and our flight into exile.

Hussa had a grudge against my family due to the fact that he was the product of a liaison between my father and a woman from a nearby village. When my mother had found out, she had forced my father to abandon the woman. At our most recent meeting Hussa had taken his revenge on my mother by sealing her in the burning Villa, destroying her in her own home – the home where he had been denied welcome. Now he was the trusted lieutenant to Aethelfrith and it was clear the Bernician king had set him on our trail.

His gaze lingered on me for a moment and my hand drifted to the pommel of my longsword, 'Wreccan', our Saxon word for revenge. I had named it so when Hussa and I had been fighting, for it was revenge I wanted so badly to have on him. Then he was gone, back into the trees where I could now spot more men forming up further back.

"It's the Bernicians all right," I said. "It's Hussa and he has found us. We need to get away." But the shield wall was now barely ten paces away and we could not run, only fight.

"Spears at the ready," I shouted, "close up the wall!"

The men drew closer together, each taking as much shelter behind the shields as they could. Spears now thrust forward towards the doorway. We were four ranks deep and three men across, a sold mass of shields and spears blocking the doorway. We were so few against the gods knew how many. I risked a final glance towards the rear door where Aedann had our other twelve men formed up. Frithwulf and Guthred had joined him

16

and were looking out into the night. My friend shook his head at me indicating that there were still no Bernicians out that way.

In front of us the enemy shield wall parted and a bald-headed man with bare arms, no armour but one huge axe, moved out towards us. He spat towards the company, roared, "Fight me cowards! Will any of you scum come and fight me?" Then he spat at us again.

"Cerdic, let me go gut the bastard," Eduard growled.

"No! That is what he wants us to do. We can't risk opening the shield wall."

The bald man turned round, bent over, bared his backside at us and then swung back to face us. Guffawing, he shook his axe towards Eduard, "Come on you fat bastard, come and try me!"

"Cerdic!" Eduard pleaded, goaded beyond reason.

"Don't be a fool lad," Grettir said. "Don't let him trick you into his game. They know that to force a way through this entrance will be suicide. They don't want to risk it."

Grettir's words were like a bucket of cold water in the morning: a wakeup call. He was right. This attack would be costly for them. Men don't want to die like that. For glory maybe, in some great battle of kings and heroes when the bards will remember you in their tales and your descendants will retell them for a hundred years and more. But dying in some gods-forsaken ruin, chasing down fewer than two score vagabonds and two runt-like princes, well there was no glory there. So, if they didn't want to die here, didn't want to attack us, what did they want? Why were they here?

Unless...

"Woden's buttocks!" I swore and pushing my way back through the men, ran across to the rear door.

17

Seeing my urgency, Edwin joined me, "What is it?"

"It's a trick, my prince. They are keeping us occupied," I answered as I peered out into the night. I rubbed my face as I tried to puzzle out Hussa's plan.

"Why?"

I did not answer but kept on studying the woods and scrub. Maybe I was wrong. Maybe the Bernicians were just foolhardy. Then I saw him: Hussa, on foot now, leading his horse and close behind him twenty more spearmen. They were creeping along, trying not to make a sound but slowly and inevitably they were moving towards the open ground beyond which lay the marsh with the single path across it. They were moving to cut off our escape route. My brother might be a traitor, but he was as cunning as a fox and he had almost outsmarted us. A few minutes more and he would have us trapped like chicken in a coop. Then the fox would strike.

"Get the villagers and the princes out, Aedann. Now!" I hissed. The Welshman looked at me vaguely, clearly not understanding what I was telling him.

"Look!" I gestured towards Hussa and Aedann's eyes widened. Then he nodded and a moment later was marshalling his half of the company to lead the way out of the rear gateway and down the slope.

"What is it? Are you mad – dividing our force like this?" Guthred shouted as he saw what was going on.

I glared at him. "We are almost surrounded. We must leave now. You must get the princes through the marsh and I will bring the rest."

Guthred hesitated. "I don't know... are we not safer in here?"

"Safe as a sheep in a meadow surrounded by wolves maybe,"

18

Lilla said, looking out of the gateway. "Cerdic's right, we have to leave." The bard hurried over to where Aidith and Mildrith huddled with the other villagers. In a trice he had them scooping up our meagre belongings and bustling along after Aedann like so many frightened chickens. I saw Aidith look back at me in confusion and then Cuthwine, still holding his sword but half asleep and bewildered, staggering along in her wake. I wished I could go to them, but I could not. I had to trust their safety to Lilla and Aedann. With a terrible ache in my heart I wrenched myself away. A few steps brought me back to Eduard and Grettir and the other men. The bald axeman was still dancing in front of them, alternatively insulting them and cavorting – his backside laid bare to us.

I smiled. This gave me an idea. I whispered to Eduard and he grinned at me. "Count to ninety, then do it, understood?" I said.

The big man nodded and I left him and climbed up to Cuthbert. My little friend was still perched in the roof cavity, arrow notched on the string as he watched the display below. "He's just out of range, Cerdic, or I'd have him."

"I know, but save your arrows and come with me," I told him and then climbed across to the decaying roof above the doorway.

"Careful Cerdic, the roof is unstable just there."

"Yes, I know... watch."

From our vantage point we could look down through the hole where the roof had once collapsed inwards and see the temple interior and also out onto the hillside. Below us the Bernician was still gesturing to Eduard and then waggling his arse at him. "Here it is..." he was shouting, "you know you want it. Come and get it!"

Without warning, Eduard stepped through the archway. "Very well arsehole. Here I am: fight me if you want," he roared.

His opponent saw Eduard's huge frame clearly for the first time. He seemed to hesitate and then took a step back "What is the problem? Full of words but got no balls?" Eduard jeered. Behind him the Wicstun lads laughed and cheered.

"Oh, I've got balls. But I am going to cut yours off!" the Bernician replied, moving forward up the slope, swinging his axe back and forth.

Eduard stood stock still, his own axe and shield at the ready.

I waited until the bald man was a few feet away and then shouted, "Now Eduard!" At the same time I leaned my shoulder against the unstable section of wall and roof above the doorway. "Cuth help me – push!" I panted. He moved to help me and together we heaved.

After a moment the stonework gave a great splintering sound and toppled away from us. Below us Eduard leapt to the side and his opponent moved to follow. Then one of his companions shouted a warning and the brute looked up. His face barely had a chance to register shock and surprise before half a ton of stone and masonry smashed him into the ground.

Beyond the bloody remains of their champion, the Bernician company were silent, stunned by the brutal suddenness of his death. Before they could react I raised my sword and shouted, "Wicstun Company, attack!"

With a roar Eduard and the dozen warriors at the door, led by Grettir and carrying our wolf banner, hurtled down the slope. Cuthbert let fly two arrows in rapid succession, each finding the throat of an enemy. I jumped down to the ground, pulled the dead man's great axe out from under the rubble and ran after my men. Fleetingly I wondered how many more arrows Cuth had left. No time to worry about that now.

A moment later we were on them. Grettir smashed his shield boss into the face of one youth and then impaled another with his spear. Eduard jumped into the gap this caused and I joined him. We hacked about us, sword and axe cutting through bone and flesh. Sixty heartbeats before and thirty warriors had stood in formation full of confidence from their superiority in numbers. Now five were dead and we – using height advantage – were attacking with a fury that only desperation can grant. In the end we were still outnumbered and a determined leader should have been able to defeat us. But the leader was dead and Hussa was on the other side of the temple. These men were not expecting a fight this night. They were expecting that, surrounded, we would surrender. They had reckoned on taking whatever loot we carried and then enjoying the women that accompanied us. Certainly they had not expected to die here. We had no choice and nothing to lose – it was kill or be killed – but they, seeing their numbers rapidly diminishing and given the choice of fighting or fleeing, dropped their weapons, spun round and fled into the woods.

I was not surprised, but my men jeered after them and then turned to cheer Eduard and me. "Come quickly," I shouted. "Five of you, loot the dead. We need gold and food. Bring their armour and weapons. The rest come with me – you too Cuth!"

I led the men through the temple to the rear exit.

"Damn!" I swore when I saw that Aedann had been too late. Hussa had brought his other twenty men across to the path through the swamp and now he had them formed up, shields and spears ready, blocking the pathway. Our dozen warriors were also in tight formation, with the women and children and the princes behind. I saw Aidith looking at me anxiously as we ran past.

As I neared Aedann he turned to me, "Sorry, Cerdic, he beat us to it!"

"Never mind, I have the rest of us here. Form up!" I bellowed and the other men ran to join the shield wall. Now, including the princes and the lords, we had equal numbers. But Hussa barred the way. I looked towards my half-brother and saw him staring at me.

"Give it up, brother. You cannot escape," he taunted.

"Traitor!" I spat at him, "Murderer!"

"Ah, how touching: you do remember me. Come now. This is hopeless. We block your path. I have another thirty men behind you. To the left and right is marshland. What will you do? Surrender – no one has to die here. I need only the princes and the rest of you may go."

The five men I had tasked to loot the bodies ran up, carrying chain shirts, swords and helmets. One of them tossed me a pouch, "Old Roman silver coins and some gems," he gasped.

I thrust it into my belt then turned back to Hussa. "See this?" I shouted holding up the large two-handed axe, "I took this from your champion. He is dead as are another five of your men. The rest are running away like the gutless cowards they are. Move aside or we will do the same to you!"

Hussa considered the axe for a moment and then shrugged. "They will come back. If we stay here all night they will return. I need only hold you here until they do."

Lilla leant over to me. "He is right. Men scare easily but once they have run the fear out of their legs they will likely come back

22

to their companions."

I nodded at him and pushed my helmet more tightly on my head. "Then we cannot stay here, nor can we retreat. Eduard, raise the wolf banner high! We attack!" Relishing a fight, he grinned at me and waved our banner over his head.

"Right men," I turned to my companions, "we don't have time to dawdle here. We are going to smash a gap through their line and get on our way. Cuth, where are you?" I called, searching for my small friend.

"Here Cerdic! Cuthbert replied. He was with the five men I had left behind to loot the bodies.

"How many arrows do you have left?"

"Five now," he answered.

"When I give the word I want you to shoot the lot, fast as you can, towards that bastard with the blue shield," I pointed at one man in the middle of the Bernician shield wall. "You let fly then we attack. Eduard, Aedann, form a wedge with me. Eduard you take the lead."

"My pleasure," the big man replied with a grim smile. "Grettir, get ready with your spear," he added and then passed the banner to another man as we prepared to attack.

Discarding the champion's axe in favour of my sword and spear, I led my two friends in front of our small shield wall. I stood on the left, Aedann to my right and in front of me loomed Eduard, his murderous axe at the ready. The wolf banner was still rippling over our heads. Grettir moved to the centre of the company just behind me. "Move out of the way Hussa, I won't warn you again!" he shouted.

My half-brother, still on his mount behind the Bernician's shield wall, looked amused. "Are you serious? We still outnumber you and yet you plan to attack us? Why are you so keen to throw your life away?"

"Cuthbert – now!" I yelled.

Cuth had moved to our flank and stuck his arrows in the ground at his feet. He let fly with the first arrow and before it had reached its target had pulled another out of the ground. In less than a count of twenty all five had been shot. Two buried themselves in the blue shield, but one caught the unfortunate foe in the throat and two more struck his neighbours in the shoulders. The blue-shielded warrior fell to the ground, gurgling, whilst both his neighbours cried out in pain and dropped their shields.

"Forward!" I bellowed and the shield wall advanced.

Ahead of us, his mocking words dying in his throat, Hussa looked stunned, but quickly recovered and began shouting orders. The wounded men were pulled back out of the way and the Bernicians hurried to close up the wall. But now we had arrived. Eduard swung his axe up and brought it down, but not at the new warrior's head. Instead he hooked the axe head over the enemy shield and pulled down. "Grettir now!" he shouted, but the old veteran was already thrusting with his spear, impaling the man.

Spears stabbed back at us and one point grazed my shoulder, but our shields now clattered against those of the enemy and once more we were locked in the trial of strength that is shield wall against shield wall. This was how battles were decided – the heave and push of both sides until one finally gave way in exhaustion. That was, however, not my plan today. I did not have time for that. I needed this finished quickly before Hussa's fleeing men returned.

"Keep moving!" I ordered and Eduard stepped over the

body of the first man and hewed at the next rank. Aedann and I pushed in behind him. Our wedge was now biting deep into their line. A sword struck my helmet, the blow leaving my ears ringing. I thrust back with my spear and caught the sword's wielder in the arm. The man dropped his weapon, but as he bent to retrieve it Eduard brought his axe down on the swordsman's neck, decapitating him. We were old companions, Eduard and I and fought instinctively as a pair.

Then we were through the shield wall. It was only a few men deep and we, equally few, had ripped it asunder. In an ordinary battlefield not only would there be more ranks behind those at the front, but the foe would bring more men over to seal the breach. But this was no ordinary battlefield. Hussa had deployed his men merely to block the path across the marsh, but the path was narrow and we now stood on it, so there was no route to bring in more men. We had split Hussa's company in two and pinned the wings against the marsh so that now only my traitorous brother was in front of us.

We kept pushing, bringing more men through the breach and now we turned to attack the rear ranks of the enemy. This was too much for the Bernicians. They broke and fled either to the east or the west, along the edges of the bog and towards the shelter of the nearby woodland. They left behind six dead men. We had four men wounded, but mercifully none was dead.

"Keep moving. Get the villagers ready. Grettir form a rear guard," I panted, marching down the path towards Hussa. Not a fool, he tugged on his reins, dug in his heels and with a venomous look back at me, galloped away.

"He has a long way to get back to his men – all the way round the marsh!" Eduard commented.

"Serve him right," I grunted, wishing I had killed the bastard while I had a chance.

"Well done, Earl Cerdic," Prince Edwin said as he came to join me, his teeth flashing white in his dirty face as he grinned at me. "So, what now?"

Chapter Three
Tamwerth

"We must march on and find some shelter further along," I announced.

"What now? It's the middle of the night." Guthred countered. "Can't we just sleep in the temple?"

"Those Bernicians won't keep running for long. When they stop they will probably come straight back here. Who knows whether there are more of them nearby? We have to get away before they have a chance to rally." I looked around at the company and the villagers. Exhausted faces stared back at me: people whose spirits were almost broken. I did my best to encourage them, flashing them a grim smile. "It won't be far. Come, follow me." So saying, I set off, adding over my shoulder, "We will find a new place to camp along the path, you'll see."

This was easier said than done, though, for the land around us was marshy and we had to continue walking for much of what remained of the night before the path began to climb up out of the bog. At last, as the moon was beginning to set, we found dry land in a wood atop a small hill and with the sound a solitary blackbird heralding the coming of dawn, we collapsed. Then, as if to prove that anything bad can always get worse, it started to rain.

After a damp, miserable and thoroughly uncomfortable rest we pressed on. We had little food; what there was we gave to the children and for a while it kept them quiet, but I knew we could not go on much longer without sustenance. At sun-up we came to a Roman road. I glanced up and down it, but honestly had not the faintest clue as to which way to go. Having no better idea, I was about to toss my dice – in fact they were a roe deer's ankle bones that I had carved and kept for gaming – meaning to let the fates decide which direction to take.

As I threw the bones in the air, Lilla caught them and, shaking his head, handed them back. "You don't need those when you have me."

Before I could ask him what he meant he turned to the left along the road and stomped on, Sabert moving up to walk at his side.

"Where are we?" Guthred asked, his voice revealing his irritation as he addressed Sabert. "It seems to me we are just marching on through bog and moor with no plan in mind."

"We do have a plan. We find Tamwerth and talk to Pybba," the old lord replied.

"But where is Tamwerth?" Guthred asked me.

I shrugged. I had not a clue where we were in these foreign lands, but his question gave me an idea and as we walked along, I delved into the bag Aidith was carrying and retrieved my map. It was one of my most treasured possessions, very old, drawn by the Romans. It had once belonged to Lord Wallace, the old Lord of Wicstun, who gave it to me before the battle of Catraeth. I unrolled it, staring at the parchment, still with a degree of wonder at what it showed: Roman roads and settlements, rivers and hills. I studied it, trying to make the surroundings fit its lines and shapes. I could see where we had crossed the Humber two and more weeks before. But as to where we were right now, I had no idea.

I showed the map to Lilla. "Is Tamwerth marked on it?"

The bard studied it for a while then shook his head. "No, but I am not surprised. Tamwerth is an Angle city. The nearest Roman settlement is shown, however. See there," he gestured at the intersection of two roads. Near it was a Roman fort – once used by their legions. I could see it had a name: Letocetum.

"I have been through here once before," Lilla said. "When Sabert mentioned Tamwerth I told him I could get us there. The old Roman town is not that far from Tamwerth. If we can find it we can follow that other road to it."

So then, if Lilla was right, we were travelling along one of those roads that intersected at Letocetum, walking southwards. I felt a fraction calmer as I always do when I know where I am.

"How far is it though?" Frithwulf asked. "We are starving and tired."

He was right, this could not go on for much longer, but we plodded on, all the time aware that Hussa might at any moment be back on our trail, this time with more men. In the state we were in we would never be able to fight him again. I had begun to despair and was just considering talking to Sabert or Lilla about what we should do when the rain finally stopped and we cleared some low hills. Just at that moment the sun came out, shining down on us from the middle of the sky and making our damp clothes steam. Sabert looked around at us and smiled. I gazed past him and in the distance we could just see smoke rising from several buildings.

"There," he pointed. "There we shall rest, buy food and ale and consider the next step." The effect on our spirit was instant. Cuthbert laughed with joy and Eduard grinned, clearly considering his stomach. We upped the pace and in about a mile turned off the road into a fair-sized village, which comprised two dozen huts as well as a headman's hall much larger than the rest. Beyond the village were more huts and a Christian church, all clustered near a small pool. The presence of the church suggested this was a British, rather than an English settlement – perhaps under the rule of the Angles in Tamwerth. Further along the Roman road I could see smoke rising from another town, perhaps a mile or so further on. We could have made it, but agreed if we could obtain shelter and food here in return for a little coin we would do so.

The locals were at first wary of us, staying hidden inside their huts, except for a dozen men who emerged and were armed, for the most part with pitchforks although one man did have a rusty old sword. He brandished it at us as we stood back a hundred paces from the village and considered our options. "That sword would not do him much good if we attacked, and those men would be little threat to us," Eduard commented.

"Maybe, but a fight is the last thing we need. We might suffer more injuries and we cannot afford that," I replied, looking round at Aidith's white, drained face, little Cuthwine in her arms. "We have to consider the women and children."

"There is another way," Edwin suggested. He slipped behind us so as to be out of sight of the British villagers, all of whom were studying us. When the prince re-emerged I noted with some surprise that he had changed into his best clothes – those he had been wearing on the night of the attack on the king's hall. Over the last two weeks we had bartered for clothes and shared them around, but there was no doubt we looked a ragtag group. Edwin, though, had thought to preserve his fine blue tunic for just this eventuality. With its gold weave on neck and cuffs he looked quite the nobleman. "Well, here we go," he muttered and arms held wide to show he was unarmed, he moved forward.

I signalled that the company should remain outside the village for the moment and so only Sabert, Hereric, Lilla, Guthred, Frithwulf and I followed Edwin, each of us keeping our hands

30

well away from our weapons. By the time we caught him up, the prince was addressing the headman.

"We are not bandits but travelling Angles from the North." He spoke in English, not having much British, and I had to hope these people had enough of the language to understand. "We mean you no harm and merely want shelter and to trade for food," he said in a very polite tone.

This did not seem to impress the headman who stood, staring suspiciously at the prince, his sword still held at the ready.

With a sigh, Edwin pulled out from his belt pouch a few of the old Roman silver coins we had looted from Hussa's dead warriors and which now comprised our meagre treasury. He handed one to the headman. "See, we have silver," the prince said.

The British man examined the silver coin, looked back at Edwin and then, suddenly, smiled. "If you have more of these, then my village is yours tonight," he said in badly accented, but perfectly comprehensible English, sliding his sword back into his belt and waving us on. "Welcome to Licitfelda, my name is Alfonwy."

Once they were reassured we would not burn their village or slaughter and enslave the inhabitants, the people were welcoming. We traded a little and secured accommodation, food and ale along with a fresh horse to carry our possessions and supplies come the morning. After a tasty meal of lamb and bread washed down by a very acceptable beer with a pleasantly spiced aroma, Alfonwy invited Edwin to walk with him to the pool for a breath of air. I wandered along behind with Cuthbert and Eduard.

Close by the pool, to the rear of the village was a cluster of small hovels nestled against a decaying stone temple with a cross carved above the door: a Christian church by all appearances. There were a few abandoned ones in Deira and I had seen more in the Bernician lands and in Elmet of course. The pool was fed by a spring. Alfonwy told us that the Romans had used it almost four hundred years before as a rest stop for their legions marching up the road from Letocetum. Later, when the Romans adopted this new faith of Christ, a group of monks had set up a little community around the well.

"The water can heal you see," he explained, "so the monks care for the well and we care for the monks."

I wondered how this small Christian and British community had survived the arrival and influx of the pagan Mercians over the last century. Most of the Welsh had been forced west into Powys and Gwynedd. I asked our host this.

"It's true that during my lifetime bands of Angles and Saxons have raided deeper and deeper into these regions over decades and they have settled further and further west. In some regions our kindred have been killed or driven away but in others we have been able to reach an accommodation with our new lords. We maintain the well as a service to the king in Tamwerth. Providing we allow travellers to stop and fill their water skins and also take a rest along the road then he is content. As a result we have so far been left alone to serve our God."

I had never thought much about religion. As a child it had been so easy. My grandparents and parents had worshiped the gods of our ancestors: Thor, Woden, Friga and the others. We named our days after them and our villages. We wore their devices on jewellery and our weapons. They governed the seasons and were called upon to bless birth, marriage and war and in the end we committed our dead to them. I had not doubted them – I had no reason to. I knew that Aedann's father, Caefydd, had not followed our gods, but worshipped the Christian God, as did Aedann and his mother. As children he had once told us of this Christ, who had taught his followers to turn away from killing and greed and to put others first, but in the end had been crucified by the Romans six hundred years ago. I eventually dismissed this as a foolish fairy tale and always considered Caefydd's a strange faith – when I had given it any thought at all, which was not often – but as I grew older I realised that to the British this religion was not nonsense. I had seen them bearing the cross on their war banners at Catraeth and noted how the Goddodin cavalry had fought that day as if their God were driving them on. Yet how could I reconcile my own belief in the gods with the Christian view that theirs was the only one? This Christ could be just another god, this heaven they spoke of just another amongst the Nine Worlds. That seemed clear enough to me and I now made the comment to Alfonwy.

He looked askance at my suggestion. "There is only one God. There is but one heaven and for those who do not find a place in it there is one hell."

It all seemed very confusing to me. Religion was used to give kings justification for their actions, to give hope to the dying and the bereaved and to explain much of what goes on around us. The lightning and the rain is Thor's doing. Women's fertility is a gift from Friga and its absence a punishment. Religion helps make sense of the world. Is that all there was to it? Did it really matter what a man did in his life? Was this brief existence all there was? We pagans, as the Christians called us, believed that when we warriors were slain in battle we would go to Valhalla and feast with Woden. Those who died naturally went to the realm of Hel. But what if Alfonwy was right and Valhalla did not exist and everyone went either to this heaven or to Hel? Could that really be true? I pondered this mystery at length. I knew that for a few of us there was always the possibility of immortality in the poets' tales – at least for as long as there were poets to tell them and people to hear them. But for most of us there was just oblivion. Within a couple of generations we would be forgotten, just as the westward push of my people across Britain was destroying the memory of the folk whose land it had been before us. Thinking about the Christians' belief in this heaven, I supposed that, farfetched as it was, there was actually some comfort in it.

"Cerdic!" – a voice calling my name brought me back to the present. I roused myself from my thoughts and realised I was staring down into the well. It was now getting quite dark and Edwin and the others were walking back to the headman's hall for the night. I started after them, but to myself I made a promise: if this life was all there was I would make of mine a story that the bards would sing for many lives of men.

When I returned to the corner of the hall, which I was sharing with Aidith and Cuthwine, I found my son wrapped up in my cloak but still awake. I went over to him. He looked up at me sleepily and as I pulled a blanket over him, asked, "Father, when can we go home?"

"I don't know son. But I will keep you safe, I promise."

"I know," he murmured, his eyes closing.

As he went back to sleep I looked up to find Aidith frowning at me. "What is it?" I asked.

She lifted her eyebrow, "Can you be sure?"

"Sure of what?"

"Sure you can keep him safe."

Now it was I who frowned. "Don't you think I would protect him?"

"Of course, you would give your life for him, for me too,

34

but..."

"Well – there you go then," I said, sitting down on the bench and pulling off my boots.

"But that wasn't what I asked," Aidith murmured, getting into our bed – really just a collection of furs and a straw mattress, but it felt like sheer luxury after the days of sleeping on the damp earth.

Puzzled, I shook my head, "What do you mean?"

"Oh, nothing," she said, then added, "and for the princes too?" She emphasised the word too in a way that made me look up. I sensed trouble.

"Yes, if I had to. I made a promise to protect them."

"What if you had to make a choice? What if you could not protect both us and them?"

"Aidith I..." my words trailed away. It was an impossible question to answer and I was tired.

"I want a home, Cerdic."

"So do I, but our home is burnt. We can't go back there. One day maybe but not yet – you know that."

"Somewhere else then," she said with a yawn.

"Well yes, Mercia maybe. Yes, Mercia," I repeated. I too yawned then and rolled into bed alongside her and Cuthwine. Clasping her to me, I whispered in her ear, "You will see at Tamwerth tomorrow..."

The following day we passed the remains of the old Roman settlement of Letocetum. A number of decaying houses clustered around two larger buildings – a sort of town hall and the baths, which were much larger than the small bath house we had used occasionally near the Villa. Nowadays Letocetum was inhabited by a small group of Britons, descendants maybe of the Romans who had once lived here long ago. The road we were following intersected another east to west road near the village and when we reached the junction Lilla turned us eastwards along it. We passed more stone-built villas to the north and south and dotted here and there the newer, wooden houses of the Mercians. It was difficult to tell exactly who owned this land, the Welsh or the English. I said as much to Lilla.

"You are right; these lands are much more confused than those in Northumbria. These Mercians have not so long ago come here – indeed, maybe seventy years ago all this was still British. Our own people up in Deira have had much longer to make a mark on the land than these Angles have. 'Land on the border' – that is what the name Mercia means, did you know? It marks the border between the Angles and the Welsh, but it's a pretty vague border too. Ah – but look, there is Tamwerth."

I gazed in the direction of his pointing finger. The road we were following was running along a little way south of a river – the Tame, I learnt from Lilla, who was as ever happy to share his knowledge. Up ahead the road passed over another river, which flowed out of woodland to the south to join the Tame. On the north bank of the river, close by the intersection, was a small hill and upon it a fortified hall. Around it, like piglets being suckled by a sow, were gathered the houses and workshops of a fair–sized town.

We shouldered our shields and hid our weapons as best as we could so as not to provoke suspicion from the local population and the Mercian warriors who guarded the king's hall. Lilla, Sabert and I went ahead of the company as we walked through the streets, aware of the curious as well as cautious glances from the inhabitants. The town was unfortified but the king's hall had a ditch and palisade around it.

Half a dozen guards stood at the gate. As we approached they stirred and brought their spears and swords to the ready. "Hold there stranger and speak your name and purpose," barked one tall, gangly fellow with a ruddy complexion and an entangled, filthy beard.

"Good warrior, I am Sabert, advisor and minister to Princes Edwin and Hereric of Deira, whose party this is," the old earl replied politely. "We seek an audience with King Pybba."

The gangly man glanced over at another guard, this one stumpy and fat. They did not say anything but it seemed there was a meaning in that exchange. I wondered if they were about to deny us entry and was about to argue with them, when the fat one pulled open the gates and led us inside.

The hall of Pybba, King of Mercia, was surrounded by stables and workshops. The building was single-story and possessed elaborate carvings over the doorway, which I saw were the shapes of animals and the runes of Woden, Thunor, Tyr and Freya. It was similar, albeit smaller, to that of Aelle and Aethelric and I saw Hereric looking at it sadly as he no doubt was reminded of his father's hall and the moment when we had last seen Aethelric alive. I might have said something to comfort the lad, but we had now arrived at the doors into the hall.

"Hand over your weapons," the guard ordered and indicated a table near the entrance on which other weapons were piled. We reluctantly complied. Unarmed I felt almost naked and could only hope that we were not making a big mistake.

"Just the princes and their lords may enter," the guard said. "The rest of you wait here."

I glanced at Aidith and smiled at her in an attempt to calm her fears, but she returned my look with an anxious expression and held onto Cuthwine tightly.

37

A few moments later we were herded into the hall of King Pybba. We had clearly arrived during a gathering of the thegns and earls of Mercia as the room was busy with dozens of finely dressed men sitting at benches down the long sides of the hall. At the far end, resting on a high–backed chair, a thin, scraggly man in his early forties appeared almost startled by our presence, his gaze darting back and forth as we were announced. I assumed this was the king and to my eyes he seemed overly nervous given we were unarmed.

"For what reason does Edwin of Deira come to Mercia?" he asked after a few moments of scrutiny.

Edwin bowed slightly to show his respect for royalty. "I am Edwin, Prince of the Royal House of Deira and brother to Aethelric the king. This is Hereric my nephew and son to Aethelric. By deceit and tricks did Aethelfrith of Bernicia usurp my brother's throne and murder him. Against my wishes was I forced to flee and seek aid and shelter outside my lands," Edwin explained politely, but with a suitable degree of drama in his voice. Lilla had apparently been giving him lessons.

"What reason do you have to expect that you will find aid and shelter in Mercia?" the king asked.

"Mercia and Deira have been friends in the past. We hoped that would still be so," Edwin retorted.

"Well, trading in times of peace is one thing but supporting you in war against a powerful warlord is another," the king said firmly.

"Are you saying you will not aid us, my Lord?" Sabert asked the king.

"That is so. Mercia is not in a position to help you."

"I am disappointed to hear that," said Edwin, his voice bitter. "I had thought you would have realised the wisdom in opposing Aethelfrith."

"Indeed we should, if my counsel be heard," said a strong voice from amongst the king's advisers. In his late thirties, the speaker was a sturdy, well–built man with bright, intelligent eyes and a slightly greying beard.

"Lord Ceorl," the king snapped, "we have heard your advice when we received the... er, messenger yesterday. We know your opinion and you know mine."

"But... Sire..." stammered Ceorl.

"Enough Ceorl, if you cannot control yourself get out of here," shouted the king, leaping to his feet and gesticulating violently towards the door.

Ceorl flushed, hesitated then stormed past us and out of the hall. The king glared after him for a moment then seemed to notice us again. He was just opening his mouth to say something more to Edwin when I interrupted. "Sire, you mentioned a messenger just now. May we know whom you mean?"

The king looked a little discomfited and dropped his gaze. Then, in the ensuing silence I heard a familiar voice and my heart sank. "Well, dear brother, he means me."

"Hussa!" I spat, moving forward as my brother stepped out of the shadows beside the king.

"Oh stop with your bluster Cerdic. You are unarmed, and besides which, you are too late. I have King Pybba's protection and his agreement."

"What agreement would that be, snake?" Sabert asked him.

Hussa laughed as he walked towards the old advisor.

Sabert glared at him and repeated the question.

"What agrrement?"

"I would have thought that was obvious, Earl Sabert. He has agreed to consider handing you all over to me. If he does, then tomorrow we leave for Deira and a meeting with Aethelfrith, who is most anxious to greet the princes – and the rest of you will all be coming along!"

Chapter Four
Ceorl

"If I agree, Lord Hussa: only *if* I agree. I have said I will give it my consideration, no more," Pybba corrected my brother. "These men have come here asking for shelter. For me to deny them such and hand them over to you would breach the hospitality customary to a visiting prince. Such a breach would weaken our position with other kingdoms. When they learned of it they would be hostile to me."

Hussa bowed. "Of course Sire, it is your choice. I say only that should Aethelfrith extend his protection over Mercia you would have no need to fear their hostility."

Sabert stepped forward, coming to stand next to Hussa but pointedly ignoring him. "Heed not this snake, Sire. He is a traitor and his master is so too. Can you not see that if you agree to this you put yourself under the influence of Aethelfrith? He surely desires to be Bretwalda and this will take him one step closer. It will extend his authority south of the Humber. By this act you would recognise that authority and put yourself against Aethelberht of Kent."

"Be quiet old man," my brother hissed. Then, turning to Pybba, he bowed again. "Sire, consider this: Aethelberht is old and will die soon. Aethelfrith is strong and still young yet. Who is better to lie next to – the old wolf or the young?"

"That depends on whether you are the sheep!" Eduard muttered by my side. As ever, his rumbling growl could be heard by everyone in the room evoking a buzz of comment, some heads nodding in agreement.

"Enough!" Pybba shouted and we all fell quiet. In the sudden silence we could hear the babbling voices of the village children outside the hall – some laughing and some crying. Pybba frowned at the racket. Then he started coughing again and it was obvious to me that he was not well. We waited until he recovered. When he spoke again his voice was weary.

"I will think on what you have all said. I will decide on my actions in the morning. For tonight one of the houses here inside the fortress will be given over to Prince Edwin, Prince Hereric, their earls and thegns, together with their immediate families. The rest of the party – that gaggle of women and children outside my door, along with the prince's warriors – will be accommodated somewhere else." A mischievous expression crept across Pybba's face. "Indeed, since Ceorl is so concerned about these visitors, he can entertain the camp followers. He has a house down in the town does he not? Very well, the rabble can take their noise there! It is making my head ache. I will retire now and deliberate on what to do with you all." With that he walked away towards his private rooms.

I looked around the hall, considering whether we might want to make a quick exit before night came, but with a clattering of equipment a dozen guards advanced on us from the rear of the hall and we were forcibly escorted past our stacked weapons and out into the courtyard. There we were briefly reunited with the rest of our company and villagers, the women folk looking strained and anxious until they saw we were unharmed.

As Pybba had ordered, we were all led under guard to a large house near the gatehouse. Amongst the villagers a baby was squalling for the breast, but for once Cuthwine and the other children were silent, most of them dead on their feet with exhaustion. Then, though, there was pandemonium as Pybba's men tried to separate the villagers and the bulk of the warriors from the prince's immediate party. They were none too gentle about the matter to be honest, driving into our ranks and using shield and spears to divide us. Gwen, Aedann's mother, looked terrified as she backed away from one of the spearmen. Next to her Guthred's youngest daughter slipped and fell against the man's shield. The shield boss cut her lip and she squealed in pain. At the sight of blood dripping down her chin and onto her gown all the other children started wailing and the girl's older brother, Frithwulf, waded in and began screaming abuse at the Mercians.

Meanwhile, Eduard and Aedann were being pushed into the other group and away from us and I could see my large friend's face grow red as he argued with one Mercian spearman. A moment later Eduard's fist came up; he was waving it about an inch from the man's nose. Grettir waded in to support him, his old face suffused with anger. Fleetingly I remembered how fearsome I had thought him when I was a lad. His word had been law back then. It saddened me to see him now as a tired old man, but I could see the situation was getting dangerous and I was anxious that before long we could suffer more than just a cut lip. Gulping in a lungful of air I roared, "Quiet!"

My sudden shout stunned everyone into silence and they all turned to look at me. Surprised, I seized the initiative, speaking quickly before the dispute could resume. "Eduard, Grettir, back off. Everyone calm down, please. We are just being taken to houses for the night. Trust me: it will be all right."

Frithwulf and Eduard looked ready to argue but I glared at them both and after a moment Eduard turned away. "Come on everyone," he said to the villagers and with a disgruntled glance back at me, led the anxious throng away under guard and out

43

of the gateway.

Whilst they were being taken away, Edwin, Hereric and I, together with the other lords and our immediate families, were pushed inside the nearby house and the door slammed shut. We were now in a substantial room with a fire burning low in a fire pit. Another door led further into the building.

"What's happening, Cerdic?" Millie asked, "Why have we been locked in here?" I glanced at her and then at Aidith and realised that all eyes were turned towards me, everyone waiting for my answer, Prince Edwin glowering belligerently.

I sighed, thinking, '*Why me?*' but I answered as best I could. "Hussa got here before us. He seems to have swayed Pybba towards handing us over to him. The king is undecided and will let us know in the morning what he plans to do with us. In the meantime we are to be held here." That triggered off an outbreak of panic and I raised my hands in an effort to calm everyone down.

"Hussa here!" Millie exclaimed. "Where is the traitor? I want to see him."

"We can't Millie, not till morning."

"Cerdic, that bastard brother of ours killed our mother!"

"He killed my cousin also, as well as Eduard's brother," Cuthbert growled.

I nodded at them both but spoke so everyone could hear. "I know what he has done and I know many of us owe him an unpleasant end – but we can't do it here. He is under Pybba's protection. We will get our revenge. I swear it, for the village and for the king - and for us too," I added more softly to Millie and Cuthbert. "But not tonight," I said, moving across to the interior door as I spoke. Opening it I found another large room, this one also illuminated by the light from a fire pit. The place felt warm and dry. I gestured that Millie, Cuthwine, Aidith and Guthred's family should go through that way. "Tonight we all need to get some sleep and you must trust us to sort this out. Guthred, please help me."

Exhausted as he was, he did not argue and together Guthred, Cuthbert and I led the frightened women and children through to the rear room and settled them down for the night. I helped Aidith spread out some furs and our cloaks as a bed in one of the corners and then, promising to return soon, I went with Guthred back into the outer room. Edwin still looked stunned by what had happened in Pybba's court, he seemed totally lost and Sabert obviously had no idea what to say. We had all been so certain we would be welcome here.

"Now what do we do?" asked Guthred. He seemed to have quickly recovered his antagonism towards me for now he was glaring at me again, as if he held me personally responsible for our misfortune. "We should never have come here. You have led us here just so your brother could carry us away."

I shook my head, too tired to argue – and besides, what could I say? The man had seen us with his own eyes running away from Hussa. Indeed, he had helped us to escape so why he was thinking I was in league with my brother was quite beyond me. I guessed he was just so tired he was babbling. Thankfully, Lilla, though neither earl nor thegn had somehow managed to include himself in my party - even in this situation it seemed his silver tongue held sway! He winked at me and said, "I suggest we just get some sleep and see if we can talk again to Pybba in the morning."

With a grumpy toss of the head Guthred took one look at him and stomped back into the other room to lie down with his wife and children. I nodded my thanks to Lilla and then I too went to find my bed. In another corner of the room Cuthbert and my sister were talking softly to each other. Mildrith said something to my friend and he kissed her and then noticed me watching and blushed. I smiled to myself. The man was married to the girl and yet he still seemed like the same shy youth who would stammer whenever she spoke to him.

"They look happy despite all that has happened, don't they?" Aidith said as I joined her and Cuthwine. I lay down next to her and threw my cloak over us all.

"They have not been married six weeks yet, so of course they are happy. I imagine the only problem is not having a room to themselves."

"Well I can understand that," she replied coldly.

I sighed, knowing I was about to get another earful. "Is this about what I said last night?"

My wife stared at me, accusation in her eyes. "Well you did imply that all would be well when we reached Tamwerth and yet here we are, locked up and likely to be carried away in chains come the morrow."

"That is not my fault!" I snapped.

"Not yours, no, just your bastard brother again! Why did you not kill him before now?"

"Thunor's balls, woman, I tried! Look, I'm sorry all right!" I moved angrily away from her, rolling over and presenting her with my back.

"Cerdic," she said softly, reaching out a hand to touch my shoulder.

"What now?"

"I'm sorry. Let's not quarrel… it's just that…"

"What?" I asked stiffly.

"It's just that I don't want our child born in a ditch some-

46

where."

"What child? What are you talking about woman?"

She did not reply and then it dawned on me what she had said. "You mean you're...?"

"Yes."

I rolled back over. The room was almost dark, but I could just make out the outline of her face in the fire's glow and could tell that she was smiling. "When?"

"I imagine when you came back to the Villa before the attack on the palace," she teased.

"No, no – I meant when will the baby come?"

"Next spring I expect – around Eostretide."

I drew her close to me and kissed her. "Then before that time we will have somewhere to live, I will make sure of it. We will be safe and in our own home, I promise."

"Another promise, Cerdic? How can you say that when it seems likely Hussa will lead us away in chains come the morrow?"

"We don't know that for sure," I replied, expressing a hope I did not really feel. "Now go to sleep, my love, and we'll see what happens in the morning."

Lying on the cold, hard floor that night I found it hard to sleep. The morning might come too soon if I did and I was fearful of Pybba's decision, doubly fearful as I thought he had already made up his mind and I suspected what his choice would be. I reached inside my shirt and found the symbols of Woden, Thunor and Tiw, the one–handed God. They were the Gods of Fate, Thunder and War. In them I had put my trust in the past and I still lived didn't I? Yet there was another symbol I carried, the symbol of a snake, the symbol of Loki, the trickster God. I had

47

trusted in him before and he had saved Aidith's life when she lay stricken with the plague. After that moment, though, my fate had unravelled. Loki had tricked me, used my brother to betray me and I would be a fool to trust in him again, wouldn't I? Yet, as I finally drifted off to sleep I murmured to myself, "Gods of my fathers please help us now. Please let our second child be born free and safe." I did not exactly say the gods' names, but I meant Loki just as much as the others.

Then, far away, I seemed to hear laughter.

I was dreaming. I was walking along a road: a stone, Roman road. I came to a junction. One way was barred by a hideous troll and I could not go that way. The other way lay towards the setting sun. It was hard to look that way into the dying sun's brightness, but I squinted and could make out two figures on the road. One was Loki, beckoning to me, a mischievous grin on his face. The other was Tiw. The warrior god also waved me towards him and then turned and threw a spear. It vanished in the sunlight...

"Cerdic! Cerdic! Wake up."

"What is it Aidith?" I mumbled, blearily opening my eyes to find it was still full dark.

"Lord Sabert wants you in the other room right away. Guthred has gone through already," she whispered.

"What for? It's the middle of the night," I grumbled.

"Hush, you'll wake Cuthwine. I don't know. Go and see," she gave me a little push.

Feeling for my tunic I pulled it on and staggered through to the other room. Here the firepit was still glowing and I could make out people's faces. The princes were awake, as were Sabert, Guthred, Frithwulf and Lilla too. There was another man

48

with them. It took me a moment to recognise Lord Ceorl.

"What is it," I asked, "has something happened?"

Ceorl turned to me, "I must be quick, the king will not agree to me helping you."

"Helping us – you? How?" Still half asleep I was confused.

He nodded. "You cannot stay here, but I believe it is right to aid you," he explained. "There are some things you do not know. Firstly, the king will refuse to help or shelter you because he has been threatened already by Aethelfrith. Three days ago a messenger arrived from the warlord. The message was quite blunt: if we should aid or shelter you Bernicia will wage war on Mercia. Our army is not strong and has been fighting far down on the Severn Valley. We are in no position to defend ourselves against an army the size of Aethelfrith's. He insisted that if you were to come here seeking shelter we were to turn you over or at least turn you away. Pybba promptly declared that no aid would be given to you. He had intended to send you on your way, but then yesterday, when Lord Hussa arrived, it forced his hand, which is why he has kept you under guard."

I glanced at Edwin. His face was pale.

"However," Ceorl went on, "that does not mean that I cannot aid you a little, albeit against the king's wishes."

"How can you help us?" I asked, wondering why he would want to. Still befuddled with sleep it occurred to me that this might be a trap intended to lead us to Hussa, and yet his sincerity seemed genuine. I waited in silence for his answer.

"I have been responsible for talks with the kingdoms of Gwynedd and also of Powys to our west. The talks are going badly with Powys and we are almost constantly fighting with them along the Severn Valley. Right now we have a brief truce but I doubt it will last long. We are often at odds with Gwynedd too and only a few months back clashed near Legacæstir. Iago – the king there – and most of his lords, do not trust us and will not entertain peace. However, I do have good relations with Iago's son, Prince Cadfan. I have reasons to wish closer ties with Gwynedd and helping you might make that possible."

I glanced at Edwin; his face was a mask of confusion. These names were known to us, but only as remote Welsh lands. I was unsure what good a band of Northumbrian warriors would do as a diplomatic effort. There was in any case another concern on my mind. "Won't they just seize us and hang us as bandits or at least treat us an enemy warband loose in their country and attack us? Chances are that is what we would do if the roles were reversed."

Ceorl produced a parchment. "This is a letter of introduction to Cadfan. Make sure you get that to him and I am certain he will shelter you, at least for a while. He is a man of honour and not vindictive so would not strike out of instinct, but would listen to your tale first. Furthermore, I will supply you with some baggage ponies, a sack of old clothes and a little food to help get you there. Your weapons are already loaded on the ponies in fact. I can give you some money too. We don't have much time. Rouse your families and come quietly," he ordered.

He waited while we did so and then led us all out into the courtyard. "The guards... won't they stop us?" I hissed, hesitating.

Ceorl shook his head with impatience. "These men are mostly my own or those I have bribed to look the other way. In the morning they will each swear that they were on duty on the East Gate. No one will admit to being on this gate, he pointed to the West Gate out of the compound.

"What about the Captain of the Guard?"

"He is drunk on my best wine and will wake with a thumping head and a lot to answer for. Serves him right for getting drunk on duty! Now come," he urged us as he opened the gates, "the rest of your company is at my house further down the hill, far enough away for us not to be heard, but keep everyone quiet until we get there."

As we passed through the gate, Cuthwine stirred in Aidith's arms and I lifted my finger to my lips. "Hush, child," she said, swinging him gently to lull him back to sleep.

In the ghostly glimmer of moonlight we walked on down a dark street lined with workshops and thatched huts – a place not unlike Wicstun. As we walked along I turned to Ceorl and whispered the question that was on my mind.

"Why? Why do this? Won't you get into trouble?"

Ceorl thought for a moment then nodded towards Sabert. "I am sure the noble Earl can surmise my reasons," he said.

I glanced at Sabert. He held his hand out to silence me. 'Leave it for now, Cerdic,' he was saying.

"Here we are," Ceorl hissed, opening the door of a building at the end of the street. I followed him into his house: a long structure similar to the mead hall Aidith and I had built at the Villa, but with its own stables and outhouses, almost an estate in fact. Inside we found Gwen, Eduard and Aedann sitting at one of the benches, warming themselves at the fire that burnt low in the firepit. They jumped up as soon as they saw us. Around them the company and the villagers slept fitfully under cloaks and furs on the floor of the hall.

"Thank the gods," Gwen said, "we were afraid we would not see you again."

Aedann put his hand on his mother's arm. "I told you they would be all right."

Once we were inside Ceorl turned to us. He gestured at a sack on the tables nearby. "In there are some clothes. They won't fit all of you, but at least some of you can change and look less like vagabonds! Wake your people and get them ready then come through this way," he pointed at another door. "It leads to the stables. The ponies are already loaded with food and money and your weapons. My house borders an orchard. We will lead the ponies out that way."

A short while later, re-provisioned, the more ragged of us re-clothed in a selection of worn but serviceable woollen tunics and breeches we prepared to follow Ceorl out of the stables. Most of the children were quiet, too stunned with exhaustion to do more than stare wide-eyed at their parents, though one or two, I noticed, looked excited at this big adventure taking place in the middle of the night.

When everyone was gathered around the ponies, upon which we had mounted some of the younger children, I turned to address them. "We cannot stay here, we are not welcome. But we have a path to follow and a letter of introduction to another kingdom. We must get away whilst it is yet dark. If we are caught my brother will take us back to Deira and we all know what that means," I glanced around the party. The warriors nodded, they knew that Aethelfrith would not be likely to be merciful to us. The villagers looked frightened at what lay ahead, but knew, surely, that horror and death lay behind us in Deira. No one argued. "So then, we must get out of here quietly. Parents keep your children quiet. Children keep your parents quiet too," I added with a wink that drew a giggle from three of the little ones.

We set out through the stable doors. Sure enough only fifty yards away we could see the shadowy outlines of apple trees, standing dark against the star-strewn sky. The moon was already sinking behind us but I figured we could still get five miles away before dawn.

I let everyone go past first so I could count them all. Sabert wearily took the lead followed by Hereric and Edwin. Then Guthred and his five warriors went by, along with his wife, Frithwulf, his oldest son, his younger twin boys and three daughters, each staring fearfully at the darkness. Eduard and Aedann led the rest – the nine other survivors of the Wicstun company and the ten men Sabert had brought with him. Then, finally, Cuthbert, Aidith, Cuthwine, Gwen and Millie stumbled along with the ten other village women and their children. In all fifty–two souls padded out into the night. Somewhere in the distance a hound barked and I froze, expecting a cacophony of noise to follow, but the sound subsided.

The orchard stretched as far as the start of a belt of woodland that curved from the northern approached to Tamwerth and around to the west. In the faint light of the moon, moving through the undergrowth was heavy going, but Ceorl was able to find a track he said his huntsman would often follow when hunting deer nearby and that proved much easier once we were on it. At the end of the woods was a stream we had to cross, the children squealing at the touch of the icy water, but by now we were a good two miles from Tamwerth so I was more relaxed about the noise. Once across the brook we emerged into an open field, its crop of barley still short and stumpy.

Finally, just as the sun was rising in the east, and after stumbling through the fields for another mile, Ceorl led us out onto the same road we had arrived by and directed us west along the path that would take us past Lichfielda and out of the English lands into regions that the Welsh still held strongly.

I thanked Ceorl profusely for his help and generosity, still wondering what was behind it and determined to question Sabert when I had an opportunity. After seeing us on the road, he bade us good luck and turned back towards the dark shape of Tamwerth, while we carried on along a path that I had never intended us to follow. I could not help wondering what Loki had in store for me – yet again.

We paused to retrieve our weapons from the ponies' panniers and then, relieved to be armed again, I walked at the front with Sabert, Lilla and the two princes. The women and children, the younger ones doubled up on three of the ponies, followed in the middle of our group, their menfolk bringing up the rear. We walked slowly, not wanting to raise the alarm until we were well out of earshot. A half dozen trotting ponies makes a good deal of noise, believe me. However loyal Ceorl's guards might be, Hussa was not one of them and I somehow doubted he would be drunk and senseless. I could only hope he was sleeping peacefully back in Pybba's hall.

"Well then, Sabert, are you going to tell us what Ceorl meant when he said you would know why he was helping us?" Around me I could see most of our companions perk up and listen.

The old Earl scratched absently at his beard before answering, "Pybba is not well."

"I could see that, but are you saying he is dying?"

"Well, not yet maybe, but he is sickly certainly."

"Does he have an heir?" Lilla asked.

"A good question and the answer is he does have an infant son called Penda, not yet a year old."

"Not old enough to rule or even inherit then," Hereric said.

"No," Sabert replied.

"So if Pybba dies in the next few years, who will succeed

him?" Edwin asked.

"Well, that is open to question. Ceorl is only a cousin, but of those that are king worthy he is the closest blood relative to Pybba."

A glimmer of understanding entered my tired brain. "So he is likely to be king?"

Sabert nodded then stared at Edwin and Hereric. "Think about it. With the rising power of Aethelfrith in the North, other Saxon lands in the East and South and the Welsh lands in the West, Mercia is right in the middle. Ceorl wants above all a strong Mercia. He must find a way to oppose Aethelfrith. But to do that he must find an accommodation with the ancient enemy of Mercia – with the Welsh."

Edwin's eyes widened in realisation of what Sabert was saying, "He is using me like a stone on a Tafl board, like a piece in a game. He hopes that I will find a way to reach peace with the Welsh and then he can brag about how he made it happen. He is a playing a game."

Frithwulf and his father, walking behind us and listening to our conversation, leaned forward. "We must not go," Frithwulf said.

"Indeed it is madness," his father agreed. "To go willingly into a Welsh kingdom whose people really have no reason to welcome us and every reason to distrust us – you cannot be serious. Again I say that we should go south to Wessex or Kent. This Ceorl might want us to play a game, but I say this is a game we don't have to play!"

"We are all playing a game whether you like it or not," I commented. "It's a deadly game and a very serious one. The trick is to play it our way. We are in hostile territory. If we go south we will be caught. It is a long way to Wessex. Pybba and Hussa will expect us to flee that way. So we change the rules of the game. The border with Gwynedd is closer. We go west and we play the game and we win."

Edwin nodded and looked at Hereric, "Well nephew, what do you say?"

Hereric looked confused. "Do whatever you think is best," he said eventually. His vagueness was so like his father's that I almost laughed.

It seemed Edwin thought the same, for he smiled and said, "Very well, we go west – to Gwynedd."

It was a critical decision. At the time we would not know quite how important. Not just for our immediate future but far beyond. The path Ceorl had nudged us toward and Edwin had chosen to follow would set in motion events that would unfold for the next thirty years. But I speak in hindsight and of course none of us knew this at the time. The reaction amongst the company was mixed: Frithwulf and Guthred looked grim at the decision, Hereric just puzzled and Lilla excited at the thought of travelling to new lands. I glanced over my shoulder to see if Aidith had heard what we were saying. She looked scared, her face white in the grey light of dawn. I smiled to reassure her, but she looked quickly away.

However we felt about it, none of us had the slightest idea of what to expect. Edwin summed up all our feeling as we continued along on the path Ceorl had sent us. "Well, my companions, does it not strike you as odd that for generations we have fought the Welsh and killed them where we could, to the extent that their enmity to us is implacable. Yet it is to these people in our most desperate hour that we turn to get aid against fellow English?"

I saw that Aedann was grinning at me and wondered if I alone among our company remembered that he was Welsh through and through. I raised my eyebrow at him before turning back to Edwin. "Odd, yes indeed my prince. And yet, since we woke at Godnundingham to the sounds of battle I have felt carried along by events like a man who has fallen into a rushing, surging river and is helpless to oppose its current. In fact, he knows that to do so only leads to drowning. His only hope is to ride with the water and try to keep his head above it."

Edwin gave a bark of humourless laughter, "Well then, let's hope we can all swim!"

Nobody else laughed. Yes, I thought, swimming is what we were doing right now: swimming in the seas of politics and warfare that at times swept like a flood across the land. There was a strong current in that sea and the current was taking us west, along the road that the trickster god Loki had beckoned me to follow him and along the path down which the warrior Tiw had thrown his spear - west, towards mischief and war. I could only hope the Norns who governed our fate and our destiny were on our side.

Chapter Five
Gwynedd

I have lived eighty years in this land. Ancient I am by any standard. Yet great age has given me a perspective on the change in the shape and boundaries of lands that few today possess. Indeed, if you start with the tales of my grandfather and father and go through to the present day, I have a view of some one hundred and twenty years. In that time, since say about the year 540, the layout of the land has altered beyond belief. Many proud British kingdoms such as Pennine and York have vanished without trace. English enclaves have grown and expanded and swelled until we have roughly seven large Saxon kingdoms of my old age. The surviving British lands have also coalesced so today the borders of lands are a lot less confusing, more formal and better defined.

If you took a man of my old age back and made him walk across the lands of my youth he would be bewildered and quite lost to see the myriad of splintered realms and kingdoms – some no larger than a single valley. Then again, to be honest, I was confused and bewildered back then, when I tried to guide fifty souls through warring, divided and utterly alien lands in that long ago year.

From the few words of advice Ceorl gave us coupled with Sabert's knowledge we knew that to the west of Mercia was Powys – a British kingdom which had been at war with Mercia but recently had reached some sort of accommodation with Pybba. That peace was fragile and would probably be short-lived and Powys was by no means likely to welcome wandering Saxon royalty. Beyond Powys in the mountainous area along the north coast of the Welsh lands was Gwynedd. King Iago of that land was reputed to feel it his duty to protect and succour disinherited royalty as he had taken some of Rheged's princes under his wing. Most importantly it was Aethelfrith's expansion that had led to the downfall of Rheged and forced these princes out. It seemed possible that a king who would shelter one enemy of Aethelfrith might shelter another.

Until recently Gwynedd would have been completely blocked to passage from Mercia by the bulk of the kingdom of Powys. However, Powys and Gwynedd were also often at war and the year before Gwynedd had captured Legacæstir from Powys. Legacæstir, which once upon a time had been a city of the legions and an important fortress, lay at the far end of the Roman roads out of Tamwerth heading northwest. So we walked and walked, avoiding the parts of Powys we passed, until we moved from Mercia into the confused area where Powys, Rheged and Gwynedd came together.

The area was wild and the way poorly trod. As a result greenery and foliage had overgrown much of the road, cracking and separating the bricks that the Romans had so skilfully laid an age ago. In places it was hard to follow any path but we made progress, albeit slowly.

This was an anxious march. We might have had thirty armed warriors but since the time we became a warband overnight, during the flight from Deira three weeks before, we had failed to form a strong bond. The trouble was that we were not just one group. Some men were from the Wicstun company and loyal to me. A few were Aethelfrith's huscarls and felt a duty to the princes alone. The rest were Guthred's huscarls and they had no loyalty to me at all. We had suffered many hardships and secretly, despite the brief moment of optimism when we had declared Edwin our king in that wood south of the Humber, I am sure most of us were all too aware of the near impossibility of returning either Hereric or Edwin to a throne. As a result we had no unified purpose to keep us strong, save survival alone. Along with us were a score of women and children. Our journey had started with most of us scared and numb at the horror of the Villa fire where many had lost loved ones. The flight across Mercia had added the fear of pursuit, and the rejection in Tamwerth was yet more to endure. But we had survived and the men had at least grown to feel protective to the women and children. In return they had provided a reason to work together.

As we marched along we grew cautious and never wandered alone whether to collect firewood, hunt or even to deal with bodily needs. Thirty warriors might be hard pressed to defend themselves and their charges against the masterless bands of brigands who roamed the wilds between the realms south and east of Legacæstir.

I often found myself wishing that we were more numerous and probably as a result of that tension my mind played games with me. Was that sound of hooves in the distance the first signs of pursuit? Was that a rock on the hillside or Hussa crouched low, watching us pass by? Those shapes in the woods – were they old tree trunks or an army lying in ambush?

I tried to think of other subjects, but all that did was make me ask questions of myself. Should I have tried to gather more men in Deira before fleeing? Should we have followed Guthred's advice and gone south to Kent and Wessex rather than west to Mercia? What had happened to Earl Harald and his companies? Harald was the Lord of Eoforwic. Just before the attack on the king's fortress that had resulted in our defeat and flight from

Deira, he and Sabert had left Godnundingham along with several hundred men intending to reinforce Eoforwic. They never reached the city as they were ambushed on the road by Aethelfrith's men. Although Sabert had joined us with pitifully few survivors we had heard nothing about Harald since the fall of Deira. Was it possible he had survived? But what if he had? There seemed little hope of us ever meeting with him. Even so, I continued to wonder about his fate.

I was musing on these issues a few days after setting off from Tamwerth, on the day we expected to reach Legacæstir, when suddenly the road ahead was filled with dozens of warriors who streamed out of some woods to the side. We abruptly halted and stared at them.

"Bandits?" enquired Sabert expressing our worst fears in one word.

"Possibly," I answered. Then after a pause I went on, "No, not bandits. They are too well clothed and equipped and they also look like a trained fighting force. These men are regular warriors, not masterless vagabonds, I am certain."

"But whose warriors?" Edwin wondered. "Aethelfrith's, Pybba's?"

"They are British," said Cuthbert whose sharp eyes picked up much that we missed, "they look more British than Saxon and also some have the cross on their shields." He referred to the Christian symbol I had seen at Goddodin.

"But which British I wonder," I speculated. I moved slowly toward the unknown warriors, my arms widespread to show I was not armed. Sabert moved with me as did Edwin. I waved Aedann forward to join us.

A few words in the Welsh tongue from a short, stocky warrior stopped us. His accent was strong and despite having learnt some Welsh, I initially struggled to understand. "Lay down your arms, English raiders, you are our prisoners," Aedann translated.

Sabert, whose Welsh was better than mine, went on to speak several sentences. Twice he pointed at Edwin, once at me and then swept his hand toward us all. He then retrieved the parchment Ceorl had given us by way of introduction and offered it to the Welsh leader. The man hesitated a moment then strode forward to take it. He examined it, but did not seem to understand it. The Welshman considered us for a long moment then nodded and muttered something to Sabert.

Sabert came back. "We are invited to accompany him and his men to a place called Deganwy which I believe is one of King Iago's strongholds on the coast three days from here. We are permitted to hold our weapons, but must march in the centre of the company," he explained. Edwin nodded. The Welsh had no reason to trust us but the letter to Cadfan seemed to be enough to keep us safe as far as Deganwy.

As we started on the journey I spotted Aedann looking around him with something approaching wonder on his face. "What are you thinking?" I asked him after watching him for a while.

He smiled at me, "It is strange to be walking in lands free from your people."

I nodded at him. The lands we now walked through had never fallen to the invading Angles. These were truly Welsh homelands and Gwynedd was at the heart of them – a mountain fastness that I doubted we would ever conquer. "If you had been born here we might never had met."

Aedann shrugged. "Had I been born here I would be a free man."

"You are free, Aedann."

"Only because you have made me so – here I would never have been a slave. I wonder what life would have been like."

"You can always stay here. I released you once from my service and the gods know that you have done enough to choose your own path."

He looked at me sharply. "My path is with you, Cerdic."

I shook my head. "You don't have to tie yourself down. You must feel free to choose."

"I have chosen. I made a mistake last year and I will never do that again," he said, referring to the time when he had seriously considered transferring his loyalty from me to another lord, one who had offered him so much more than I was able to do.

"Prince Theobald's offer of land and name was a good one, Aedann. I do not blame you for that. But I am glad you changed your mind and are still with me."

"As am I, Cerdic," he said and fell into silence as he stared around him again, his eyes once more distant.

To begin with, the road the British took us along ran through low lying lands not unlike the plains we had just crossed between Tamwerth and Legacæstir. Then, gradually, the landscape changed and soon we followed a long, gently curving coast line to our right, whilst to our left, hills sprang up in increasing numbers, heavily forested at first, though as we marched west the hills grew higher, the trees thinned out and we spotted the first signs of the Welsh mountains. Here and there we saw brooks and rivers snaking out of them and plunging down in a froth of white water that would eventually empty into the sea.

"Is this your idea of getting a safe home for us?" Aidith asked peevishly as we marched on. I knew she was anxious, but she was also starting to annoy me so I ignored her.

63

"Have you been to Deganwy before?" I asked Lilla when we paused for the night, the Welsh having allowed us to set up shelters and light fires. Even so, they watched us sullenly, their hands never far from their weapons.

As I expected Lilla shook his head. "No but I have heard of it and know more or less where it is. The clue is in the name: Deganwy means 'Fort on the River Conwy'. We should be there tomorrow if my geography is correct."

True enough another day's march brought us to a wide estuary. On the east side of the mouth of the River Conwy, as it opens to the sea, was a tall hill with twin peaks. One peak was slightly larger than the other. The kings of Gwynedd had fortified these hills as one of their strongholds. On the larger hilltop was a great hall surrounded by other lesser buildings all built of stone with, in some cases, wooden upper stories and thatched roofs. A stone watch tower stood on the lesser hill. An earthen embankment, topped by a battlement made from dry stones piled up into a solid barrier, ran round the base of both peaks, whilst an inner wall lined the north and south edges of a saddle of land that connected the peaks and where various workshops were dotted around. It was an impressive fortress and certainly very defensible.

"What's with all the stone?" Eduard asked with a shiver. Like most of my race he considered such structures, like Roman buildings, with deep suspicion and disapproval, preferring a good wooden hall to anything made from stone. "I don't like it!" he added.

"Oh, I don't know," I replied wistfully for there was something about the king's hall that reminded me of the Villa.

The commander of the warband approached us. "Your warriors, women and children must stay here. Shelter will be found for them shortly. The princes, lords and their huscarls can come with me."

As ever when I left them, Aidith shot me an anxious glance, never quite certain if I would return and if in the meantime harm would come to her and Cuthwine. I put a hand on her shoulder to comfort her but she shook it off. A moment later she turned back, her face apologetic and kissed me on the cheek. "I am sorry, Cerdic ... it's only that I'm worried."

I nodded. "I know my love. I just hope we can find a welcome here." I held her hand for a moment and then followed the princes into the hall.

In that late summer of 603, King Iago of Gwynedd was 55 years old. The kings of Gwynedd had always been, so the tales were told, tall and strong men who had fought great battles. Gwynedd's fortunes had matched those of its lords. Indeed, in the days of Iago's grandfather, Gwynedd had been the most powerful of the British kingdoms, at times holding sway as far as York and Penrith as well as far to the south.

This was no longer so, for Northumbria's rising sun was matched with Gwynedd's sunset – or so it seemed to its people. They were not to know that many of them would live to see a bright, fiery new dawn. But neither was I back then. That is another story of another later year along the path we were following and as tempted as I am to reminisce, I must confine myself to my present telling of the year 603.

And so, contrary to what I had expected, Iago was in fact a short man with thinning grey hair and a paunch of a belly. Indeed, in many ways he was unremarkable and reminded me a little of Aethelric – a man who in another life might have been a baker or a farmer. Yet despite his lack of majesty, when we arrived in his long hall, I for one was apprehensive and the rest

65

of the company even more so. This was the first time many of us, apart from myself and Lilla, had visited the palace of an unconquered British king. We were, after all, the invaders of this land: all the lands that my people owned had been taken from these people. Yet Edwin, Sabert and I held our heads up high and acted the part of a royal party as we walked along the hall, past benches filled by stony-faced warriors and lords who studied us with ill-concealed hostility as we waited to be presented.

What delayed us was that Iago was talking to a group of Irish merchants who were discussing a contract to deliver richly embroidered cloth. Once the agreement was reached the traders, having been invited to stay the night, were found a place at benches down the far end of the hall. Finally we were invited forward and brought out our letter of introduction from Ceorl.

Iago was sitting in a high-backed chair flanked by a slightly taller man in his thirties and standing on the other side, a youth on the verge of manhood. This younger fellow was already taller than the others and broad in the shoulders. He regarded us intently with a fierce interest that chilled me, although I did not know why. Sabert surmised, correctly, that it was the elder of the pair to whom our letter was addressed.

"Prince Cadfan?" Sabert enquired bowing and then handing over the document.

Iago regarded us suspiciously as Cadfan read the letter then turned to speak to the king. "Father," he began in a strong, confident voice, "these people are recommended to us by Lord Ceorl of Mercia, a friend of mine. He asks that we give them shelter. They are from Deira and …"

Iago interrupted. "Mercia is no friend of ours, my son; neither are princes of Deira beloved by us. Why should we welcome them to our court and why give them shelter?"

"Shelter from whom, Father?" the youngest of the three asked, his dark eyes still intense in their gaze upon us. Cadfan glanced at him and then back to the letter.

"Well, Ceorl goes on to say that amongst the party are Prince Edwin and Prince Hereric, brother and son to the late king Aethelric whose land and crown was … so Ceorl claims … usurped by Aethelfrith of Bernicia."

The murmur of whispered conversation rolled around the hall. That was a name that was known to many just as, apparently, was the name of Deira.

Iago glared at us. "So you are Deiran? You sent an army to Catraeth and killed Owain of Rheged. He was a great hero of the old North, why should we shelter the people who murdered him?"

Edwin stepped forward. "I am Prince Edwin, son of the late King Aelle. I admit we did send an army to Catraeth. I admit also that Owain was killed – in battle, not murdered – by one of us. Yet such things happen in battle. Deira and the British kingdoms present were at war. That war is in the past – six years ago. Today the greatest enemy you could face would be Aethelfrith. He seized our land and our crown. We will take it back from him but we need shelter for a while until we are ready to do so."

Iago studied Edwin without comment for a long moment and then turned to his son. "What do you say, Prince Cadfan?"

Cadfan looked up at us from the document. "I think we can listen to their tale at least, Father," he replied.

Iago nodded. "Very well, let us hear the tale. Come princes, let a chair be brought for you each and tell me the tale of your travels," and he waved Edwin and Hereric forward. Cadfan himself took a chair from the side of the hall and placed it to one side of the king's and gestured that Edwin should sit. He then pointed to the youth who stood to Iago's far side. "I introduce to you my son, Cadwallon ap Cadfan." Cadwallon nodded in our direction, but said nothing.

Mead was brought out for us to drink and Edwin, sometimes speaking through Sabert or Lilla when his Welsh failed him, spoke of the wars in Deira, of Aethelfrith's invasion and treachery. Iago and Cadfan listened without at first commenting, but then later asked a few questions about Aethelfrith. Cadwallon said nothing, but from his eager expression when any battle was described, he was apparently more interested in the description of the fighting than in the politics.

Edwin may be young and rash at times, but he had learnt some statecraft and diplomacy from Aethelric or Aelle and perhaps some of the art of telling tales from Lilla, for he told what seemed to me a convincing tale of how badly he had been wronged and how either he or Hereric was the true and rightful King of Deira. The question on my mind, though, was how convinced were Iago and his son? At no point did they express their opinion on the princes' claims. By the time the tale was told dusk was fast approaching and preparation was made for the evening meal in the hall.

Iago now stood and addressed the entire hall. "Prince Edwin has told us a tale of treachery and betrayal in distant Northumbria. I have not yet decided what my response to his request for shelter will be, but whilst I consider it, I will permit him and his followers to stay - for a while at least." He turned to us, "Edwin, Hereric, princes of Deira, I bid you welcome to my hall. It is our tradition and custom to accept into our protection princes and sons of princes. You and your company are welcome to stay here for a month whilst I decide on what then to do about you," Iago said. "We will celebrate your visit with a feast tonight."

Edwin bowed. "You have our gratitude, my Lord King."

It seemed to be going well on the surface, but I was still anxious. I had seen dark, distrustful expressions on the faces of the British lords lining the sides of Iago's hall. Certainly many of them did not approve of their king's choice of guest. Indeed, they looked as if they would sooner Iago had strung us up from the beams of his hall than feast us in it.

"If you will excuse me I will withdraw until the time for the feast is come. My steward will show you to your rooms," Iago was now saying as he got up from his throne. Edwin rose too and gave a respectful bow, as did Sabert. Hereric and I quickly followed their example.

The British royal party turned and passed through a side door into what I assumed were their private quarters. When they were gone, a thin scrawny man with wild black hair came over to us and spoke in hesitant English. "My Lords, I am Belyn, King Iago's steward. If you would care to follow me, the guest rooms are in another building outside. The warriors along with the women and children of your party are already there."

We followed him down the hall and past the Irish traders. As we passed I noticed they were studying us intently. When they saw me looking at them they turned away and started a whispered conversation.

"Come with me, Lord Cerdic," Belyn called impatiently from the hall doors. So I turned away from the nosy Irishmen and gave them no more thought. We passed out of the hall into the dark night. Belyn turned to take us around the great hall to the north and across an open space toward an older building. "This is the old hall. It used to be the hall of king Iago's forefathers of old. We use it now for guest quarters and for some of the king's relatives," Belyn said.

We were about halfway across the hundred–yard gap between the buildings when there was a shout of alarm from behind me. I turned to see Cuthbert at the rear of our company sprawling in the mud. Above him wielding a great sword was a British warrior, clearly a seasoned veteran in his late thirties, his bearded face twisted in fury, his dark hair thinning and already streaked with grey. He was swinging the sword back over his head ready to deliver the death blow. On either side of him twenty or so other warriors were spreading out around us. They were all armed, all with murder burning in their eyes and all clearly ready to strike.

"No!" I shouted, starting towards the fight but knowing as I ran that I could not possibly get there in time to prevent Cuthbert's death. Around me some men stood frozen in surprise or shock whilst others stirred to action. Weapons were drawn from sword belts. Edwin was somewhere to my right also moving forward. I had lost sight of Eduard and Aedann.

As I was moving to Cuthbert's aid a British warrior stepped in front of me and desperate to get to my friend, I prepared to plunge my sword into his belly. Beyond the warrior, Cuthbert had now turned over and was lifting his hand up to ward off the blow. Yet I knew that his action was futile. I had seen men cleaved in two at Catraeth and at Degsastan and knew a hand would never stop the blade!

Chapter Six
Eisteddfodau

With a monstrous roar, a commanding voice broke across the scene. He first shouted a word in Welsh then, "Stop!" in English.

As one the British halted in the middle of their charge towards us. Though they still held their weapons at the ready and eyed us warily and with hatred smouldering on their faces they actually backed off a little. The warrior standing astride Cuthbert spat at him, but did not move, the sword arrested in its downward swing.

To a man all of us English turned our heads to look at the owner of the voice that seemed to have had such a powerful effect upon our would-be Welsh assailants. The voice had come from the shadows off to the south towards the king's hall. After a moment the man who had intervened stepped forward. I did not recall ever having seen him before. He was young, I guessed in his twenties and dressed in fine clothes, like that of a lord, and yet he bore no weapon, not even a shield and spear. He moved to stand over Cuthbert and glared up into the face of the warrior. Although a slight figure by comparison, the young man did not flinch nor show any signs of fear, but addressed the warrior, who now slowly lowered his sword. "Prince Eidyn, please put your weapon away." He then turned to look at a bald–headed fellow who stood nearby and who, whilst unarmed and not fighting, was obviously accompanying Eidyn. "Prince Rhun, I am surprised that a man in your position would allow this to have happened. I must insist that you both back away." He spoke in English and then snapped a few words in Welsh.

My Welsh wasn't up to much, but I understood the fellow called Rhun to say, "Come away, Eidyn, leave them be."

"Rhun sees sense at least," the newcomer said. "Do as he says, Eidyn, please."

Eidyn shook his head and snarled a reply. The younger man took a step closer to him and once more hissed a few words. Whatever they were, the Welsh warrior looked away from him, apparently embarrassed and shamed. Then he gave a curt nod and with a final poisonous glance at Cuthbert he and his companion shuffled away into the shadows. The man stared after them for a moment and then extended a hand to help Cuthbert back onto his feet. Startled, Cuth mumbled his gratitude, which the young Welshman acknowledged with a nod before coming over to join the rest of us. He glanced up and down our group and then, his gaze settling on me, he moved across to stand in front of me.

"I know you, Angle," he said in very good English, looking me up and down, "Indeed it was my recognition of you that saved your party."

I looked at him more closely but was certain we had never met. "I am grateful of course, my Lord, but I do not recall a meeting between us," I responded.

"I am not surprised by that. The last time we were close I was in Goddodin armour and there was an army between us!" He spoke with a sad almost mournful smile. "You were holding the gates at Catraeth. The day you ... the day you slew Owain," he added in a soft, hesitant voice.

"You were there that day ... at Catraeth?" I let out a low whistle. I thanked the gods that this man's memory of a brief encounter some seven years before had stirred when seeing me through the gloom all these miles away.

"Ah, it is because you were at Catraeth that I have saved you. I am a bard you see. I am composing a song about Catraeth. There are few surviving British who were there. I saved you so you could help me with my poem."

"Woden's balls, but I've never been so glad of poetry!" Seeing him more clearly now I knew of his calling, there was something about his bearing that reminded me of Lilla and I wondered if it was the gift of all bards to look so much better groomed than the rest of us. Under his scrutiny I felt unkempt and ragged.

Looking around I saw that most of the Welsh warriors had melted away now the promise of a fight was over, but Edwin, Sabert and Hereric had come to join us in the company of the king's steward. "My Lords," Belyn was saying extending a hand to Cuthbert's saviour. "May I present to you Aneirin the king's poet and bard."

Aneirin bowed. "Princes Edwin and Hereric of Deira I gather," he said a little coldly. Whatever his feeling toward me he obviously felt suspicious of these princes whose kingdom had been part of the downfall of his army. Edwin felt it too and stiffened slightly so I hurried to intervene.

"My Lord Prince, Aneirin was present at the Battle of Catraeth. He charged with the Goddodin cavalry. Most of his fellow warriors died there," I explained.

Edwin gave a slight nod. "I was too young to see that battle but I have heard tales of your valour. As to our enmity with your people there, I now have ample reason to regret the alliance I had with Aethelfrith of Bernicia. Chance and fate now decree that we might be allies," he responded.

Aneirin looked a little surprised then gave a laugh. He slapped Edwin on the shoulder and said. "Nicely put indeed.

Come princeling. I have quarters in the old hall too. Let us break open a cask of mead together," the bard said, leading Edwin away.

I looked at Sabert and caught him winking at me. I nodded back. We were both thinking the same thing. Was this the spoilt brat of only a few months ago? Edwin had certainly matured these few last weeks through the horrors of Degsastan, the downfall of Deira and our flight into exile. Perhaps the young prince might really make it as king one day.

"You unhurt?" I said to Cuthbert who was walking past me, brushing the dirt and mud off his tunic.

"Yes, but I think I might need to change my britches, Cerdic, I almost wet myself!"

"Really?"

"No ... not really. I was joking but merciful Woden I am grateful that Aneirin came when he did," he replied.

"Yes, me too. What made Eidyn go for you like that?"

Cuthbert shrugged, "I have no idea."

"Ah well, we will have to watch out for him and his mate, Rhun. They look like trouble to me. Come on, I will get you a cup of Aneirin's mead," I said and led him towards the old hall.

Later that night we were called to the table of Iago. Edwin and Hereric sat between Cadfan and Cadwallon just to the king's right at the high table. Sabert and I were close by. When we entered and took our seats the old king rose to address the assembled warriors. This time he spoke slowly enough that I could follow most of his words, but in any case, Sabert leaned in behind Edwin and whispered a translation loud enough for us both to hear.

"Warriors of Gwynedd," Iago started in a growling voice. "You have taken oaths to me as Lord and I have treated you well and housed you and fed you. Does all that mean so little to you?" Around the hall I could see not a few mouths open in astonishment and surprise.

"These princes and their party I have invited as guests. I have promised them safety and shelter for a while at least. What I have promised holds you also by virtue of the oaths of loyalty you have made." Now I could see anger on many faces and hear the mutters of discontent. The king slammed his goblet down onto the table and the commotion settled.

"This prince has come here seeking shelter," he continued after a moment. "He might be the prince of an enemy nation but his nation is now occupied by Aethelfrith."

At the mention of that name many men hissed and spat. Iago moved over to lay one hand on Edwin's shoulder and the other on Hereric's. "Prince Edwin and his nephew Hereric claim to be the rightful heirs to Deira. I have not made any claim in support or opposition to that claim, but these men are princes and for the present I extend hospitality to them. So I say to you, obey my commands. Let no harm come to these men or their party. Raise a hand to any one of them and you are raising a hand to me."

He stared for a long time around the room, his glaze finally coming to rest on Eidyn and Rhun. "As for you, Prince Rhun from Rheged and Prince Eidyn from Manau Goddodin, I acknowledge that your realms have suffered the most at the hands of the English. However, you too are guests at my hall. As such I ask you to obey the rules of hospitality. You will not lay a hand on these Angles whilst they remain under my protection. Is that clear?"

At this Rhun said nothing but gave the faintest tilt of the head to show he understood. Eidyn grunted and nodded although rather curtly, and I again thought to myself – *'Cerdic my lad, you will have to watch these fellows.'* The king did not seem to have noticed anything untoward and indicated that the feast should resume, calling on his steward to bring in a great quantity of mead. Soon any ill feelings were drowned in liquid cheer and I confess I do not remember much of the evening that followed.

The following day I emerged rather later than normal into the – in my opinion – over bright midmorning light, my head pounding and with a terrible thirst. Iago's hall had its own spring piped from the hillside to fall into a soak away. I walked over to it in a rather unsteady manner and plunged my head under its icy waters. That started to revive me. As I stood up again I was aware of a commotion near the gates. Glancing over I saw a crowd of perhaps fifty men and women gathering there. There was much talking and chatter. I wandered over and saw Aneirin among them. He was standing with Lilla.

"Ah Cerdic, a good morning to you," he said nodding his head happily.

"You look cheerful this morning Aneirin, I thought you Welsh bards were supposed to be gloomy and reflective, unlike our English ones," I said with a wink at Lilla.

The Welshman laughed. "Yes, I suppose our style and speech can come across that way. We do after all have much to be sad about. But no, today I am happy. We have just heard that a great friend of mine and a mentor is due here at any moment."

"Really – who is that?" I asked. One or two of the Welsh who presumably spoke some of my tongue or else grasped my meaning gave me incredulous glances.

"Ah my pagan friend of the barbarian English," Aneirin replied, "I speak of the greatest bard who ever lived. He has seen much of the wars of the last half a century. He was a friend of

76

Urien of Rheged. Some say he is a wizard. Some say he is Merlin himself. I speak of Taliesen of the Flowing Verse."

"Ah," said I, "I see." I didn't, but I nodded my head and tried to look intelligent. I must have failed.

"Truly you are an ill–educated race!" the young bard said, seeing that the name meant nothing to me. "Taliesen has composed much of our greatest verse. And he is coming here. You see there is to be a bardic contest right here in the next few days. The foremost bards are coming to tell stories and sing songs. It will be a great event."

"A contest? Will you have a go then Lilla?" I asked my friend.

"I think I must – if only to prove to the Welsh that not all of us Angles are barbarians," he replied, raising an eyebrow at me.

"What about you, Aneirin, will you participate?" I asked.

He looked at me as if I was an idiot. "Yes, Cerdic. I do believe I will."

My attention was brought back to the main gate by a commotion. I saw a number of Welshmen pointing earnestly and smiling. Aneirin and I pushed our way to the front. Then I could see the cause of the row, for walking through the crowd toward the king's hall was an old man. "Ah ...Taliesen, he comes," Aneirin sighed next to me and moved forward to clasp the old man's hand. They were clearly acquainted for they greeted each other warmly.

I saw a man who must be in his seventies at least, his face wrinkled beneath bushy eyebrows that were as silver as his hair and beard, both of which reached down perhaps a foot. He wore a chaotic assortment of colourful but extremely tatty clothes, most of which did not match each other and were heavily patched. 'So not all bards are tidy', I thought, hiding a smile. Taliesen was not actually that tall, although what he lacked in stature he made up for in terms of charisma. He had an aura about him; something that reached out from him and made you aware he existed. Indeed, it was hard to be other than aware of him. Glancing around I saw that he had the rapt attention of the entire crowd. He must have seen me looking bemused, for he pointed at me and asked Aneirin something. Glancing in my direction, the young bard said something in reply and the pair came over to me.

"I understand that I am addressing the Lord Cerdic from distant Deira," the old man said in a deep, melodious voice. He too spoke good English, but his tone was unfriendly and challenging.

"Yes sir," I replied, not sure how best to respond.

"I am Lilla... an English bard," Lilla said at my side, extending his hand. Taliesen ignored it and continued staring at me.

"You are truly the man who killed Owain, son of Urien, at the Battle of Catraeth?" He went on in a whisper so only the three of us could hear, "Also I gather you were present at Degsastan when there was a great slaughter of our people."

"I do not deny any of this," I replied.

He sniffed. "I gather that Iago has granted you hospitality here despite all that." He was now speaking normally and many of the crowd were paying attention.

"He has."

"Is Prince Rhun aware who you are?"

I frowned, "I ... well, he knows my name," I replied, uncertain how to answer.

"But not about your defence of the gates at Catraeth?"

I shrugged, "He may do. I have not told him. Why?"

Taliesen said nothing in reply for a long moment. Finally he sniffed again and ignoring my question, said, "I see. Well I am not sure I approve." Then with no more words he turned his back on me and wandered off towards the king's hall leaving me standing. I was aware that many in the crowd were sneering at me.

As Lilla and I walked away, Aneirin caught up with us,. "Oh dear," I said, "I don't think your friend likes me.

The young bard shook his head. "He has little reason to. Taliesen was a close friend of Owain and his father. He wrote many poems about their bravery. You will find that here you and your people are the monsters. But the man who killed Owain would excite a special kind of hatred that you will have to work hard to overcome."

I pondered this as I asked another question. "Why did he ask about Rhun and whether he knew who I was? What is so special about Rhun?"

Lilla swore. "Thunor's balls, but have you never listened to any of my stories, Cerdic?"

"I don't recall you ever mentioning Rhun. What do you mean?"

Aneirin stared at me incredulously. "You really don't know who Rhun is, do you?" he asked after a moment.

"Know what?" I snapped, growing frustrated now. "Who is he?"

"Rhun is not just any old prince of Rheged. He is the young-est son Urien and the brother of Owain."

I gawped at him, "Merciful Woden!" I swore. "Does he know I killed his brother at Catraeth?"

Aneirin shrugged. "That is what Taliesen was wondering, but I don't think so – at least not yet."

I was getting increasingly confused. "Well what is he doing here, if Owain is dead? Owain had no children did he? So should

Rhun not be king in Rheged?"

"Rhun abdicated and joined the Church as a bishop soon after Owain died, so the crown passed to Rhun's son Rhoerth, who clings onto the last vestiges of Rheged, harassed by Aethelfrith all the time, whilst Rhun grieves for his lost brother and takes comfort in the Church here in Gwynedd, far away from anything that would remind him of his loss. He and Owain were very close."

At Catraeth I had been the hero: the man who held the gates against the British hordes – the man who killed the golden king of Rheged, Owain. In Deira I had been feted and cheered. Here, if they knew who I was, I would be the villain. Here, I was the man who had destroyed their dreams. When - for surely it was not a question of if - Rhun found out about me, was I in for more trouble? I imagined so. "Perhaps we should not have come here," I said to Lilla, who shrugged.

Aneirin was nodding. "Many here are asking why you did. We are not fools, Cerdic. We know why Ceorl sent you here. The man who will one day be King in Mercia hopes to win our friendship. I have to say he might have chosen better ambassadors," Aneirin said. Then the smile was back on his face and he slapped me on the shoulder. "Well, my good Englishman, while you are here we will have to see if we can broaden your horizons a little. Barbarian you might be but when I have finished with you we will make an educated man of you. You are lucky to be here for the Eisteddfodau," he said, sounding proud.

I had no idea what an Eisteddfodau was. I did not say so, but Aneirin could tell. He laughed gently. "You really are barbarians. An Eisteddfod is…" he began, but Lilla, eager to show that we were not all ignorant, continued the explanation.

"An Eisteddfod is the Welsh name for a bardic competition –

such as that we were talking about earlier. They take them very seriously and they are well attended."

"Very good," Aneirin complimented Lilla. "It was actually Iago's great-grandfather who instituted the tradition. He was Maelgwyn and a great king was he. He lived about ninety years ago. Slightly before my time," he grinned. "The king was so keen to have his own bard win that he had all the other bards swim across the river Conwy. When they came to play, all their instruments were wet and made a terrible noise."

Aneirin looked worried for a moment then added, "I hope Iago does not get any foolish ideas to emulate his ancestor. I can't swim!"

We all laughed at that. Then, my head spinning and not sure what I was going to see when this Eisteddfodau occurred, I left the two bards talking about poems and went to seek out Aidith for some sympathy, along with a dose of the powdered willow bark she kept in her medicinal supplies. I found her, Gwen and Millie sitting a table in the old hall, sorting through the gowns and tunics, which we had managed to buy from the Welsh. Cuthwine and Theobald, one of Cuthbert's nephews, were sitting under the same table playing with some wooden warriors I had whittled for them during our journey. Aidith scowled at my request.

"It's your own stupid fault you have headache, Cerdic, you drink too much!" Nevertheless she poured some of the powder into a wooden cup and added a little wine and honey before thrusting it at me.

A few nights later the king's company and guests were called to Iago's hall for a feast to mark the bardic contest. The hall was crammed full of warriors, nobles and the king's servants, and all drank and ate well. Then Iago rose and welcomed all to the event and in particular the bards who would participate in the competition. There were about a dozen of them including Taliesen and Aneirin. I learned later that these great meetings are actually quite rare. The Welsh were a race for bards and poets, but they were a solitary lot. To have so many in one spot was remarkable.

The contest began. Some sang while others recited speech. I tried to get Aedann to tell us what was going on but he stared in wonder and listened so intently that I left him entranced and asked Sabert to translate, as best as he could, those words we could not understand. Eventually Aneirin came over and sat by me and explained not only what the poets were saying, but what their stories meant and who the characters were: something Sabert was, of course, unable to help with. Even when I did not understand the words, the music spoke to me, plucking at my heartstrings, and looking around the hall I could see tears standing in the eyes of even the hardest warriors. Stories were told of ancient times before the Romans came, then of later years when a king they called Arthyr united the British against the Angles and Saxons and won a great battle a hundred years ago at a place called Badon. Further poets spoke of dark times as their lands and people slowly fell to my own race of marauders – the Angles and Saxons – and of great times when almost godlike warlords and princes, fighting under Christian banners, forced us back.

Then Taliesen rose and performed a poem. It was about Urien, the king who led the attacks against Lindisfarne. He had been a great man who had fallen in the wars against us and who was considered a holy warrior. Through these tales it became obvious that our hosts belonged to a race that had a rich history and culture from far back in time right through to the present.

Through it all was woven a note of sorrow at what was lost and above all, the idea of heroic defiance even when the odds were against them.

"Were a foe in a hill,
Urien will stab him;
Were a foe in a dale,
Urien has pierced him;
Were a foe on a mountain,
Urien conquers him;
Were a foe on a hillside,
Urien will smite him:
Foe on path, foe on peak,
Foe at every bend...."

And so it went on.

When Taliesen finished speaking there was an awed silence. The Welsh seemed to be under a spell. Even to me, via a translation, the bard's words were powerful, and I and everyone around me were sure he would be declared the champion.

Then it was Aneirin's turn. Getting to his feet he began a poem that no one had heard before, but which he had composed in the years since he had spotted me with my short sword in my hand, standing over the body of Owain at the gates of Catraeth. In a haunting voice he told of the last ride of the Goddodin. He spoke of how they had feasted together and how they prepared for battle. He described how their armour and weapons shone in the sunlight and how they slew their opponents with the wrath of the Almighty, only in the end to fall to the superior numbers of the enemy. His verses named all his companions one by one, describing their valour and courage before describing their deaths.

"…Shield flashing fire, he bowed before no one,
He nursed his thirst for glory…
… I saw blades in the swarm fighting with a savage foe…"

When he finished Taliesen and the other Welsh were in tears. Aneirin had written a masterpiece and all there knew it. It seemed he had not needed to ask me much about Catraeth after all, for it was all there and even I, the enemy, was transported to that place and time, filled with pride and sorrow.

Taliesen came forward and presented Aneirin to us, declaring him the Champion. The British nobles rose and cheered, stamping their feet and applauding. We Angles clapped politely, although most of us had understood little. Yet it was clear that above all else the one thing the poems and songs of the Welsh were about was the great enemy: the English. Looking around that room I saw many a glare in our direction, many with a hint of threat in their eyes. I spotted Rhun studying us … or was it me in particular? His murderous expression made the hairs rise on the back of my neck.

"Powerful words," Sabert remarked, apparently noticing the same thing.

"Indeed, such poems are used to stir up their enmity against us," Lilla commented.

Sabert nodded, "We need to find a way to make them feel better about us if we are to stay."

Lilla looked thoughtful. "Leave this to me," he said and stepping forward raised his voice to ask, "May an English bard be permitted to speak at this noble event?"

"We don't need to hear your words," Eidyn hissed.

"Let him speak," Aneirin answered.

Taliesen did not look happy, but shrugged.

Lilla bowed to Iago and then came to stand in the middle of

the hall. He spoke in fluent Welsh and once again Aneirin translated his words for the benefit of our company.

"Lo, I tell the tale of the noblest of us all. I tell the saga of the one born a mere servant who became the great Enchanter..."

Taliesin looked up sharply as the tale began, recognising himself in Lilla's words. It seemed our English bard was going to tell a story of Taliesen himself! Merciful Woden, I prayed, don't let Lilla bugger this up. If his tale was disrespectful or insulting we could all be dangling from the timbers far above us before the day was done. My anxiety must have shown on my face for Lilla winked at me before launching into his tale and it was soon clear that I had worried needlessly.

"Once, long ago, Taliesen was called Gwion," – so Lilla's tale went – "and he was a servant to a certain Lady Ceridwen, an enchantress in the days when King Arthyr ruled. Once day Gwion drank from a cauldron containing a mystical brew she had made and he became extraordinarily learned in various arts and full of the spirit of prophecy. Yet Gwion was afraid for he knew Ceridwen would be angry," Lilla continued. "Indeed, when she returned and discovered what he had done her temper became uncontrollable. So he fled by turning into a hare and darting over the grassy land and she became a greyhound and charged after him..."

Lilla was acting the part now, jumping across the hall like a hare then barking like a dog. The Welsh watched him with bemused expressions on their faces.

"...To escape the hound Gwion transformed himself into a fish and jumped into a river, but Ceridwen then turned into an otter and continued the pursuit. Leaping out of the water Gwion took flight as a bird in the air and in response she became a hawk..."

85

Lilla now swam through the air like a fish, leant over a table and pretended to paddle and then clambered onto the table and leapt off it whilst flapping his arms like wings. I could not help but chuckle as I looked around at his stunned audience.

"…When Gwion became exhausted by the chase Ceridwen managed to force him into a barn, where he turned into a single grain of corn and she in turn became a tufted black hen and ate him. She appeared to be triumphant. Yet this was all part of Gwion's plan, for as a result of his powers she became pregnant and the grain turned to a child within her…"

As the tale went on, the icy glares of the Welsh lords gradually softened as they watched the antics of Lilla and then, one by one, despite themselves their faces cracked. Starting with a titter and rising like a great flood, laughter grew and grew, especially now, when Lilla stuffed a cloak up his tunic and waddled like a heavily pregnant woman around the hall.

"…Ceridwen resolved to kill the child, knowing it was Gwion, but when he was born he was so beautiful that she couldn't, so she had him put into a hide–covered basket and thrown into a lake. The basket floated across the lake and was found by Elphin, the Lord of Ceredigion, who was fishing for salmon. Naming the child Taliesen, Elphin soon discovered his great powers and boasted that his bard was the best in the land. They had a competition in which Taliesen was able to use sorcery to make the other bards dumb and then he sang, and of course he won."

Coming to the end of his story, Lilla looked across at Taliesen and smiled. "I have to say that I am rather glad you did not use these powers today or I would not have had a chance to speak, and nor would Aneirin," Lilla said, giving a brief bow to the assembled warriors and a much deeper one to his fellow bards.

In the end even the stern–faced Taliesen was smiling and

coming forward extended a hand to Lilla. Only Rhun and Eidyn were not laughing. Rhun's expression was unreadable whilst Eidyn stared at us, his arms stubbornly crossed, implacable hatred standing in his dark eyes.

"Princes Edwin and Hereric," Taliesen said, "it has been said that I am the most powerful weaver of words in the land, yet today it seems you English also have your share of poets of great power. For the sake of Lilla and his words, today let us forget our enmity and drink together."

Edwin nodded and with a cheer Aneirin poured them each a goblet of mead. "Nicely done, Lilla," I whispered to the bard. "We might not be safe here yet and those two need to be watched," I glanced at Rhun and Eidyn, "but whilst an hour ago the whole company was ready to lynch us, now I think they will leave us alone for a while."

Lilla grinned at me, accepting the compliment but saying nothing. More mead was served and the feasting continued. I yawned and was just giving thought to calling it a night, thinking that by now Aidith would be tucked up warming the furs for me, when the doors to the hall flew open. The winds outside blew a cold gust at us and all heads turned that way.

A bedraggled and extremely dirty but vaguely familiar figure walked in. He glanced around the hall until he saw Edwin and came over towards us. My hand went to my dagger in alarm. Was this an assassin?

But then, sharp-eyed as always, Cuthbert gasped out, "By the gods it's Lord Harald!"

With a shout of joy we all recognised him then.

The travel–worn man bowed slightly and said to Edwin, "Any chance of a drink my prince, I've been on the road for weeks and you are a frigging hard man to find!"

Chapter Seven
Earl Harald Returns

An hour later we Angles were all gathered together in the old hall. Harald had brought a number of men with him and these were found places in the rooms provided for us. Once food and drink had been supplied to his men, Harald agreed to tell us his tale of events that had occurred since Sabert had last seen him weeks before, on the road outside Eoforwic. Harald took a gulp of ale. This appeared to revive him for he seemed once more the strong lord of Deira's largest city, a man who had even been considered a possible successor to Aelle until he had turned down the offer in favour of Aethelric.

"When the Picts attacked us it was... well, it was a frigging disaster, to be honest. I took two hundred men along that road and Sabert just as many, but the Picts had double our number and smashed into us. We lost so many, almost all of us killed. It was hopeless. I could see no sign of Sabert and had no idea what had happened to him or even if he was still alive and so, with those few men I could gather about me, I made a break to the West. My own estates are outside Eoforwic and I headed for them, thinking to get back to Godnundingham somehow, but the following day I learned that the palace had been attacked and that..." he glanced at Hereric and Edwin, "King Aethelric was dead. I did not know if any had survived, only that Aethelfrith had taken the crown, declaring himself King of Deira and all of Northumbria."

Hereric stared into the firepit and said nothing. Edwin swore. "I will kill the bastard. One day I will!" No one else said anything. What was there to say? Harald continued his tale.

"It was chaos after that. Then I heard that the princes had escaped and that Aethelfrith was scouring the country for them. That lifted my spirits I can tell you. The Picts and Bernicians were all over the place, but none came to my estates, though it was obviously only a matter of time and I had to decide what to do. Then I heard rumour of a boat crossing the Humber with at least one of the princes on board. That decided me. I had to find out if it was true. I asked for men willing to follow me. I had some gold for payment and that, plus the promise of more, persuaded some. Others came out of loyalty to me or to old King Aelle and his heirs. Anyway, to cut a long story short, I set off to seek you out and here I am."

"And right good it is to see you. How did you find us?" Sabert asked.

"We headed for Tamwerth and arrived two days after you had left. Apparently that bastard Hussa was in a right state when he discovered you'd gone; threatened dire punishment to anyone who was found to have helped you. He was hopping mad when no one would admit to knowing anything about it. Lucky for us he went off in a huff before we arrived - otherwise I think that might have been the end of my travels! As it was, Pybba seemed embarrassed by our presence and we were shooed into a house and left under guard for a day. I think the king was trying to decide whether to tell Aethelfrith about us or send us away. The next day, though, a lord came to see me and told me where you had gone, so we saved Pybba the trouble and left of our own accord."

"Ceorl?" I suggested.

"Yes ... Ceorl, that was the fellow."

"It was he helped us to escape," I explained.

"So, he moves a few more pieces onto the board..." Edwin muttered as he too now stared into the fire. After a moment he looked up at Harald again. "So my brother the King is truly dead then. I assumed it to be so, but I had hoped..." Edwin's voice sounded flat as it trailed into silence. Then, perhaps trying to hide his emotions, he went on, "Sounds like you have had quite the adventure Lord Harald. Well done indeed to get here. How many are you?"

"Twenty-five, my Lord, plus me," Harald replied.

"Will they follow you, these men?"

"They will, my Prince. They will pledge themselves to you and follow me, I am certain of it, if for nothing else, then for a chance to get revenge on Aethelfrith. After all, they were with me when we lost almost two hundred men. Many of these men's brothers or their friends lie dead outside Eoforwic. So whether they do it for honour or for revenge they will follow us."

"So we now number fifty or so men. Best part of a company. Not much – but it's a start," Edwin mused.

"We need allies my Lord," observed Sabert.

"You know the British better than I, Lord Sabert. What do you think of these people?" the prince asked.

Sabert took a deep breath and considered that question. "They are a proud people and somewhat strange, but it seems they are basically honourable and I do not believe that Iago will betray us once he has accepted us as his guests. However, it will take more than a sense of honour to persuade some of the other British. We must look for opportunities to impress. I think we must also offer our service to Iago until such time as you can regain your throne."

Edwin looked startled by Sabert's opinion but then gave a small laugh. "A month ago I was a prince of Deira. I was heir to the throne perhaps after my brother. Or at the least if Hereric had become king I would have been his most powerful advisor. Perhaps even a sub-king. I was rich and owned many treasures, horses and clothes. Here, I am leader of a refugee army of less than sixty, I have only one good set of clothes and we have half a dozen nags between us. We are forced to depend on the good will of the enemies of my race. Even more than that, you are now saying we must offer our service to him as if we were mercenaries."

Sabert went to speak but Edwin raised his hand. "Relax, Sabert, I know you are right. We must do whatever is needed to survive and gain our strength. I was just amused by what the die of Fate has rolled us."

Later that same day Belyn came to see us. "Iago requests your presence in his hall," he announced.

"What about?" I asked.

"There is a Saxon messenger arrived and I think the king wants your opinion."

Sabert and I exchanged an anxious glance, both thinking it might be Hussa.

"Of course we will come," Edwin answered and accompanied by Lilla, all the lords and a number of our warriors we walked across to the king's hall.

As the doors opened I looked around the room, seeking sight of the one man I hoped had not tracked us down. Near the king's high chair a small party stood. There were in fact five men, four I assumed from their chain shirts were escorts or huscarls, although here in the king's presence they were unarmed other than with their seaxs. The fifth man, I was relieved to see, was not Hussa. The fellow was about thirty-five and wore a long brown tunic and a hooded cloak, which was thrown back to reveal a head of red hair, a bald circle shaved on top of his scalp, which Lilla informed me was a monk's tonsure. It was the first time in my life that I had seen a monk and I scrutinised him closely as we came near.

Iago looked up as we approached. "Ah, Prince Edwin, Prince Hereric I wanted you here. This party is from another of your English kingdoms – that of distant Kent, so I thought you might like to hear their message. This man calls himself Father Bartholomew."

"You come from the Bretwalda?" Edwin addressed the monk.

He turned to look at the prince then shook his head. "Not exactly – we come from Augustine," he replied.

The name clearly meant nothing to Edwin, who glanced at me for guidance but I just shrugged in ignorance never having heard the name. Sabert coughed and stepped forward. "If I may, Sire"

Edwin nodded.

"I have heard of Augustine. As some of the ports on the coast of Deira were in my earldom I occasionally received news from traders. Before your father died I mentioned this Augustine to him. I also talked to your brother about him. A few weeks after Catraeth a merchant of fine cloth from Flanders put in at Dorsa before coming north. He told me that when he had visited the court of Aethelberht a while ago, a party of priests and monks had recently arrived there from Rome. They called themselves Christians and their purpose was supposedly to convert the Saxons and Angles to the religion of their Christ God. The Bretwalda had permitted them to stay. Then, not so long ago I heard from another trader that Aethelberht had himself become a Christian and renounced Woden and the gods of our people."

92

Sabert's voice was condemning and disapproving.

"Praise God that he has seen the light of Christ and embraced the faith," Father Bartholomew intoned. Sabert glared at him but did not respond.

"So what are you doing here, monk?" Guthred asked.

"We are tasked by Pope Gregory himself with reaching out across the lands of the Angles, Jutes and Saxons. That work, which was begun in Kent and has now moved into Wessex and Sussex has, by the grace of God, already born fruit. But the Pontiff has also granted us authority and commission to make contact with the bishops of the Church in the lands of the Britons. Our task is to bring the Church under one authority and one primate in Britain."

"I imagine that would be this Augustine you speak of?" I asked.

The monk fixed me with a cold stare. "He is appointed both by God and by Gregory as their representative in Britannia, so naturally it would be he."

"How convenient," Eduard muttered from just behind me.

"But it is in fact fortuitous that you are here, Prince Edwin," the monk continued, either not hearing or ignoring Eduard's dry wit, "for it is God's will that your land must also hear the gospel, embrace the word of God and join the brotherhood of the Church."

"Why must it?" Sabert retorted, but Edwin held up a hand to interrupt him and addressed Bartholomew.

"I am afraid that I am in no position to do such a thing. I am in exile. Aethelfrith murdered my brother and usurped the throne of Deira. Even if I wanted to become a Christian I should still be far from able to invite you to found a church there. I have but a small force of men."

The monk's eyes narrowed. "That need not always be the case."

"What do you mean?" Guthred asked, coming forward to join Edwin.

"I mean that God would surely look with favour on the efforts of a wronged prince who embraced the faith, and perhaps such a man would find allies amongst the faithful."

Guthred turned to look at me, his eyebrows raised and a sneer of triumph on his lips. I knew what was coming and shook my head to silence him before he could say, 'I told you so. We should have gone to Kent.' Perhaps he was right, but the die was already cast and we were here, there was little point in discussing it further.

Iago tapped his knuckles on his chair to regain the monk's attention. "What of this meeting of bishops you mentioned earlier?"

Bartholomew moved back towards the king. " I am instructed to ask, Majesty, if you will agree to send your bishops to a meeting two weeks from today. The other Welsh bishops have already agreed to attend."

Iago glanced across at Rhun who stood nearby. "What do you say to this invitation, Bishop?"

"We will go," Rhun said after a moment. From his unenthusiastic expression I judged he was not keen on the idea, but maybe he could think of no reason against it.

"Very well," said Bartholomew, his lips curving in a satisfied smile as Iago nodded his agreement. "There is an oak tree on a small hill where the borders of Mercia, Gwynedd and Powys come together. My escort will tell you where the place is. There we shall meet." He turned back to Edwin, "And you, Highness, will you come and meet Augustine too?"

Edwin glanced at Guthred, Sabert and me. Guthred was nodding enthusiastically, Sabert shaking his head, not keen on the idea. I shrugged noncommittally. Edwin frowned at the mixed advice he was being given and then appeared to make up his mind. "Very well, we will come and hear what he has to say."

"Can't Cuthwine and I come too?" Aidith asked later when I told her that I would have to leave Deganwy for a couple of weeks. She was sitting at a table in the old hall, sorting through our spare clothes, searching for damage to repair. On the table lay her needles and thread. I shook my head.

"Sorry, my love, but we are only taking a small party as escort for the princes. I get the feeling that Rhun was not at all happy when he heard I was going too. He sent instructions that we are to limit our numbers."

Aidith put my tunic down and stared at me. "Why do you have to go at all? Why can't Guthred provide escort… or Harald now he has arrived? Why is it always you?"

She had a point and I gave thought to going to Edwin and suggesting that I stay behind, but then I recalled my promise to King Aethelric that I would care for the princes. I reminded her of this.

"That was to do with them being in danger was it not?" she said crossly. "They are just going to a conference of churchmen. Surely they will come to no harm in such a gathering?"

I shrugged. "Who is to say where the danger is these days?"

Aidith frowned at that and I thought we were about to argue, but then her shoulders slumped in acceptance. She sighed and put her hand on mine, "Oh very well. You be careful though, Cerdic. The way that Rhun looks at you makes me shiver."

"Of course I will be careful." I smiled to reassure her, but I knew exactly what she meant.

We travelled through the Kingdom of Powys and then down the Severn Valley. Having agreed to the meeting, the Welsh bishops had extracted promises from the kings of Powys, Gwynedd and the other kingdoms we passed through that there would be a cessation of fighting and a truce honoured for the duration of the conference, and that we be allowed safe passage to and from the meeting place. Even so, I was anxious about this expedition, travelling as I must in the company of Prince Rhun.

The journey took five days and although Prince Edwin's small party had been permitted to travel with the Welsh bishops it was clear they did not welcome our company. Each day we rode a little way behind them and each night set up our own camp if outdoors or, if staying in monasteries and abbeys along the way, we were found quarters separate from the bishops. When we had first set out I had watched Rhun from a distance, my tension rising as I wondered if he yet knew for what I was responsible and more to the point, how he would react when he did, for sooner or later someone would surely tell him. As the days went by and he did not seek me out I decided I was worrying unnecessarily. Lulled into a false sense of security I began to relax, so was taken by surprise when the day of reckoning came.

Rhun left it to the day before we were due to arrive at the meeting place when I was returning to the campfire from emptying my bladder in the woods. Before I reached the circle of light given out by the flames, he stepped out of the trees ahead of me. My hand went to my belt, but I had left Wreccan at Deganwy and whilst I had brought Catraeth along, it was with my pack by the fire. My fingers found my seax and rested upon the hilt. Rhun saw my move and shook his head, "You do not need any weapons. I am unarmed and mean you no harm – today at least."

"Indeed?" I replied, searching the woods for any men of Rhun's who may be hiding there.

Seeing my anxiety he gave a bark of mocking laughter. "Nor will I instruct my men to harm you."

"*Today* at least?" I asked.

"Quite so, but I did want to talk with you. I do indeed know who you are, Cerdic son of Cenred of the Villa. I know that you killed my beloved brother at Catraeth."

I hesitated, considered lying, but decided in the end to be honest. "It was a fair fight, in the middle of a battle. It is not like I murdered him," I protested, "he could as easily have killed me."

"I know," he said.

I waited for him to say more, surprised by his apparent calmness, but he seemed to be content just to look at me, which unnerved me. "So what do you want... if not to kill me that is?" I asked after a long pause.

"I am a man of God. I try to avoid fighting and I will not kill you in revenge, but know this: after Catraeth and Owain's death a darkness took me. I hated your people and in particular I hated the man of whom I heard rumours, this Cerdic son of Cenred. You! The madness took my soul and would have destroyed me. I started raising an army, intent on marching at once to this Villa they told me of and laying waste to all I found there."

As he spoke an image of the destruction Hussa had wrought at the Villa came to me. Rhun was motivated by the same burning desire for revenge as my half-brother. I looked around me again. Was I *really* safe today, or was he lying?

He watched me for a moment and then glanced away from

me into the shadows gathered between the boughs of ash and oak, his expression distant. "My advisors and my son argued against this. They told me the truth. After Catraeth Rheged was not able to go to war again for our army was destroyed and we had no allies. I did not want to listen. I raged and shouted at them. Then one day the darkness did take me and I fell into a deep, abiding melancholy that nothing, not even thoughts of revenge, could lift."

He paused to wipe his hand across his face and for the first time I felt a twinge of sympathy for his distress, which was plain to see.

"At least in that despair I finally saw the truth," he continued. "I knew I could not go on as king, so I abdicated and Rhoerth took over. I left Rheged and travelled to Powys first and then to Gwynedd and in time embraced the Church and became a bishop here. I turned away from anything to do with your people – your race. Only in my faith did I find solace and the strength to go on. Slowly, day my day, I improved and regained purpose."

"I am glad to hear that. I am sorry about your brother..." I started to apologise.

He held his hand up. "Stop! I did not say I forgave you for what you did. I never have. I just buried those thoughts away and turned to God's work. This I could do for there was little to remind me of you and your people."

I nodded, "Until now you mean?"

"Yes... until now. Until the day that very same Cerdic, son of Cenred, Lord of the Villa and Earl of the Southern Marches came to Iago's court leading his rag–tag collection of princes, warriors, women and children."

"I see."

He shook his head and stepped closer, his eyes filled with

venom. "I don't think you do see, Cerdic. I feel... I feel the darkness rising once more. I want to kill you. My hands yearn to close around your throat. I want to spill your blood as you spilled Owain's then watch you die. Keep away from me, Cerdic. Take your people away from us and be gone before the madness overtakes me and it is too late."

Then, with no more words, he turned on his heel and stomped away into the twilight leaving me alone wondering what I should do about him. I was still wrestling with the problem as I returned to the campfire and tried in vain to get some sleep before the final day of our journey on the morrow.

The bishops' meeting place became known as 'Augustine's Oak' or in later years, 'Holy Oak' when the Christians renamed everything so that it referred to their God and their Church. When I was born we English believed in the gods of our fathers. That is how I was raised, but it seems that by the time I die, which cannot be long now, we all will believe in this single God – this Christ about whom we were meeting on that distant day beneath the boughs of an ancient oak tree which, according to the local Christians, had been alive since the crucifixion of their Christ. How did it happen?

As we sat at benches that had been placed around its broad, gnarled trunk, I asked Sabert the same question about Kent and how its people had abandoned the beliefs of a thousand years, turned away from their gods and become Christian.

"Politics, my dear Cerdic," was his response, "simply politics."

"Why?"

"The King of Kent is married to a princess of the Franks. The Franks are Christian and aided Augustine in his journey from

Rome. Francia is more powerful than Kent and so Aethelberht seeks its favour. By becoming Christian, by allowing and assisting this mission, he appeases his father–in–law and increases his influence. Politics – that is all it is. Did you think he had *'seen the light'?"* Sabert asked with a cynical sneer.

I shook my head although I really had no idea about all of this.

"It is for the same reason that we should agree that if we return to Deira, Augustine can send a mission," Guthred put in, leaning forward between us from the bench behind.

Sabert turned to reply, his face screwing up into a scowl. Before he could say anything though, I tapped him on the shoulder because the bishops of the Welsh and the English had approached and were entering the circle of benches, taking their places at the front. In the middle of the Welsh contingent was none other than Prince Rhun. It seemed he had risen to high prominence in this role. He glared at us as he took his place and then turned his scowl on the English party from Kent, which was now entering the circle. Leading them was a man in his mid–forties with a black beard and a shaved head. He wore a finely embroided cloak over a long tunic. For a moment his expression seemed almost cold as he studied the ranks of Welsh bishops and priests. Then he turned to sit down at a space that had been left for him in the middle of the English.

Bartholomew stood and unrolling a parchment, cleared his throat and began reading so all could hear. "Gregory, Bishop of Rome and Primate of Christendom himself confirmed Archbishop Augustine here with the charge of the Holy See of Canterbury and Primacy in Britain. Our purpose this day is to unite the remnants of the Church in the lands of the Britons with the Church established anew in Kent and spreading out across the lands of the Saxons."

This was almost exactly the wrong way to start the meeting. The Welsh began muttering amongst themselves and I heard Rhun chuntering about "remnants". He got to his feet. "The monk can be forgiven for ignorance of the situation in Britain, given he represents a Church that comes from *Rome*. Yes, Rome, which abandoned these islands two hundred years ago! Now you come here suggesting that we be united with you? No – more than that – that we bow down and accept your primacy over us. What we find hard to accept is that you come from the lands of the Saxon invaders and were accompanied by these invaders. You chose to take your mission not to Welsh lands first, but to pagan English lands."

Augustine pointed a finger at Rhun. "We followers of Christ are commanded to witness to all men. If you had been doing this then my mission would not now be needed here at all."

"You are suggesting that we should preach to the heathen – to the very people who enslaved our forefathers and took their land off them?"

"That is exactly what I am suggesting. Forgiveness is divine. You should do just that. *Love your enemies*, saith the Lord."

"Easy for a Roman to say," Rhun spat. "Your land was not taken from you by such as they." He pointed a shaking finger at Edwin, "Your fathers were not slain by them, nor your... brothers." This time his gaze drifted across to me.

Augustine shrugged. "That may be so. Nevertheless, this is what we are commissioned to do. As the book of the Apostle Matthew tells us: *'Go ye therefore, and teach all nations, baptizing them in the name of the Father, and of the Son, and of the Holy Ghost.'"*

Rhun shook his head, his hands curling into tight fists, but before he could reply, Augustine spoke again. "There are other matters in addition to your approach to missionary work that we must address."

"Oh? Such as?"

"The dating of Easter. Your calendar is in error. The Church of Rome has decreed and calculated the correct date for the celebration of this feast. It is critical that all Christians celebrate it at the same time."

Rhun shook his head. "How can you be so sure that you are right and we are wrong?"

Augustine gave Rhun a look that a father might give a child making some basic error. "You are still using the Jerome Computus, Bishop Rhun. That is simply not accurate enough. I have here," he reached back to take a scroll from one of his priests and passed it to Rhun, "the current computus by Dionysius. If you adopt this, your practice will be brought in line with the wider Church."

Rhun unrolled the scroll and examined it before passing it to another bishop. "I do not see why it matters so much…"

"Matters? Matters? Of course it matters! It is imperative that the Church in your Welsh lands be brought into the same practice as we in Rome."

"Is it just Easter that you wish to discuss?"

Augustine blustered. "I have hardly begun. There is your conduct of baptism; your approach to mission to the pagan English, which I have already addressed; then, of course, the tonsure."

"The tonsure?" Rhun glanced around at the other bishops and then back at Augustine "You are concerned about the way we cut our hair?" There was a thread of disbelief, almost of amusement in his voice.

"I've had enough," Eduard muttered from behind me. "I have no idea what these idiots are talking about and I care even

102

less. I am going to find a beer and a woman in the nearest town. You will find me in an ale house. Coming Aedann?"

Aedann shook his head. "No, I want to listen."

"You do?" I asked, sorely tempted to go with Eduard, but feeling I would have to stay and endure this.

"These are my race. I have not lived amongst them and now I want to know more about them."

We turned our attention back to the confrontation between Rhun and Augustine. "So you would have us change the way we shave our heads," the Welsh bishop was saying, "the method we use for baptism; our means of calculating Easter, and you would make us send missionaries to the likes of those heathen invaders," this with a scowl at us again. "And all you offer us in return is the right to become subservient to you, to a See in English lands?"

Augustine must have heard the cynicism in Rhun's voice, but watching his arrogant face I could see that he was puzzled by it – as if it were self-evident that he, the Archbishop, should be superior to the Welsh bishops and could not understand any objections they had. He did not deign to respond but waited in silence. None of the other Welsh bishops spoke. Their faces were dark and I could see their anger seething beneath the surface.

"Very well," Rhun said at length, "I believe that I am authorized to request time to consult with our kings and our churchmen?"

Frowning, Augustine nodded. "We are heading east to Anglia. We will be back this way in the spring before we return to Kent. Let us meet here again at Easter... Easter calculated our way that is!" he added with a tight smile, clearly not able to resist.

As the Welsh bishops moved away from the benches, Bartholomew said something to Augustine, who then stared at Edwin, nodded and walked across to us. I noticed Rhun, his gaze on Edwin, drift a little closer, presumably so he could overhear the exchange.

Bartholomew introduced us. "Princes Hereric and Edwin, of the house of Aelle and Aethelric, kings of Deira, may I present to you his Grace, Archbishop Augustine."

"Your... Grace," Edwin stumbled over the unfamiliar title.

"Highnesses, I am delighted to meet you. His Holiness would wish it that all the lands of the English receive the good news."

"Good news?" Edwin asked, obviously confused.

"Why, the good news of the salvation of mankind by the death and resurrection of Christ, of course. Men need not fear death now for they are assured of resurrection to life eternal."

Sabert snorted. "What need have we of your Christ, man of God? Woden promises us the same. If we die in battle we go to feast at his side. We live out eternity fighting during the day and celebrating our victories at night. Why should we convert to your religion?"

"All other religions are false. There is only one path to God, one route to life eternal and that is belief in the son of God," Augustine replied.

"You truly believe that don't you?" Sabert replied. "I had heard that you Christmen were arrogant, but to say that our gods are false – even we would not deny the existence of other people's gods. Let them have their gods and we ours, I say."

"They and you are wrong!" Augustine said in a voice that suggested no doubts.

"Maybe we should at least consider his words," Guthred said. "Perhaps we should go to Kent and see what King Aethelberht says?"

The Archbishop nodded. "We rejoice that the Bretwalda has accepted the word of God. Why not go and meet with him? I will pray that with God's grace you also may see the light." His face became suddenly thoughtful, "And who knows, mayhap God would then talk to Aethelberht and suggest that he aid you in your present strife?"

Hereric beamed at Augustine, "We will," he said with enthusiasm.

He was about to say more, but Sabert, with a quick glance at the young prince, cut across him. "The prince means, of course, that we will consider your suggestion, Archbishop," the old Earl put in.

"Indeed. Then come here again in the spring and I will pray that Eastertide will inspire you and show you the right path to follow." With that he turned and left us.

So, it seemed we had a choice: we could go and see if the Bretwalda would aid us, but the price would be our conversion to this new religion. Sabert was scowling and I knew he would resist such a move. Nor did it appeal to me. Guthred and Hereric, however, looked thoughtful – both watching Augustine as he made preparations to leave.

Prince Edwin made no comment, but I was conscious of his gaze on me. "What are you thinking, Cerdic?" he asked after a moment.

I shrugged, about to reply and then I noticed that Rhun was still watching us and must have overheard the Archbishop's suggestion that we go to Kent. Rhun said nothing but he glared at me and his expression spoke volumes.

"What I am thinking, my Lord Prince, is that we all have a lot of thinking to do!"

Chapter Eight
Hand Them To Me!

"What would you advise that I do, Cerdic?" Edwin asked me again for the tenth time. We were on the return journey to Deganwy and in fact after four days we were finally in sight of the twin hills, which even now were silhouetted against the setting sun. We were riding along the coastal road towards Iago's stronghold, as ever trailing behind the official party of bishops and monks, which included Rhun, who I could see up ahead of us. Throughout the ride our party had thought about and discussed only one subject. When we met Augustine again, come the spring, should we go with him to Kent? More importantly, should we abandon our own gods and embrace this strange religion of just one God?

Sabert had been utterly opposed to the idea the previous night when we sat a little way apart from the Welsh bishops and stared into the flames of our own fire. "Woden, Tyr, Thunor and Freya have been good enough for our fathers for a thousand years. They blessed us with land and made us victorious in battle. Now, because things have gone wrong, we seem very quick to abandon them."

Guthred scowled at him through the smoke. "I always thought you the cunning politician, Sabert. It seems in your old age you have lost all your skills."

"What do you mean by that?" Sabert snapped back.

"We don't have to abandon our gods. We just make pretence of accepting this new religion to get Augustine's support. Then, when he has talked the Bretwalda into helping us to defeat

Aethelfrith, well then we can forget all this nonsense."

"That seems reasonable, don't you think?" Hereric asked Sabert.

"I do not favour even the pretence that we are laying aside our gods, Highness," Sabert said.

"Anyway," I spoke at last, "there is more to this than which god we bow before. There is also the matter of who would do more to aid us – Iago or Aethelberht. As I have said before, Kent is a long way from Northumbria. Gwynedd is much closer and almost on Aethelfrith's doorstep, but if Rheged finally fell it would quite literally be on the doorstep and in that case Iago would have more interest in opposing Northumbria than the Bretwalda would."

"Not if Aethelberht felt he could extend his overlordship beyond the Humber," Guthred said, repeating his earlier argument.

"I am not happy to bow down to some foreign king as overlord," Edwin said.

"Are you certain of that? What if that was the price of getting Deira back?" Hereric asked.

Edwin shrugged but did not answer. He was clearly asking himself the same thing.

That had been the previous night's conversation. Now, as we approached Deganwy, he stirred and asked me that question again.

"What would you advise that I do, Cerdic?"

I sighed. "As before, I can't tell you what to do but I have a feeling that our wyrd led us here to the Welsh. I think we should see it through and find out if an alliance with them is possible. In any event we have all winter. It is eight months until the meeting with Augustine in the spring. Let us put it aside for a while at least. Come: we are back at Deganwy. It is not so bad here even if some of the Welsh do not want us here," I added as we approached the gates. I had just seen that up ahead of us Rhun was being welcomed back by Eidyn. I watched as the bishop jumped off his horse, the two men talking animatedly. After a moment they both turned to look down at us as we climbed the slope to the gatehouse. There was something about their expressions that suggested they knew something we did not and I guessed that whatever it was, it was not to our advantage.

When we reached the gatehouse Eidyn stepped out and with a nasty little smile addressed Edwin. "Highness... you have a friend here. He apparently arrived last night. He is most eager to renew his acquaintance."

Edwin paled and then glanced at me his eyes wide with concern. "Do you think it's...?" he started to ask, but I shook my head to cut him off. No need to let Rhun and Eidyn know our fears. Rhun was looking pleased, as if this visitor was the answer to his prayers. I felt my heart sink with the certainty that what we feared had come to pass: my half-brother had finally found us.

Without a word we pushed past the two Welsh princes and entered Iago's hall. Sure enough Hussa was there, dressed in a weatherbeaten cloak and accompanied by half a dozen huscarls. He saw me enter and inclined his head in greeting, but then turned back to the king. Iago was already an old man, but he seemed somewhat older today: his careworn face wrinkled into a frown as he listened to my brother's words. His sombre gaze, though, was on Edwin and Hereric. As we approached, Hussa stopped talking. What had he been saying? I was pretty sure I knew.

Iago sighed as if he did not want to have to deal with the

issue in front of him. "Prince Edwin, Prince Hereric – this is Lord Hussa who…"

"We know who… and what he is, Majesty," Edwin said coldly.

"Do not interrupt the king!" Rhun shouted.

"Forgive me, Sire," Edwin continued, ignoring Rhun, "but you must know that this man is a traitor, a snake and not to be trusted."

"That may be so in your eyes, my dear prince," Hussa answered with a lazy smile, "but I carry the seal and commission of Aethelfrith, King of Bernicia and Deira."

"Usurper of Deira your mean!" Hereric spat. "King Iago – this man comes from Aethelfrith who murdered my father and seized my kingdom through trickery. He cannot be allowed to speak!"

"I decide who may speak here, Hereric of Deira," Iago replied, a tinge of anger in his voice.

I put a hand on Hereric's arm. "Caution, Highness," I whispered. Hereric glared at me and looked ready to continue his tirade with all the uncontrolled anger of a youth, but it was Edwin who spoke first.

"Our apologies, King Iago, this is your court. Please continue," he said in a placating tone.

Iago nodded. "Lord Hussa has brought a message from King Aethelfrith that I must consider. Repeat to the princes and lords what you said to me."

Hussa bowed. "With pleasure your Majesty." He turned as though to address the assembled nobles, but his attention was all on Edwin and Hereric.

"Until this day there has ever been enmity between the English in Northumbria and the Cymry," I noticed his clever use of

109

the Welsh phrase that meant 'brethren'. It was what the Welsh called themselves. It was designed to make Hussa seem almost one with the audience rather than an agent of their enemies.

Hussa was walking now, stalking the hall like a wild cat prowling a forest glade. "For almost two hundred years we have fought each other. Our blood stains fields like Degsastan, Catraeth and a hundred others. Yet my master feels we can share this land – this Britain. He wants only peace. There need be no more bloodshed. There need not be a repeat of the bloodletting of Catraeth nor the slaughter of Degsastan. I say again: Aethelfrith wants peace. He asks but one thing in return."

Now his steps carried him towards us and his hand came up so he was pointing first at Edwin and then at Hereric. "He asks that these two be handed over to him. That is all: two youths, two princelings that have no kingdom and no army save a few homeless men. Do that and he will agree to come no further into the West. Moreover, hand them over to him now and he will give back the lands he has of late taken in Rheged and will withdraw across the mountains. That land can thrive once more under the rule of Rhoerth map Rhun. That is what my king offers: peace and more land. The price is very low – just these two boys."

He had now come closer still and stood less than a sword's length from me. My fingers twitched and I would have struck him down had I not left my sword at the door to the king's hall. "You bastard!" I hissed so only he could hear.

"You know, brother – that insult is getting worn rather thin," he replied, a humourless smile playing on his lips as he turned away.

"*You are right*," I said under my breath, "*I will have to think of a new one.*"

"I say we give them over to Aethelfrith," Rhun shouted and

at once the hall was full of shouting and calls of, "Agreed, I too!"

Hussa smiled at the noise and his eyes shone with exultation.

"Silence!" Prince Cadfan shouted from where he stood next to his father. "Let each man speak in turn. Prince Rhun: you first."

"Our reply is self–evident. What are these men to us other than vagabonds on the road running from their own defeat? They have no power and no influence. Aethelfrith is the power in the North. We hand these boys over and not only do we appease Aethelfrith but we regain my land, Rheged. We take land back from the invader."

Rhun glanced once at me and I knew that whilst he was putting the argument in terms that would appeal to the Welsh, he had another motive. If this arrangement went through I would be out of his sight and maybe his darkness would subside once more.

"You believe that Aethelfrith would honour this arrangement once he has the princes in his hands?" Cadfan asked Rhun.

"It seems unlikely that he would yield up all the land he has occupied in Rheged since Degsastan as the price for two boys," Iago mused.

Rhun shrugged. "In the end we lose nothing by trying. The alternative is to gain another enemy. Gwynedd already fights Mercia, is on poor terms with Powys in the South and of late the Irish have pestered you raiding from the West. Would you add a fourth power arrayed against you?"

Iago did not reply, but his expression suggested he was asking himself just that same question. Mighty Bernicia, swollen and powerful through the lands it had conquered would be a fearsome enemy. Dare Iago offend Aethelfrith and bring his wrath down upon him? Rhun could sense the king's indecision

111

and so could the lords in the hall for muttering started up again.

"Sire, your lords feel as I do," Rhun said. "We should hand these princelings over!"

The mutterings broke out again into shouts of agreement. Iago seemed to be wavering and I feared that he would indeed hand us over to my brother. Then I noticed that Aneirin was standing up and coming to face Iago. He bowed deeply and as he did so the noise died away.

"Sire, princes and lords: such a decision would be contrary to the traditions and laws of our fathers and our people. We have ever offered hospitality to travellers and shelter to those of rank. You two know that more than most," he added, this last comment directed at Rhun and Eidyn.

"We are the Princes of Goddodin and Rheged, members of the Cymry," Eidyn protested. "They are not," he pointed at Edwin and Hereric. "Shelter to kings and princes does not extend to the invader."

"One might argue that it is our Christian duty to extend shelter to them," Cadfan said.

"With respect, Highness, those sound like the words of Augustine. These men are not Christians, so our faith does not come into this matter," Rhun replied.

"You interpret the word of God, lord bishop, but kings define laws and bards pass on tradition," Aneirin said. "Do you deny tradition?"

"No – tradition is everything, but I would argue that you are incorrect if you say tradition means we should give these men shelter."

"You would question my authority?" Aneirin said.

"I would and I do. You are yet young, master poet."

"And what if a Council of bards were assembled to judge on

112

the matter? Would you accept their judgement?"

Rhun hesitated, realising he had been manoeuvred by the bard into a dead end. "Yes... I suppose so," he acknowledged reluctantly.

"Then Sire," Aneirin bowed towards Iago, "with your permission I will call upon the bards and poets and men of wisdom to assemble and judge on this matter."

The king nodded, a look of relief passing across his face as the immediate decision was taken out of his hands, but Hussa looked less than happy. "When will that be?" he asked, anxiety straining his earlier confidence.

"Well, Taliesen and I are already here, of course," Aneirin said, "but we are not enough. I will send a message out at once, but some of our bards are far away, we cannot expect a response from all of them before the winter. Then they must make plans for travel. I will call the Council at the Vernal Equinox, which should give everyone time."

"When will that be?" Hussa asked.

"Late March, just before Easter," Aneirin answered after a moment's thought.

Hussa's face grew red. Struggling to control his temper he turned away from the young bard to address the king. "Sire, my master will not be happy waiting six months for a reply on this matter!"

"I am aware it is a fair time, but even I am bound by the traditions of our people," the king said. "Until the matter is ruled upon I will grant Prince Hereric and Prince Edwin shelter and the freedom of my court, but with the undertaking that they do not leave my realm until the hearing. If the Council decides that our tradition of shelter does not apply to the invader, then I will in turn decide on our response. You can reassure Aethelfrith, however, that I do not wish to get involved in the affairs of the English, so I will do what I can to reach accommodation with him when my hands are free to do so."

"Is that your final word, Sire?" Hussa asked his voice tense.

"It is until the spring."

"Very well, I will pass that message on. I hope that the outcome in the spring frees you to act in the *best interests* of your kingdom," Hussa added, with a nasty emphasis that suggested defying Bernicia was certainly not in Iago's best interests. He bowed to the king and then, as he walked out of the hall, he passed very close to me. "Enjoy the winter, brother. It may be your last," he hissed and was gone.

"You want me to follow and kill him?" Eduard murmured in a pleading voice.

I hesitated; it was a tempting thought, but would certainly not help our cause. Reluctantly I shook my head, "Best not. Not yet at least."

Eidyn was staring at us with undisguised hostility. He wandered over. "Your friend the bard helped you then, but do not think you are out of the woods, Prince Edwin," he said. "Many of the bards are very traditional and one tradition we all share is our enmity with you. If enough of them feel that way the decision could go against you. Do not get too comfortable here." He stomped off with a stony-faced Rhun in his wake.

Aneirin joined us. He was accompanied by Taliesen, both looking glum. "I fear he is right, noble prince," Aneirin said.

"Why?" I asked the younger bard. "I thought you knew what you were talking about. You certainly sounded like you did."

It was Taliesen who replied. "I am afraid there are two schools of thought on the matter. Some feel as Aneirin does, but some would argue that you are our enemy. I felt that way at first. Still

114

do to an extent, but I find I have mellowed slightly, thanks to the clever words of your own bard," he nodded at Lilla who bowed in acknowledgement. "I am willing to be persuaded to Aneirin's viewpoint, but there are many who will not be so easy to convince."

"So, our friend Aneirin has bought us six months. Six months for us to find a way to swing the argument," Lilla said.

"Or find another reason for Iago to keep us here," I said.

"If we had gone with Augustine we could be away from all this," Guthred pointed out.

"Well, that choice is still before us, assuming we still have the freedom to choose come the spring and are not in chains being dragged along behind Hussa on our way back to Northumbria," Sabert countered.

Edwin groaned. "All I want is a home for a while."

I thought of Aidith and our baby, due at around the same time as the Vernal Equinox: the start of spring, when we celebrated the birth of lambs and the return of the sun and the flowers and the leaves. The Christians called it Easter, but they got the word from us. Eostretide we called it – named after Eostre, the Goddess of new life. My wife desperately wanted a home for when her time came. Could I find her one and would Eostre be a time of new life for us, or would Edwin, Hereric and I be dead, and Aidith's and my baby born a slave to Aethelfrith?

Chapter Nine
Boars

I had drunk rather a lot of beer the night after Hussa's visit. The following morning I was barely up and dressed when Aneirin burst through the door. He was wearing bright, cheerful clothes, mostly orange and red. Just by looking at him I felt a headache come on. He bounded up to me and slapped me on the back.

"Good morning Cerdic. You look a little green. Our drink too strong for you? You had a lot last night after that fellow Hussa left. We will have to train you to take it."

He spotted Aidith sitting with Mildrith across the other side of the hall, both with their necks bent as they repaired a torn tunic. With a laugh he leapt over to them, "Gracious ladies, how are you both this morning?"

Mildrith giggled at Aneirin whilst Aidith gave him a stern look. "If you must ask, I am feeling tired actually and a little queasy."

"Ah, that will be the child. I am sure I can mix up a remedy for that," the bard said brightly.

"Aneirin what, apart from being noisy, are you doing here?" Edwin asked. I gathered he too was nursing a headache judging by the way he was rubbing his temples.

Aneirin turned to Edwin and Hereric and gave a flourishing bow. "Noble princes, I am commanded to invite you to accompany Prince Cadfan and his son Cadwallon on a hunting expedition south into the mountains. There is much game to be found there with spear or bow. Will you come and show us your English skills?"

Edwin immediately forgot about the headache, gave a broad smile and replied, "Aneirin, I would be honoured."

"An hour then and we depart. We will be gone twenty days. Bring with you only six companions." Then, with another bow, he was off.

Eduard groaned a little. "That man has a little too much energy for such an early hour. And he is certainly too loud!"

Sabert did not look happy. "My Lord, I am concerned. You are to be away for twenty days with only six of us to protect you. This could be a trap," he said.

Edwin objected, "Hereric and I are the king's guests. He has given us his protection at least until the spring."

"Maybe, but he could, of course, see this as an easy way out: an accident in the mountains, miles from anywhere. The few witnesses would not last long. But even if, as I am sure is the case, he has no ill intention toward you, can that be said of the other nobles?"

Edwin considered this. "No, but Sabert I must go. This is a risk I must take if I am to prove myself worthy of their trust. Cadfan will be bound by friendship to Ceorl as well as his father's instructions. But choose six companions who will protect me best. In case you are right, though, I think Hereric should stay here with you and Guthred, then if the worst happens one of us is safe."

So it was that an hour later, Edwin stood ready outside with me, Eduard, Cuthbert, Harald and two of his company: Alfred and Horsa. Sabert was to stay behind and make sure the others did not get into fights. He confessed that in any event he was getting a little too old to be involved in hunting expeditions to the mountains. He promised to watch over the children and women as well as the company and try to keep all out of trouble.

Cuthwine, Aidith and Mildrith came to see us off. "Take care brother, come home safely," Millie said to me as she fussed over Cuthbert's pack. "Make sure you bring all your companions back," she instructed. Her gaze flicked momentarily to Cuthbert who smiled at her.

"Can't I come as well, Father?" Cuthwine asked, his voice high–pitched with excitement as he saw the hunting party preparing to leave.

"I am afraid not. One day I will take you son, I promise."

My son looked disappointed then brightened as he had a thought. "Will you bring me back a boar's head Father?"

"Of course I will – with lots of blood?"

"Oh yes please!" he replied, eyes widening now.

"Very well – run along now."

He scuttled away and was soon stalking a cat that was hiding in the shadows beneath the hall. When I turned back to Aidith I spotted that she was giving me one of her disapproving looks.

"What is it?" I asked.

"You do realise that all the while you are having fun in the mountains, all I will get from him now is talk about your wretched boar's head?"

I laughed then straightened my face, "Sorry... and I'm sorry I am going to be away. I love you.

Her frown dropped and she pulled me closer and kissed me. "I love you too you big oaf. Just be careful do you hear?"

"I will," I replied and kissed her again.

Aedann, who was staying behind, led a horse out for me to ride. "Look after Aidith and Cuthwine," I asked him.

"Of course I will, Cerdic. You be careful."

Edwin was given a horse by Cadfan and would ride with him toward the front of the company. Apart from the Prince of

118

Gwynedd there was also his son, Cadwallon. There were twenty or so British warriors present and also, to my dismay, both Rhun and Eidyn. I pointed them out to Harald and also told him of the attack on Cuthbert on our first night here.

"Well Cerdic my lad, we will have to keep an eye on those two," was all he said.

A young woman had emerged to say goodbye to Eidyn. With long black hair she had a serious but strikingly attractive face. I waved Aneirin over to me. "Who is that?" I asked him.

"Eidyn's daughter, Bronwen, she came with him along with others of the Goddodin court when Aethelfrith extended his power into their land."

"She is beautiful," Aedann said, looking wistfully towards her. I grinned at him, but Cadfan was calling us to order up ahead and before I could tease my Welsh friend, we were off.

Aneirin and Taliesen accompanied us. The former's boisterous nature, which both Britons and Saxons enjoyed, seemed to unite the company. Taliesen was more restrained, more sombre, but he attracted no less respect, at least from the Welsh, in the appreciation of the master bard that he was.

Cadfan led us down from Deganwy to the coast and then across to the west bank of the River Conwy. We then followed the river inland and southwards. As we rode along we moved closer to the mountains that covered the western half of Gwynedd. Here the land became rocky and more barren with few trees, and yet at the same time it held a kind of stark magnificence. Here and there were farms and crofts clinging to the mountainside or tucked in small vales in between. We camped overnight in the ruins of a Roman fort that Taliesen told us was called Caerhun. The next day we covered a lot of ground – perhaps twenty or thirty miles – and the sun was already set before we stopped for the night. In the morning we Deirans were surprised to find we had slept only fifty yards from a huge cairn. I asked Aneirin if his people or the Romans had built it.

"Neither, Cerdic, my friend. There are many such structures in these hills. They have been here for as long as our race can recall, certainly long before the Romans. Perhaps more than a thousand years. It and many more were built by the old people that were here before my race arrived."

"So your people once invaded this land and took it from the occupants just as we English are doing," I observed.

Taliesen looked across startled at this and then irritated. "That's completely different," he said quickly.

"How so?"

"Well, that was then and this is now," he said, and with a toss of his head stomped off to find himself some food leaving me smiling after him.

Cadfan now called us all together. "Prince Edwin, we have now come as far as we can by road. To the west of here, maybe ten miles across the mountains, is a group of isolated lakes. It is good hunting ground. It will take us most of today to reach there, but tomorrow, my guests and companions, we will hunt."

As we moved off across rocky and gradually rising ground I noticed that Harald seemed glum. I moved up beside him, "I would say from the look on your face that you are thinking the same as me," I suggested.

"Oh? What's that?"

"Here we are, going far into the barren mountains. Just seven of us and three times that number of British."

Harald nodded. Then he glanced behind me and his eyes narrowed. I turned and saw Eidyn looking at us both. There was the hint of a grin on his scarred face and his dark eyes held a hungry look. A moment later he turned away as we prepared to move west, away from the Roman road and into the wilderness.

The going was not easy. We toiled slowly over ridges and along valleys – leading our horses as often as riding them. Although Taliesen was the oldest present he strolled along as if we were in the fields around the Villa, yet some of us, such as Eduard, puffed and panted a little under the exertion. Eduard had refused to abandon his spear or his wooden shield. "You don't know when we might need them, Cerdic," was all he would say.

But whether strolling at ease or puffing in exertion, we made steady progress through the hills. Here and there we passed long barrows and cairns: more evidence of the old people Aneirin had referred to. In the early afternoon we reached a track leading north–west into a small valley between two hills and we followed it. On our left a stream babbled and giggled in its bed alongside us. The track curled past a hill to the north and then we emerged from behind yet another cairn, its rocks having grown mossy and worn over the ages, onto the rim of a wide bowl of land. All around us a ring of silent hills looked down on the shallow dip in the midst of which was a small lake, perhaps half a mile long and wide. From the western side, the far side from us, a small river trickled away through boggy land past more lakes and pools toward a forest, maybe five miles away. On the northern edge of the lake was a collection of huts and a stone hall.

"Welcome to Ogwen Lodge, Prince Edwin," Cadfan said, "it belongs to the kings of Gwynedd who have long hunted here." He led the way down the hillside on the last part of the track to the remote hunting lodge that was our destination.

Ogwen was a pleasant place to stay. Indeed, had I not been

keeping one eye on our hosts and the other on Eidyn and Rhun I would have enjoyed being back in a smaller community again, one not unlike the Villa. Yet I have to admit that Cadfan was generous with his hospitality and we enjoyed good food and ale. Taliesen was entertaining and Aneirin continued to teach me Welsh. My basic knowledge of the language was improving and I was now able to grasp some of its more complex phrases. During the day we hunted in the vales and hills and westwards into the forest. A number of the huge wild oxen we called Aurochs still survived in these remote parts. They had been hunted out of existence in the more populated eastern lands, but in these western hills could still be found. We kept an eye out for them, they stood two yards high and possessed a fearsome pair of horns and although they tried to avoid us, if forced to fight in their own defence they were determined and dangerous beasts. One of the British warriors was badly injured when an Auroch charged him. But it was boar we were after and we left the wild oxen alone.

As the days went by and no threat to Edwin emerged I relaxed a little. Even Eidyn seemed to have stopped glaring at us in hatred and instead simply ignored us. So too did Rhun. The bishop's temperament seemed lighter despite my presence and I surmised that these days of living the simple life away from Iago's court suited him and helped his dark moods. Then came a day that achieved what Edwin had hoped for, but which in one unforeseen moment almost destroyed our plans.

That morning we had travelled the few miles west to the forested area that bordered the lakes, Cadfan having assured us that wild boar were to be found among these woods. The land undulated gently between hillock, low ridge, dell and vale and was densely wooded with ash, beech and oaks that were surrounded with much undergrowth, including blackberry bushes now laden with sweet fruit. The party had spread out into small groups and Cuthbert and I were walking along a low ridge that ran east to west. To our south, in a little dip fifty yards wide, was Edwin and the young Cadwallon, along with two British warriors and Harald. On the slightly higher ground on the southern side of the valley were Eidyn and Rhun with two of their men. On the other side, to our north and out of sight in the next dell, were Eduard, with Cadfan and some of his men. The rest of the party were spread out further north and scattered over a mile in all. We were all moving slowly east, acting as a huge net in which to drive and catch our prey.

I was, for once, intent on our task and anticipating roast pork and crackling that night back at the lodge. We had been moving for quite some while and with little talk to distract me, so it was no surprise that my concentration was waning and my mind wandering. Suddenly I was catapulted out of my day dreaming by a shout from the far ridge to my right.

I spun round to see Eidyn, Rhun and their men charging towards us into the dell, swords and spears at the ready. 'This is it Cerdic, you fool,' I thought to myself, 'they are attacking, and you are twenty yards from Edwin!'

Edwin himself seemed stunned by the sudden movement, but as I leapt towards him, Harald moved quickly in front of him, his boar spear aimed at Eidyn's throat.

"Not us, you English idiot!" Eidyn shouted in Welsh. "Look behind!" He gestured over his shoulder.

Harald did not understand Welsh, but he did not need to, for now Eidyn's meaning was plain. A score of strange-looking warriors had come into view surging over the hill at his back. One of Cadfan's guards roared, "*Llynii!*" and turning to face them took up a fighting stance. Others did the same.

Eyes narrowed, I studied the newcomers, who were now moving more cautiously towards us. They looked wild and unkempt with straggled hair and beards that were for the most part dark and long. They were not tall, but stocky, their torsos naked aside from the open woollen jackets they wore, dyed red or unstained in shades of brown and black. Unlike our longer, Saxon trousers their britches were short and brightly coloured in stripes of reds, greens and blues, covering their legs to just below the knee and leaving their calves and ankles bare. They were armed with short stabbing swords, javelins and small, leather–covered bucklers. One or two of the warriors - perhaps the better off amongst them - looked less wild. These few, who carried shields with large central bosses rather than bucklers, had taken the trouble to trim their beards and wore short, reddish-brown tunics and woollen cloaks, but I noticed that even these men had nothing on their feet, despite the rocky ground hereabouts.

So it was that we Angles met the warriors of yet another of this island's splintered races. We didn't know it at the time, but these people came from Llyn, a peninsular lying along the coast to the west of Gwynedd and inhabited by one of its rivals. Taliesen kindly educated us later that day. Llyn, he told us, bordered Gwynedd only a few miles south and west of where we were hunting and these warriors were in fact Irish, from Hibernia, a strange land beyond the sea to the west. Just as my own people had come to these shores from across the eastern sea, so had the Hibernians crossed the western sea. When Rome's power waned they had begun raiding the coast of Britain and were one of the reasons the British had invited my people in to help defend their lands, but Hibernians had begun settling the western coast and although Iago's ancestors had mostly driven them out, a few had lingered. They had been a thorn in Gwynedd's side for generations, Taliesen told us.

The warriors charging down on us now appeared to be a raiding party that had wandered across the border to burn a few farms and loot a few villages. Was it fate that brought them to the spot where we were hunting, deliberate intention, or just chance? Whatever it was, it was clear they had no wish to talk peace! I charged down the dell towards them already knowing I would be too late to reach Edwin before they did.

Cadwallon was furthest south. Next to him was Edwin with Harald standing in front of him. Eidyn, Rhun and their guards were running past to stand to Edwin's right. Nearest to me as I hurtled toward them were two more British warriors. I could see that Cadwallon was in the most immediate danger.

"Cadwallon, back off!" I shouted.

The youth, however, was either stupid or courageous and surged forward against three Irishmen. He thrust and impaled one on his spear, but then lost it as the man toppled backwards. Cadwallon stepped back and drew his sword bringing it up to parry a javelin thrust, then leaping to his right to avoid a sword cutting across him. Elsewhere the Llynii had reached our party. Harald cut down one veteran warrior but then was winded by a spear butt to the midriff and went down in a crumpled heap. Eidyn and his companions were soon in the thick of the fight with the odds against them. Over my head buzzed an arrow toward the enemy. From the corner of my eye I saw that Cuthbert had arrived and was firing down on them from the ridge line. I could hear him shouting over his shoulder, calling Eduard and Cadfan to our aid. But would they be in time?

Three of the Llynii ran round Rhun straight at me. I lunged at them with my sword and cut a gash open down the flank of one. Another fell with one of Cuthbert's arrows in his chest. The third warrior and I circled each other watchfully. He was a few years older than me with sharp eyes and a face that reminded me of fox, and just as cunning, I thought. He was studying me intently looking for my weakness, but he was also watching Cuthbert, wary of the archer who had killed his fellow warrior a moment before. I spotted this and used it against him, stepping to the side to expose him to Cuthbert's fire. He dodged to stand in front of me in an attempt to use me as a shield. However, I had anticipated this move and thrusting out my boot, tripped him up. As he fell I plunged my sword into his neck. The look on his face before he died was one of irritation at having been tricked rather than pain.

Panting hard, I glanced about me and took stock. Six Llynii were wounded or dead, but we had lost two of our warriors and Rhun was injured. Moreover, Cadwallon was surrounded by five of the enemy. I moved towards him, but he was fifteen paces away and before I could reach him he was knocked down, bashed by a huge shield sporting a fearsome iron boss in its centre. Blood flowed from a cut on his temple and he was temporarily blinded by it. As he shook his head trying to clear it from his eyes three Llynii warriors closed in for the kill, one brandishing a short stabbing sword such as the Romans used, rather like my Catraeth. Just then Edwin leapt into the midst of them. His initial attack took them by surprise and knocked two to the ground while he engaged the third. They soon recovered, but the attack had saved Cadwallon, who scrambled back onto his feet. Together the two young princes held off the enemy. I arrived soon after this and slashed at one of the warriors, drawing blood and driving him back, away from Edwin. An arrow from Cuthbert downed another. The Irish charge had failed to sweep us away and we were holding out. They had taken more losses than we and I could sense their commitment to the fight was waning.

At that moment Cadfan and Eduard arrived on the scene, advancing over the hill to our rear with a half dozen more of our men. They charged down into the dell, Eduard bellowing and swinging his huge axe over his head. An enemy javelin hit his shield with a thud and impaled it, but Eduard ignored it and hurled himself on down the hill, Cadfan and the Gwynedd guards on his heels. This broke the enemy's spirit and they stepped away a pace or two before finally turning to flee. Eduard went charging after them closely followed by Cadfan and his men. My big friend reached the slowest enemy warrior and hacked down with his axe. The man fell screaming, but Eduard did not stop to deal with him, running on past and leaving the man to be finished off by a guard with a thrust from his boar spear. Then Eduard, still waving his axe and bellowing war cries, was gone, running over the hill to the south, he and his companions full of blood lust in pursuit of the defeated Lynii.

Prince Cadfan, however, turned back and came over to where we were stood still catching our breath. He went first to Cadwallon and patted him on the shoulder, looking with concern at the nasty cut on his son's head caused by the shield boss. Calling for one of the warriors to hand him a flask of water, Cadfan washed away the blood. Underneath it the wound was swollen and bruised, but not deep. The prince relaxed with a sigh. "That will need stitches, lad, but you will then boast a warrior's scar." He grinned, "Well, my son, so what do you think of your first taste of battle, eh?"

Cadwallon held up his blooded blade and stared at it as if only then realising what he had done with it. Then a slow smile

127

lit up his face and quiet but determined, he said, "You know Father, I think I rather liked it." The look in his eyes seemed almost spiritual in its intensity and I shivered slightly.

"You will make a fine warrior, son, but you must learn caution." Cadfan now turned to Edwin. "I saw from the top of the hill that you came to Cadwallon's side when you might have been killed. You risked your life to drive away some of the enemy and probably saved my son's life thereby."

Cadwallon looked surprised at this and seemed about to argue, but his father extended his hand to Edwin and tightly grasped it. Cadwallon's face grew red. He clearly believed this was his moment of glory, his first battle and yet this foreign prince was being given all the credit. It seemed to me that he was not happy at the way attention was shifting to Edwin.

"You have my thanks, Prince Edwin," Cadfan said. "There are some among us who doubted my father's wisdom in protecting you and some, indeed, who wanted your blood. Now they must see that he was right all along." With these words he stared for a moment at Rhun and Eidyn, who were only a few yards away.

Rhun shrugged then nodded slightly but Eidyn glanced away. I could see from his sour expression that he knew he had lost any opportunity to turn the Gwynedd Royal House against us – at least for the present.

Cadfan seemed angered by Eidyn's meek response and I think he would have said more, but at that moment Eduard and the others returned from the south reporting that the enemy survivors had got away and were fleeing fast to the west.

"Who were they Prince Cadfan?" asked Edwin, squatting to clean his blade on the grass.

Cadfan spat. "Ireland, they come from Ireland," he explained.

"We have been rivals with them for many years although open warfare occurs only occasionally. Last autumn we gave a small army venturing east a bloody nose and were able to recapture several villages from them. This is the first time they have come across the border since then. It might just be a raid or it might be a prelude to a more determined move against us. My father will need to know about this. We must be ready to leave in the morning and return home."

I saw Eduard grinning at me. "What's up with you?" I enquired.

He pointed at the javelin still projecting from his shield. "I told you it might come in useful," he replied smugly.

Soon after that the hunting party was abandoned. No self–respecting boar was going to hang around once they'd heard us fighting. We had caught only two beasts, and those mere young-sters. So we returned to the lodge and feasted, and although we had barely enough to go round, at least they were tender.

In the morning we were all up before dawn preparing for the journey back to Deganwy. We sent a messenger ahead to tell Iago that we would be arriving soon and by the time we got back to the fortress, Sabert was anxiously waiting at the gates.

He looked very relieved when we came in sight still alive and apart from a few minor wounds, unhurt. His relief turned to surprise when Edwin rode up beside Cadfan, the two of them laughing and joking like old friends. Sabert's quizzical expres-sion made me laugh and I winked at him. I looked forward to telling him how Edwin had made the impact we needed. Not only had the prince's bravery won us allies, but our position was stronger by far than when we had set out a few days earlier.

Glancing back I happened to see Cadwallon riding with Eidyn. They were deep in private conversation, but there was no disguising the frustration on Cadwallon's face, as well as the hatred on Eidyn's. Edwin may now have won us friends in Iago's court, but clearly he had enemies also.

Chapter Ten
Retaliation

The news of the Irish raiders caused a great stir in Deganwy after we had returned. Indeed it was not only Sabert who had come out to meet us. Iago emerged soon after we rode through the door and inspected both Cadfan and Cadwallon, anxiety etched on his aged brow.

"We are unharmed Father," Cadfan said.

"We fought a battle against the Irish!" Cadwallon said proudly.

"In which you might have died were it not for the Angles," Cadfan pointed out and then turning to Edwin he extended an arm and drew him towards Iago. "They fought by our side and Prince Edwin here saved the life of my son."

Cadwallon screwed up his face at this comment, unhappy it seemed at the implication that his life had needed saving, which it had, but the fact of it clearly bothered him.

Iago did not notice and swept past Cadwallon to grasp Edwin's hand. Clasping it warmly he said, "I thank you for saving the life of my grandson." Then, raising his voice so that all those present could hear, he added, "I see that my decision to allow the Deiran princes to stay has been vindicated."

Nearby, Eidyn looked away in disgust, then his face twisted into a mask of rage and he started off across the courtyard. On the far side of the fortress I spotted his daughter, Bronwen. She was laughing at something a man next to her was saying. As he spoke, he turned and waved at me and I saw it was none other than Aedann. Ready for trouble I followed Eidyn, who was clearly fuming as he reached his daughter and my Welsh friend.

Bronwen smiled to see him. "Welcome home, Father. Are you unhurt?"

"You ask me that now?" Eidyn thrust an accusing finger at her. "You deign to ask me that now you have finished cavorting with this man."

The smile wiped from her face, Bronwen took a step back. "Father please, there has been no impropriety."

"I should hope not. You will not talk to this man or any other in the Deiran party. They are the enemies of our blood."

Bronwen looked confused. "But the king said—"

Eidyn cut her off. "The king is confused, led astray by personal feeling. He needs reminding that we Britons should stick together and have nothing to do with the Angles.

"But Father, Aedann is a Briton! His ancestors were lords in the Eboraccii."

Eidyn snorted. "Is that what he has told you? He lies! He is a companion of Earl Cerdic."

Aedann stepped forward now. "That is no lie," he said hotly. "I am Aedann ap Caefydd of the Eboraccii, freed slave and now a free man in Cerdic's service."

"Huh, you admit that of your own choice you consort with Englishmen. That proves you are a traitor to our blood."

"Lord Eidyn, I protest!"

"Shut up! Come with me Bronwen. You will not talk to this man or any other in the Deiran company ever again. Do I make myself clear?"

"Yes Father," Bronwen replied in apparent obedience. Yet as she and Eidyn walked away she risked a final glance back at Aedann. He winked at her and I saw her lift a hand to her mouth to stifle a giggle. Her father flicked his disapproving gaze over her and then back at Aedann before placing his hand on Bronwen's shoulder and propelling her in front of him towards his quarters.

As I reached Aedann's side he was looking after them, shaking his head. "What was that all about?" I asked.

"Typical isn't it? Your father took a dislike to me because I was Welsh and a slave. Now, Eidyn takes offence because I am in the company of the English. I can't win, Cerdic."

"Has he a reason for being offended? Just how much 'consorting' were you guilty of?"

Aedann glowered at me, "I am a honourable man and Bronwen is a lady. What are you implying?"

"He is asking whether you've tupped her lad," Eduard said as he came to join us. "Not that I blame you if you have." He grinned and with a dig of his elbow into Aedann's ribs, added, "Know what I mean?"

"You leave her alone!" Aedann snapped. Then he shrugged, "Sorry Eduard, it's just that I do really like her. No, Cerdic, in answer to your question I have not tupped her. But you have been away almost three weeks and I have spent a lot of time with her. Let's leave it at that, but I will be damned if Eidyn will prevent me from seeing her."

"Aedann," I began, "he is her father and a prince, you—"

"So what!" he cut across me, flaring up again.

"Just be careful, that's all," I smiled.

Mollified, he winked at me. "I am always careful."

Behind Aedann's back Eduard made a face. I was still laughing when I spotted Aidith, Mildrith and Cuthwine emerging from the old hall.

"Father, have you brought me a boar's head?" Cuthwine

asked, running up to me.

"No, because we were interrupted before I was able to catch one. BUT I do have an auroch's horn in my saddle bag. Let me kiss your mother and I will show it to you."

"What's an Or...ruck?" he asked, stumbling over the unfamiliar word.

"It is a giant bull even taller than me. Bigger by half than any of the cows we used to have at the Villa. Almost as big as a horse and with horns as long as my legs!"

Cuthwine's eyes sparkled. "Let me see!" he begged, tugging at my tunic sleeve.

"For three weeks he has talked of nothing else but you and hunting," Aidith said with a tired sigh. I pulled her to me and kissed her and then held her at arm's length. Cuthwine was still tugging away at me – now at my belt.

"Let me look at you. Is there a bump yet?" I asked, glancing at her belly.

"Maybe a slight one, but enough about me: what about you? I hear that you can't even go hunting without starting a war!"

I frowned. "That's a bit exaggerated my love. It was only a little skirmish."

"Well a small war then!"

"Best you don't worry about it. It's over now and it won't bother us anymore."

"You promise?" She sounded far from convinced.

I hesitated. "I thought you complained I was making too many promises lately. Let's just say I hope it is over," I added hastily as I noticed her eyes narrowing.

Cuthwine was now jumping up and down and so, to avoid further discussion with his mother, I let myself be dragged to my horse, but my mind was not on the Auroch horn. It was on the Lleynii. Had it really been just a meaningless skirmish or the sign of something more serious? The way my luck went these days I was beginning to wonder.

Later that day Sabert and I went to see Taliesen. Other than our encounters with the Scots of Dal–Riata – another Irish clan – we had little knowledge of the peoples from Hibernia and so that we could advise Edwin and Hereric I decided we needed to know more. Taliesen was tuning a lyre when we knocked on his door. Once he had found us some mead and we had sat down, I asked him where the Irish who attacked us had come from.

"Had they just come across the sea?" I suggested.

Taliesen shook his head. "Not directly. Ultimately that is where they are from, of course, but during the fall of Roman Britain, the Irish had settled Ynys Mon – a large island off the coast to the north – as well as the peninsular called Llyn. But once the whole of this area was under their control – so the tale goes – the High King of the Britons, Vortigern, decided to drive them out and sent for help to Manau Gododdin in the North, beyond the Roman Wall. They not only sent an army, but also lords and a king. That king was Cunedda and he stayed on and founded Gwynedd."

"So Iago's ancestors are Gododdin? I had not realised," I commented.

Taliesen nodded. "So now you see why many of the lords and even the king were hesitant about your coming," he said, with a grave expression.

I nodded. We had destroyed the Gododdin cavalry at Catraeth. If Iago and his people were kin, however distant, to those men in the blue armour, it was small wonder they had doubts about our presence here.

"Anyway, it took successive campaigns by Iago's distant ancestors more than a century ago to drive them away. Even so, small settlements persisted in the coves and bays along the coast and these grew in strength and began to raid inland. Yet it is a while ago that they last troubled us," the old bard explained. "I wonder why now," he pondered.

"What will Iago do?" Sabert asked.

"What he must do. Arm his warriors and drive the Irish away again," he replied.

Indeed, a war council was called for the following week, once the majority of Iago's nobles could be gathered. On account of his valour, Edwin and his lords were invited to attend. I noticed Rhun and Eidyn looking glum at this. There was much debate about the action to be taken, but in the end it was decided to muster a force of the nobles' spearmen, push west along the coast into the Llyn peninsular and clear out the Irish settlements.

"But autumn is here and it is harvest time and the men will be in the fields gathering the crops. After that the weather will most likely permit only a few weeks for a campaign," pondered the king. "Nevertheless, I am resolved to strike back before the winter comes – let the Llynii know we mean business."

This left Edwin and Hereric with a decision to make: whether, and to what extent, we would support Gwynedd's campaign against the Irish. The night after the council we held our own meeting in the old king's hall.

Guthred spoke first. "Saving Cadwallon was fortuitous I will admit that. It certainly gave us a few more friends in Iago's court, but it is not enough to keep us here. Actually though, it may now be enough to permit us to leave. Whilst Iago is feeling warmer towards us we should ask for leave to depart and go to

Kent."

Sabert shook his head. "We need an ally and this act by Edwin could be the start of our gaining Gwynedd as one, but I agree it is not enough in itself. We must do more. I say that if we aid Iago against the Irish it can only help our position."

Frithwulf shook his head. "My father is right – we should not get caught up in these Welsh matters. What if the fighting goes wrong? We don't have many men and can't afford to risk those we have on side ventures. We should preserve our fighting men for when we return to Deira."

"There will be no return to Deira unless we get a sponsor, shelter and support," I pointed out. "We have made a start here. We have made friends."

"We have made enemies too, Cerdic," Harald observed. "Counting Guthred's men, you and I between us have fewer than sixty spears – barely a company in fact. Many have had a tough year with the campaign up north, then the fall of Deira. It will not be easy to persuade them to risk their necks again for this Iago."

I shrugged. "Admittedly, but did you expect this to be easy, wherever we went I mean? We are not exactly welcome any-where. Wherever we go, Aethelfrith's eye will follow. No land will welcome us easily, but this one at least has a reason to fight Aethelfrith, for now he represents the enemy and we... well, we just might offer a new ingredient."

"So you are suggesting that we help Iago against the Irish and perhaps that might persuade him to support us?" Lilla asked. "You do realise that many in his court will see this as us just try-ing to ingratiate ourselves. "

I nodded. "Aye – that is true, but let our enemies worry about how to react to us. If we go, then we put ourselves in a position to take what chances are offered. If we stay – or leave Gwynedd – then those chances are gone."

"I agree," Edwin said at last, "what do you say Nephew?"

Hereric glanced across at Guthred, which concerned me. I had spotted in the time since we left Deira how much more he listened to Guthred than to Sabert. It seemed that during our absence Guthred had used the opportunity to gain even more influence over the younger prince.

"I… I am not sure," Hereric said after a moment's hesitation. "Maybe Guthred is right and we should seek permission to leave for Kent."

His response confirmed my suspicions. How like his father he was, I reflected. Aethelric had ever been vague and easily influenced, unlike old King Aelle, Edwin's father.

Edwin studied Hereric for a moment and judging by his heavy sigh he was entertaining similar thoughts to my own. "You do what you want, Nephew. I am for going with Iago," he declared.

Aidith and Mildrith did not exactly greet with enthusiasm the news that their menfolk would be going away again so soon. "You have only just come back from the mountains and you are off again. You could be killed and then what will happen to us – to your son, to your unborn child? Have you thought of that?" Aidith complained. I could see from Mildrith's arched eyebrows as Cuth told her the news that she was taking it similarly well!

"What would you have me do, woman?" I said, feeling frustrated yet guilty all at once. "Would you have me abandon Edwin and Hereric? Would you have me leave them and just go with you? I made a promise to Aelle and to Aethelric that I would watch over their heirs. How can I leave them now when the circumstances are so desperate?"

She walked over to me and put her arms around my neck. "No, of course you can't. I just wish… I just wish we could be left to live our lives in peace."

"My love, those are the very words I say to myself every day," I replied and kissed her.

Chapter Eleven
Into Llyn

Eidyn and Rhun were dispatched to call up the Fyrd as well as scout out the land west of Deganwy and establish where the enemy were. Cadwallon accompanied them as squire to learn more of war and continue his education. That concerned me a little. On the journey back from the mountains the young prince and Eidyn had spoken often and I was concerned that he was being drawn into the camp of those who were far from happy with our presence. It would be some weeks for the *Alldaith* – the Welsh equivalent of the militia or Fyrd – to be summoned. As Iago had said, this would not occur until the harvest was gathered. Around Deganwy the villages and farms were soon busy collecting the harvest and many of the estate workers from Iago's fortress lent a hand. Here was a task that those of us from the Villa and Wicstun could be genuinely useful at helping with and so we volunteered our services to Iago. His steward, Belyn, soon had us collecting sacks of grain from the threshing barn or leading cattle and sheep to the slaughter house.

Meanwhile, Aidith, Mildrith and Gwen helped out with the smoking, drying, pickling and sealing of fruit and vegetables in jars and pots for the winter ahead.

The weather was kind and it was a pleasant few weeks. I enjoyed the familiar routine of it all. Days without spears and shields made a refreshing change to what had come before and what was yet to follow. I put all such thoughts to one side and enjoyed the long days of productive work followed by warm nights wrapped up with Aidith. For that month I lived in the moment.

Someone else who lived in the moment was Aedann. Throughout the day he laboured alongside us, but come evening time he would sneak out of the king's hall whilst the rest of us were eating or drinking, and either just beforehand or just afterwards I would spot Bronwen stealing along the shadows at the side of the hall, or scuttling across the courtyard to a barn or workshed. It was obvious to me what was going on and occasionally I would mutter something to Aedann, urging him to be careful, or Eduard would dig him in the ribs and say something like, "Sleep well last night did you mate?" and Aedann would shrug and say nothing, but I would catch a smile flit across his lips. It could not go on of course. Sooner or later they would get caught.

In early October the harvest was finally all gathered in and stored away and the king held a feast in celebration and to reward and thank everyone. That night Eidyn and Rhun returned. It seemed that Eidyn had caught wind of the ongoing liaison between his daughter and my Welsh friend in his absence, because whilst Rhun stood to give thanks to his God for the harvest and call upon His blessing for the military endeavours that would follow, I noticed Eidyn staring at Aedann, his expression dark with foreboding.

The prayer said, we attacked the roast meat with gusto, but after a while Aedann got to his feet. I frowned at him, "Maybe not such a good idea tonight, Aedann. I think Eidyn suspects something. Look, he is watching you right now. Sit down," I advised.

Glumly he did so, but later, when the minstrels took up their lyres and harps and began singing of the legends of Arthyr and Myrddin and their campaign against the Saxons a hundred years before, Aedann slid off the bench and sidled down the hall and into the shadows on his way to the door.

My friends and I watched him leave. "He must be very keen on her," Cuthbert muttered.

"Or else she is very good, if you know what I mean," Eduard added crudely and then belched.

"Do you think Eidyn noticed him leaving?" I asked.

We all glanced up the hall to where Eidyn sat close to Iago. Bronwen was behind him, pouring his mead. Like many of the ladies of the court she would often serve the lords' drinks during the feasts. Soon after Aedann had gone, she put down the jug and hurried out of the hall. At first Eidyn did not seem to have noticed, but he then drained his goblet and held it up for a refill and when Bronwen did not appear at his shoulder he turned to look for her. A moment later he flashed a glance towards us, spotted Aedann's empty seat and was on his feet moving towards the main doors and barking out orders to his men. Followed by half a dozen warriors, all of them buckling on their swords, he passed out into the night.

"Shit!" I swore, getting to my feet. "Eduard, Cuthbert, come with me. Grettir, you follow with two more lads."

Grabbing up our weapons from the pile outside the hall, we spotted Eidyn and his men hastening to one of the leather workers' workshops on the other side of the courtyard. They must have noticed some movement or heard something there because two of the men kicked the door open and rushed in. A few moments later one of them came hurtling back out, blood gushing from his nose. Next thing Aedann and the other guard tumbled out, arms locked around each other. As they stopped rolling one of Eidyn's thugs stepped forward and kicked Aedann in the ribs. He shouted in pain and released his opponent. Eidyn's

142

other men dragged Aedann to his feet and pulled him over to their lord, who drew a vicious looking dagger and placed it at my Welsh friend's throat.

"Father, no!" Bronwen shouted, emerging from the hut. At her appearance I was reminded of the time when my father had caught Cuthbert and Mildrith canoodling in the old barn at the Villa. Father had been hopping mad and it had taken all my skills to prevent him from slaying Cuthbert on the spot. Now here I was, once again attempting to save a friend from imminent disaster and for the same reason.

"Stop!" I bellowed running forward.

"Keep out of this, Angle. I warned this man to keep away from my daughter and he ignored the warning. I mean to geld this piece of scum right now."

Next to me Eduard's axe was out of his belt and in his hand. Catraeth was soon in my own. In a flash Eidyn's men were also wielding swords and it was clear things were about to get very nasty indeed.

"Enough!" bellowed a strong voice and Cadfan came running from the king's hall. "I command you to put up your weapons immediately. Just what is the meaning of this?"

"My Lord," Eidyn shouted, "Cerdic's huscarl has been cavorting with my daughter. I am taking action to see it does not happen again. It need not concern you."

Reaching him, Cadfan gazed at him and then at Aedann. Finally he looked at Bronwen. "Such might be your right, Eidyn, if he forced himself on her, but not if she chose him of her own free will. Did you, Bronwen?"

"My Prince... I protest..." Eidyn spluttered.

"Protest all you like Prince Eidyn, but if your daughter consented then it is her affair and you have no hold on this man's life."

We all stared at Bronwen. Her cheeks flushed scarlet and she turned away. For a moment I thought she would deny Aedann in order to save face, but then she turned back and nodded. "Yes my Lord Prince, I took him as a lover of my own free will. Release him Father."

His face like thunder, Eidyn thrust Aedann to one side so violently he almost fell. "Harlot!" he spat at his daughter then without a backward glance he stomped away, followed by his men.

Cadfan watched them leave and then turned to me, his face grim and disapproving. "Lord Cerdic, we depart for the West and war tomorrow. I need all the spears at my father's command to be fit and healthy. We cannot afford division among the men. I would thank you not to provoke Prince Eidyn and to see to it that your men do not do so either."

I nodded. "Of course, Prince Cadfan," I replied as he turned back to the hall.

I let out a long breath and then rounded on Aedann, "You idiot! What were you thinking of? Make your fairwells to Bronwen and then get to bed. And by that I mean your *own* bed and on your *own*!" Aedann glared at me, but made no comment.

I made a slight bow to Bronwen and murmured, "Goodnight my lady," then sent the others back to the king's hall. Rather than join them I made my way to the old hall. In just a few hours we would be off and I wanted to spend the time that was left with Aidith and Cuthwine.

Iago had mustered five hundred spears to march against the Irish raiders. Edwin agreed to go with our fifty or so men, and despite Hereric's reluctance and Guthred's opposition we went. Of the Deiran men, only Sabert remained behind – the aged counsellor

144

now getting rather old for battle. We set off one bright but cold and frosty autumnal morning. The entire household turned out to see us off and grant us good hunting. Millie and Aidith were amongst them, their faces pale and tense with worry.

Shivering, I pulled my cloak around me to keep out the penetrating breeze and cantered my horse to catch up with Edwin near the front of the column as we marched toward yet another enemy: the Irish.

Iago led us west along the coast while his scouts raced ahead to alert his nobles and villages in the area. Eidyn and Rhun, accompanied by Cadwallon, had spent some days scouting the region and had discovered that there were indeed several Irish raiders present and settlements not only along the Llyn peninsular but also on the Isle known as Ynys Mon.

"That is unprecedented in my lifetime," Iago said. "Not for a century have they been so bold as to invade the Isle. Just what has provoked them thus, I wonder?"

There was no answer to his question but in the end Iago chose to divide his forces. He commandeered boats and led half his men across the Menai Straits, the narrow strip of water that separated Ynys Mon from the mainland, while Cadfan, Cadwallon, Eidyn, Rhun and Edwin went along the coast with the remainder, including our Saxon spears.

The Irish settlements were isolated with some miles between each one. Cadfan's plan was to destroy them one at a time, preventing them from communicating with each other and alerting the rest to our attack. So, as we approached each village, a hundred of the men under Cadwallon and Eidyn would encircle the habitations to the landward side and position themselves to prevent escape, whilst Cadfan's and Edwin's half – about two hundred men – attacked the village from the other side. What usually happened is that the Irish warriors would move to face us on their ramparts and the children and women would try to escape to the next village.

At the start of the campaign we had the advantage of surprise. Indeed, the Irish apparently had no idea we were approaching and we aggressively assaulted their earthen banks and wooden palisades. Often their warriors were outside working the fields, the gates wide open. No mercy was shown. The men were cut down as they stood fighting in small groups trying to buy a few minutes for their families to escape. We then surged on to set fire to the huts and hovels and capture any food and supplies that we could find. For the families there was no escape. Cadwallon and Eidyn intercepted them, slew any older boys and the men protecting them and dragged the children and women back to their burning homes. Here they were chained and led off east under guard to slavery.

Did any of us show any compassion and pity to our captives? Precious little is the truthful answer. This was just what the Irish would have done to us had they captured us during the raid the previous winter. It is just what the British did to Saxons and what we English did to the Welsh. Does that make it right? Probably not, but in a time of danger and confusion the only sensible course of action is to destroy your enemy before they get a chance to do the same to you. You kill the warriors and enslave their women and children. In doing so you reduce the capacity of their race to replace their losses and seek revenge on your children. It is simple survival.

And I hated every moment of it. I could see Aidith in each woman we captured and recognised Cuthwine in the terrified faces of the children. I was reminded that I had never wanted to be a warrior. 'Farmer' is what Edwin had called me, and at heart that is exactly what I was. And yet I was also skilled with a sword and understood the tactics of battle and the need for survival, and so I guess I was always torn in two.

The season dragged on with us moving from settlement to settlement. Despite how cold it had been on the morning we set out, it turned out to be unusually warm that autumn and my men began to grumble and complain. They were tired and dirty and a long way from home. To us Saxons the coastline we now followed was the ends of the earth and these mountainous lands seemed so very far from the woodlands and fields of distant Deira. More than one man could be heard to ask what in Woden's name we were doing fighting for the accursed British against a group we had never met before and certainly posed us no direct threat. Indeed, if they were the enemies of the British, surely we should be their friends? My old retainer, Grettir, was, of course, as loyal as ever.

"It is enough that Lord Cerdic and Prince Edwin and the others order us to do this. I try not to think too hard on the whys and wherefores of it all and I advise you to do the same," I heard him say one night as I passed by the men's fire on my way to relieve myself among the trees.

"You don't think at all Grettir," Frithwulf's voice rang out, "and as for Cerdic, he will just do what Edwin tells him – whatever the cost to the rest of us. I tell you, my father was right to oppose this. We could have been far away from here and safe in Kent by now had he and I had our way."

The group around the fire hushed him and pointed at me moving past, but Frithwulf stared defiantly at me and then smiled across at his father who was sitting at a nearby fire. I knew I was going to have to deal with him and his father sometime. Their very presence was dividing the company.

The rumbling of dissatisfaction among our men was only one of the problems that concerned me as we continued our campaign. Eidyn took every opportunity to complain about us in his efforts to convince Cadfan of the folly of our presence. It didn't get him anywhere: the act of bravery on Edwin's part in saving Cadwallon's life was enough to keep Cadfan viewing us as allies. Eventually Eidyn left off those attempts and instead chose the easier target of Cadwallon. In this he was joined by Rhun.

The Welsh bishop had accompanied the army at Iago's request to give spiritual support and to pray for our victory. Yet that meant he spent more time in our presence, which he no doubt disliked, particularly since it brought him into contact with me. As he had made clear on our way to Augustine's Oak, this was to be avoided lest his desire to see me dead became too hard to control. Each day he would stand and stare at me in silence, his face growing dark and his hands balling into fists. Then he would spin on his heel and hasten away as if afraid of what he might do. It was obvious to me that the man was not right in his head and others too were beginning to notice. His prayers, such as I understood them, became darker and frankly depressing. He would refer to the wrath of God and bringing down destruction on the Irish like God had done to Soddom and Gomorrah, wherever those places had been. Pointing to the nearby Irish-occupied village he would say, "Lo, the angel of the Lord speaks to me and He says you will wreak terrible destruction today in His holy name." Rhun was implying this was what the Welsh were about to do to the Irish, but he often looked at me as he was speaking these words and I suspected that it was my destruction he meant, seeing in his mind the image of me dead at his feet.

I became increasingly convinced that the darkness of which he had spoken was returning to him and I think he was aware of it too because he tried to have me sent away, suggesting I scout to the south. Cadfan resisted this as he wanted to keep his strength together, which is probably why Rhun joined Eidyn in trying to turn Cadwallon to their point of view, perhaps in the hope that he would persuade his father to send we Angles packing. They seemed always about him whispering and scheming and it was of some concern to me where that would lead.

Tensions amongst the leaders of the army were obvious to the men themselves. It was natural then that men would begin to take sides. Eidyn's men in particular were aware of their master's feelings about us and would tease and taunt us Saxons. My own men only naturally snapped back. Whenever I saw that happening I would tell them to keep quiet. We had to be careful, outnumbered as we were five to one.

Yet, in that unseasonably hot October, it was inevitable that the tensions would erupt eventually and on one particular day so they did. We had been marching for many hours through the heat and were running low on provisions and water. It had been a few days since the last raid on the Irish and tempers were short. I was polishing my sword and generally relaxing after the hard day when I noticed half a dozen of Eidyn's henchmen approaching Eduard and Cuthbert, who sat on a fallen log by our fire. I could not hear what was said, but I saw Eduard leap suddenly to his feet and throw himself at the Welsh. All seven of them collapsed in a heap with my friend on top. A dozen more British warriors from nearby rushed over and a similar number of my folk joined in the fight. In a second fists and feet were flying and a furious battle was at hand.

I rushed over to try to intervene as did Cadfan. Cadwallon, I noticed, kept back and was standing next to Eidyn, who was pointing at Eduard. I saw the youth nodding eagerly at whatever

149

Eidyn was saying and it was clear to me that as I had thought, the young fool was firmly in the older man's sway.

When I reached the fray there were fully forty warriors involved. Half a dozen were slumped nearby with bloodied noses. One was spitting out a tooth in a glob of blood. In the melee I saw a sword drawn and another man with a spear. Taliesen, Aneirin and Lilla were all shouting at the men to lay down their arms, but to no avail – the bards' influence over the men for once proving ineffectual. Then Earl Harald, Cadfan and I surged in amongst them and started pushing men apart and bellowing for them to stop.

In the end it is only by the will of the gods that no one died. One man lost an ear and two others a finger each, but that was as serious as the injuries got. Alas, the most injured of all was Eduard, who had been set upon by a half dozen warriors. Apart from losing two teeth, he had taken a nasty sprain to the right shoulder, which meant he would struggle to wield his axe for days. However hard the bards, Cadfan and I tried to keep the peace between our people, we were clearly not succeeding. Put simply, they did not get on. The different races were like oil and water and sooner rather than later that was going to lead to disaster, I could feel it in my bones. How Loki must have been enjoying himself! I could almost hear him chuckling.

Some days later we approached a large village towards the east end of the Llyn peninsular, which we believed to be held by the Irish. The mild autumn weather of the previous weeks seemed to be fading and the air was cool with rain in the air. Winter was approaching and soon men would be looking to head home. Cadfan had received word that Iago had more or less completed his campaign in Ynys Mon and having driven the Irish away, intended crossing back in a week, rejoining us and being home in Deganwy within a fortnight.

"One last raid and then home for Christmas," was what Cadfan promised. "After that, if there are Irish left in Llyn, we will have to wait till the spring to sort them out."

The village was typical of the Welsh settlements the Irish raiders had captured this autumn. It was built on the thin strip of flat land between the mountains to the south and the sea, whose waves even now crashed upon the sand to the north. It was surrounded by fields where a few cows and goats grazed. However, there were no folk in sight. This was odd as typically someone would be repairing a fence or a roof or just watching over the animals. Their absence should have warned us that all was not quite right. Hindsight again! Perhaps it was that we were complacent because this was the last raid and soon we would be going home.

Beyond the fields was a circular ditch and an earthen embankment. This was topped by a wall built from stones that were in such abundance in the mountains that ringed the settlement on the landward side. The gates to the enclosure were open and faced east, towards us. Within the walled perimeter were eight round stone huts and a larger headman's house. There was also a simple stone chapel. Smoke was rising from a half–dozen cook fires and also from the baking pit, but other than that there was no sign of life anywhere.

"I don't much fancy this," Cuthbert muttered to Eduard. My larger friend rarely showed dissent at all, but I saw him nodding to his companion. His arm was still giving him pain and that made him more grumpy that usual. It wasn't only Cuthbert who was uncertain. Several men were studying the ramparts with a growing sense of unease.

Cadfan was not stupid and he was certainly wary of the quiet

151

settlement with the wide open gates. "I don't like this son," he grunted to Cadwallon.

"Let me go Father. I'll take Eidyn's men and scout it out. If there is any danger we can spring the trap and you can rush to our aid."

"No, Lord Cadfan," interrupted Edwin, "it is too dangerous to risk the young prince. Let me go with my men." Edwin had spoken rashly, doubly foolish indeed, because not only had he put himself and us in danger – it is one thing trying to show valour and loyalty to earn allies, but another to risk your own plans on a petty Irish village – but also, he had in effect clumsily insulted Cadwallon's honour.

The youth bristled with indignation and the days of listening to Eidyn and Rhun's poison showed through. He glared at Edwin, "I am no coward! It is for me to go, not you," he snapped.

"I agree. After that fight in the camp I would not trust these English," Eidyn murmured, rubbing salt into Cadwallon's wound.

"We have been nothing but loyal during this campaign, Eidyn of the Gododdin!" Edwin countered.

"Enough!" Cadfan ordered. "We must resolve this disunity. Both Edwin and Cadwallon will take fifty men each and scout out the camp. I will remain here ready to bring the rest forward on your signal."

So there was nothing else for it. Looking daggers at Eidyn, Edwin signalled to me and Harald and we led our men forward. I noticed that Rhun had joined Eidyn and Cadwallon and they and their fifty marched out alongside us towards the Irish village. At least as many English as Welsh were looking at each other with distrust as we approached the village gates. "Keep your hands on your weapons, men," I hissed, my own hand

152

tightening around Catraeth.

We English seemed to be moving a little faster than the Welsh. True the latter were walking across muddy fields rather than along the hard earth track that we followed. But afterwards I wondered if this was deliberate. In any event we reached the gates fifty yards ahead of Cadwallon and his men. Edwin stopped and turned to look back, perhaps wondering if he should wait, but at that moment he caught sight of Eidyn, who wore a cynical expression as if to say: *'What are you waiting for? Afraid of a little village are you?'*

Edwin's face grew hard and he spun round and stomped on through the gates, apparently working on the basis that it was better to risk danger than be accused of cowardice. As he entered the gates with a couple of the men from Harald's company, I followed. I was missing my two friends who would customarily be at my side. Eduard, still nursing his injured shoulder, was away in the rear ranks and Cuthbert was keeping him company rather than scouting out in front as usual. We paid dearly for the lack of Cuthbert's hawk–like eyes that day, but I was so preoccupied with the escalating anger between Edwin and Cadwallon that I never gave a moment's thought to calling him forward to where he belonged.

Suddenly, a dozen or more Irish warriors burst out from where they were hiding behind each gate and lunged straight for Edwin. One brute hacked at him with a sword and I saw the blow glance off the prince's temple in a fountain of scarlet as he stumbled back. Dismayed, I charged forward bellowing and skewered his opponent. By now, our men had come up and were engaged in a vicious fight around us. I grabbed Edwin by the shoulder, spun him round and pushed him back through the gates. Stunned and bleeding copiously from the scalp, but still

153

carrying sword and shield, he staggered a few yards off the path into the fields and then collapsed.

"Edwin!" I shouted after him. He did not answer. "Edwin!" I shouted again. There was no movement. I swallowed hard. Was he dead? I was about to run after him to check when two more Irish came roaring at me. Alive or dead, I could not help Edwin now, so I brought Catraeth up and prepared to fight for my life.

Chapter Twelve
Deception

The enemy's surprise attack had thrown us into disarray. I saw one of our lads from the village stumble backwards, blood spraying from an open wound in his chest. The Irish surged out of the gates, hacking at us with their broad, two-handed blades.

"Form up! Form up," I bellowed, "Shield wall – now!"

The men hurried to obey. Aedann was first to arrive by my right side, overlapping my shield with a clatter. Grettir moved next to him and Harald arrived on my left. Guthred and Frithwulf joined us, bringing Hereric. Moments later Cuthbert too arrived beside me, but not Eduard. When there were twenty of us formed up I shouted an advance and levelling our spears we stomped forward, driving at the Irish.

The enemy saw us coming and forming their own shield wall moved to engage us. The distraction provided a respite for the rest of my company who scattered to the right and left out of our path and then re-joined us, expanding the shield wall and adding depth.

Gradually our numbers rallied until there were as many English in formation as there were Irish and then more. The Irish attack had taken us by surprise, but we now outnumbered them and despite the lack of participation of Cadwallon's company, which had still not joined us, we were shoving the enemy back towards their village. I swung my sword at the throat of a yellow-haired youth. He leapt back, cursing as the point nicked his neck and blood ran down onto his chest.

I sensed movement behind me and turned to see someone

pushing through the ranks at my back. With a surge of relief I recognised Edwin. Still blinking blood from his eyes, his face starkly pale, he came up beside me and slotted his shield into the wall. Giving me a curt nod, he advanced another step and said, "Thank you. That was a close one. It seems we have come through the ambush easily enough, though."

"Yes it does," I replied with a sudden sense of foreboding. Had it been too easy? It had been reckless of the Irish with only half our number to attack us as they had, albeit with the benefit of surprise. Had they been overconfident or was something else going on? Was it a trap?

"Keep alert lads!" I shouted, peering beyond the retreating enemy to the village. It still looked deserted and I saw nothing suspicious there. Nevertheless, something was not right: the hairs on the back of my neck were standing up and I could feel my skin prickling with the tension. Were these outnumbered Lleynii attacking us simply to give their families a chance to escape – just like every other village we had encountered? Or was that the point. Were we supposed to believe that was what they were doing when in fact they had something else planned for us?

To our front the Irish continued to give way and so we pushed on. We were almost in the village now and it seemed as if the fight had gone out of the enemy. I was sure they were falling back a little too easily – almost as if they wanted us to follow them. As soon as I had that thought, I knew I was right. They weren't giving way because of pressure from us. We were being drawn in deliberately. But why do that unless...?

"Hold! Stop advancing!" I shouted. No one responded. Still smarting from the sudden attack that had struck down several of our company the men were bent on revenge. "Friga's tits!" I bellowed. "I said halt, you bastards!" I swore even more loudly and this time the company reluctantly obeyed, staggering to a standstill and glaring at me in confusion.

"What the Hel is it lad?" Guthred sniped. "Lost your nerve have you?"

"What's up Cerdic?" Harald asked, his gaze taking in the retreating enemy and the empty village. Then his eyes narrowed as he too perceived something was not right.

"Hold the men here and let me look," I said to him, turning to peer away from the village.

To the north Cadwallon's company was still standing off in the middle of the field – watching us and not committing to battle. I waved at them and gestured angrily that they should join us. Rhun stood impassively, dark eyes watching us and arms folded across his chest. Eidyn waved back but made no move towards us and Cadwallon stared at me then looked pointedly the other way as if I did not matter. The arrogance of the youth took my breath away; he was clearly under Eidyn's sway. I spat in their direction and turned to study the surrounding land. Further to the east I could see the shadowy forms of Prince Cadfan's men in amongst the trees - ash and beech, bare of leaves now - but I could not make out the prince and was uncertain where he was.

To the south, the land rose towards the mountains which this late in the year had the hint of snow on their peaks. A flock of crows wheeled overhead and flapped away towards the west. The land seemed deserted and I figured I must be imagining things, yet something was making me jumpy. After another moment I shrugged, turned back to the company and was just opening my mouth to give the order to advance once more, when Cuthbert shouted.

157

"Cerdic! Look up there!"

He was pointing southwards up a valley towards the mountains. I turned my gaze back that way. "What is it, Cuth?" At first I could see nothing save the empty hillside. Then something moved and I saw what he had seen.

A man stood alone on a rocky outcrop about a couple of hundred paces south of the village. Even from that distance I could see he was impressively tall, maybe six-foot-three, with wide shoulders, legs like oak trees and powerful, muscular arms. He stared down at us, one hand holding a broad, two-handed blade and the other stroking a luxurious red beard. Behind him a green cloak flapped in the breeze. I was to learn later that this was Garrett, Lord and Chieftain of the Lleynii, but even before I knew that, I would have guessed he was a chieftain by his appearance. He studied us for a moment and then thrust one finger in our direction.

A huge roar echoed off the granite mountainside around him and from a dip in the ground a horde of Irish warriors emerged, cresting the rise on either side of their chieftain and surging down the hill towards us. There were perhaps three hundred… no I was wrong, there were at least four hundred of them!

"Merciful Woden!" I cried, "We've been tricked!" Mesmerised, I was unable to do anything but stare in horror.

"What do we do, Cerdic?" Edwin shouted, clearly as stunned as I was by the terrifying sight.

I came to my senses, glanced at him and shouted an order. "Back! Get back towards the trees. Stay together. Keep the shield wall intact, but back off!"

We started retreating. To our front the small party of Irish in the village emerged and pelted us with slingshot, threatening to charge if we broke ranks and fled. As we pulled back we were horribly aware of the Irish Chieftain and his men thundering towards us. A hundred paces away the woodland beckoned as a sanctuary and the urge to turn and run for the trees was intense, yet if we did and were overtaken by the fast approaching horde, most of us would not make it. Turn your back on a charging enemy and you are asking for a spear between the shoulder blades. Better to fall back in order and hope that help would come to us. I risked a glanced toward Cadwallon's company. Eidyn, Rhun and the Gwynedd prince were staring open-mouthed at the approaching Irish.

"To me!" I yelled at them.

Cadwallon blinked and looked at me. He seemed to be in shock, uncertain how to respond. Suddenly there was movement in the trees not far from where he stood and a voice bellowed, "Attack, don't just stand there!"

It was Cadfan. Yelling at his son, he led the rest of the men out from the cover of the woodland and came running to our aid. Cadwallon stirred and began shouting orders then moved forward onto our right, just as Cadfan was forming up on our left.

The Irish were fifty paces away now. They were still covering the ground at speed, making no attempt to form up into any shield wall, and bellowing war cries in their strange tongue as they came – a sound that fair chilled the blood.

"Spears ready!" Cadfan shouted in Welsh and I echoed the order in English. Spear shafts were braced between arm and chest whilst our left hands held tightly to our shields.

"Here they come!" I shouted. "Skewer the bastards!"

Each of us picked one of the oncoming warriors and thrust his spear at them. Anticipating this move the Irish swerved and dodged as they came at us. But when a man is running he cannot

159

change direction as easily and at least one in five of our spears found its mark. Razor sharp spear points buried themselves in chests or bellies and screaming in agony dying men fell to the ground. Others deflected the spear points with their shields, but still cried out in pain from the impact. Still more caught the point in their shoulder and were knocked off their feet. Only lightly wounded, these would live, though would do little more this day.

Then the enemy were upon us. Shields smashed against shields and men, carried by their own momentum, tumbled into our ranks. At most spots the shield wall held, but at the gap between our own men and those of Cadwallon, where the warriors were wary of each other, the shields had not overlapped. This then was the disaster I had envisaged: a shield wall will only hold if it is impenetrable, but it requires absolute trust to keep it so, each man working with those on either side of him. This day we paid the price for that lack of trust.

The Irish burst through the gaps, breaching our shield wall. Cadwallon's fifty men were now trapped between the village and the Irish. Cadfan had started pulling the shield wall back and there was a real danger that his son would get cut off and surrounded.

"My Prince," I gasped to Edwin, "I must go there. Keep the men retreating and keep in pace with Cadfan. Aedann, Cuth to me..." I began then hesitated, for now I saw that Eduard had come up behind us. I shot him a relieved smile, knowing that even injured he was stronger than most and I had need of his strength right now. He knew it too and hefting his axe he grinned at me.

"Aedann, Cuth, Eduard, follow me," I cried.

I led my three friends across to the right behind our own company, to where the Irish were spilling out through the gap and lapping around Cadwallon. I charged in first with my longsword in my right hand. While Catraeth was perfect for the confined spaces of a shield wall, here the fighting was more open and Wreccan's long blade gave me an advantage.

Focused as they were on surrounding Cadwallon and his men, the Irish did not see us coming and we took them by surprise. I slammed my shield into the flank of one youth and as he stumbled away from me, I slashed Wreccan across his face. He fell to the ground squealing in pain and Eduard, showing no mercy, buried his axe in the lad's back. I saw my friend wince in pain, his injured shoulder jolted by the blow, but he had recovered enough to fight once again with the weapon of which he was such a master and I sent up a prayer of thanks to my gods.

Side-stepping a spear point I followed inside its reach and thrust Wreccan into the neck of the veteran who held the spear. An arrow sped past my ear catching another man in the shoulder. He dropped his shield and I saw Aedann come round to my right and hack at the man's unprotected arm.

We had reached Cadwallon now; next to him stood Eidyn and Rhun. "Come with us!" I bellowed. As my friends and I held the breach in the line, Cadwallon shouted to his men to form back on us.

Then a shadow fell over me as a huge man stepped between me and the sun. I gawped up as the Irish Chieftain and Lord of the Lleynii seized my tunic and pulled my face up close to his own – so close that I could smell the previous night's stale ale and garlic on his breath.

"Angles?" he demanded, bellowing the question over the noise of battle.

I struggled to get free.

161

"Angles?" he shouted again.

"Yes I am an Angle, you Irish bastard!" I hissed at him. "So what?" I wrenched myself free and stepped back, bringing up my blade.

He grinned and it was not a pleasant grin. "All this is because of you!" he roared and before I could fully comprehend his strange words, he charged again and swung his huge axe at my head. I parried the blow with my shield and staggered backwards out of his reach.

We were drastically outnumbered. The red-haired chieftain was leading a dozen enormous houseguards, heavily armoured and like their master equipped with gigantic axes, which they wielded with efficient brutality as they cut their way through Cadwallon's ranks. Eduard, the only one of us who looked as though he might hold his own against them, joined me and we locked shields, but the heavy wood would not hold the immense power of their blows for long. As the chieftain advanced on me once more I became aware of movement behind me. Risking a glance that way I saw Cadfan leading a dozen of his warriors towards Cadwallon's position, desperately trying to rescue his son from the onslaught of the red-headed barbarian and his frenzied companions. Then I spotted Taliesen and Aneirin, along with Lilla – the three of them helping the wounded away from the slaughter. It must have been obvious even to the Irish that these were bards, for none touched them, their persons sacrosanct in all British cultures. I caught Lilla's expression and felt a chill. It was the first time I could recall ever having seen such desperation etched on the poet's face.

Over the noise of battle I heard Cadfan shouting at his son, "Get back Cadwallon! Get back to the woods!"

My nose was filled with the stink of blood, faeces and spilled guts while my ears rang with the bellowing of war cries, the screams of the wounded and the roar of battle – the full fury of which had been unleashed upon us by this Irish warlord. My own bowels loosened as I struggled to control my fear. It is a myth that warriors do not feel fear. No man, unless he be insane, can face this without terror and I could not recall being more terrified than I was at that precise moment. I daresay I said much the same after Catraeth. It is odd how one forgets: each successive moment of terror always worse in one's mind than the last.

I felt a sickening blow to the back of the head, which knocked me to my knees. I was vaguely aware of Eduard standing over me swinging his axe to keep the enemy at bay. Wreccan had fallen from my hand and I reached back to feel my scalp, my fingers encountering a sticky liquid. As I brought my hand forward I realized in horror that it was blood – my blood! A moment later I felt an agonizing pain in my right thigh and at the same time an instant of overwhelming nausea. The world seemed to spin away and I slumped forward face down on the bloody soil and then remembered no more.

Nothing more apart from those words. Those incomprehensible words roared at me in fury and hate: "...*because of you!*"

Chapter Thirteen
Because of you!

I woke up in a darkened room feeling incredibly thirsty. My head hurt and an excruciating pain was shooting up and down my leg. I was lying in a bed, that much I could tell, but I could make out little else. "Where... where am I?" I managed to mutter.

As my eyes started to adjust I saw a shape move in the darkness. It crossed to the shutters and opened them letting in a dull grey light. Outside I could hear rain beating steadily on the ground and thunder rumbling overhead. Just then a crack of lightning briefly illuminated my surroundings and I squinted at the figure standing in the window. It was a woman. Almost at the same time I recognised the room as Aidith's and mine in the old hall at Deganwy. So, we were back at Iago's fortress, but how had I got there?

"Aidith?" I muttered.

The woman came closer and I saw it was indeed my wife. "Who else did you think it would be?" she retorted. She sat on the bed and held a cup of water to my lips. It tasted like nectar and I drank greedily, emptying the cup. Taking it from me she reached out to examine the bandage that I could now feel swathing my scalp. "How is your head?" she asked. Hearing a particular tension in the tone of her voice I took a deep breath. I knew that voice: it was the one that meant I was in trouble. Maybe not right now, but soon.

"It hurts." I sat up in bed and then wished I had not. A spike of pain shot down my leg making me gasp. The limb felt as heavy as a tree trunk. Frowning, I threw off the furs to take a look. My right leg was heavily bandaged and splinted with two wooden sticks. "Thunor's balls! I broke my leg," I swore.

"Eduard said you were lucky not to lose it!" Aidith said tartly.

"Why, what happened?" I was utterly confused. The last thing I remembered was being struck down in the fury of a pitched battle in a foreign land, outnumbered by a fearsome horde of Irish and about to die. Yet here I now was, apparently alive and safe… or was I dreaming? "What happened?" I repeated. My wife's eyebrows rose into a severe arch and she glared at me. *'Oh dear,'* I thought, *'that was obviously the wrong question!'*

"What happened?" Aidith repeated softly, "What happened?" she said again, this time her voice rising to a higher pitch.

'Uh-oh, Cerdic my lad, you are in for it now,' I said to myself. "Is… everything all right?" I asked tentatively. Her eyes narrowed and I knew at once that I had made another a mistake. I sighed and waited for the tirade.

"Of course everything is not all right!" she snapped. "There is an awful lot that has gone wrong in fact, but I will let your friend tell you about that. What bothers me most, Cerdic, is that you could have died. *Died!* You could easily have lost your life, not just been injured, but died in some gods-forsaken, flea infested Irish warren, helping the Welsh to fight the Irish instead of standing back and letting them kill each other, which would have been the sensible thing to do." She paused to take a sobbing breath, tears spilling from her eyes. "I could have been left with no husband, a young boy and a baby who would never know its father, dead on some battlefield before he or she was even born! Did you think of that when you went marching off to war that you love so much? Do you ever think of those you leave behind?"

"I… that's not fair, Aidith… I think of you all the time."

I stammered out the words, but she was not listening. Getting to her feet she fixed me with a stern gaze. "Cerdic… why are we here?"

Before I could answer her there was knock on the door. It opened and in the frame stood Eduard. His expression grim he studied me then ducking under the lintel came fully into the room, his clothes dripping rainwater all over the floor. Aidith glanced up at him and then back at me. Without another word she stepped out through the door and shut it firmly behind her. I looked up into Eduard's worried face and my skin crawled. Something was very wrong here.

My big friend stomped over and threw himself down on the stool by the bed with such force that the wood cracked. "Well," he said, after staring at me for a while, "I reckon Guthred was right!"

"What?" I asked, perplexed by his approach. "You mean about attacking the Irish? Well obviously it went a bit wrong, but—"

"A *bit* wrong? Bollocks to that. Do you think 'a bit wrong' really sums it up?"

"Why, what do you mean? And anyway, how in Hel do I know?" I was beginning to get angry now. "It may have escaped your notice, Eduard, but I've been out of it for however long - how long is that by the way? - so are you going to tell me what has happened?"

Eduard frowned and glanced back at the door, "You mean Aidith has not told you?"

"No, I have only just woken up. Told me what?"

"About the battle. Guthred said we were sticking our necks

166

out and should never have gone to fight the Irish didn't he? Well maybe he was right."

I stared at him. Eduard had never been so animated before – certainly he had never questioned me so blatantly. "Yes I know he did," I said at length, "but we needed to impress Iago and try to gain him as an ally. Fighting his enemy seemed a good way to go about it. If you remember we all agreed on that."

Eduard shook his head. "Oh, and that worked so very well didn't it?" he said bitingly. "And not all of us agreed, Cerdic. Some of us didn't get the option!"

Stung by his sarcasm, I pounded the bed with my fists in frustration. "Eduard, will you please tell me what in the name of Thunor's balls is going on? The last thing I remember is Cadfan coming to help our shield wall and that Irish brute coming for me," I said with a burst of recollection. "And then... then it all went black."

Images of the battle flashed across my mind: that huge chieftain roaring at me, Cadwallon's company cut off; Cadfan coming to the rescue; Lilla's worried expression... I had a sudden alarming thought. "Gods! Did Cadwallon die?"

Eduard stared at me, once more shaking his head. "Is that really all you can remember?" I nodded and was quickly reminded why that was a bad idea, the pain hammering in my temples. I ignored it and waited for my friend to speak. He took a deep breath. "Very well then, no, he didn't die. Cadfan managed to get him and Eidyn out of the way, but then Garrett, having smashed your brains out – or so it seemed – attacked us and—"

"Garrett?"

"The Irish Chieftain - and stop interrupting if you want to hear the rest. At that moment the Welsh decided they'd had enough and started running for the woods, which was—"

"Gods – what about Edwin? Did they get Edwin?" I broke in again.

Eduard sighed. "No. The prince is fine: Hereric too. The company got them both out safely. But…" his voice trailed away and he looked down at his big hands.

"But what?" I asked, my tension rising.

"Well, when we saw you had been struck down we rushed towards you. Lilla and I managed to pick you up between us and drag you away, but when we got back to the woods we realised we had…" Eduard swallowed hard.

"Had what?" I demanded impatiently.

"Lost Cuthbert and Aedann."

"*What!*" I cried, aghast. "Dead?"

He shook his head, his face grim. "The battle was lost and we were running. It was chaos. I stopped everyone I could to ask about them. Nobody had seen them struck down, yet we could not find them anywhere. Then later, someone said he had seen them alive and being led away by enemy warriors. Not just them but Cadfan, Rhun, Taliesen, Lord Harald and some others too. The Irish won't hurt the bard, of course," he grimaced, "but the gods know what they'll do to the rest. Aedann and Cuth have been captured, Cerdic, and all because of this damn fool attempt of Edwin's to impress the frigging Welsh."

Now I could see why Eduard had changed his tune and was so critical of Edwin's - or my - decisions. I did not know what to say. I was still trying to think of something when he added, "And since Cadfan and the others have been captured, you can well imagine what mood King Iago is in!"

The news was so bad I hadn't got around to thinking about the implications, but I did so now. "Gods, does he blame us?"

Eduard shrugged. "It is likely. Eidyn blames us certainly and

Cadwallon is singing his tune. Some in his company admit that you were first to go to their aid. It has to be said that as many are blaming us, though." He sighed, "I suppose it could be worse."

"I find that hard to believe! How so?"

"Well you could be dead for a start, or at least have lost a leg."

"Yes, so Aidith told me. I have you to thank that I'm here. How did you get me back alive, by the way?"

"It was Lilla as much as me. After we had retreated from that village, he stitched up your head wound and set and splinted your leg. Then he gave you some of that white powder he carries and said you'd live, but were likely to remain unconscious for several days, so we carried you on a shield between us. The Hel of it is that we'd not gone far when we came across Iago's companies. They were only a couple of days away. Had we just waited a day or two instead of attacking that last settlement, we would have outnumbered the Irish and beaten the bastards.

"Hindsight is a wonderful thing," I muttered glumly. "Eduard... I am so sorry. Is there word about Cuth or any of them?"

"No, Cerdic. We don't know if they are alive or dead. We got back yesterday. Tomorrow there is to be a council. Best you get your arse down to it." He got up and moved towards the door.

After he had left I stared unseeing at the wall. Only a few days before we had felt we were getting somewhere. Cadfan and Iago had been content to let us stay it seemed, and we had even started to garner friends and support amongst the Welsh lords. Now it had all changed. The campaign was a failure and everything we had striven towards we had lost in that one brief but terrible battle. I didn't see how we could be held to blame for it, but at the present that did not concern me. What mattered far more - to me at least - was the loss of Cuthbert. He and Eduard were my oldest friends and it wrenched at my soul to think of him being badly treated, or worse, killed. I felt hollow inside. I also grieved for Aedann, who whilst not as old a friend as the other two, was nonetheless precious to me.

I was still lost in thought when the door opened again and Aidith came in with my sister. I could see Mildrith had been weeping, her face swollen and red. I held out my arms to her, "Millie… I am so sorry. I…" my voice trailed away. What else was there to say? She came hurrying over, collapsed next to me on the stool by the bed and leaned into my arms. I held her to me in the way our mother used to hold us when we were infants and had been hurt or upset.

"I am frightened, Cerdic. What will they do to him?"

At first I did not reply. In my mind I saw the shape of my old enemy Felnius standing over me. I recalled the pain of the beatings when he had captured me and my brother Hussa and held us chained in a dungeon the winter before. Were these Irish any better than he had been – or were they just as cruel? Eventually, thanks to Lilla we had escaped, but not before Felnius had tortured us. I did not hold out much hope for Cuth. He was a lot less robust than I, but of course, I said none of this to my sister. "I don't know, Millie. But he will be all right." I said it to reassure her, but my words sounded hollow and she pulled away and stared at me.

"You don't know that. Not for certain, do you?"

"No, I don't," I answered honestly. "What I promise though is that when this leg is healed I will go and get him back." It was a damned stupid oath to make. I had no idea where he was and no knowledge of the lands he may be in, if indeed he was still alive. But I wasn't lying. Somehow, I would go and get him back - or if not him, his body.

170

The next day Grettir and Eduard helped get me across from the old hall to Iago's throne room - my leg was agony, but I tried to hide it. The moment we were admitted I could see the change in the king's demeanour and even had Eduard not told me what had happened I would have known something had gone gravely wrong. There was even more tension between the Saxons and the Welsh than before. We had not been exactly welcome when we came here, and still hanging in the air over our heads was the decision on whether we would be allowed to stay or in the spring be handed over to my brother. After our cooperation with Iago's campaign, I had hoped the king would look favourably upon us, but the expression on his face when I came in was dark.

With the two lads' help I hobbled over to a stool between Sabert and Edwin, unable to conceal a wince of pain as I lowered myself onto it. Iago studied me for a moment and then turned to address the whole hall.

"Well, you all know why we are here," he said in a sombre tone. "Less than a week ago the campaign against the Llynii went disastrously wrong. After weeks of success everything was thrown away when Prince Cadfan's force was ambushed. Now the princes Rhun and Cadfan..." his voice faltered as he said his son's name and if anything he looked even more aged and weary that he had before. Next to him Cadwallon stood motionless, staring stony-faced at the ground. Iago coughed to clear his throat and continued, "...the bard, Taliesen, and a half dozen others are lost to us. What is more, the winter storms have begun and I have been obliged to disperse the militia. As a result there is no possibility of renewing the campaign until the spring. The men will not respond to a summons until the fields are sown."

171

"I counselled against trusting these Angles, Sire," Eidyn hissed. "They should be held accountable."

"Accountable for what, exactly?" I snapped. "If we are accountable for anything it is saving your worthless hide! If your company had supported us at that village and not hung back in the field we might have all got away."

Eidyn glared at me. "You refer, I believe, to Cadwallon's company. If so, perhaps you are implying the king's grandson is a coward?"

Cadwallon looked up at me and then over at Prince Edwin, his expression murderous. Aware I had made a serious mistake I felt all eyes in the room turn to stare at me and knew my face had reddened under their scrutiny. "I spoke in haste, Lord Eidyn. I certainly meant no offence to Prince Cadwallon," I said quickly.

"Be quiet worm!" Eidyn demanded. "What is true is that you blundered into an ambush that a blind man should have spotted. Call yourself a seasoned warrior?" He spat onto the floor.

"That is enough!" Iago snapped irritably. "Blame may be accounted one day, but we have more important matters to attend to. Sit down Eidyn."

The Gododdin prince threw me another malevolent glare and stomped back to his place.

"Sire," Edwin got to his feet and addressed Iago, "I stand ready to lead my men on a rescue mission. Permit us to go."

Behind him I saw Guthred scowling. He was not the only one. There was little enthusiasm in either Angle or Welshman for another campaign. Near to Guthred, Hereric was shaking his head. Iago said nothing in response.

"Go where?" Eidyn hissed. "You do not know the wild lands west beyond that village and have no idea where the Irish would be holding Prince Cadfan – if indeed he is still alive."

"That may be true, but we can try!" Edwin replied hotly.

"There will be no trying!" Iago shouted. Both princes fell silent and turned to the king. He held up a parchment. "I have a message here from the Chieftain of the Llynii. It came with one of his bards this morning. Garrett speaks plainly. He says that it is his intention to establish a permanent kingdom here in Gwynedd, in the lands once owned by his forefathers."

"Does he say why he attacked at this time?" Eidyn asked.

I blinked as the words Garrett had snarled in my face came back to me. "Because of you!" he had said. What had he meant by that?

Iago shook his head. "He makes no mention of that, no. Anyway, Garrett goes on. He says the captives are unhurt and safe in his fortress and will remain so until Eastertide."

His words brought such a feeling of relief to me that I almost cried out. I glanced at Sabert and saw he felt it too, but the king was still speaking.

"By then I am to agree to yield over Ynys Mon and all our lands his people have occupied, and to publicly recognise his dominion over them. If I do that then Cadfan, Rhun, Taliesen and any others he is holding will be returned to us unhurt. If I do not..." he hesitated, "...then my son and the others will be executed!"

Chapter Fourteen
Desperate Measures

This announcement threw the assembled company into pandemonium. Some lords, completely at odds with their apparent sentiments of moments before, were shouting "Attack now!" Others bellowed out, "We shall never give away our land!" Meanwhile other, perhaps cooler, heads looked sympathetically at Iago and were offering their support should he decide to bargain with the Irish.

"What will he do?" Edwin asked Sabert and me.

"If he gives away land to retrieve his son he will appear weak to the Irish, yet to not do so condemns his own blood. It is a hard choice for any leader," Sabert answered.

"Yet no choice for any father," I murmured.

After permitting the chaos and noise to go on a few moments more, Iago got up from his chair and the throng fell silent. "I will make no choice or decision in the heat of emotion today," he said. "I will go and pray to God for guidance and would ask that you all do the same." With that, looking weary and broken, he withdrew to his own quarters.

"If he prays to his one god what answer does he expect to hear?" I asked scathingly. "Walking on water and forgiving one's enemies are of no use here. He should pray to our gods. They would all tell him to buckle on a sword and go and rescue Cadfan."

"Hush Cerdic," Sabert muttered, placing his hand on my shoulder and nodding towards Prince Cadwallon, who flicked an outraged glance in my direction as he walked past us to follow his grandfather.

"Great, now you've gone and done it," Guthred said in my ear. "He probably thinks you have just insulted the king now and only moments after you had a go at him."

"He won't have heard what I just said – and anyway, I didn't have a go at him, Guthred. Eidyn *did* hold Cadwallon's company back at that village and everyone who was at the battle knows it," I protested.

"Maybe, but Cadwallon commanded it, at least in name. He's a proud young man and you made him sound like a coward."

I shook my head, glancing at the young prince's retreating back before saying to Guthred. "That was not my intent. He is inexperienced and under the older man's sway. It is Eidyn who is the coward, not Cadwallon.

Guthred snorted. "Don't matter what your intent was, that is how it sounded and if that were not enough, you just said much the same thing about his grandfather."

"I doubt Cadwallon heard," I said, hoping that was the case.

"I wouldn't be so sure, "Eduard muttered, pointing towards the door that led to the king's chambers. Eidyn was walking towards us, accompanied by Cadwallon.

"King Iago wishes to talk to you," Eidyn said. He addressed his remark to Edwin, but indicated that I, Sabert, Guthred and Hereric were included in the summons. They each looked at me accusingly and I felt like a cur with its tail between its legs.

"Sometimes I wish I would just shut up," I muttered to myself as leaning heavily on Sabert I limped along at the rear.

Once inside the chamber I saw that Iago was talking to Aneirin. The king's chief minister, his steward Belyn and various other advisors were gathered around him and it was clear that Belyn was not happy with something the king was saying. There

175

was a brief exchange of words and then the steward bowed his head in acquiescence.

"Despite what I said just now out there," Iago said, raising his voice and turning away from his advisors, "I have in fact made up my mind what my response to Garrett will be. I have asked you here to my chamber, Prince Edwin, along with your nephew and your lords, because what I now have to say is for your ears alone and not for the wider audience." He moved to sit on a chair and we five exchanged glances, each wondering what he was about to tell us.

"Belyn here, Princes Cadwallon and Eidyn and others of my advisors do not agree with my talking to you about my decision," the king began, "but several of your men are held captive by the Irish chieftain, their lives in danger, and since the policy I choose will affect them as well as my own people, I feel obliged to share the information with you."

"What information, Lord King?"

"Garrett sent his message for a purpose and contrary to how it may seem, that purpose was not to give us a chance to ransom the prisoners. He knows full well that the price he has asked is not only too high, but impossible."

Edwin frowned, "Too high? Surely for your own son, if not for Prince Rhun and my own people, you would be willing to pay any price?"

"Of course I would, were it only that simple."

"I don't understand. Why is it not?"

"The lands and estates in Western Gwynedd are not mine to give, Prince Edwin. My family's own lands are here and in Ynys Mon, but the other lands the Irish want us to yield to them belong not to me but to powerful lords, whose men number one in three of the spears at my command. Belyn here is one

176

of them. I trust him and know I have his confidence, but others who would be less supportive are out there," he pointed to door leading back into the hall. "They are the ones most energetic in their call for war. They will not agree to us merely handing over their domains. If I tried to force them I would find myself with civil war on my hands. No… yielding those lands is not a viable option for me and Garrett knows it, damn his eyes."

"Then why did he ask for them?"

"Because he knows that I will refuse. Oh, I will try for peace by offering payment in gold and silver. I can probably find some estates near their own enclaves that are in my possession and offer him those, but in the end it will not be enough. Anything I offer will be rejected."

"I still do not understand. If he knows that then why ask it?"

"It is strategy. If I refuse his demands Garrett can claim that he is in the right and justify his actions in the spring." Iago paused to pick up a parchment from his desk. He held it out to Edwin, "These are written accounts of the statements of fishermen who report an increase in the sightings of enemy shipping between here and Ireland. The Irish have been bringing men and supplies across to our coast. They are building an army on my doorstep, Prince Edwin. This hostage issue is just a way they can argue that they tried hard to negotiate peace with me and that I rejected them, thus forcing them to go to war."

"Sire, the Irish are a great and terrible enemy, but despite the disaster at the ambush we have defeated them before and we Angles stand ready to help you again. If you reject Garrett's offer you condemn your son and his fellow captives to death. There has to be an alternative."

"Yes I know that. It is why I asked you to come and see me. Cadwallon told me what Lord Cerdic said about buckling on a sword and rescuing Cadfan..."

Iago stared at me as he spoke and I felt my face flush under his scrutiny. I started to stammer an apology, but he held up is hand to stop me. "Don't worry, I may be getting too old for fighting, but I agree with the sentiment, Lord Cerdic. I will not hand over these lands, but nor will I meekly stand back and let the hostages die. That is why—"

"Forgive me, Sire," Eidyn interrupted, looking anxiously in our direction, "but think a moment about what you are about to say. Once you tell these men our plans, what is to prevent them from betraying us to the enemy in exchange for their own people's lives?"

I heard Edwin's gasp of anger and saw his face flush scarlet, his fists bunching at his sides as he struggled to control his reaction to this most heinous of insults. Somehow he kept silent and it occurred to me once again how much he had matured in recent weeks. What a king he would make - did we ever succeed in winning back his kingdom.

Iago's eyes narrowed. He glanced at Edwin before considering Eidyn for a moment then he frowned and shook his head. "No, I will trust them. We are in this together." Eidyn's face darkened, but he said nothing more and after a brief pause as though choosing his words, the king continued speaking.

"I plan to send a raiding party into Llyn in the midst of winter when the coldest weather comes and there is ice on the ground. At this time the raiders will be able to pass unnoticed deep into enemy territory. They will find Garrett's fortress and then attempt one of two things: either free the captives or, if they cannot do this, seize Irish hostages of sufficient rank to be useful in bargaining with their chieftain. If successful we will then go to the table in the spring with a stronger position in the game. In the meantime I will stockpile weapons and try to raise more men in case war becomes inevitable."

I asked the question that was on all our minds. "I assume, Sire, because you are telling us this, that you want us to be part of the raiding party?"

Iago nodded. "Indeed, that is exactly my desire."

"My Prince, I would advise you not to go," Guthred said to Edwin. We were back in our quarters in the old hall, Iago having agreed to let us withdraw to think about our decision.

"I don't see how we can refuse," Sabert said.

"All along I have argued against this Welsh enterprise, Earl Sabert. It would have been better for us to have gone to Kent when I said, or when we met Augustine, or when our fortunes were highest after Prince Edwin saved Cadwallon's life, but no one listened to me. So far not only have we failed to gain support here in Gwynedd, but indeed, we have lost some of our number - Lord Harald among them. You must know that I both like and respect Earl Harald – he is a brave and honourable man - but we cannot sacrifice any more of the small army we have in order to get back a mere handful of men."

"It is too late for all that now, Guthred," I said. "We are here and whatever you think might have been better or not is irrelevant. We must decide what is best to do now. Iago has asked us directly to help him. If we do this and are successful we may rescue everything we have lost and more besides."

"And what if we fail?" Guthred retorted. "We risk everything also!"

"Not necessarily," I said and looked across at Edwin.

The prince raised an eyebrow at me, "What are you saying, Cerdic?"

"That it would be foolish indeed for us all to go – for once Lord Guthred and I are in agreement there. But I also agree with Sabert that we cannot refuse this request."

"What then do you suggest?"

"We send only a small number of men and suggest to Iago that he does the same. A large party would be too easy to spot in any event. A small one would have more chance of success." I hesitated, looking towards the door to my room where I could see Aidith lingering. Beside her in the shadows was Millie. "Let me go in your place, my Prince. I will lead the raid," I finished.

"Your leg is broken, Cerdic!" Edwin pointed out.

"It will mend. We won't be going for a few weeks anyway – not until mid-winter. Sire, I have to go."

"Why you?" Hereric asked.

"Because the men captured were from my company, save for Harald himself. Also, I am the most experienced commander, apart from Sabert and he is…" again I hesitated.

Sabert smiled, "You are trying to say 'too old' without insulting me, but do not worry, Cerdic, you are correct. Like Iago, I am getting too old for this sort of enterprise."

"Well, perhaps," I agreed. And not only that…" my voice trailed away as I turned to look at Millie's strained white face in the shadowed doorway.

"Go on," Edwin prompted.

I shrugged, "One of the captives is my brother-in-law. I promised my sister I would get him back."

"Well damn me," Guthred sneered, "we are planning policy based on Cerdic's family arrangements now are we?"

Edwin ignored him. "So be it," he said to me. "Who will you take with you?"

"Us," Eduard shouted from the side of the room, indicating

180

himself and Grettir. "We will both be going."

"He means, with your permission, of course, my Lord," Grettir added respectfully. I smiled. Grettir was at least as old as Sabert and yet he did not seem so and I knew I could rely on him.

"Well I am going whether I get permission or not!" muttered Eduard, earning him a glare from our old trainer.

"Your friends are loyal, Cerdic," Edwin commented.

"Always, Sire." I exchanged a glance with Eduard and nodded at him.

Edwin smiled, "So that's three of you - anyone else?"

"We will both be going too," Lilla's voice came from the doorway. He was accompanied by Aneirin, who nodded. "Taliesen is my friend," he explained.

"Aside from which, you need someone who can speak Irish, Cerdic," Lilla said with a smile. He had a point!

"Very well," Edwin nodded. "That makes five. Lord Sabert, please inform Iago of our response and suggest he fields a similar number."

Sabert went at once to see the king. When he returned a short while later his face wore a worried expression. "What's up?" I asked him.

"Iago thanks you for agreeing to be part of the raid and wishes me to inform you that none other than Eidyn will be going as well, with half a dozen of his men."

"Eidyn?" I asked gloomily. "Gods! Couldn't he have sent someone else? That is just great!"

"Well, this is going to a jolly outing," Eduard said to no one in particular.

Chapter Fifteen
Winter Raid

"So, my love, aren't you going to tell me not to go?" I asked Aidith. It was later that night and we had retired to our room. I lay back in our bed and looked up at her. Cuthwine was snoring softly under his furs against the far wall - I had waited until he was sound asleep before I told Aidith about the raid. Sitting on the edge of the bed she stared in silence out of the window at the sickle moon, which was still climbing the heavens to its zenith.

When she did not respond I asked again. "Well, aren't you going to lecture me about putting family first and tell me not to go?" There was an edge to my voice. I was being unfair and I knew it, but it seemed as if the world had come crashing down around us and because everything else had gone wrong I was half expecting the same thing to happen between myself and Aidith.

This time she turned to look at me and said with a sigh, "I will not lie to you, Cerdic. I just wish life could be different. I wish we had a farm and naught but the crops to worry about. If it was just Prince Cadfan who was missing I would say to Hel with this kingdom of Gwynedd and forbid you to go. But Cuth is family, and Aedann near enough as makes no difference. We have both known them all our lives." She laid a hand on my knee. "Of course you must go. Just come back again, Cerdic. I won't ask you to promise, just come back alive, do you hear?"

"That thought is at the top of my mind, believe me," I grinned and held out my arms to her. She climbed in beside me and I wrapped them around her and held her tight throughout the night, my mind busy until dawn thinking about what was to come.

Every year when the nights are longest and the daylight shortest, Christians and pagans alike celebrate and feast. For those who believe in the old gods of our fathers it is Yuletide. We would drive away the darkness with our light and our warmth. We ate roast boar - the beast of the God Freyr - and drank ourselves senseless. The Christians chose the same time to celebrate the birth of their God and called it 'Christmas'. Whether Christian or pagan, the aim was the same: to seek solace from the bitter winter and to raise our spirits with joy and song. This Yuletide or Christmas, however, while others were drinking and feasting, I and my friends would be setting out with hostile companions into enemy territory.

There had been doubts when I suggested this plan and I had some talking to do to persuade my own men, let alone Eidyn and Iago. "This is the moment when folk bar their doors and drink more than usual," I explained. "Those that are awake huddle by their fires to sing songs and tell tales. If they hear a noise in the night will they go and look or merely sip from their cups and draw closer to their women? No one will expect us and if they see dark shadows pass by their doors they will not want to come and look." Iago had pondered on my words then nodded his head. And so it was decided.

Before dawn on the day before the winter solstice we set off. There were twelve of us in all, evenly split between Deirans and Welsh. With me were Eduard, Lilla, Grettir, and also Wilf and Eldrick, two huscarls from Harald's company. With Eidyn were four of his warriors and the young bard, Aneirin. It was bitter-

183

ly cold and despite thick furs and well-made cloaks, within an hour of our departure I was regretting my idea to set out in the midst of winter. Behind us the sun was rising on the far side of Iago's hilltop fortress. Tonight they would feast there and the halls would be lit up and warm. Somewhere right now was a warm bed with Aidith and Cuthwine still in it. I felt an ache in my insides thinking of what I was leaving behind then I pushed those thoughts out of my head and pulled the cloak tight around my shoulders as my horse plodded on through the frozen grass, west into the darkness of the unknown.

To avoid thinking gloomy thoughts and hankering after my wife, I pondered on the task that lay ahead of us. Iago and Edwin had insisted that this be a joint venture: Angle and Briton. I had not objected to that, but since learning that Eidyn would lead the Welsh I had been anxious. To me this seemed the height of folly. Eidyn and I were not exactly close companions. Indeed, I blamed him for the fiasco at the Irish village. If he had not persuaded Cadwallon to keep out of the way and instead we had co-operated, we might have escaped without the catastrophe that ensued. What of him? I knew he was of Gododdin descent as well as related to the kings of Gwynedd, but it seemed he had a very personal hatred for us – or at least, for me. Before now I had not had any particular reason to be bothered to find out why. Now though, whatever the cause, it could endanger the entire raid and I decided to bring things to a head in an attempt to resolve the issue and find some common ground between us.

That morning, as the party forded a stream a dozen miles west of Deganwy, I pulled my horse in next to Eidyn's. The prince stared at me coolly but said nothing.

"We need to talk," I began.

"Do we? Why? The plan is clear. We know our parts. What

need is there to talk?"

"If we are at odds we put all at risk."

He gazed at me coolly, "What is it you are seeking, Cerdic? Friendship? I cannot offer that."

I shook my head. "We don't need to be friends, Eidyn, but we cannot afford to be enemies."

His face flushed with sudden anger. "We will be nothing but enemies until the end of time. Thus it has been for the lives of our fathers and forefathers. So it is in our time..." he hesitated then added, "and that of our sons."

"Our sons? I know of your daughter, of course, but I did not know you had a son."

His eyes smouldered with barely controlled rage. "I do not. Not any longer. Not since Catraeth." With that he dug in his heels and galloped his horse past Eduard and into the lead. His warriors followed, leaving me at the rear, my head spinning.

So, like Rhun, Eidyn had also lost someone close at Catraeth. But whilst in Rhun the result was a deep melancholy, in Eidyn it was bitter hatred and rage. So here at last was the reason for his enmity. I could not blame him. I knew that were our positions reversed and Cuthwine had been killed I would feel no different. Indeed, I recalled only too well my desire for vengeance against the Welsh brute that had killed my older brother, after whom my son was named. Catraeth had changed lives for so many people. For us it had been salvation, whilst for the Welsh it had been a catastrophe.

I caught up with Aneirin who was dozing on his horse, and nudged him with my elbow. "You might have told me!"

"Told you what, Cerdic?"

"That Eidyn's son died at Catraeth. "

He frowned. "I thought you knew. I did sing about it at the

bardic contest."

"Oh did you? My Welsh was not good enough to catch it all. Did you really think poetry was the clearest way to let me know?"

Aneirin looked confused, "Well… yes, of course. Is it not Lilla's stories and poems that have kept you informed of news over the years?"

"Yes but…"

"So it is the same with us."

"Oh, very well! How did he die? Remind me."

Aneirin closed his eyes and was silent for a moment. I thought he might have gone back to sleep. Then he opened his eyes and looking at me he spoke a verse in Welsh.

"*O gollet moryet ny bu aessawr*
Dyfforthyn traeth y ennyn llawr
Ry duc oe lovlen glas lavnawr
Peleidyr pwys preiglyn benn periglawr
Y ar orwyd erchlas penn wedawr
Trindygwyd trwch trach y lavnawr
Pan orvyd oe gat ny bu foawr
An dyrllys molet med melys maglawr"

It was a verse from his poem 'Y Gododdin', but although my Welsh had improved since I heard it first, I could make out only some of the words. Seeing I was struggling to understand, he repeated the verse in English.

"*Having sustained a loss, Moried bore no shield,*
But traversed the plain to set the ground on fire;
Firmly he grasped in his hand a blue blade,
And a shaft ponderous as the chief priest's crozier;
He rode a grey stately-headed charger,
And beneath his blade there was a dreadful fall of slaughter;

186

When overpowered he fled not from the battle, –

Even he who poured out to us the famous mead, that sweet ensnar-
er."

Aneirin looked at me a moment as I absorbed his words and then he explained further. "You know that Eidyn is a prince but what you may not know is that although his father was Idwal, Iago's dead brother, his mother is a sister to Mynyddog, King of the Gododdin. He is a prince of both kingdoms. Eidyn had a son called Moried and doted on the boy, taking delight in all he did both in peacetime and war. Seven years ago Mynyddog put out a call for warriors to join the army he was assembling to fight for Owain at Catraeth. Whilst, at Iago's insistence, Eidyn stayed in Gwynedd, Moried was permitted to join that army. I met him at the feast that Mynyddog held on the eve of our journey. The boy was very keen on mead and if anyone's cup was drained he would rush over and refill it, at the same time topping up his own. It amused us at the time, but the next day when we set off to Catraeth we were all a little the worse for wear, none more so than Moried."

Aneirin closed his eyes as if recalling the battle and I too let my mind drift back seven years. I saw again the thundering charge of the cavalry in their blue armour. Had their swords been blue too, I could not remember. Dreadful slaughter, Aneirin called it. Indeed it had been. I shuddered at the memory. "What happened to him?"

"As it happened I was with Moried in the very front of the charge. We broke through your lines and were sure victory was upon us. Then, as you fell back to the camp I was separated from him. When I last saw him he was surrounded by your spearmen. He was still laying about him with his sword, but then he gave a cry and was pulled from his horse. I saw no more, but I knew

187

he must be dead."

I glanced ahead to where Eidyn was riding. "So that is why he hates us so much. He blames us for Moried's death and me in particular."

"Maybe, but I think he is also angry at himself for not being there beside his son. Then again, if your race had not invaded there would have been no battle, no need for him to have died."

"Oh I don't know, not then perhaps, but there has always been war. I imagine there always will be - until the wolf released at Ragnarök swallows the sun and the earth is renewed."

"*And there will be a new heaven and a new earth and there shall be no more death, nor sorrow, nor crying,*" the bard muttered. "*There shall be no more pain, for the former things have passed away...*"

"Is that what you Christians believe will happen? Seems like we all want the same thing," I said. "Yet will it ever come to pass?"

Aneirin shrugged. "Who can say?"

"Well anyway, I understand Eidyn a bit more now, thank you. I will try talking to him again, maybe later tonight when we make camp."

We rode west all day. For the time being we were still passing through land owned by Iago and his family. Even so, because we wished to avoid news of our approach reaching Garrett, we steered clear of the villages and towns and that night camped out in hills overlooking Ynys Mon, not far from Llanbeblig. We lit a fire and roasted some chickens we had bought from a farm earlier in the day and drank ale the same farmer had been happy to sell us.

After taking a swig from the jar, Eduard screwed up his face. "This Welsh ale tastes like rats' piss, mate. No wonder that farmer was happy to flog it you cheap, Cerdic."

"I wouldn't know, Eduard," I grinned. "I'm not in the habit of drinking rats' piss!"

He made a rude gesture at me then took another swig, longer this time.

"I thought you didn't like it, lad," Grettir observed.

"Well, no point it going to waste. It gets better the more you drink actually," he replied with a belch.

After we had eaten, Eidyn came over to discuss our plans. "Tomorrow we will ride to Clynnog Fawr," he said. "That is the name of the village where we were ambushed. Beyond it lies the Llyn peninsular. When the Irish were here in my ancestors' time it was in Llyn that their strongholds were. Even after King Cunedda and his sons broke them up and drove them away, small groups of Lynii lingered there. In the hills of Llyn there are still fortresses that date back before the Romans. The old people built them, but after the Romans left the invading Irish used the forts. The largest of those and the one from all accounts that remains in the best condition is Vortigern's old fortress, Tre'r Ceiri – sometime called City of the Giants. It is actually not far beyond Clynnog Fawr, which is possibly why they arranged that ambush there. If the Irish are back in strength that is where they will be."

"Vortigern – you mean the British King who invited Heghest and Horsa and the first of our people to Britain nearly two hundred years ago?" Lilla asked Aneirin, excited by the news.

"Indeed. That is where he ruled from – at least some of the time. It is also where he is meant to be buried," the younger bard answered.

"How will we get close to the fort without being spotted?" I asked.

Eidyn shrugged. "I suggest we get nearer and then lie low

189

until after dark. Tomorrow is the longest night and like us the Irish will be celebrating the winter solstice along with Christ's birth." He grimaced, "At least we would be, were we at home and not freezing our balls off in the middle of nowhere."

"So you are hoping they will be drunk and not paying too much attention to who is creeping up on them?" Grettir asked.

"Yes."

"Seems a decent enough plan," Lilla said, adding with a wry smile, "they are Irish after all!"

Around the fire there was laughter from Angle and Welsh alike at Lilla's comment, all except Eidyn, who waited frowning until the laughter died then said, "And then we sneak in, try to locate the prisoners and free them."

"Actually, this sounds disturbingly like my plan to get Cerdic and Hussa out of Dunadd," Lilla commented.

"Did it work?" Aneirin asked.

"Well I'm here aren't I?" I replied.

"Then clearly we bards are clever fellows and it's about time our genius was recognised afar," Aneirin responded with a grin.

"Frankly I cannot think of any better idea," Eidyn said. "All right then, get to sleep everyone, you won't get much tomorrow night."

The party started to settle down. "I will keep first watch tonight, Prince Eidyn," I offered.

"Very well," he answered gruffly and turned away from me to settle himself on the ground.

"Aneirin told me about your son," I said suddenly.

He twisted back to glare at me. "Well, what of it?"

"I know he died at Catraeth."

"Yes, he was killed by your kind, just as you killed Owain."

"I did that, I accept it. I did not kill your son though – nor

190

any Gododdin that I recall. But whatever happened, it was war, Eidyn. It was not personal. People die. It could as easily have been me."

"Easy for you to say, sitting by the fire with your ale while my son lies cold beneath Catraeth field."

"I am sorry he died."

"How can you be? You did not lose a son."

"No, but I lost a brother! The Welsh from Elmet attacked my home and killed him a few weeks before Catraeth. He was dear to me and I miss him – even now seven years later. So believe me, Eidyn, I do understand."

He did not reply, just stared into the fire, but the tension left his body and I could see his anger was waning a little. After a moment he said, "War seems glorious when you are surrounded by your fellows. Clad in mail and well-armed you feel invincible. Then a day comes when your son dies and you realise how pointless it all is. We fight the Angles, the Irish and our fellow Welsh. It is always fighting, always war. Does it change anything? Does life get better? What is the point of the struggle?"

I looked at him in surprise. How often had I thought the same? He might have been me expressing these views.

He finally looked up at me and his face seemed softer somehow, the burning hatred held at bay for once. "Damn you Cerdic," he said softly. "Till now I have kept going by believing you are all monsters. Then you come along with your honour and courage and I don't know what to believe."

"Just believe that tonight I am not your enemy and sleep well, Prince of Gwynedd," I said, and now he did turn away and wrap himself in his cloak. I sat down on my log near the fire, chewed on a piece of chicken and pondered what had just happened.

Chapter Sixteen
The Longest Night

The following morning we carried on along the coast road. Snow started to fall, light at first but heavier as noon approached. The road was deserted. Small wonder I thought. Sensible folk were keeping well out of the weather and were no doubt snug and warm by their fires, preparing themselves for pleasant days full of food and drink and with few cares. Still, at least this meant that we passed seemingly unnoticed, just as I had planned – or at least, had hoped.

Around noon we were once again at Clynnog Fawr. The village was abandoned with no sign that the Irish actually lived there – they had clearly chosen it only as an ambush point. The bodies of the fallen were gone, I assume either burnt or else tipped into a mass grave after their weapons and armour had been stripped. This was as far as our armies had reached during the previous autumn's campaign, so from now on we became more cautious. All the land west of here was potentially occupied by the Irish raiders.

The coastal road would have taken us directly to Tre'r Ceiri, the hill upon which it stood visible in the distance, but Eidyn and I agreed to avoid that route. Instead, we turned south into the very mountains the Irish had attacked us from a few weeks before. We took a route between two hills which brought us to a valley south of Clynnog Fawr and due east of Tre'r Ceiri. We climbed to the top of the western slope to scout ahead.

As we emerged onto the hilltop, we got our first look at this so-called 'City of the Giants'. It was yet a couple of miles away and the snow was still coming down, but for a few minutes the storm abated. As the skies cleared we could make out the huge perimeter wall of the fort atop a plateau, which rose a few hundred feet above the hill where we stood. The side from which we approached appeared to have no obvious route up, the main entrance being – according to Eidyn – on the far side. The land around the fort was barren and covered with scree, piles of rocks or expanses of heather and moss.

"Impressive," Eduard observed. "Going to be a steep climb though."

I nodded. "Come on, let's get closer," I grunted.

We left our horses under the guard of Wilf and Eldrick at a ruined farmstead close to the hills. We had brought spare mounts with us in the hope and expectation that they would be needed for our rescued friends. Then, using all the available cover as much as possible by moving from rock pile to rock pile and keeping undulations in the ground between us and the fort, we approached cautiously, circling the fort to get around to the west side. We moved slowly and so it was getting dark as we stood together in a rock-strewn hollow only two hundred yards from the base of the hill. The slope was so steep that we had now lost sight of the ten-foot high wall that ran around the perimeter of the plateau. Signs of life were evidenced by smoke, which could be seen rising from dozens of fires – possibly inside huts, although these were also out of our view. From our present location we could see that whilst the south and east slopes were almost sheer in places, the west and north walls were approached by a saddle of land beyond which another mountain loomed. This saddle dipped down towards the surrounding landscape and allowed access to the main entrance which, as Eidyn had told us, stood on the northwest side not far from where we were and was approached by a steep path that nipped back and forth before it reached the gate.

"Stone walls – they don't make it easy," I observed to Eidyn.

He grunted at me, "Lots of granite around here, plenty of material for building walls. In addition, I think the Romans used the fort at times and probably improved the defences during their years here. They always built with stone if there was a choice."

"Well I don't much fancy sneaking in there, do you?"

The Welsh prince shook his head, "Yet that is what we have to do," he replied, "and here come the scouts."

Whilst Eidyn and I had led the patrol through the hills to this agreed meeting spot, we had sent Grettir around the fort in one direction and one of Eidyn's men in the other. They must have met up on the far side and had now returned together.

Grettir nodded respectfully at me and Eidyn then launched into his report. "The gate on the north side looks to be the main entrance and too well guarded for us to approach unseen, but there are three lesser gates, one at each compass point more or less. They appear to be less well guarded. Each one leads to a narrow path that winds a little way down the hillside and meets up with the others at a spring, which is likely their main water source."

Eidyn's man added, "Yes, and from what we can tell, the enemy's fires run between the west and east entrances and are around the middle of the camp, so some distance from the north and south gates."

I thought for a moment then turned to Eidyn. "From what they are saying, and assuming the fires mark dwellings, our best bet might be to approach from the south. Once inside, we can steal up on the camp and see what we can find," I proposed.

"South is closest to where we are and would avoid going past the main gate or marching a long way round the fortress to get to the other side," Grettir added.

"Agreed," Eidyn responded. "Right men, get some rest. We will go in after dark."

We waited until it was well after midnight. It was snowing again as well as being extremely cold, so we huddled together under our cloaks, ducking down in the lee of the rocks to take what shelter we could from the wind and snow. We dared not light a fire but passed around what remained of the farmer's ale and chicken from the night before then watched the moon rise and fall whilst we attempted to seize some sleep.

It was the longest night; the shortest day. The sun was far from earth and all over the Saxon kingdoms boars and cattle would be slaughtered. Their blood would be used to coat the walls of the temples and the idols of the gods. Particular care would be taken to appease Freya and her brother Freyr. These were the Vanir gods of fertility. My people would pray to them to send back the sun and to bless us with good crops and a fair harvest in the year to come. Then we would feast on the flesh of the animals and drink our mead and ale and there would be laughter and joy. As we sat and shivered in the cold I reminisced with Eduard about Yuletides past. I noticed Eidyn was listening to us and shaking his head.

"You are a strange people, Angle, to believe you must appease your gods so. We believe that one must simply have faith in God and all will be well. The Almighty sent his son to Earth to dwell amongst us and on this night was He born, or so the tales go. Man must merely put his trust in Christ and the Father will care for him."

"As simple as that is it?" I asked, unable to keep my scepticism out of my tone.

"As simple as that," he nodded, glaring at me.

I dropped my gaze. It was not for me to challenge another man's faith, but it seemed much too simple a choice to put all one's trust in this new God. I was reminded that it was a choice we had yet to make. I was not happy that Augustine had asked us to choose his God over our own gods, but the Bretwalda and many other minor kings had already made that decision and I wondered what Edwin should do. When it came to it, what choice would he make?

More immediate concerns were mine this night. Whether one was pagan or Christian this was a holy night, but what I had planned was far from holy. This was not about new life and the return of light to the world. This night I might have to fight and kill in the dark. I might also be killed... and what then? Would all my questions be answered? I pushed these thoughts out of my mind and focused on cleaning Catraeth's blade and my seax while I waited.

Before the moon had set, we crossed the crisp, snow-covered ground to the south of the great fort and under the waning moonlight we clambered up the steep slope. This was the most dangerous part of the plan. There was every chance a sentinel up on the wall of the City of the Giants might look out on this slope, spot us and call out the guard. We could be heading right to where fifty Irish warriors were waiting for us. But the gods, it seemed, were looking out for us and there was no cry of alarm as we approached. After toiling up the steep hillside, ploughing through knee-deep snow, cursing as we slipped on ice-covered scree or rocks that lurked beneath it, we could now see the gate in the wall. At this point we came across a spring emerging from the hillside, its fountain of water cooling quickly and becoming a frozen stream mere feet below. A small pathway led from it up to the gate, just as the scouts had described, and this proved easier to ascend than the rock-strewn hillside.

When we reached a spot just beneath the wooden gate, Grettir snuck up to it and tried the big iron handle. It was likely to be locked of course, but worth a try. He shook his head at us and Eduard, Lilla and I joined him. Between us we gave the bard a leg up so he could clamber over the top. I held my breath as he vanished from sight, expecting to hear a shout of challenge at any moment, but none came. A moment later, with a scrape of wood on ice the gate slowly opened a little way before appearing to jam. Through the gap I could see Lilla struggling with it, but Grettir gave it a shove and suddenly the gate gave way, crunching against the frozen snow piled up behind it as it opened. I held my breath expecting to hear a shout, or maybe a pack of hounds raising the alarm, but there was a deathly silence. After a moment, Eidyn waved his men forward and we followed.

Once through the gate we could see about twenty paces away a single hut, a faint wisp of smoke rising from it. It seemed to be a guard hut. I imagined its occupants, convinced that no one would attack this night, were inside enjoying a drink and whatever warmth there was to be had. Even as I thanked the gods for the guards' apparent lack of anticipation, I tucked the lesson away in the back of my mind. No matter how inclement the conditions, one should always be ready for the unexpected. It demanded strict discipline to keep one's men alert all the time – a discipline the Romans had had in abundance, which was probably why the legions had been so successful. But these were Irish, not Roman and for that I was thankful.

We moved around the hut and looked along the top of the plateau. The fort was vast, stretching some five hundred pac-

197

es from the south entrance off to the northeast. The high stone wall surrounded it and now I was on the inside I could see platforms and steps dotted around allowing access to the top. Many looked in a poor state of repair – dating back to the time when the Irish had lived here over a century before, but some were still in good order and from these elevated positions an army could rain havoc on any attacking force.

Within the wall we could make out the shadowy outlines of scores of stone huts – each made from blocks and sheets of granite and extremely thick-walled. No doubt they were warm in the winter and cool in the summer. There seemed as many as a hundred-and-fifty huts, although many were in a decayed state with the roofs caved in and in some cases the walls collapsed. Yet over fifty were inhabited as evidenced by the smoke rising from them.

I raised my eyebrows at Eidyn, wondering how we were to find our men in what amounted to so large a city. He saw me looking, shrugged and leaned over to me. "Search for huts with a guard?" he suggested. I nodded and scuttled away to give the orders.

Leaving two men to watch the guard hut inside the gate, the rest of us moved quietly across the plateau. Stealthily sneaking from hut to hut looking for guards and when finding none moving on, I realised after a while that we were now deep inside the forest of hovels. If we made too loud a sound or the alarm was raised we would be caught like fish in a net. It seemed extraordinary that as yet no hounds were barking. Perhaps the Irish did not keep them, but it seemed unlikely. I felt panic begin to rise at the thought of capture. These Irish were the same race as those that captured me in Dál-Riata and it was another Irishman, Felnius, who had tortured me and treated me very harshly. Then

I thought of poor Cuth suffering the same fate and felt some of my resolve return. I wasn't going to abandon my friend to these men. Whether they were merciful or cut from the same sadistic cloth as Felnius, I would find him and get him out of here.

As we searched I wondered again about those words Garrett had used as he attacked me: 'Because of you!' Had he meant us Angles? Was the raid sparked off in some way because of our presence? Or was it more personal than that? Had he meant something in the past was our fault – maybe the defeat of the Irish Scots at Degsastan? Were these folk kin to the Dál-Riata and blamed us? What did he mean?

As I continued to scout a small cluster of huts I spotted a movement in the corner of my eye. Turning I saw that it was Eduard alongside Grettir, standing on the far side of the same hut circle waving at me and pointing. I looked to where he indicated and saw off to the side a slightly larger hut with an iron door. A guard was standing outside, leaning on a spear and swaying slightly as if drifting from half asleep to half awake. I nodded at Eduard and gestured that we should approach from either side. As I moved forward, I drew my seax. There was a faint scrape as I did so and I froze, terrified. Surely it must have been heard? I expected the guard to shout and from all around us hut doors to burst open and the Irish to appear. Yet mercifully the guard remained dozing. And then I remembered what night it was and guessed that, as I had hoped, they were all dead drunk.

I breathed out a long breath of relief and moved closer. As I did so, Eduard and Grettir closed in from the other side. Just then, Grettir stepped on a loose fragment of rock, slipped and cursed. The guard's eyes flicked open and startled he stepped out of the doorway to seek the source of the noise. He saw my friends and opened his mouth to shout for help.

199

I did not give him the chance. Stepping forward I clamped my hand over his mouth and then brought my seax up to his throat. The guard dropped his spear and with a lunge Eduard caught it before it could clatter on the ground.

Pressing the tip of my seax into the man's neck I hissed, "Quiet!" I spoke in Gaelic, the rudiments of which language I had picked up the previous winter when I had stayed as an unwilling guest in the dungeons of Dunadd. "The key – where is it?" I asked.

"I ... don't have it. The guard captain has it."

"You're lying!" I said, letting my seax dig into his skin.

"I swear that I don't have it. By Jesus, please don't kill me."

"He says he has no key – search him," I instructed Grettir. He did so, but found no key. "Damn it – he must be guarding something. Eduard, try the door. Can you see inside?"

Eduard moved to peer through the door. It was a wrought iron affair with bars allowing a view of the interior. "It's hard to see, but I think it might be them," he whispered.

Thrusting the guard ahead of me, I came up behind Eduard and tilting my head looked through the bars. The stub of a single tallow candle guttered inside the hut, its glow barely visible from outside, but from its meagre light I spotted a number of figures. All appeared to be chained up and asleep, huddled together for warmth. As my eyes grew accustomed I could make out Cadfan, Cuthbert and Harald nearest the door. My first feeling was one of immense relief that my friend was alive. I searched for Aedann and saw him amongst the other captives at the back of the hut. Next to him, the only man awake in fact, was Rhun. His bleak face turned to me and all I saw there was despair. The darkness, it seemed, had returned to him with full force in this evil place.

Eduard tried the door. It was solid. He then tried bending the bars, but to no avail. Then he stepped back, hefted his axe and flexed his shoulder. It looked as though he was preparing to barge the door down. "No!" I hissed. "You will wake up the whole camp!"

At that moment we heard a shout of alarm some distance away on the other side of the city. Another voice answered. Then it came nearer and there was a flash of torch flame casting light over huts that were barely a hundred yards away. We had been heard but not yet spotted and I let myself hope that in their drunken state the Irish would take a while to respond, yet common sense told me that in the event of an attack someone would surely come to check on the prisoners. We probably had only moments before that happened. If we were going to release our friends we had to act fast.

"That's it! We've been discovered. All right Eduard – barge it down!"

Bracing himself, by big friend charged the door. There was a clang as he slammed into it and with a curse he came staggering away. "Frigging thing's solid!" he grumbled.

The noise had shocked the prisoners awake and Cuthbert was peering up at the bars. "Cerdic?" he asked sleepily. Then wide awake, "Cerdic it is you!"

"It's me, Eduard and Grettir," I said.

Cadfan was staggering to his feet. He did not get very far before his chains tugged him back, but his face lit up as he saw me. "Thank God! Father's sent you on a rescue mission."

"So we'd hoped, my Lord, but the door's locked solid and the guard's not got the key so we can't get in and now the enemy's coming for us. We are too few to make a stand against them. It'll have to be just a scouting mission this time – sorry," I said miserably, seeing his expression change to one of despair. "We will get you out, only not tonight." As I spoke I could hear the Irish coming ever closer, their cries of outrage spreading across the city, torches being carried aloft. "Damn!" I hissed, "Damn it all!" The guard I was holding gave a sharp yelp and I realised that in my frustration I had tightened my grip on my seax and nicked his throat.

"You must go – get away now!" Cadfan ordered and yet, hearing the disappointment in his voice, I hesitated. "Cerdic: it's no good. You have to get away." Cadfan shouted.

"Go now!" Cuth yelled hoarsely. "Please, Cerdic, while there's still time!"

I nodded, knowing they were right. "I… I'm sorry," I said again and turned away from the cell door, unable to bear it that their hope had so quickly melted into despair, a despair that matched the look on Rhun's tortured face. I had brought them a brief moment of comfort only to crush it again. Was that all I had achieved this night?

"Go, Cerdic. You must go." Cuthbert said again. "Just tell Millie that I love her."

"You can tell her yourself soon, I promise," I said over my shoulder. I brought the seax away from the guard's throat and slammed the hilt into his temple. I am not sure what stopped me from simply slitting his windpipe. Perhaps fear of recriminations against the prisoners, but if I am honest, I have never liked killing for the sake of it. Without a sound the guard crumpled unconscious to the ground.

"Come on!" I urged my companions, turning away from the hut.

"But what about Cuthbert and Aedann?" Eduard protested, looking desperately past me into the cell.

202

"I know, I am sorry, but we can't help them now. Leave it Eduard, come away. You too Grettir. *Now!*" I could hear from the shouts and sound of running feet that maybe a dozen men were making for the prisoners' hut. We had only moments before they were upon us.

"Woden's balls, but it has been a frigging waste of time," Eduard grumbled with one last kick at the door before following me and Grettir away.

We ran between two more huts only to find we were in the next stone circle. At first it seemed the huts' inhabitants had not yet been roused by the hue and cry we could hear coming ever closer. Then, as I led my companions across the open space to the far side of the circle of huts, four Irish huscarls emerged from one of them. Each man was shrugging into a chain shirt and carrying a two-handed blade. They spotted us an instant after we saw them and both parties froze.

We stared at each other for what seemed like an age but could have been only a few heartbeats. Then, to my side, Eduard recovered first, shouted some incoherent challenge and charged two of the huscarls. As he swung his great axe, one of the Irishmen managed to bring up his sword to parry Eduard's strike. Yet so powerful was Eduard's arm that the axe cut on through the air with only the faintest deflection and caught the second huscarl in the side of his neck, cleanly decapitating him. His mouth was open in a silent scream as the head fell bloodily to the ground and rolled, but I had no time to dwell on the sudden nausea than cramped my guts. Coming to my senses I leapt forward to follow Eduard and reached the first huscarl before he could recover from his parry. Bringing Catraeth up into his belly and shouting a torrent of abuse, I buried the blade to the hilt before ripping it back out, bringing blood, bile and stinking guts along with it.

Grettir passed by me on my right side and thrust a spear at the third huscarl, who deftly backed away, swatting the spear point to one side with his sword. The fourth huscarl came between me and Grettir and sliced at the old retainer's flank. Grettir roared in pain as the sword point laid open his skin, but mercifully it went no deeper. By now my own foe had fallen to the ground and I leapt over him, seized Catraeth in both hands and stabbed down into the fourth man's spine, snapping the vertebrae and paralysing him. The last man standing turned and attempted to escape, roaring and shouting for help. He managed five paces before Eduard snatched a seax from his belt and tossed it end over end. It caught the warrior in the shoulder, knocking him to the ground. Before he could get back on his feet, Grettir had reached him and this time his spear found its mark as he punctured the huscarl's lungs. The man gasped for breath and then slumped back dead. I glanced at Grettir, assessing his wound. He was holding his side and blood was oozing between his fingers, but he saw me looking and indicated by a nod of his head that he was not badly hurt.

"Come on, got to keep moving!" I hissed at Eduard, who had stopped to retrieve his seax. We continued our flight, but now I could hear shouts and curses directly behind us. I led the way, weaving between the huts, keeping the buildings between us and the pursuing Irish. Suddenly I drew up sharply and gasped. Behind me Eduard cursed as he almost piled into my back.

"What now?" he asked leaning to look at what had halted our progress.

"I… don't believe it!" I said.

Ten paces away, staring straight at me, having just stepped out of a hut, was Felnius, lieutenant to Áedán mac Gabráin,

King of Dal-Riata. Felnius: the very man who had tortured me throughout the previous winter and whom I had last seen escaping the battlefield at Degsastan.

He fixed me with an intense glare and in his eyes I saw a glimmer of recognition. His hand went to the hilt of his sword, but before he drew the weapon Eduard had charged past me and piled straight into him, knocking him down. My large friend had his seax out and in a flash it was at the Irishman's throat.

"Don't kill him!" I hissed.

"Why, just another guard ain't he?"

"No – that is Felnius..." I gasped, "more use alive than dead!"

Eduard's eyes glimmered, "Isn't he the one who tortured you in Dunadd?"

I nodded.

"Right," Eduard said in a chilling voice, "in that case..." and then, instead of cutting Felnius's throat, he treated him to a stunning back-handed blow that knocked the man off his feet and drew blood from his lips. Then Eduard leant close to him, the seax still pressed against Felnius's windpipe, "Listen, you: any trouble and I will kill you, you hear?"

Felnius was still suffering from the blow to his face and was clearly disorientated, yet still managed a faint nod of the head in acknowledgement. Eduard grunted and drawing the Irishman's own blade he pointed it at him and barked, "You're coming with us mate. On your feet, dog turd!"

The captured Irishman staggered to his feet then took two steps towards another cluster of huts. We could see the flare of torches immediately behind them. Eduard aimed a swift kick at the back of Felnius's knee. His legs gave way and he stumbled. "Not that way you bastard," Eduard hissed. "Don't try anything or this knife goes up yer arse."

205

We moved away from the approaching torches, slipping between unoccupied huts and back into the open area that ran across to the south entrance. The two guards in the hut there had obviously emerged when the alarm was called, but Eidyn's men must have jumped them. One guard was dead; the other wounded and slumped against the hut. When we reached it we saw that Lilla and Aneirin were still there, but there was no sign of Eidyn or his men.

"Is that who I think it is?" Lilla said, as we led Felnius into the light that splashed out of the hut doorway. "Lord Felnius! My word, so it is."

A few moments later Eidyn and one of his men came running out of the darkness. "We got ambushed," he gasped. "I've left two men dead back there. In amongst the hovels we managed to lose the enemy, a dozen or so, but it won't take them long to find us!"

Even as he spoke, men carrying torches were beginning to emerge from between the huts and out onto the plateau. "Come on, we must get away," I said.

Eidyn nodded then spotted Felnius, his hands now bound roughly behind his back – goodness knows where Eduard had found a rope in all the kerfuffle – but my big friend was grinning with satisfaction as he thrust the prisoner ahead of him and slipped through the south gate, followed closely by Grettir, the bards and Eidyn's remaining two men.

"Who is that?" Eidyn asked as bringing up the rear we started down the path towards the cover of the rocky hollow we had hidden in earlier.

"Iago gave us two choices, did he not? Rescue our men or bring along a hostage of rank. We failed in the rescue attempt, but that is Felnius and he is none other than lieutenant to Áedán mac Gabráin, the King of Dál-Riata."

Eidyn's eyes opened wide, "Then…"

"Yes, it seems that Dál-Riata has a hand in the Irish coming back to Llyn. We share a common enemy, Prince Eidyn. Think on that!"

High above us we could see torchlight flaring at the gate and knew there were men up there now, but we had covered the ground with speed and already reached our hiding place. The moon had set and little light fell on the snow-covered slopes, so our footprints would not be too obvious. Nevertheless, it would not be long before a patrol emerged, following our trail.

"Come," I gasped, out of breath, "we cannot afford to linger. We must reach our horses and be away from here." I led the way out of the rocky hollow and further down the slope towards the place where we had left our mounts with Wilf and Eldrick. "We will take our guest along with us and see what he will tell us about Irish plans." I turned to glance back at Felnius. He looked barely conscious, stumbling along, Eduard jabbing the handle of his axe into the prisoner's shoulders to keep him moving. I had no sympathy, for him, the man was a cruel, sadistic bastard and my fingers itched to bloody his nose – and worse. But then, I pondered — enjoying the thought of what I might do to him and sore tempted to take revenge for the hurt he had done me the year before — Felnius was a man of rank and important to Mac Gabráin. He must also be important to Garrett's plans, whatever they might be, or he would not have been there in the City of the Gods. Was he important enough for the Irish to bargain for his life? And if so, would that bargain good enough to free our friends? I prayed that it be so.

Chapter Seventeen
Felnius

Felnius, still suffering from Eduard's blow, had not made much noise since being captured. Now though, it seemed he was recovering rapidly because shortly after we reached Wilf and Eldrick in the hills east of *Tre'r Ceiri*, both men looking bored with inactivity and delighted to see us, he started struggling with his bonds. I barked at him to be still but he turned to me and spat, "You're making a big mistake taking me prisoner. "

"How do you figure that?" I asked as Eduard and Wilf bundled the protesting prisoner up onto one of the spare horses and tied his wrists to the pommel. With a grunt of effort, Eduard then pulled himself up onto his own mount and taking the reins of Felnius's horse in one hand prepared to lead him back to Deganwy.

"Well, do you really think you will get away with capturing me, Cerdic, you fool? You will regret this, I promise you," Felnius said.

"All we want is to get our people released and end the fighting. We did not ask for this war," I said.

Despite his predicament, Felnius actually laughed at this.

"What is so funny?"

"You're even more of a fool than I thought you. Don't you realise that everything that has happened is because of you, Cerdic?"

I gawped at him. Those damned words again. What in Woden's name did they mean? I opened my mouth to ask, but Eidyn clicked his fingers at us and gestured that we should be underway.

As we moved out I pondered what had happened. We had failed in our attempt to rescue the prisoners, yet we had this captive who might give us leverage. It still gave us the hope of negotiating their release, yet I felt an acute sense of disquiet. Felnius was too confident by half and whilst I was eager, of course, to reach Deganwy to be with Aidith and Cuthwine, I was haunted by those words *'Because of you'*, which kept echoing through my mind as we galloped away.

When we halted that night I was exhausted and so, when Eidyn offered to keep watch, I gratefully accepted the opportunity to catch some sleep having had little for two nights, but I was restless and during the night I woke to hear murmured voices. Drowsily I glanced towards the campfire where Eidyn and Felnius – the latter tied to a fallen tree – were deep in conversation. I tried to listen in on what was being said, but they were talking in Irish and I understood only a little of that language. Both the bards were fast asleep so I had no one to translate. The conversation went on a long time and I spotted Eidyn looking my way more than once before I fell into a doze.

In the morning I asked Eidyn what he and Felnius had been discussing. He grunted that he was asking about the size of Garrett's army, but there was something about the way his gaze slid away from me as he answered that made me sure he was not telling the entire truth. I pressed him, but he would say little more and soon ordered that we mount up and be on our way.

As soon as we had galloped in through the gates of Deganwy, Eidyn took our captive, Felnius, to present him to Iago. Meanwhile, I headed towards the Old Hall with the intention of reporting to Prince Edwin and his nephew. However, before I spoke to them I knew I had first to go and see Aidith and my sister. As I expected, the latter took the news badly. I watched her expression of hope turn to one of despair and could have wept for her.

"So it was all a complete waste of time!" Mildrith sobbed. You don't have Cuthbert and you may even have made his plight worse!"

"I am sorry… really I am. We tried, but there was nothing we could do."

Millie was still angry and she glared at me as she shouted her next statement. "You will be even sorrier if because of you your nephew has to grow up without a father."

"My *nephew*?" I stared at her and then at her belly. "You mean…?"

"Yes, Cerdic, I am pregnant."

I sighed as I took her into my arms and held her for a moment. Aidith looked on with a sympathetic frown, clearly unsure what to say. I drew back and looked down at Mildrith, holding her gaze with my own, "Take comfort from the fact that he's alive, Millie. We saw him. I am so sorry we could not get him out, but he looked well enough and he sent you his love."

"Won't they hurt him now though? That is what I am frightened of - that they will take reprisals for your raid by killing the prisoners."

I shook my head. "No, we captured a high ranking hostage, Felnius. He is our safeguard I think. They won't harm the prisoners until they have him back. He is too important to the Scots." I was still both surprised and discomfited to have found Felnius hobnobbing with the Irish chieftain. Yet he was, without a doubt, mac Gabráin's most trusted lieutenant. The Scots king would want him back unharmed.

"What happens now then? Aidith asked.

210

That is what I am going to find out," I answered as I let go of Millie. "Iago is questioning Felnius. I came to tell Edwin and take him to join them."

A short time later I made my report to the princes and their lords, who listened in silence until I mentioned the name of our captive.

"Felnius *here*?" Sabert's eyes widened, "Then Áedán mac Gabráin must be seeking an alliance with Garrett. Felnius is an evil bastard, we must question him closely, find out what's going on."

"Shame one of us did not kill the sod at Degsastan when we had the chance," Edwin commented.

"Believe me I tried," I grimaced, "but there were rather a lot of men with him and mac Gabráin, if you recall."

Edwin nodded, "I do indeed," he said, his voice distant.

The two princes and I, along with Sabert, Guthred and Frithwulf, walked across the courtyard to the king's hall, but when we got there I found to my surprise that we were being denied admittance. Two guards crossed spears in front of the doors barring our entrance and then stood stony-faced as we demanded to be let through. Our raised voices soon summoned the guards' sergeant, who came forward to speak to us.

"I am following King Iago's instructions," their potbellied officer stated. "He wishes to talk further with Lord Felnius of Dál-Riata."

"*What*?" I asked. "I captured the man. He is as much our enemy as yours – more so really - why will you not let us in?"

"All I can tell you is that King Iago wants to speak alone to Lord Felnius. I cannot permit you access at this time. I am sorry that is all there is to it." The sergeant's tone suggested he was far from sorry and indeed, the self-important little toad was rather enjoying obstructing us.

"My uncle and I are princes of Deira – who are you to deny us passage?" Hereric said in a pompous tone. The sergeant drew himself up and Edwin stepped forward and pushed past Hereric, fists bunched. Things might have got nasty and I was about to intervene when at that moment the door scraped open and Eidyn emerged.

Ignoring me, he addressed the princes, "Iago wishes to speak to Felnius alone because he now believes that although the Scot may be your enemy, he might not need to be ours."

"What?" I gasped again, gaping at him.

"I am sorry, Cerdic, but you must go back to your room. I will send for you when he says he will see you." Turning on his heel, he went back into the hall and slammed the door shut in our faces.

The sergeant stepped forward and pointed towards the old hall. Hereric raised one finger and looked about to argue, but Edwin placed a hand on his shoulder and shook his head. "Come, there's no point arguing right now."

We turned away and retreated to our quarters. Once there Guthred began immediately to complain. "I told you we should have left here! Each month we have stayed has brought us more and more ill luck."

"All right, you've made your point. What would you have us do now?" I asked, my temper simmering. I'd had enough of Guthred's constant carping. I'd had enough of this whole gods' forsaken situation in fact and I was mystified as to what was really going on here.

"Perhaps we can still leave. Maybe Iago would allow that?" he suggested.

"Without Harald?" I asked. "Without the others?"

He nodded, "We need to do what is best for ourselves and the princes. This entire Welsh enterprise was a mistake. We must cut our losses."

Edwin took one look at my face and stepped between us, shaking his head. "I've said it before and I'll say it again: I will not leave without Earl Harald. He gave his loyalty to my father and deserves no less from me."

"Nor will I leave without my brother-in-law," I added.

"What of you, Nephew?" Edwin asked Hereric. "Are you with us?"

The younger man glanced across at Guthred, as usual turning to him rather that to Sabert or me for advice and wisdom. "I think Guthred speaks sense..." He hesitated then said, "Maybe... maybe we should split up, Edwin. Perhaps with you and me in separate kingdoms there is a chance one of us can muster enough support to get home to Deira?"

Before Edwin could reply, Sabert shook his head. "I advise against this, Sire. If we divide our small force into two even smaller ones we risk losing both."

Guthred held up two fingers, "But two eggs, two baskets. Twice the chance one will survive."

"We can discuss this possibility later," Edwin said. "The point is I think we should first see if we *can* leave. Whether we want to or not, it may be that Iago has other ideas."

Sabert shrugged, "You could well be right. We should at least find out. There is perhaps no harm in that."

So Guthred did just that. He went back to the king's hall to ask Iago for permission to leave, but returned shortly afterwards, his face grim. "He won't see me. I went to the outer gate, but they would not let me pass. The council is in progress and they will not be disturbed. King Iago's instructions apparently.

"Why must we get permission anyway," Edwin mused. "We could try to break out like we did at Degsastan." I knew he was remembering when we had been surrounded by the Bernician army after the battle of Degsastan earlier in the year. They were supposed to be our allies and we had just fought a terrible battle together. Yet once the battle was won, we learned that having used us to help him defeat the Scots, Aethelfrith planned to turn on us and invade Deira. As part of that plan his Bernicians had surrounded us, or so it had seemed at the time. We managed to escape at night by creating an elaborate diversion, but in our present situation there were several significant differences, which I now voiced.

"In the first place we don't know for sure that Iago will not simply let us go. Secondly, Degsastan was an open battlefield. This is a fortress. Thirdly, there we had only warriors with us. Here we have women and children - I can't say I fancy our odds of sneaking out with them in tow," I observed.

Edwin grimaced. "So all we can do is to wait for Iago to send for us."

"We can pray to the gods, trust in our wyrd and wait," I replied.

So wait we did. Later, Lilla went back to the King's hall hoping to see Aneirin, but even our bard was denied access. He left a message with the guards, but Aneirin did not come to us. Bronwen did try, however, most likely find out how Aedann was, but halfway across the courtyard she was intercepted by Iago's guards and turned away, protesting loudly.

"It seems we are cut off, denied any knowledge or contact and unable to leave," Lilla said. "It is extremely frustrating." I glanced at him. The bard's stock in trade was knowledge and stories and as we weren't getting any of either, Lilla was becoming quite bad-tempered – a new emotion for him evidently.

Iago did not send for us that first day or the day after. In fact it was a full week before Prince Eidyn appeared at our hall: a week of kicking our heels, repeatedly trying to gain admission to the King's hall and being turned away. Our men were becoming bored and fractious and I had my work cut out to prevent them fighting amongst themselves. The women too were beginning to complain, none more so than Aidith, so despite our past differences it was with great relief that I saw Eidyn standing in our doorway.

His gaze slid off me and centred on Edwin. "King Iago will see you now. Follow me."

He led us across the central courtyard to Iago's hall where this time the guards stood aside and Eidyn led us inside.

"I don't like the way this is going," Guthred muttered.

"For once I agree with you," I replied.

The greater part of Iago's council was assembled in the hall and I did not find the expressions on many of their faces encouraging. After Cadfan had been captured the progress we had made with the Welsh seemed to have been swept away and the failure of our mission to free the prisoners had apparently caused even more harm. Yet I had hoped that capturing Felnius would help. He was such a prominent figure amongst the Irish Scots of Dál-Riata that surely they would offer much for his safe return? I still had no idea what he had been doing in Garrett's camp, though guessed it concerned negotiations for an alliance of some kind. It annoyed me intensely that it had been we Angles and not the Welsh who had seized him, so surely we should have some credit for that? However, there was no warmth in the faces of the Welsh lords. I wondered then what Felnius had told them.

215

I was expecting to find him being held in chains, such as those he had put on me the year before. Given he was part of a hostile army that had caused Gwynedd much harm I would have expected them to treat him harshly, if not tortured the bastard, at least neglected him. Imagine my astonishment to see him standing in the hall, not only unchained and unbound, but adorned in rich garments that were certainly not those he had been wearing when we captured him. My mouth must have fallen open, for the moment he saw me he grinned in a most unpleasant way, mocking me with an exaggerated bow.

We had now reached the front of the hall where Iago was sitting in his high-backed wooden throne. Cadwallon was close at hand as was the King's steward, Belyn, and not far away, Aneirin, who studied us, a worried expression on his young face.

"King Iago, you have finally sent for us, though we should have been here before. That man there," Edwin pointed at Felnius, "was our prisoner and yet we have not been permitted to question him. Why not?"

Cadwallon, standing next to Iago came forward, "You presume to tell the King whom he may question in his own home?" His voice was harsh and cold.

Edwin stepped back, clearly surprised by Cadwallon's tone. I was too. Edwin had rescued the Welsh princeling only weeks before - saved his life in fact. Granted he had been swayed by Eidyn and Rhun, doubtless influenced by their poisonous remarks against us, but now he appeared to be directly attacking Edwin. I could not be sure if Cadwallon's anger was simply because his father had been captured or because we had failed in our attempt to rescue him – but I now wondered if something else was going on as well.

"No, of course not, Prince Cadwallon," Edwin said, his tone

equally cold. "I merely seek to know why we have not been included in the interrogation of the man we captured."

None of the Welsh answered him. Instead, Felnius moved towards Edwin and smiled into his face. I had seen that cold, taunting smile before, deep in in the dungeons of Dunadd. Now, seeing it again, I suppressed a shudder and with a sudden feeling of premonition was not eager to hear what the sadistic Irish Scot had to say. As though sensing my thoughts, he glanced at me and his mocking smile grew broader before he turned back to Edwin.

"Maybe I can enlighten you, Prince Edwin. It is perhaps because I revealed the fact that the very reason – indeed, the only reason – that the Lleynii attacked you was because we – that is to say, my King, Áedán mac Gabráin – persuaded them to."

I gaped at him as I took in the full implications of his words. Áedán mac Gabráin, King of the Dál-Riata Scots and Aethelfrith's sworn enemy, whom we had defeated at Degsastan, must indeed be attempting to forge an alliance with Garrett. But why? It made no sense… or did it? Go back far enough and the Scots and Irish had been one race.

Felnius sneered at me, "Oh they didn't take much persuading. They were keen to return to lands their forefathers had conquered after the Romans left, before losing them in turn to Iago's ancestors. Yes indeed, they were happy to return to the shores of Gwynedd, but having been soundly defeated by the Welsh in the past, they feared them and had no eagerness to come back without aid. So we gave it to them. Mac Gabráin sent me with two hundred spears to assist the Lleynii in taking back their lands here."

"Why?" Edwin retorted, "What would you stand to gain?"

I thought I had probably worked out the answer to that ques-

217

tion, but I could see that when it came it took Edwin by surprise. Felnius grinned again, "You, my dear Prince Edwin. You and your princeling nephew!"

"*What?*" Edwin stared at him.

"It is simple enough," Felnius shrugged, "mac Gabráin was angered by his defeat at Degsastan by you Deirans and Aethelfrith's Bernicians. My king wants revenge and has looked for an opportunity to strike back ever since, but Aethelfrith is too strong for us at present. Then we heard rumours that as soon as he had no more use for you, the Bernician king turned on Deira, defeated you and killed your father, Aelle. Not long afterwards news reached us that you and your nephew had escaped and were in flight with a few companions." Felnius paused and turned his nasty grin on me, "I might have known you would be one of them *Lord* Cerdic! We paid our spies to bring us news of you. Then earlier in the summer one of our traders happened to be here at Deganwy when you arrived. He passed word back to us. When mac Gabráin heard that you had taken shelter with Iago, he persuaded the Lleynii to attack Gwynedd. As I said, they took little persuading. Our only requirement in return for our aid was to have you two princes and your lords captured alive and taken back in chains to Dunadd."

I thought on this in the ensuing silence. What benefit was there to mac Gabráin in seizing Edwin and Hereric? He surely would not go to all this trouble out of a petty desire for vengeance? But, of course, the answer was staring me in the face. It wasn't about vengeance, at all. It was about strategy. While the two Deiran princes remained alive they were a constant threat to Bernicia. The Scots King must have it in mind to use them to weaken Aethelfrith, or else to bargain with him. Either way, it was not looking good for us.

After a moment, Iago spoke. "So you see how it is, Prince Edwin. The Irish would not have attacked us had you not come here, for without mac Gabráin's aid they are not strong enough. It all happened because of you."

'Because of you...' those words again. At last I understood them.

Edwin shrugged. "Perhaps that is so. But attack you they did. Must I remind you, King Iago, that Prince Cadfan is in their hands, along with Rhun and Taliesen too? Surely whatever the original reason for the attack you must consider what action to take now?"

"We have," Cadwallon replied, coming to stand beside Felnius.

"You have?" I asked with a growing sense of foreboding.

"Indeed, it is very simple. We hand over Felnius and agree to the Lleynii staying within the bounds of their little peninsula and in return we get back my father and the other captives," Cadwallon said.

"Is that all?"

"Well, not quite all," Felnius smirked at me. "The arrangement also requires that all the Angles currently here at Iago's court are handed over to me. That means Prince Edwin and Hereric and all their thegns and huscarls. And that, most definitely, includes you, Lord Cerdic," the Scot added, flashing his dark eyes at me.

Chapter Eighteen
Prisoner Exchange

"I protest!" Hereric shouted. "We are guests in your court, Sire. We came here asking for your hospitality. Are you proposing just to throw us to the wolves? So much for tradition," he spat, added, "and so much for your fabled Welsh hospitality!"

"You were hardly seeking us, your traditional enemies, out of a desire for friendship, Prince Hereric," Belyn observed. "You only came here because you were in flight from powerful enemies. We thought that just meant we would have to deal with Aethelfrith of Bernicia, which was bad enough, but now it seems we must contend with Áedán mac Gabráin too. Would you have us take on the North in its entirety?"

"Need I remind you that I saved Prince Cadwallon's life," Edwin said.

"My life would not have been in danger in the first place if the Irish had not come looking for you," Cadwallon retorted.

He had a point. Edwin flushed and fell silent as around the hall there were shouts of agreement. Iago raised a hand to silence them and addressed us. "This war was brought upon us by your feud with the Scots King. I am not happy about giving the Irish back any of the land my forefathers took from them, but not only do I want my son returned to me, I do not want Gwynedd embroiled in a war brought upon us by outside interests that are no concern of ours!"

I could understand Iago's point of view and indeed, had some sympathy for him, but it boded ill for us. I caught a movement out of the corner of my eye and turning my head saw that Eidyn had stepped away from the guard who had accompanied us from the old hall. Iago nodded at him, giving him permission to speak.

"Sire, I am uncomfortable with us handing over the Deiran princes and their people to this man," he gestured at Felnius.

"You are?" I asked, gawping in astonishment at the Welsh prince.

"You are?" Iago echoed, his voice also tinged with surprise. "Was it not you and Prince Rhun who were so outspoken in opposition to my granting them shelter in the first place? Is it not you two who have reason above all others to despise these Angles: to not trust them. Indeed, you two have cause to want revenge on them. Have you forgotten Catraeth so soon, Eidyn?"

"I have not forgotten, my Lord King, nor will I for as long as I live. Yet I have reason to believe these men are honourable. I also agree with Prince Hereric that it would violate our traditions of hospitality to do what Lord Felnius is suggesting."

Once again there was a buzz of mutterings and comment from the lords and warriors in the hall, but this time their emotion was one of obvious disbelief. Iago gave a bark of humourless laughter and then shook his head, "I would remind you that it was you and Rhun who argued loudest and longest that those traditions do not apply to these men. "

"I have changed my mind, Sire, and in any event, that matter is in dispute pending the bards' decision in the spring."

Iago shook his head. "More important matters override our traditions, Eidyn."

Aneirin was now on his feet, "Sire… more important than traditions?

"Indeed, master bard. This kingdom needs its prince back. I

am old and Cadwallon young. You all need a man full grown to follow me. That has to be more important than our tradition of hospitality wouldn't you agree? We need Cadfan. He is my heir and the only one suited to lead Gwynedd when I'm gone. My ruling is that you, Eidyn, and you Cadwallon, will both ensure that Princes Edwin and Hereric and their entire household are confined until they can be handed over. There are to be no exceptions."

"But your Majesty," I cried out, "my wife is pregnant, my sister too. Surely, for decency's sake they can stay here?"

Iago hesitated then shook his head. "No exceptions. We do this and we get Cadfan back."

I could see now that this aspect alone was weighting the king's decisions. Who can blame a man for doing all he can to get his son back? Before we had brought Felnius along with us Iago had been uncertain how to act, but now, in the light of what the Irish Scot proposed, he had fixed on a route to follow. He would get his son back, keep most of his land and avoid a war. What price was a remote rocky peninsular and three score Angles set against that? Cadwallon too was clearly thinking along the same lines, but it was clear from Eidyn's expression that surprisingly he was torn.

"When will all this happen?" I asked the king.

"A messenger has already been sent to Garrett to agree on a meeting. As soon as it can be arranged the exchange will go ahead. You may stay in the old hall until that time. Do not try to leave. Should you do so, less pleasant accommodation will be found for you. Do I make myself clear?"

"But my Lord…" Edwin protested.

"Enough!" Iago shouted. "I have reached my decision. Now go!"

The guards closed in around us and we were herded towards the door. I glanced back to see that Iago's face was determined. He looked like a man who knew he was doing something wrong but felt it was justified. Cadwallon's expression revealed no such doubt. Both Eidyn and Aneirin were looking on with disapproval as we were led away. I finally caught a glimpse of Felnius and saw that he was sneering at me, triumph etched on his features. I cursed myself for bringing him back as a hostage. Could I only have the time again I would slit the bastard's throat without a thought.

"I am sorry, my love," I said later to Aidith. I had felt that I needed to tell her and Mildrith what was to happen to us. Aidith pulled Cuthwine to her and started to cry. The lad was confused and kept asking her what was going on, but she was too upset to explain.

"You promised to find us a home," she sobbed. "Huh! Some home: we are going to be slaves!"

"I am sorry, my love," I repeated, "but we are not slaves yet. We will find a way out of this."

"I don't want Cuthwine or our new baby to be slaves," Aidith went on, not listening to me.

"Aidith!" I shouted, seizing her shoulders and gently shaking her. "Listen to me. It will be all right. Trust me."

She stared at me and I could see her framing the words, 'Why should I?' I could not blame her; I seemed to have let her down at every turn. But she did not speak them and at least she had stopped crying. I turned away to Mildrith before Aidith had a chance to say anything else. In contrast, my sister was not reacting badly. Indeed, she seemed almost content. I knew why.

"Maybe we will see Cuthbert. Maybe the Irish will let us be

223

together," she said hopefully.

"Maybe..." I was not sure about this, but if believing this made her feel safer I was not going to argue.

Iago had guards posted all around the old hall and it was plain that we who had been his guests were now his prisoners. All our weapons were taken from us. I was reluctant to hand over Catraeth and Wreccan, but Eidyn promised to keep them safe and supervised the storage. It seemed strange to me that of all the Welshmen, Eidyn was the one who treated us with most respect, as though he were reluctant to be taking part in our downfall, but he was Iago's man through and through and as much as I had disliked him, I could not blame him. Indeed, our respect was mutual.

Edwin, Hereric, Sabert and I discussed trying to break out, but it was clear that any attempt would be futile. Instead, we waited day after day, wondering when we would be taken away. I was told that the rest of our party, principally the warriors and villagers, were becoming increasingly troublesome, all of them wondering why they were being so closely confined. I pleaded with Eidyn to ask Iago if he would consider letting them go, since they were no threat in the scheme of things. But perhaps they were valuable as potential slaves. In any event, my pleas had no effect, other than to ensure we were all guarded even more closely. In fact it took a full three weeks for negotiations to be concluded between Iago and Garrett as to the location and circumstances of the forthcoming exchange of prisoners. We learnt this from Aneirin, who was permitted to visit us occasionally. Finally, in the middle of the month of Fillibrook, or February as the Welsh called it, Eidyn came to see us, his face grim.

"Tomorrow we set out to meet the Irish. Iago is keen that none of Garrett's men pass any further east than is necessary, so instead we are going to them. In fact we are going back to *Tre'r Ceiri*, but this time our entire army is accompanying us. It is going to be a spectacle as the kings, lords and chieftains of both kingdoms are to meet. Then the prisoners on both sides will come forward and be exchanged. Afterwards, Iago and Garrett will agree a treaty that ends the war. You and your people are to be ready at dawn."

"So that's that then. There is no possible alternative?" I asked. "Are you happy about all this, Eidyn? Handing us over and trading land for Cadfan?"

He shook his head. "You know I am not, nor is Aneirin and if truth be told others too, though they will not admit to it. You have made an impression on us. It is easy to hate a faceless enemy, but we have got to know you and were just starting to realise that you are not as bad as we had believed. So no, I am not happy, but Iago is king and Cadfan his son. So I can do nothing – and were it my son, I would do no different. I am sorry." He turned away, but Lilla called him back. "What is it now?" Eidyn said. "It is no use protesting, bard. You know I would help if I could - but I can't. "

With a glance at Edwin, Lilla drummed his fingers on a table, his face thoughtful. "Lord Eidyn, you say the entire army is going to *Tre'r Ceiri*?"

"Indeed, and in their best clothes complete with banners and armour! Garrett enjoys playing the part of a king, lording it over a great occasion and I imagine Felnius and Iago are content to have it so, providing they both get what they want out of it."

"What if there was a way to get Cadfan back without handing us over and giving away land?"

Edwin laughed, but there was no humour in it. "What are you suggesting Lilla? That some miracle occurs?"

225

Lilla smiled, "That is exactly what I am suggesting."

Eidyn looked from Edwin to Lilla and snorted, "Come now," he said, moving towards the door, "I don't have time for your games, bard."

"I thought it was you who believed in miracles," Lilla called after him. "You say that a man can walk on water and turn water into wine. Is that not so?"

Eidyn hesitated, his hand on the door handle. "Well... yes, but not any man. I hardly see how..."

"You also believe that if a man has faith then anything can happen?"

"That is *their* religion, Lilla, not ours," Edwin observed, his cynical smile fading to be replaced by a look of irritation. "Why should their God help us?"

"We are in their land and have been asked to consider their religion, have we not? Is that not the choice before you, placed there by Archbishop Augustine? Maybe we should test it. I believe we *can* see a miracle if we have faith," Lilla said, then turning back to Eidyn he added, "let me speak with you alone."

Edwin looked put out by this request, but I, knowing Lilla of old, was intrigued. He clearly had some trickery in mind. Eidyn hesitated then, with a nod of his head, indicated that Lilla should follow him. As the bard got up to leave, I noticed he was fiddling with his necklace – the one from which hung the pendant of Loki and which matched the one I also wore, as did my brother, Hussa. In my mind's eye I saw Loki up in the heavens bent over the game board, a look of cunning snaking across his ancient face, whilst here in 'Midgard' his servant Lilla winked at me and left with Eidyn. I shook my head to clear the image that for an instant seemed almost real to me.

"What in Woden's name is he up to?" Eduard asked.

226

'*More likely in Loki's name,*' I thought, but I shrugged and said nothing, for I had no idea. And yet, for the first time in weeks I felt hope: faint and distant, but a tingle of hope nonetheless. I remembered the dream I'd had back in Tamwerth, when it seemed that both gods, Tiw and Loki, had beckoned us west to mischief and war. Well, we had had our fill of war so perhaps it was now time for mischief. I sat back at the table in the old hall and waited for Lilla to return. Eduard, who had been unusually quiet, poured us both a cup of mead and waited with me.

Chapter Nineteen
Broken Leg

In fact Lilla did not return that night. Eduard and I stayed up late hoping he would come back with news of some clever plot to win our freedom. I thought about going to bed but knew if I did I would have to face Aidith again. She was angry with me for coming here, angry at me for the risk I had taken for my princes, which put her and our family in danger. I should have gone to her but, damn it all, I was fed up with being blamed by everyone when things went wrong. Lilla's words gave me hope and I preferred to stay awake and drink with Eduard and wait for the bard to return, than go to bed and face Aidith's despair. Yet we finished the jug of mead and opened another and sat together for several hours with no sign of his return.

It was still dark but not far from dawn when I was awoken, stiff and aching from sitting all night and with a sore head. What woke me was Eidyn who, accompanied by Cadwallon, hammered on the door to the old hall and without waiting for a reply marched in with thirty of his spearmen. Lilla had still not returned, but when I asked where he was, the only reply I received was a grunt and, "You will see him soon enough." My feeling of hope vanished and suddenly I was anxious. I stood up and moved towards Eidyn, but one of his spearmen intercepted me and pushed me roughly away.

"What in Hades have you done to him?" I demanded as I staggered back against the table.

Eidyn shrugged. "Me? Nothing: he injured his leg last night and needs to be carried in a cart to the meeting with the Irish."

I glanced at Eduard – he looked as sceptical as I felt.

"What do you mean he injured his leg? How? Is that why he did not come back last night?" I demanded, but Eidyn was already leaving the room and turned a deaf ear to my questions.

Cadwallon lingered, "Wake your people, Cerdic. Then get them outside. All of you – and right away," he shouted as he walked through the door and beckoned in a group of spearmen.

Anxious about Lilla, I turned to Eduard and shrugged. "Come on, nothing to be done. Rouse everyone."

We walked around the old hall, hammering on doors to wake the company and their families. This triggered off alarm in several of the children, a number of whom burst into tears or started screaming at the sight of the armed Welshmen looming over them. Their fathers or mothers held them close as Iago's spearman herded them through the door.

Outside the sun was just visible to the east – a sliver of light beyond the king's hall. A cold wind blew between the twin mounds of Deganwy. I carried a still sleeping Cuthwine and reached out to hold Aidith's hand, but she shrugged me off and glared at me. Her eyes were red and swollen. She was not crying now but I felt a stab of guilt as I realised she must have done so long into the night while I had been drinking myself into a stupor. Now she just stared around fearfully, wondering no doubt what would happen to her. She was over seven months through her pregnancy and I worried about her making this journey, about where the baby would be born... about whether I would be alive to see it happen and to hold my child. I wished I had not stayed up with Eduard drinking, but had gone to her and tried to comfort her. Who knew when I would have the chance again?

In the space between the two halls, two hundred of Iago's huscarls and the local fyrd were gathering. Belyn, Eidyn and

Cadwallon were there, inspecting the men and their equipment. Cadwallon glanced across at us briefly then looked away without comment, his face showing no emotion.

A few moments later, with a clatter of wooden wheels, a cart was brought out of the king's hall. Lying on it, his leg splinted and bound, was Lilla. He winced when the cart went over a bump and his face paled. I was surprised to see that he was accompanied by Bronwen, mounted on a horse. Did she hope somehow to persuade the Irish to let Aedann go? He was a Welshman after all. I nodded at her. "My Lady, is it wise that you come with us?"

"My father has said the same thing, yet despite his dislike of Aedann he loves me and I have persuaded him to allow me to ask for Aedann's freedom. He is Welsh, not Angle so I hope Garrett will agree."

I had been right, but I didn't think she had much chance of success. I knew Felnius very well and from my brief encounter with Garrett I doubted that either of them would be merciful with any of our party, whether Angle or Welsh.

She must have seen doubt flicker across my face because she grimaced. "I have to try, Lord Cerdic, do you understand? I love him."

I glanced at Aidith and Cuthwine. "Oh yes, I understand, my Lady," I replied. I turned to Lilla and grimaced at the splints. I knew full well how much pain he must be in. "You broke your leg? How did that happen?" I asked him as he was wheeled past us.

"Oh, I slipped in the dark and my foot went down a badger hole."

"A badger hole?" I said flatly, not believing a word of it. "Who has done this to you Lilla, Eidyn?"

"Nobody - you know me, clumsy as anything," he said with a shrug.

"No, you are not," I shouted after him. Lilla was the most graceful man I knew. For him to fall down a badger hole seemed most unlikely. In any event I had seen no badger sets on the top of Deganwy. Filled with fury that anyone should deliberately harm our bard, I looked across at Eidyn, but he avoided my gaze.

"Well I was clumsy last night so leave it at that!" Lilla replied tersely. He would say no more and soon his cart was moved on towards the front of the column.

"Damn!" I cursed.

"What is it?" Eduard asked.

"I hoped he would be with us so I could ask him what he said to Eidyn last night. All that business about a miracle... what was he playing at? And now the bastards have broken his leg and yet he denies it. What's going on Eduard?"

"Maybe we can talk to him wherever we camp tonight?" he suggested.

"Yes, hopefully," I replied shortly, still seething with anger on Lilla's behalf.

It took some while for the king's army to gather fully. Felnius was brought out, under guard but unbound and walking freely. He was led to a horse and allowed to mount whilst we Angles were obliged to walk. Finally, Iago emerged, looked over the ranks lined up for his inspection, flicked his gaze at us and then dragged himself up onto his horse. With a tug on his reins he trotted off towards the gate, Eidyn and Cadwallon in his wake. Then with a bark of orders the army followed, along with ourselves bringing up the rear and surrounded by as many spears as we had men.

"Doesn't look good, does it?" Eduard commented as he fell

into step beside me.

I shook my head, but then put a finger to my lip and nodded at Aidith next to me.

"Sorry," he grunted. "Frigging Welsh hospitality, eh?"

We marched all day with few breaks and little food or drink. Riders had gone ahead to warn the villages and towns between Deganwy and Lleyn that the king was on the road. As we passed the settlements, people would emerge and watch us and then the local fyrd would come out and join us – swelling our ranks and increasing our numbers. By the end of that first day the army had grown to five hundred spears – each man wearing his finest tunic, his weapons polished and buckles shining brightly in the spring sunshine. A forest of flags and pennants flapped in the breeze above our heads and the whole effect reminded me of the Northern progress of Princess Acha's marriage escort in which I had been involved a couple of years before. Today would have been thrilling and exciting to me, a younger Cerdic, and it was still a grand spectacle to be part of, had it not been for the fact that as far as we were concerned it amounted to little more than a brightly decorated funeral procession - and it was *our* funeral we were most likely on the way to!

At night the march was broken at one of Iago's lesser halls, which was perched on a craggy hill overlooking Ynys Mon. Here, in lieu of rooms or even a prison cell, we were pushed into a corral alongside the cattle and closely guarded. I had hoped that this night might allow a chance of escape into the mountains and the roads south in the direction of Powys, but it was clear this was not to be so. The guards were well armed and always alert – being rotated very frequently so as to keep them bright and fresh. Eduard and I casually wandered around the perimeter, looking for a gap in the corral or more importantly – because we could have always climbed over the wooden fence if we needed to – a blind spot where the guards were not in attendance.

"That one is following us," Eduard said, nodding at a particular guard – a lanky youth with long black hair. As we moved around the corral he trotted along a few yards behind us, always with his gaze fixed upon me and Eduard.

"It's as if someone has given him orders to keep an eye on us," I replied as we gave up our search for an escape route and returned to the centre of the corral.

"Well?" Edwin asked. "Any ideas, Cerdic? As I recall the tales, you led the escape of the Wicstun Company from Calcaria when you were seventeen and I well remember the flight from Degsastan last spring. You must have *something* in mind?"

I looked around the company and realised that every face was turned towards me. I missed Lilla; he had always been someone to bounce ideas off, but he was nowhere in sight, the cart in which he had travelled standing empty outside the hall wherein were the king and his thegns. Frithwulf and his father Guthred were looking cynically at me, waiting no doubt for a chance to prove how my plans and my leadership had led us to disaster. Edwin, Sabert and Hereric, along with the great bulk of the company, had a mix of fear and desperate hope on their faces. After all, I had rescued them at Calcaria, held the gate against Owain's army at Catraeth, led them to freedom at Degsastan and then brought then through the death and blood of Godnundingham into exile. Always I had the answer, they believed. Now, once again they looked for me to achieve a miracle. Never had I felt the burden of leadership more. Grettir and Eduard gazed at me, sympathy standing in their eyes. One a veteran the other my right-hand man, both as loyal as the day is long, both knew there was no chance of escape. But their sympathy did not help me. If anything it made me feel worse somehow. I think, though, that it was Aidith's and Cuthwine's faces that were the hardest to bear. Cuthwine's held an unshakeable faith in his father. He knew – was utterly convinced – that I would win because I always did. It wrenched my soul to contemplate how he would feel in a day or so when what I feared had come to pass and I had failed.

I closed my eyes imagining the horror of Aidith being raped, our unformed child being ripped from her belly, my little son being dragged away into slavery. I would most likely be dead before then. The images turned my stomach and I was gripped by despair as I realised I had but one choice to prevent that from happening. But could I ever bring myself to kill my own wife and child? Opening my eyes I looked at Aidith and realised she alone was not looking at me. Her eyes were downcast and her face a mask of despair. She had given up. To be frank so had I … almost. And yet… there was still Lilla and that glimmer of hope.

"Prayer, the only thing left is prayer…" I said to them, and then I added Lilla's words, "and a miracle."

In the morning, again before the sun was fully in the sky we were herded out of the corral and were soon on the road. I looked for Lilla, but as before his cart was away amongst the royal party and when I tried to join him I was pushed back into line with a spear butt in the belly. If anything, conscious no doubt that this was the last opportunity for us to break away, Iago had increased the guard upon us and when a man from Wicstun strayed out of the line he was brutally beaten and thrown down onto the road in our midst. We fell into silence and marched along having given up any hope of making a break for the hills.

So it was that at the end of another long, exhausting day we came again to the land below the great City of the Giants. Now, in mid-February, the lands around us had thawed and the streams and brooks were flowing fast – fed from the hills by the melting snows. We followed the path all the way around the east side of the fortress, which loomed above us throughout the latter part of our journey. We then were led up the rocky trail that climbed the steep route to the high saddle of land. Coming from this side we could see the fort ringed by its tall stone wall and, lower down, running from north to south, just about where the steep hillside met the saddle, we could see the outer wall that protected the actual approach to the main entrance. The path we followed took us towards that main gate, but we could make out the smaller southern entrance that we had used at Yuletide.

Before we entered the gap between the inner and outer walls we halted on a relatively flat area of the saddle beneath the fortress. The sun was going down as camp was set up around us. Eidyn led us to several tents near the centre of the camp and then spoke to us.

"The exchange will be tomorrow. The Irish chieftain, Garrett, will come down bringing the Welsh prisoners. The kings will meet and then the exchange will occur."

"Eidyn, please: Is there nothing we can do to prevent this?" I implored him.

"Iago is set upon this. His mind is made up."

"And you… is your mind made up?" Edwin asked.

Eidyn hesitated and looked around us before he answered, as though fearing he would be overheard. "What if I were to promise you a miracle tomorrow? Would you believe in my God then, Prince of Deira?"

Edwin's eyebrows shot up and he looked at me.

"What do you mean, Eidyn?" I asked.

He opened his mouth to reply, but at that moment Cadwallon appeared. "Come Eidyn, my grandfather wants you."

"Stay close to Lilla in the morning," Eidyn hissed in my ear as he turned away.

"Why?" I asked, but he was gone.

Lilla was not with us – Eidyn's huscarls had always kept him closely surrounded. I could not ask Eidyn what he meant, nor could I get to Lilla to ask him, for I was now certain the 'miracle' Eidyn mentioned had something to do with the bard. The guards gestured that I should go into the shelter that we had been allocated. There I found Aidith, Millie and Eduard still awake, Cuthwine asleep on a makeshift cot behind them. After the long, rough journey on foot and the steep climb, they were all beyond exhaustion. Aidith's face was pale as snow, her eyes sunk into deep hollows. The sight of her twisted my heart.

"What will happen in the morning?" she asked. Her first words to me all day. I took her in my arms.

"We will be handed over to the Irish as part of Iago's exchange, unless..."

"Unless what?"

"Unless there is a miracle."

"What do you mean? What is all this talk of miracles?"

"Nothing, my love... or maybe everything."

"Cerdic, you are not making sense."

"Something is going on. I don't know what it is, but something is going on. I am sure that Lilla has something up his sleeve."

"Huh! If he is involved it will more likely be a trick than a miracle," Millie commented.

"If it works does it matter whether it is a trick or a miracle?"

But even as I spoke the words I did not really believe them. What miracle could there be? Would this Christian God deliver us? Would we receive – what was the word Aedann had once used – 'salvation'. What was Lilla up to? Wherever he was involved, I felt Loki's hand. So was it really Christ or Loki that guided our fate? Was it salvation or mischief: the Cross or the Snake?

Or both?

Chapter Twenty
The Miracle

The following morning we were paraded out of the tents and gathered under guard in the centre of the camp. Around us the entire Gwynedd army was assembling, company by company, under their banners and pennants. All of the Angles looked anxious, staring about them wide-eyed, heads jerking around at any sudden noise, such as the clatter of a Welshman's spear against his shield as he tramped by. There were whimpers from the children and terror on more than one face, male or female. Edwin, grim-faced, took in the scene around us and appeared to be no less resigned to our fate than the rest of us, but then he seemed to stiffen and grit his teeth, turning to address us all.

"I am a Prince of Deira, of the bloodline of Aelle, son of Yffi. I will not go to my fate like a coward. We will face it like warriors and like kings. Form up men of Deira!" he commanded.

"Does it matter? If we are to die, does it matter a damn how we look?" Aelfwulf from Wicstun grumbled.

"Form up! You heard Prince Edwin… your king!" Grettir bellowed and we all, noble or commoner jumped to obey the man who had trained so many of us and whose presence still commanded our instant respect.

We enclosed the women and children from the village. Aidith, Cuthwine, Millie and Aedann's mother, Gwen, along with the others standing in the centre – we like a wall around them. We would give them such protection as we could, futile though this seemed. I guess we hoped they would feel some comfort if only for a short while and we in turn, glad to be doing something, drew solace from that. If we were to be slaughtered or to be handed over into slavery at least we would do it with pride.

Hereric now stirred. He might have been dull-witted and easily led, and like his father, Aethelric, incapable of making decisions, but he had also inherited Aethelric's unquestionable ability to raise his voice and sound heroic at moments like this. "You are the men who destroyed Owain at Catraeth, the men who against the odds smashed the Scots and British at Degsastan. Never forget that and stand firm, men of Deira!"

Edwin turned to me and spoke so all the Angles could hear. "Well, Lord Cerdic," he said, "here we are at last. There has been a lot of talk of a miracle these last few days. It seems only a miracle will save us now. Well I do not know what value I put on faith in the old gods, nor this new Christ, but for whatever worth there is in it, I place my future in their hands."

There was a clattering sound and Lilla, still in his cart, was wheeled out to join us. He was guarded by a dozen warriors led by Prince Cadwallon, who glanced over us with no show of emotion and then sat his horse a few yards away, observing us and waiting for his grandfather to emerge. Aneirin wandered out of a tent and came to stand by Lilla's cart. Spotting the Welsh bard reminded me that I had not seen much of him for several days. I moved closer and asked him, "Where have you been then?"

Aneirin shrugged. "Oh, here and there," he said noncommittally with a quick glance at Cadwallon.

I frowned at him and he winked back at me. 'He knows,' I thought. Whatever Eidyn had hinted at and whatever Lilla was planning, Aneirin knows too. I looked at Lilla who smiled at me. "How is your leg today?" I asked.

He shrugged, "Just as you would imagine, Cerdic," and he too winked at me.

"Will one of you tell me what is going on?" I hissed.

Lilla spread his arms. "I have no idea what you are talking about," he answered. Then he leant closer and murmured, "Not in front of Cadwallon."

I bent my neck and whispered, "Oh come on, Lilla. You are planning something, with Eidyn, I know you are. Tell me!"

Before he was able to reply, Iago emerged along with Felnius and Eidyn. The king looked across at us. For a moment it seemed that his gaze lingered on me and Aneirin huddled beside Lilla's cart. Then he turned away, mounted his horse and started off towards the Irish fortress. His warriors fell into line behind him and then our guards closed in around us and we were herded along in the wake of Iago's army. My hand found Aidith's and she came close to me so that we walked hand in hand beside the cart.

At the base of the path coming down from the fortress was a flat patch of ground covered in moss and bracken. We were marched into one side of this open area and then the rest of Iago's army took up positions behind us along its edge, nearest to our camp. Iago, Cadwallon, Eidyn and Felnius were up in front with us. I saw that Lady Bronwen had come too and ridden out to join them.

On the far side of the space the Irish Llynii chieftain and his house guards were already gathered at the bottom end of the path leading down from the main entrance. Behind them were ranged the bulk of the Irish warband, those warriors who the year before had been raiding Gwynedd. In the midst of the Irish, near to Garrett, stood Prince Cadfan, Rhun, Taliesen and the other captive Welshmen. None of our Deiran men were present. Cadfan was looking hopefully towards his father like a man who believed he was about to be freed. Rhun, I noticed, was staring at the bracken, his face bleak. Had he descended further into his darkness – darkness that even freedom might not heal?

"I can't see Cuthbert," Mildrith said. "Where is he?"

"He will still be locked up inside the fortress along with Harald, Aedann and the others. I imagine the plan is that we will join them soon enough," I replied.

With a shout at his guard captain, Iago moved towards the centre of the field. The guards pushed us along with their spears. Lilla was lying on a pile of sheepskins, his injured leg stuck out in front of him, the cart, pulled along by his horse, rattling across the uneven ground. The horse seemed to be struggling, which seemed odd given Lilla and his pile of furs were by no means a heavy weight, but I thought no more about it for suddenly the cart hit a dip and there was an almighty clatter as the wheels got stuck.

Lilla cried out loudly as he was jolted, but there was something about his shout of pain that did not ring true, almost as if he were trying to deflect attention from something. The guards hastily got the cart free and we were away again, but that clatter stuck in my mind. It was a noise I had heard before. I sidled up to the cart and murmured, "Lilla, what have you got under the rugs?"

He smiled at me but did not answer at once. Then he said, "I am recalling another cart in another place – that Roman Fort, Calcaria?"

"Calcaria? You mean when Samlen One-Eye stole our weapons and Aedann and I got them back?"

"Yes, do you remember what happened?"

I nodded thinking back to that crazy night when I had escaped the clutches of the man who had slain my brother and taken Millie and others prisoner. We had pursued his warband

241

back over the border into Elmet, but then it had all gone wrong. Samlen had captured my men, stolen our weapons and strung me up, leaving me to die. But Aedann, who was still my slave in those days, had tracked us to Calcaria and in the night had cut me down. Together we had released my men and retrieved the cart full of our captured weapons. As we carefully manoeuvred toward the shed where the men were locked up, some of the weapons had fallen out of the cart and clattered to the ground, raising the alarm. We had fought our way out of the fortress in the running battle that ensued, but it had been touch and go...

Lilla broke into my reminiscences, face bland with innocence, a twinkle in his eye. "It would be a kind of miracle if this cart were full of our weapons now wouldn't it?" I stared at him, realisation dawning. Before I could speak, he bent closer to me and hissed in my ear, "You are correct that we have been plotting. I can tell you now that Iago's men *will* fight with us today, *but* Cerdic, they will not act until Cadfan and Taliesin are free. That part is up to you. You have to get them away from the Irish. Do you understand? Now: at the back of the cart is something you *will* need. Be ready!"

"*What*?" I gasped, my head spinning. But Lilla did not reply because we had reached the Irish chieftain, whereupon Iago stepped forward and approached him. Beside this huge warrior-chieftain in the prime of his life, Iago looked ancient and tiny. Garrett glanced across at us, his gaze lingering on me and then returning to Iago.

"We are here as we promised and we bring the Angles you asked for along with Lord Felnius," Iago said.

"Here is Prince Cadfan along with your countrymen. Let us exchange them and then we can agree our peace," Garrett replied.

Before they could proceed, however, Bronwen, who had ridden her horse forward a few paces, spoke up. "King Garrett, there is a Welshman you have prisoner along with the Angles, Aedann by name. Will you release him too?"

Garrett frowned. "He is not from Gwynedd is he?"

"No, from Deira, but he is Eboraccii not Angle. Welsh not English," Bronwen replied.

"Was this man in the Angle's army at Degsastan?"

Bronwen hesitated. "Yes, he was."

Garrett looked across at Felnius, "Well?"

"All the Deiran party are to remain prisoners. My king wishes to meet those behind the slaughter at Degsastan," Felnius replied.

"But he—" Bronwen began, but got no further.

"Enough!" Garrett said. "The man called Aedann is not part of this exchange."

"Go to your father, Lady Bronwen," Iago commanded. Bronwen looked ready to argue, but she could see there was no point. Her shoulders slumped in despair and she turned away. She did not ride to Eidyn. Instead she rode only as far as the cluster of villagers and there she joined Millie, leaning down from her horse to talk to her. I wondered what about, but they were speaking softly and I could not hear what they were saying, so I turned my attention back to King Iago and the Irish chieftain.

"Well then, are we now ready?" Garrett asked impatiently.

Iago nodded his compliance and Garrett turned and gestured at the Irish houseguards, who brought Cadfan, Taliesen and the others out from the ranks. On our side, Iago's guards who were leading Lilla and his cart pulled it forward and we Angles walked along behind. I beckoned Eduard and Grettir to come closer to me and surreptitiously moved forward until I was di-

243

rectly beside the cart. We halted when we reached the two kings so that now, in the centre of the field, were Iago, Cadwallon, Felnius and Aneirin, and under the guard of a dozen Welshmen, we Deirans. Facing us were Garrett and the dozen houseguards who were escorting the Welsh prisoners. Both armies, each five hundred strong, were formed up a hundred paces away from us in either direction. As a single body, we Deirans outnumbered everyone else in the centre of that high moor, not that it made any difference, of course, given that we were unarmed. Unless... I thought of Calcaria and glanced again at Lilla.

Still wearing the hint of a smile the bard slanted his eyes down at the lumpy furs beneath him. I placed my hand on the side of the cart and casually let it slide under the rugs where Lilla indicated. I felt the cold touch of steel. I lifted the rug a couple of inches and saw swords and spear heads, the edge of a shield and... I saw Catraeth. My heart pounding in my chest, I let my fingers curve around the hilt.

Felnius passed by close to me and I seemed to feel his sharp eyes piercing my back. I turned to look at him and saw his face was full of suspicion. His gaze drifted downwards to my arm, my hand... and then his eyes widened in alarm.

"Betrayal!" he shouted. The ruse had been spotted.

"Now!" I yelled and as Lilla rolled to one side, I pulled back the sheepskins. Catraeth was in my hand now and in an instant Eduard and Grettir were also armed. "Get the prisoners!" I said to them, jumping forward at the guard leading Cadfan.

The Irishman shouted in surprise and tried to bring his spear down to attack me, but I thrust Catraeth into his belly and before he fell I was already moving on to the next guard. Eduard bellowed and Grettir roared as they charged the guards on either side of Taliesen and Rhun. With a hack and a slash the Welsh bard and the bishop were free. In the time it takes to blink three times, four Irishmen were dead and we were standing clutching our bloodied weapons in the middle of the field with Cadfan, Rhun and Taliesen safely in our hands.

Garrett and his entire Irish-Scot army were stunned by what had happened, but I knew their inactivity would last only moments. I had to act now. "Men of Deira, to arms!" I shouted and suddenly all them were rushing for Lilla's stack of weapons, hands plunging into the cart from which the bard had miraculously alighted, his fingers working to discard the splint from his leg, aided by Aneirin.

"It *is* a miracle!" I heard Edwin say in awe. Then he shook his head as he came to his senses and hastened to the cart with the rest.

Meanwhile, Iago had rushed forward to embrace his son, who looked shaken by what had just occurred. He was not the only one. Cadwallon, though smiling as he clasped hands with his father, was clearly bewildered. It had all happened so quickly that for a moment everything was chaos: weapons clattering and clanging, confused men running and jostling, shouting incoherently. Above it all I heard Felnius bellow, "Dál-Riata to me!" He had broken away from our line and was dashing towards the Scots. I took a step to pursue him, but realised I would not reach him before he got back to the safety of his huscarls, who were now rallying to their lord.

"Men of Gwynedd, rally to the king! The Angles are our allies!" Eidyn yelled from behind us where he was leading one wing of Iago's army.

"Follow me!" Belyn shouted from the other wing and suddenly, two-hundred-and-fifty armed Welsh warriors were forming up on either side of us.

"Llynii to me! To me!" Garrett bellowed, backing towards his lines and drawing his sword. His remaining houseguards formed up around him, to be joined quickly by the entire Irish warband.

Where mere moments before there had been a peaceful meeting between two kings, now their two armies were formed up, arrayed as for battle and facing each other with murder glinting in many a pair of eyes.

"You tricked me, you Welsh bastard!" Garrett yelled at Iago from across the small battlefield.

"Oh, it was not my trick. Others can take credit for that, but I'll admit I played along," Iago shouted back. "It was too good an opportunity to miss. You Irish fool! You let me march with my army unhindered to your fortress. Did you expect I would not take advantage of that?"

Iago looked around him at the ranks of Welsh and English spearman, all well-equipped and armoured, save for our own company of Deirans who were still scavenging what they could from the cart, aided now by Lilla and Aneirin. The bards stood one on either side, their arms full of weapons. Quite how Lilla had managed to get away with concealing so many I could not imagine. He must have had a very lumpy ride on top of all those sheepskins! He whistled at me and handed me a sword. I saw that it was Wreccan and grinned at him as he passed me a mail shirt and nodded to where the shields were stacked at the back of the cart. I rooted around for a helmet and slapped it on my head. "Better odds than Calcaria," I said and winked at him.

"It's a miracle," he smiled.

"Well," Iago called out to the Irish chieftain, "it seems we are evenly matched, Garrett of Llyn. But we need not fight today. You can get on your boats and go home with no blood shed – or

246

you can give battle. Either way this war ends today."

The Llynii chieftain spat towards our ranks. "You gambled everything here, but you will lose. I will win and today all of Gwynedd will be mine old man, just as it was in the days of my forefathers!"

Beside him, Felnius was pulling on a mail shirt and being handed a buckler and sword by his Dál-Riatan huscarls. He glared at me across the narrow strip of land separating our two armies. "And I, Lord Cerdic, will finish what I started the winter before last. You won't escape me this time!"

Iago drew his sword. "Enough Irish chatter. Prepare for battle."

I turned my head to seek out Aidith and saw that she and the other women were huddled together with the children a short distance away. "Get Cuthwine back behind the lines," I shouted. "Take the women with you, get them out the way and keep them safe."

She nodded and turned away. Then suddenly she came running to me, wrapped her arms around my neck and kissed me fiercely. "I am sorry for doubting you. I should have known you had a plan."

"I didn't..." I started to say, but she was gone, shouting orders, herding the villagers away from the battle lines. She was Lady Aidith again, wife to Cerdic and full of confidence and command. Her man had delivered his miracle and now it was her job to see that his orders were obeyed. I felt guilty – Lilla's plan was nothing to do with me. I shook my head and saw the bard was watching me. "Lilla, she thinks this was my idea. But it was yours."

He shrugged, "As I told you long ago, this is your story. I am not interested in being in the stories. My job is simply to tell them."

"And to create them too?"

"Sometimes even heroes need a nudge," he smiled. "Now go and be a hero, Iago is calling the spears to arms."

I nodded at him and turned away.

We formed up in four companies. On the right was Belyn, next to him Iago, Cadwallon and Cadfan with the Royal houseguards. Next came the Deiran company and over on the left flank Eidyn's men: five hundred Welsh and English spears facing as many Irish. I found myself near Eidyn and moved over to speak to him.

"I take it from what you just said that we are no longer prisoners under guard then?"

He shook his head. "Not now. Aneiren's job was quietly to brief a few key captains and get them on board with the plan. We made sure the warriors that accompanied you would take no action to oppose you – unless things went wrong of course. We even had you watched the last two nights to make sure you did not try to escape and ruin everything."

I nodded, remembering that black-haired youth who had stalked Eduard and me. "So when did Iago agree to all this?"

"Not straight away. He seriously considered Felnius's offer. Truth be told so did I, I will not lie. In my case, my view of all of you changed a lot during that Christmas expedition, but I was still unsure what was best for Gwynedd. Believe it or not, it was my daughter who swayed my decision. Women can be very adamant at times!" he grimaced.

"Agreed," I replied, "but what about Iago?"

"Well, he was unwilling to risk Cadfan to save you Angles. But he was also far from happy leaving the Irish with their enclave here. So when Lilla approached him with an idea that could hopefully save Cadfan and at the same time end this war, he was willing to listen."

"But why not tell us – me at least?"

"In case it all went wrong. If you had failed to save Cadfan, Iago could deny involvement, turn on you and still hand you and the princes over in exchange for his son. Besides which, Prince Cadwallon was an unknown factor. We were not sure how he would react, so he was left out of the plan. Actually, that may have helped us by convincing Felnius that we were genuine."

"I see. You know, I suppose, that Edwin believes this sudden turnaround to be a miracle?"

Eidyn laughed and then looked thoughtfully at me. "You are free and with a sword in your hand, where before you were a prisoner headed for death or slavery. Now you have a chance to win a battle today. Is that not a miracle? We have a saying: the Lord moves in mysterious ways His wonders to perform..."

I frowned. "I am not sure that I believe in your Christian miracles. I make my own fate."

"Ah, but who enables you to make your fate?" he grinned at me, knowing I had no answer to that question. Nor at that moment did I have time to dwell on it. On the far side of the field the Irish were blowing war horns to call their men forward. The Llynii warband, bolstered by Dál-Riatan warriors, looked furious at what had just happened. They were moving towards us with murder in their eyes. I thought fleetingly of Cuth and Aedann, wondering where they were and whether we would ever get them back alive.

"Time to make it now then," Eidyn clasped my hand.

"Good luck!" I shook his hand, then turned back to re-join my men.

Chapter Twenty-One
Battle of the City of Giants

On one side of the battlefield the Welsh and Angles formed up into a shield wall. These huge boards of wood were our protection and we huddled together overlapping the shields and taking as much shelter behind them as we could. Spears held in our right hands were angled over the top of the shields so we projected an iron tipped forest towards the enemy.

The Irish warband facing us, much like their compatriots the Dál-Riatan Scots of Ulster, favoured individual warrior prowess and ferocity over formations and co-operation. Massed on the other side of the bare field, for the most part they carried smaller shields – bucklers - which were half the size of ours. Many of the warriors had forgone even that slight protection and despite the cool of the late winter day stood bare-chested in only short britches. For weapons men wielding axes and swords were sprinkled amongst their ranks, but for the most part they bore short, spear-like javelins – a man may be preparing to throw one from his right hand whilst holding two more in readiness in his left behind the buckler on his arm.

This was an army that was designed for agility and speed just as ours was trained to pin ourselves to the land and stubbornly resist. Hammer against anvil. Bull against gate. At Deganwy the 'bull' had broken the 'gate', burst through and all but shattered our defences. As a result, I knew full well how terrifying the next moments were likely to be. I tightened the grip upon my shield, took comfort in the feel of Catraeth in my hand and waited.

On the far side of the tiny strip of moss, rock and earth, the

Irish started clattering spear against shield, sword against buckler and chanting. Iago responded in kind and soon the Welsh were calling on their God to protect them and slay the enemy. It occurred to me to wonder which side their God would choose this day, for I was certain the Irish were doing the same. Did Christ favour the Irish or the Welsh? Next to me Eduard was chanting "Woden, Woden," and I, with a brief nod to Loki, figured that all the gods were going to be busy this day.

"*Ionsai!*" Garrett shouted. Felnius and the other Irish chieftains took up the same call: "*Attack!*"

Then towards us they came.

It was like a hare bursting forth from its warren or a deer springing into flight. As one, five hundred Irish were roaring, bellowing and screaming as they charged straight at us. Once they had reached fifty paces from our line, those carrying javelins let fly and a storm of iron burst forth upon us. Frithwulf cursed as one bolt caught him in the thigh and he fell to the ground, blood pouring from his wound. A lad from Wicstun was struck in the chest and tumbled onto his back, choking. One slammed into my shield and I stumbled back, Grettir steadying me before I could fall. At thirty paces there was another volley and this time Eduard swore as a javelin slashed past his cheek, leaving a gaping bloody wound.

Then they were upon us.

A man experiences the passage of time in a variety of ways in battle. For some the action slows down. Every motion and movement is like some elegant dance. Like dancers the warriors spin and manoeuvre around each other in a graceful, practiced performance. They can see every move and have an eternity to intercept each other. Each heartbeat gives you forever to see what is coming, and an age to fear and to feel it all.

For others, combat passes in a blur: a swirl of chaotic activity. It's all steel and sweat, stink, blood and pain and then death or life.

What is best, I wonder. Which is worse?

That day, though, my mind was not on the battle. Somewhere in that hut high up in the City of the Giants, Aedann and Cuthbert were locked away with Harald and the others of our company. I needed to get up there and free them. This battle was a distraction and an obstacle. I needed it over – and quickly.

The Irish smashed into our ranks with a crash that rebounded off the hills around us and echoed back at us. Eduard impaled a huge hairy brute that had just run, roaring like a wild bull straight at him. Grettir was knocked back off his feet when the brute's neighbour dodged deftly around his spear point and rammed his buckler into the old veteran's shield. I swung Catraeth at him ineffectually, missing his throat completely and the fellow jumped into the breach and brought his axe down, aiming to smash Grettir's skull. Eduard's shield boss shattered the man's nose, knocking him backwards and this time the back swing from my sword slashed deep into his neck. He crumpled to the ground, his blood spraying us all.

Around us the battle was utter chaos. A few paces away, Edwin, his scalp so recently healed was now bleeding from another nasty head wound and Hereric, looking terrified but still standing in the shield wall, was shouting out incoherent instructions. Yet our company had remained standing against the fury of that charge. Glancing quickly left and right I could see that the Irish had smashed through the Welsh line in at least three places. Reacting to the crisis, both Belyn and Eidyn were leading men into the breaches. Meanwhile, in the centre, where the Irish chieftain's horrific houseguards had hacked deep into the Welsh king's company, I could see both Iago and Cadfan locked in combat with Garrett. Cadwallon was beside them, his eyes shining with excitement and something akin to joy as he cut down an Irish warrior and looked around for another.

Then, I spotted something. The Irish, having almost cut though our lines in three locations, were feeding more men into the gaps, trying to burst them asunder. The result was a slackening of the pressure directly in front of us. If we could push hard enough we might break out.

"Eduard, Grettir, Aelwulf, Halig with me – wedge tactics," I shouted. Edwin heard my shout and glanced at me. "Follow me!" I mouthed. He nodded, wiped the blood out of his eyes and led a half dozen men, including Guthred, around to our rear.

When assembled, we pushed forward out of the shield wall and formed a small arrowhead projecting into the enemy – Aelwulf, Grettir and Halig in the rear row, Eduard with me in the lead. Our job was to keep pushing forward, hacking and cutting at the enemy as we went. We did not care about the flanks – we trusted that the men coming up from behind would follow up and protect our rear and sides.

A youth to my front threw his remaining javelin at me. I brought my shield up and deflected it. Then Eduard and I reached him. He was shaking with fear, but still holding his buckler. Drawing a sword. Eduard bellowed at him.

"Run – just run," I said in Irish. The lad took one long look at the bloodied Roman gladius in my hand and then another at Eduard's axe, gulped, dropped his sword, turned and ran.

Another man took his place, this time a massive red-haired veteran with gold rings on his arms, his chest bare. We had spared the youth, but took no pity on this man. As he moved towards us, Eduard hooked his axe over the man's buckler and pulled it to one side while I stepped in and rammed Catraeth into his chest. As the warrior fell to the ground, Eduard brought the axe back down and sliced his throat open. As he lay dying, we stepped over him and with a suddenness that surprised us both there was no one in front of us. We turned to cut at the men on either side whilst Grettir and the others surged out between us and moved to come round behind the Irish.

With cries of panic and alarm the warriors to our left and right began pulling back, desperate to move away from danger in the form of Eduard and me as we rolled up their line. In an instant the heroism and ferocity was gone and now terror seized them and the entire wing collapsed.

"Well done!" Eidyn roared at me as he led his company around us to attack the Irish chieftain's houseguards from the rear.

I clapped Eduard on the shoulder and smiled at him. Then my smile dropped from my face because I had just noticed a figure fifty yards away. Felnius had managed to break out from the encirclement that threatened to annihilate the Llynii chieftain. He had a dozen warriors with him and he was moving – but not towards us. Instead he was heading for the path that led to the gate into the fortress above us: the fortress in which Cuthbert and the others were still locked up!

He glanced back once towards the battle, caught my eye and gave me a nasty smile as pulling a sharp blade from his belt he turned to run up the path heading for the west gate into the fortress.

I yelled, "The prisoners! Wicstun Company, follow me!" Without waiting to check if they did or not, I hurtled towards the path, but I could hear Eduard's great feet stomping in my wake. We were a hundred paces behind Felnius, however, and even though we had broken through the Irish lines, high up on the walls of the fort I could see more warriors moving towards the gate. We would have to fight our way in when we reached the top. Then – assuming we won – we would have to find the prisoners whilst coming from a totally different approach to that winter's night raid. Deep inside me I knew it was a futile effort — but we had to try.

"Come on!" I urged the men on and we approached the foot of the path.

"Cerdic – look!" Eduard shouted, pointing up the path. Felnius had reached the gate and was going in. But it was not the Scots lord my friend was looking at. The path we followed entered via the west side of the fort. Further round – almost at the due north location – was one of the smaller gates that the scout had reported to us during that Yuletide raid. We had on that occasion taken the south gate into the fortress, but now Eduard was gesturing wildly at this northern one. Distracted by our charge the guards had abandoned it, which meant they had not spotted – for the moment at least - the pair of figures who now scuttled up the steep path towards it.

I gaped in astonishment. Two figures, both women, had sneaked around the battle then headed unnoticed for the northern gate. Against all the odds Millie and Bronwen, armed only with seaxs, were single-handedly attacking the stronghold of the Irish chieftain! Two women whose lovers lay imprisoned within these walls had gone to try and rescue them.

"They'll be caught and killed!" I gasped.

"Never underestimate the determination of a lass when her man is in danger, "Eduard said in an attempt to encourage me. However, I noticed that he picked up his pace nonetheless.

"Damn women!" I cursed and set off again towards the west

gate. I was in pursuit of Felnius, but now I also had to keep the guards distracted and their attention firmly focussed on us whilst hoping and praying that they would miss Millie and Bronwen.

"Frigging pig-headed women," I cursed again.

Chapter Twenty-Two
A Woman's Fury

Spurred on by a desperate sense of urgency as well as a terrible dread that we would be too late, we hurtled on up the path, our feet slipping and sliding, weapons clattering. The path was steep and we were carrying our heavy shields and swords or spears and soon every one of us was gasping and panting for breath. Sweat trickled down my back despite the coolness of the day. Behind me the Wicstun Company ran after me, forty pairs of boots stomping up the stony surface. I looked back at them and spotted Hereric at the rear accompanied by Guthred and a still bleeding Frithwulf limping along beside him, but I could not see Edwin. Where was he?

As we ran I glanced down at the battle on the saddle below and to our left. Our elevated position gave us a good view. The Welsh right wing under Belyn had been broken through in places and a confused formless melee was ensuing. Further over, Eidyn's left wing had now come round the back of Garrett's men and had trapped them against Iago's royal guard. Garrett's houseguards were fighting in two directions, desperately trying to break out. But Eidyn had them in his grip and would not let them go easily. The clash of weapons and the screams and roars of the men echoing off the hillside was a chilling, disquieting sound.

From their stance beyond the battlefield I could tell that the small huddle of village women and children were watching the fight with a mix of horror and fascination. It brought to mind tales Lilla had once told me about how the Romans would entertain the people by letting them watch real battles in which many of the combatants bloodily died. These days I could not imagine ever wanting to do that, yet seeing Cuthwine's little face – recognisable even from this distance peering around Aidith's skirt – and recalling my own curiosity about battle as a boy, I realised that perhaps it was understandable. Maybe the Romans had just been more honest than we were.

In the heart of the battle I spotted Garrett again. He was advancing on Iago. The Irish chieftain's head was back, his mouth wide open and though I could not distinguish his cries from the rest, I knew he was screaming and shouting like a madman. He swung his huge sword and cut down two of the Welsh king's houseguards. Now he was facing Iago. A man in his sixties, Iago was old, but he showed no fear as he hacked at Garrett. The chieftain parried the swing with a contemptuous swat of his sword and then lunged again, this time knocking Iago's blade out of his hand. And now Iago was down in the midst of the melee, one hand raised to block the killing blow. Garrett stepped forward again and swung back his sword.

Gasping for breath, I faltered, running backwards up the hillside so I could watch what was happening. Garrett never made that killing blow. Suddenly, bursting out of the maelstrom, Edwin was in front of him, parried his attack and thrust his sword into the Irish chieftain's throat. As the man went down, Edwin recovered from the swing and brought the sword back in an arc that severed Garrett's head. I saw Edwin reach down and pull Iago to his feet and now they turned to take on what was left of the Irish warband. From the field below we could hear the cheer of triumph come rippling out of the Welsh ranks.

With a shout of relief, I turned my attention back to the front and ran on. The path ahead curved and we soon lost sight of the north gate. I had no idea how far the two women had got. Millie, my impulsive and reckless sister, accompanied by Bronwen, a woman full of love and passion for her lover, were heading alone into the fortress above us. Whose idea was this suicidal rescue, Bronwen's or Millie's? I guessed that it could have been either of them. I flung a prayer at any god that would listen to watch over them both.

A slingshot bounced off my shield and looking up at the east gate I realized we were now close to it. Up on the walls a dozen skirmishers pelted us with stones or let fly with arrows. Somewhere behind me in the company a shriek of pain told me that at least one missile had found its mark. I ignored it and pressed on. The gates were still wide open – after all, the Irish had not being expecting a battle today. Those left behind had been gathered on the walls to watch the pomp and ceremony below. Now, though, the defenders were pushing the gates together. In a matter of moments they would be shut, we would be outside and Millie and Bronwen would be trapped!

"Faster!" I gasped, trying to force my muscles, which now burned and complained with each step, to make it a few more yards. Eduard passed me, still bellowing, so he at least still had air in his lungs and a fearsome sight he was too, the blood still streaming from his face wound, his raised axe filthy with encrusted entrails, bits of bone and brain. Ahead of us, just ten paces away now, the Irish were panicking as they attempted to push the gates shut. We made a final effort, but I could see they had almost succeeded and we were still five paces short.

"Woden!" Eduard roared as he jumped into the narrow gap, smashed his shield boss into one man's face and then hacked with his axe at the men on the other gate. Two men fell screaming and the others took a few paces backwards, mouths gaping at the horror before them.

Eduard burst through the gates and then I was beside him, the Wicstun Company in our wake. Each man was screaming now. The fears of the last few days, the blood and terror, released in a moment to become a type of exultation that only battle can bring.

Inside the fort the defenders had formed up into a body of fifty men. I looked from face to face and could see the uncertainty there. Below us their army was being destroyed, their chieftain had been killed and we could hear the cheering as Iago's men celebrated the victory. So, then, here they were - the remnants of the Llynii expedition. They had thought to come to this Welsh land to conquer it and now all they longed for was escape across the sea to their homeland. If I had the time I could talk them into surrender, I was sure of it. But then I caught sight of Felnius heading off between the stone huts. I saw something else – a brief glimpse only – of two women flitting between the granite dwellings in pursuit.

"Charge!" I ordered and now it was we who abandoned formation and slammed recklessly into the Irish warband. A spear head gashed across my shoulder and I, groaning with the pain, buried Catraeth into the belly of the spear's owner. As the man went down his guts tightened around my sword wrenching the blade from my grip. There was a gap behind him and I leapt through it leaving Catraeth behind.

Not looking to see if anyone was with me I pulled Wreccan from my belt. Named in our Saxon tongue for revenge, today Wreccan's blade would draw blood, for revenge was exactly what I had in mind for it.

I sped on towards the gap where I had seen Felnius disappear. Once through it I stared around. I had emerged into a small circle of huts that I did not recognise from the night raid. Which way had he gone? I heard the pounding of feet and a moment later Eduard emerged, his axe still sticky with the blood of his latest victim. In his other hand he held my old Roman gladius. "Didn't think you'd want to leave this behind," he gasped holding it out to me.

"Gods! Thank you," I said, thrusting Catraeth into my belt.

"Which way?" he asked, still breathing hard.

"I don't know," I replied, desperately peering between the huts. After a moment I made a decision. "This way," I suggested, heading towards where I thought the south gate lay.

"Are you sure?" he asked, but I did not reply because as we passed between two huts we came out into another hut circle and this one I did recognise. This was the same circle we had come to during that dark night. One of these huts was the prison cell. Even had I not recognised it, as we emerged we saw Felnius and six guards nearing the iron-barred door, one of them jangling a set of keys.

As I stepped out into the circle Felnius saw the movement. He turned to stare at me and Eduard then smiled. "You are too late. Your companions will be dead soon."

"So will you, Felnius," I hissed back at him.

"You think so?" He indicated the guards, "You seem to be outnumbered, Cerdic," he said moving towards me. The guards, all except the one with the keys, spread out and followed him. "Today I mean to finish our business begun at Dunadd where I enjoyed torturing you. I got such pleasure in your pain, Cerdic. Had you only stayed for one more day I would have taken delight in killing you, but today I will take even more."

"You are nothing but a coward and a bully, Felnius. You have lost. Garrett is dead and this little expedition of yours is a failure," I taunted him.

"So… who cares? My men and I will get away back to Dál-Riata. Another day will come when we can settle with Deira. For you, though, your time has come now!" He gave a heave of his two-handed sword. I brought Wreccan up to parry the blow. The shock was immense, the weight of his huge sword sending a surge of pain down my arm. But I held on and then pushed Felnius away with my shield. By my side Eduard was backing off as three guards tried to encircle him. He positioned himself so that one of the huts protected his rear and the guards could not get round behind him. Then suddenly he sprang forward, sweeping his axe in an arc. Two of the guards saw his move and leapt out of the way, but the third was too slow and the axe bit deeply into his flank almost cutting him in two. Spouting blood, the man screamed then crumpled to the ground and lay there twitching.

"Don't just stand there gawping," Felnius barked over his shoulder at the remaining five guards. "Kill the prisoners!"

Grinning sheepishly in response, the guard holding the keys fiddled with them in one hand, the other drawing a short sword from his belt as he moved towards the cell door while two others engaged Eduard, all of them trying to keep out of his reach with that fearsome axe.

"No!" I cried. I took a step towards the cell and then jerked back as Felnius brought up the tip of his huge blade and pointed it at my throat. I flicked Wreccan up and with a clang of steel on steel parried his blow, but I could not get past him. I was aware that one of the guards was sidling around to my left, trying to get behind me. Another had manoeuvred into the gap between me and Eduard.

I risked a swing to my right. It forced the guard to back off, but just as quickly Felnius's blade was cutting through the air towards my head. I could not recover from my swing in time so I went down on one knee and brought the shield up. His heavy blade clattered off the boss unbalancing me. Forced to use my right hand to stop myself from falling, I dropped Wreccan. Felnius laughed and moved in, looming over me so close I could smell the sweat on him as I sought to protect myself with my shield. Glancing over at the cell I saw that the guard with the keys had unlocked the padlock and swinging open the gate was bringing up his sword, about to move through the doorway.

Suddenly there was a high-pitched, ear-piercing shriek of outrage from close by and the two women I had been seeking emerged like two avenging Valkyries into the hut circle.

The blow I was expecting from Felnius never came: we all stopped fighting and stared in astonishment at the new arrivals. "Keep away from them, you bastard!" Mildrith screamed, baring her teeth at the Irish guard who was preparing to kill the prisoners.

With a bark of mocking laughter he began turning towards her, but before he could bring his sword to bear my sister, her seax ready to strike, flung herself at him knocking him sideways. No longer laughing, the guard quickly recovered his balance and moved to stab at her with his sword, but Bronwen was there now, grasping his arm, keeping the point away from Millie. Much stronger than she, the guard tore his arm free from her grasp and smashed the hilt of his sword into her chest sending her tumbling way. As Bronwen lay on the ground gasping for breath Millie's eyes widened in terror, but she swallowed hard and slashed at the guard with her seax. Now the man laughed again, tilted his head out of the way of the small blade and grasped Millie by the throat, squeezing hard so that my sister

263

was struggling to breathe. Whilst he was throttling her he fumbled with his sword and brought it round, preparing to finish her with a stab to the belly.

I glanced at the other guards to see that they were standing back grinning, clearly enjoying the entertainment and jeering at their companion as he grappled with the women. Bronwen, still wheezing threw herself forward and landed on his arm, jolting it so that he lost control of the sword, which went spinning away. His other hand released Millie, who sucked in a lungful of air and darted away. Roaring, the guard smashed his head against Bronwen's forehead and she, stunned, blood tricking from her brow, slumped semi-conscious to the ground. Yet the attack had given Millie a chance to recover. She jumped to a crouch and then with a sudden thrust leapt upwards. In the blink of an eye her seax was in the man's throat and he was staring at her in horror and astonishment. Then his eyes darkened.

As I describe it, it seems incongruous that Felnius's men did not immediately rush forward to the guard's aid, but in fact it all happened in a trice, so quickly that the rest of us were stunned into inactivity. As the man dropped dead, blood gushing from his larynx, Felnius roared, "Kill the bitches!" and the spell was broken.

Seizing Wreccan I feinted an attack at Felnius' throat and as he moved to intercept it I dropped the point to lunge instead at his belly. I was not quick enough. He rotated his body so my lunge passed him by and then he rammed the hilt of his sword into my face. There was a crunch of breaking bone and cartilage, followed by a gush of blood that poured into my mouth and down my chin. The pain in my nose was excruciating and my eyes watered so that for an instant I was blind, but I stuck out my knee and thrust it hard into Felnius's groin. The move took him by surprise. He grunted and bent almost double then hugging himself backed off, swearing at me. I spat out blood, rubbed the tears out of my eyes, blinked and looked about me.

Eduard was bellowing in rage and hacking recklessly at his four opponents. One, smaller but more agile and using his nimbleness to avoid the blows, darted in and out of Eduard's reach stabbing at him with a javelin. He caught my friend in the left elbow and though it did not look too serious an injury, the arm must have been momentarily numbed, for with a roar Eduard dropped his shield.

Felnius's guards were good fighters and it could be only a matter of time before they overcame us. We were still outnumbered, even with the women, both of whom I saw had recovered and clambered to their feet. As I watched they began retreating to the cell, but were spotted by two of the guards, who left off fighting Eduard and moved toward them.

At that moment Felnius came back at me.

Fending him off with Wreccan, I yelled, "Millie! No! You will be trapped!" My sister ignored me. Stepping over the body of the guard she had killed she crouched down and came back up clutching something in her hand. She turned and threw it into the cell and then halted at the door beside Bronwen, both women now standing side by side ready to face spears and swords with their feeble seaxs. One guard lunged at them, but Millie skipped away to one side and Bronwen to the other, momentarily confusing him. That left an opening at the doorway and in that opening I now saw Aedann, with Cuthbert standing close behind. My clever sister had tossed the dead guard's set of keys into the cell so that our men could unlock their shackles and free themselves.

Aedann dashed to the body and grabbing up the dead man's

sword, raised the blade and advanced on the two guards, drawing them away from the women. Cuthbert was as yet unarmed, but he was crouching down and I guessed he was looking for pebbles and splinters of the stone used to build the huts. Cuth always carried a sling tucked into his belt – and his aim was deadly. At his back I caught a glimpse of Harald and the other three captured Angles emerging from the cell, but by now I was re-engaged in a furious fight with Felnius and did not see what happened next. I knew though that the odds had turned and grinning at Felnius I could tell from the look on his face that he knew it too.

"I will take you with me anyway, you bastard," Felnius shouted and advanced at me again.

I say our fight was furious, but in truth we were both close to exhaustion now, our movements increasingly slow and cumbersome. We were evenly matched, but perhaps because he was tired Felnius had grown careless. His huge double-handed blade hissed through the air and slammed into my shield, but the momentum of his sudden attack brought him on towards me and I, instead of sidestepping, let him come and bringing up the tip of Wreccan let him impale himself upon it.

Eyes wide with shock and anger, Felnius slid backwards off the blade and fell to the ground. He twitched for a moment, his blood welling and pooling beneath him and then the life went out of him and he lay still.

Resting on the point of my sword to catch my breath, I looked down at my fallen enemy. I had expected to feel triumph and satisfaction at his death, but I felt nothing at all. He was just dead meat.

With Felnius dead, the three remaining guards – Eduard having succeeded in killing the little bastard with the javelin – looked at the odds, glanced at each other and dropped their weapons. Millie now took great joy in jabbing them in the butt with the point of her seax, pushing them into the same cell where her husband and the others had been incarcerated all winter. Slamming the door, she locked it and tossed away the keys then she rushed over to Cuthbert, wrapped her arms around his neck and gave him a huge kiss. A moment later she stepped back, wrinkling her nose, "You smell like a midden!"

"Sorry… but I have been stuck in there for months," Cuthbert grinned warily.

"So now you can have a bath," she said, mimicking his mother's voice as though he were still a small boy come home filthy from the fields.

His response was not that of a small boy though. "How about we share one?" he said, giving her a lecherous smile.

I gaped at him. The shy Cuthbert had changed, or so it seemed. I coughed. "There will be enough time for that later. Come on: let's check that the battle is really over."

"You came back," Aedann said to me, his arms wrapped around Bronwen.

"Promised I would, didn't I? But you can thank Bronwen. Not just for the rescue now either. I have a feeling she had a hand in talking her father into accepting Lilla's plan and I dread to think where we'd be if not for that."

"What plan?" he looked at Bronwen.

She shrugged, "It's a long story, I'll tell you later. My father can be stubborn and I still don't know if he will treat you any better, Aedann, but despite his strong feelings he is a man of honour. When King Iago said he would hand you and the Angles over in exchange for Prince Cadfan and Taliesen, I knew my father felt it was not right. He just needed a little nudging to accept that, so I gave it to him."

"So what has been going on?" Harald asked me.

"Merciful Woden, but where do I start? Come on – I will tell you all about it as we walk," I said, my voice sounding strange in my ears from my broken nose, which had quickly swollen to twice its size and hurt like Hel. But I had got off lightly and thanked the gods for that as I led my friends back through the huts and related Lilla's miracle and its outcome.

Two weeks later, with Felnius and Garrett both dead the remaining Lleynii and Scots surrendered. Iago could have kept the prisoners as slaves. It was generally accepted that this would be one's fate when caught by one's enemies, but with Cadfan's counsel the Welsh agreed to let the Irish go in return for a promise, to be sworn over the bones of a saint from a nearby abbey, that the Lleynii would never again try to reclaim their ancestral lands in North Wales.

Before they were allowed to leave, though, they were put to work. The city of *Treyr Ceiri* was slighted – the huts torn down and the fortress walls broken in many places so they would not be easily refortified. Once done, the defeated Irish, along with the few remaining of Felnius's Scots, boarded their boats and the remnants of the expedition set sail for Hibernia. As soon as they were out of sight, Iago ordered that the victorious armies return to Deganwy.

When we arrived there we found that in our absence the bards and masters of tradition had arrived. Kings ruled lands, bishops and priests spoke the word of God, but the Welsh were very bound to their traditions and beliefs. Much of that tradition was expressed in the words and sayings of the bards – men like Taliesen and Aneirin. They held sway over the hearts of the British and if they spoke against us we could even now be in trouble.

On seeing these poets, I felt anxiety jump back into my chest. We had fought bravely and many of the Welsh were now our friends and companions, but still other lords blamed us for the war in the first place. Winter was over and Easter on the way, so it would not be long before Hussa returned. Many of the Welsh still argued that our presence was disruptive and that Iago owed no duty of hospitality to English princes in the way he would do to Welsh royalty. These still urged him to send us on our way or to hand us over and be done with us.

On the night after our return, Iago called the entire court and our party to his halls. "Spring comes upon us and so there are two decisions we must soon make. The kings and bishops must decide how we respond to this approach from Augustine of Canterbury. Do we join with them and bow to the authority of these Saxon Christians or do we go our own way? "

He glanced up at Edwin and Hereric. "I must also decide how to respond to Aethelfrith of Northumbria. Do we offer our protection and hospitality to the Princes of Deira or do we let this Hussa take them away to their fate?"

Chapter Twenty-Three
'They Took Counsel With An Old Wise Man'

" I cannot believe, after all we have done and all we have been through, that Iago will just hand us over to Hussa," I said. We were in the old hall again. Edwin had called all his advisors together to try and decide on the way forward. Only Cuthbert was missing. He was in his room with Mildrith, 'making up for lost time' as Millie put it, or maybe even having that bath!

"His army is weakened with the fight against the Irish, a fight that despite the role we played in the victory many of his lords still blame us for. They blame you, Prince Edwin, and others too," Guthred said, his gaze flicking over to me. "They blame you for Áedán mac Gabráin's defeat at Degsastan. It was his desire for vengeance that brought the Scots here. The Welsh have lost brothers and sons in this war – men who might not have died had we not come here. That is why they blame us. Iago must be careful. His power relies on the support of his nobles and if they are divided our position is weak."

"Prince Cadfan trusts us, Eidyn too now – I am sure of it. We have allies," I countered.

"We have enemies too. Rhun is not our friend and Cadwallon, despite Edwin saving his life, seems to feel no gratitude towards us. I believe they will say that Aethelfrith is too powerful and that Iago dare not risk offending him," Guthred argued.

I shook my head, "What will Aethelfrith do? Will he march half way across Britannia to attack us here, less than a year since Degsastan – even less since he seized Deira? He has much to do to control what he has. He won't come. Not yet. Not until he is strong enough. Iago can agree for us to stay with little risk to Gwynedd - at least for the time being. "

Guthred shrugged, "Iago is an old man. I think he will play safe. He has little reason to support us."

"Hang on there a moment," Edwin retorted. "Have you forgotten I saved his life at *Tre'r Ceiri*? He owes me two lives now, his own and his grandson's!"

"Even so, I think if he can be done with us then his risk is removed and he keeps his lords happy. I say we leave this rats' hole before Hussa comes to claim us. If we go to the meeting with Augustine at Eastertide then we can go with him to Kent and take service with the Bretwalda - try to get his support for a challenge against Aethelfrith," Guthred counselled. "It's what we should have done in the first—"

Guthred was singing the same old song, but Earl Sabert held up his hand to stop him. "We have lost men here. We have suffered and we have fought. I am reluctant to simply abandon all that. These Welsh are natural enemies of Bernicia and could make good allies. We must persuade them that supporting us and opposing Aethelfrith makes sense. If we do, they won't hand us over to Hussa."

I looked from Guthred to Sabert and realised that they both had valid points. I favoured Sabert's position, but despite my differences with Guthred and arguing against it in the past I could see merit in his plan too.

"Those seem to be our choices. Do we stay and take our chances here or do we go to Kent?" Harald summarised.

Nodding, Edwin's young face was thoughtful. After a moment he said, "Maybe... maybe we don't have to make the choice. As Hereric suggested before, maybe we could do both. I could stay here with Sabert and Cerdic. You Hereric, with Harald,

271

Guthred and Frithwulf, could go with your men and seek help from the Bretwalda."

"Divide our company? As Sabert pointed out when we talked of this before, there are risks in that approach," I observed.

"True," Guthred agreed, "but like I said then, two eggs, two baskets: we also double the chance that a prince of Aelle's line survives and finds patronage."

"What say you, Nephew?" Edwin asked Hereric. "Would you go to Kent?"

Hereric nodded. "I will go with Guthred," he confirmed - which was no surprise to anyone present.

"Well, that at least is decided then," Sabert said, then looked at Edwin and frowned. "My Prince, you must decide what you will do about Augustine. You will recall he implied that you and Hereric cannot expect Aethelberht's support unless you embrace his religion."

"I will decide... just give me time," Edwin replied.

"Very well," Sabert said. "In the meantime we need a reason for Rhun to support us, because if he could be persuaded to do so then that would swing the influence in our favour. What would lead to him to change his mind and argue our cause; take our side when Hussa returns? It must be something to convince Taliesen too, because his word will swing the bards into line. Any suggestions?"

Lilla, who had taken little part in the discussion so far, now said, "I have an idea that will help with Taliesen. I must go and talk to him."

"That's it? You are not going to tell us any details?" I asked the bard, who was being mysterious as usual.

"Not yet."

I scowled at him, but all he did was wink at me. Damn him

and his scheming!

"What about Rhun then?" Harald asked.

I rubbed at the stubble on my chin. "Do you all know he suffers a malady of the soul? A deep melancholy? It has something to do with the loss of his father at Catraeth but I think it is more than just grief.

Lilla looked thoughtful. "I had noticed all was not well with him, certainly, but are you sure of this?"

I nodded. "Indeed... he told me so," I said, relating the conversation we'd had on the way to the bishop's summit.

Drumming his fingers on the table Lilla's expression was thoughtful. "Well now, I may be able to help there. I have some knowledge of herbs that can heal ailments of the mind. Maybe I can try some lupin, elf-dock or let me see dock elder and wormwood. Periwinkle even..."

I stared at him. "Are you saying you can cure him?"

Lilla shrugged. "Well, maybe make him feel a bit better. I will see. It's worth a try."

"If you could heal the man, he might feel better disposed to us," Sabert put in. He looked from Lilla to me, "Would that be enough do you think?"

Before I could answer, Lilla lifted his hand. "I have another idea. When you consider Bishop Rhun you have to realise that there is only one thing he values more than his nationality. Only one aspect of life that will make him – for once – put aside his prejudice against other nations, especially the English."

"You are talking about his faith. You mean Christianity?" Edwin said.

"I do."

Sabert frowned. "So we are back to that. You are suggesting the princes abandon the gods of our fathers to become followers

273

of that religion? I am not sure—"

"Why not?" Edwin interrupted. "If you look back at what has happened to us these last few months, it would be easy to say that our gods have abandoned us, Sabert. Taken our kingdom and deprived us of land."

"I know it can seem like that, but to turn away from all we believe and embrace this new god ... Are you sure?" I asked.

"Would it hurt our position for Edwin to take baptism in this new faith?" Harald asked. "I have heard many kings of our race have done so, but kept the old ways alive too. Need one abandon the gods of our fathers by accepting the new?"

"I think Rhun would expect you to abandon our gods," Lilla said. "What do you say Aedann? You are the only Christian among us," he added, turning to the corner of the room where Aedann was talking quietly with Bronwen.

Aedann looked up and smiled. "*I am the way and the truth and the life. No one comes to the Father except through me,*" he quoted.

"That from their bible?" Harald asked.

"My bible too, my Lord. It also says, '*Thou shalt have no other gods before me.*'

"Maybe I would be willing to commit to that," Edwin said. "I have lost all that I had and been forced to take service with a new king. Perhaps I should take a new god too. I don't see that it could make things any worse – it might just make things better. After all..." his voice trailed away.

I stared at Edwin. Was he thinking about the 'miracle' at the City of the Giants? Surely he knew that had been a trick of Lilla's? Then again, for things to have worked out so well that day – to get the weapons along the coast, up that hill and to the centre of that battlefield with no one noticing had taken quite a bit of doing. So many things could have gone wrong yet did not.

274

Maybe it had been a kind of miracle... but had it been as much Loki's miracle as Christ's?

"Are you serious about all this, my Lord?" I asked.

"I said maybe, Cerdic, I need to think. And make some decisions."

"So then," Lilla said, Guthred will go and seek permission to go to Kent, I will have my little chat with Taliesen and cure Bishop Rhun, and whilst that is going on Prince Edwin will ponder." The gentle mockery in the bard's tone would have got other men into trouble with the young prince, but Lilla seemed immune to such matters and was rewarded by a slight chuckle from Edwin.

I was not able to find out at the time the nature of Lilla's chat with Taliesen. Nor could I find out from the old Welsh bard himself. Even young Aneirin clammed up. Both of them were summoned to a counsel that same day. I was anxious about that at first, thinking that maybe Iago had decided to make a judgement about us at once. In fact it was nothing to do with us. It turned out that the Welsh bishops had come to Gwynedd to discuss how to respond to Augustine. They met in secret and summoned Taliesen to their meeting. Aneirin went too and afterwards all he would say is that the bishops now knew how they were going to respond to Augustine and that the bards' wisdom had been of use to them. Lilla smiled when he heard that.

"I was sure it would be," he commented as he sat in the old hall tuning a harp.

I tilted my head at him. "What have you been up to, Lilla? Your old tricks again? You've been interfering haven't you – manipulating events the way you like to? Huh, they might as well call you Loki!"

"Cerdic, I am frankly shocked at the accusation!" Lilla said, putting on a mock expression of outrage. He had just returned from taking a concoction of herbs to Rhun. The Welsh bishop had been suspicious at first but had apparently agreed to try the potion.

I would have pursued the point, but Guthred and Harald returned at that moment with news that Hereric and his party – Harald, Guthred, Frithwulf and their huscarls – would be permitted to depart with Augustine.

"Moreover, Iago would like us all to go along to listen to what he has to say," Guthred reported, warming his hands at the firepit and then coming to sit at the benches with Sabert, Edwin and me.

"Why's that?" I asked.

"I think Iago hopes that once we are there we might all decide to leave with the Kentish churchmen and save him the trouble of having to decide what to do with us," Sabert suggested. "He could tell Hussa that we absconded, which would hardly be his fault would it?"

"Iago may be looking for an easy answer, but his son does not want us to leave," Edwin commented.

"Cadfan? What has he said?" I asked.

"He had a chat with me this morning. He wanted to thank me for our part in the battle with the Irish as well as for saving Iago's life. He made an offer that could be the answer to our troubles, for a while at least."

"What offer? Guthred asked.

"I will tell you when the time comes. I need to decide my response. His is a very personal request," Edwin replied, sipping at a cup of mead and then staring into the fire.

I paused a moment, but it was clear he would say no more. "Very well then," I said, "but have you decided to stay here and try to gain these Welsh as allies against Aethelfrith as we planned, or might you change your mind and go with Hereric after all?"

"You and everyone else will know soon enough, Lord Cerdic. In fact this journey to meet Augustine is an opportunity."

"How so?"

"You will see," he said and went back to his pondering, leaving me frustrated at his unwillingness to impart his decision. We got up to leave him to his solitude. All except Lilla, who let us leave and went on tuning his harp. Then, just as I reached the door to my room I looked back and noticed that the bard had moved across to sit next to Edwin.

"My Prince ... I have a suggestion," he said and whispered something in Edwin's ear that I could not catch. I glared at Lilla, but he just smiled and waved me away.

A week or so later we set off for the meeting with Augustine in the Severn Valley. This time Iago and Cadfan accompanied us on the journey. As before we travelled to the meeting in the company of the Welsh bishops, meaning we could travel unimpeded through the lands of Powys and Demetia – both of which had been Iago's enemies in the past, but for the present were in a fragile peace.

Just as with the meeting at the end of the summer, this one was held beneath a huge oak tree, but this time workmen were erecting what looked like a large tent nearby to house the meeting in the event of bad weather, which was just as well because the skies above us were laden with rainclouds. In addition to the tent I noticed another change: it appeared that the workmen had also marked out the foundations of a building near to the tree's base.

"What is that? I asked one of them as we arrived.

"A chapel will be built here in memory of the location of Augustine's mission to the Welsh. It will mark the spot where they submitted to the power of Rome and the Pope's authority. Augustine consecrated the spot himself you know," the fellow replied.

"He does not lack for confidence, I will give him that," I commented and got a strange look from the workman.

Augustine had not yet arrived and Rhun declared that we should all withdraw from the location and set up camp a half mile away.

"What's the point of that?" I asked.

"Augustine needs to arrive first," he replied. He gave me a sharp look that suggested the conversation was over.

I didn't see it mattered, but Rhun would not give any more explanation so we set up our camp and waited overnight. There was something about Rhun that left me thoughtful. I had spotted that his eyes were again focusing fully on his surroundings. Also, his voice had lost the joyless monotony of tone I'd got used to and he was more alert and animated than I could recall his ever having been before. I mentioned this to Lilla, who nodded and looked smugly satisfied.

"Excellent, so it's working," he replied. "Now we have to see how he responds to Edwin's request."

I scratched my head. "What request?"

"Wait until tomorrow. I don't want to spoil the surprise."

"You know, I am getting mightily fed up with surprises!" I complained, but Lilla just grinned.

The next day we returned to the oak. Before we went into the tent Rhun rode ahead and established that Augustine had in fact arrived and was waiting inside. Only then did Rhun wave us forward. The Welsh bishops gathered into a procession and entered with Iago, his court and we Angles bringing up the rear. When we got inside the shelter the first thing I heard was raised voices. Then I caught sight of Augustine. He was sat in a wooden chair that was more like a throne. Sitting on either side of him were the other members of the Kentish delegations. Rhun and the Welsh bishops were, however, all standing in front of Augustine and none of them looked very happy.

Rhun was speaking and it was clear that he was displeased. "When we left this place at the end of the summer we were much vexed by the meeting we'd had with you. The assumption that you laid before us was that we needed to change, that we were wrong. Our dates for Easter, the style of our tonsure, our approach to missionary work – all was at odds with the practices that Rome dictates. This left us in a quandary. Perhaps you were right, we said to ourselves; perhaps it is we who need to change. Maybe God had sent you after all. We could not run the risk of being at odds with divine purpose."

"This sounds as if you have seen reason and come to your senses," Augustine murmured.

"Well now, the problem we also faced is that you came across as so sure of yourself and your mission," Rhun continued.

Augustine's eyebrows shot up, "If I am commissioned by God for just this mission then is that such a surprise?"

"Perhaps not and if what we saw and felt was truly the will of the Almighty then we should fall to our knees in acceptance."

Not one of the bishops moved. Augustine's eyes narrowed. "You do not seem to have accepted it to me."

"There was always another possibility, Archbishop. It could be that what we saw in you was not the Lord's countenance, but

279

simply a man's arrogance."

"How dare you!" Augustine blustered.

Rhun ignored him, "And so we prayed and we felt the guidance of the Lord telling us to seek the advice of a wise old man – the man respected amongst our people as being the wisest of us all. We did so, and he said to us that when we returned here today we should allow you to come in first. Then when we arrived we should observe whether you stood to welcome us in the manner of equals and displayed humility, or if you remained seated in the assumption of superiority. If the former, then we should treat you as a man under God's guidance, but if the latter - as actually transpired - then we would know that we deal here with a man - an arrogant, self-important man - and act accordingly."

There was utter silence for a dozen heart beats and then Augustine did stand. But he did not address the Welsh. He simply scowled at them and then turned and walked away to the exit. It was in fact Bartholomew, the priest who had brought the first summons to Gwynedd for us to attend the summer meeting, who now spoke.

"You are aware that your words and actions put you at odds with the Holy Church in Rome? By rejecting us this day you will remain in the cold outside the Church. May God have mercy on you, Bishop Rhun, and on all those souls under your protection!"

"He does, Father, every day. But whatever the consequences, we will not comply with your demands and will return to our mountains," Rhun replied.

Bartholomew nodded. "So be it," he said and then he too turned away and walked towards Augustine, who, grim-faced, watched the proceedings from the doorway. Reaching him, Bartholomew twisted round to look back at Rhun. Lifting one hand he pointed at Edwin and Hereric. "What of the Deiran Princes? Are they free to travel with us should they so desire?"

He addressed Rhun, but it was Iago who now spoke from the benches behind where the bishops stood. "If they wish to travel to Kent, they are free to do so."

Bartholomew gave a bow of the head in thanks. "Very well," he replied. Addressing Edwin and Hereric he asked, "Have you decided what you will do? Will you return with us to the court of King Aethelberht of Kent?"

Hereric walked out to join Bartholomew, accompanied by Harald, Guthred and Frithwulf. "I will come with you, myself, along with these three lords and a score of their huscarls. We wish to travel with you to Kent and be presented to the Bretwalda," said the young prince.

The priest smiled and then looked across at Edwin. "What of you, Prince Edwin, what will you do? Will you come too?"

I heard a creak of the benches as a number of the court, including Iago, tilted forward to hear his response. Guthred had been right, I thought, Iago would be pleased if we all left. It would solve his problems all right. Every pair of eyes in the tent was turned to Edwin: the Welsh kings and bishops, Augustine and his priests and every one of the Angles in Edwin's party. I can confidently say that what happened next no one was expecting, least of all me.

Edwin flung himself down on his knees in front of Rhun. "My Lord Bishop, I would ask that you baptise me, that I might worship your God beside you and receive His blessing. Then I would ask that King Iago accept this miserable sinner into his court."

Rhun appeared stunned and just stood gawping at Edwin.

281

Iago blinked in surprise and then with a faint smile he looked shrewdly at Edwin, knowing that he was to be given no easy way out after all. Edwin wanted to stay, he wanted an adopted homeland in the Welsh hills and by accepting the faith of the Welsh was now almost impossible to refuse. Next to Iago, his son Cadfan was smiling. Rhun meanwhile stared around the tent, unsure how to respond. Here, on his knees before him was a prince of the hated English. Every instinct made him want to refuse this request and cast Edwin away.

Over near the door Augustine and Bartholomew looked on with interest. You could almost see their thoughts writ large upon their faces. If Rhun refused this act of repentance and request for baptism then everything Augustine had claimed would be proven true. Rhun had no choice really. But then I noticed his gaze upon me and the faint touch of a smile on his lips. "Perhaps today can be a day for forgiveness of past sins and a new start for more than one man," he said.

I could see the confusion spread around the room, but I nodded back at him. It was I, after all, who most needed his forgiveness, even more so than my prince and our race, and what Rhun was about to do offered us just that.

He reached down and took Edwin's hand, raising him up from his knees. "So be it," he replied. "You will be baptised on Easter Sunday... Easter by *our* calculation that is!" he added with a final, slightly taunting glance towards the Roman priests.

Augustine, indicating dismissal with a toss of his head, disapproval emanating from every pore, walked stiffly out of the tent and led his party away from the failed meeting.

Thus ended the only real attempt to unify the Roman and British churches in my lifetime, although, as I write this as an old man, I recall Abbess Hild telling me recently that there is to be another meeting between the English and the Welsh bishops next year in Whitby – a full sixty years after the last one – I am indeed an old man! A synod she called it. She invited me along as the only man still alive who was present at that meeting at St Augustine's Oak. It had been a meeting that did not achieve its official purpose, but as far as we Deirans were concerned at the time, it in fact achieved all that we had needed of it.

I remember that next to me, in the tent under the oak tree, Lilla was chuckling to himself. "Well that all worked pretty much as I expected," he said.

Chapter Twenty-Four
Baptism

Augustine might have been arrogant and rather full of himself, although I suppose he was acting in what he saw as a good cause. He was right about one thing, however: there was a substantial difference between Easter in the Roman Church and that celebrated in the Welsh Church. Mildly interested in the reason for this and wondering exactly when this baptism of Edwin's would take place I made the mistake of asking Rhun. I had felt that I should approach him anyway, and did so on the morning after the meeting with Augustine. Feeling oddly hesitant as I walked up to him, I asked, "Rhun... can I talk?"

He glanced at me, "Apparently."

His short reply threw me and it was a moment before I realised he was joking. "I see you are in brighter spirits than when we spoke last," I smiled.

He nodded, "Calmer, yes and not as black in spirit. Your bard is a clever man. I am not perfect, mind you. I do get dark days but I think we all get those. Mine can be hard though," he said, looking sad again for a moment. Then he smiled. "But whereas before I saw no hope ever, there are now better days and even good ones. I thank both you and Lilla for that."

I held up my hands, "Nothing to do with me, but I am glad to hear it. So can I ask you another question... about Easter?"

It was not long before I regretted my action. Throughout a long morning's ride he bored us with a tedious explanation about lunar cycles, calendars and something called a Computus, and why the Welsh version, being based on St Jerome's calculations, must be better than the Roman one that had been written down by someone called Dionysius – but I may have got that wrong since I dozed through most of it! In the end all I was able to get out of him was that the Welsh would celebrate Easter a couple of weeks after the Romans did, so I was still none the wiser.

"Wouldn't you think," I later grumbled to Aedann, "that if this feast is all about celebrating the day this Christ rose from the dead and made several appearances to his followers, one of you Christians would remember when the darned thing actually happened?"

Aedann shrugged, "Sorry Cerdic, I don't understand it either."

When eventually Easter day dawned, the act of baptism was done close to Deganwy in the cold waters of the River Conwy, which was now flowing quickly due to the spring rains and the last of the melted snow coming down from the mountains. Edwin emerged from his room at first light wearing a long, plain white gown. He looked embarrassed and more than a little irritable. A titter from one of the Wicstun men at the sight of him was rapidly stifled when the prince spun round and glared at him. After a moment Edwin flung himself down on the bench next to me and Sabert.

"Hungry?" I asked him as I waved vaguely at the food-laden table in front of me.

He shook his head. "Alas, I am not supposed to break my fast until after the ceremony."

I hid a smile and tore a chunk of bread off a fresh-made loaf, adding it to the wedge of cheese in my hand and taking out a huge bite. "So you are really going through with this then?" I asked, my mouth full.

"I am," he replied, looking enviously at the food in my hand. Eyes narrowed he studied Sabert and me. "You realise I could insist that my lords join me?" A panicked expression jumped into Sabert's face whilst a chunk of bread froze halfway to my mouth.

"Don't worry," Edwin said at last. "I know how much the old traditions matter to you both."

"Sod traditions," I stuttered, "I was more worried about having to wear a dress and look like a…" I trailed off as Edwin glared at me. Quickly I changed the subject, "So you believe in this Christ do you?"

"What I believe is my own concern, Cerdic. What I am doing is right though."

"You mean politically? It's a clever move if so."

Edwin did not answer. The young man was playing this very close to his chest.

Once breakfast was over we all paraded down to the river bank. We Deiran warriors and lords made a fine show: in respect for our prince we had donned our best armour and polished our swords and spears – we had even cleaned the mud off our shields! The women were dressed well too – all of them had been busily sewing new clothes from bolts of warm Welsh cloth since our return from Lleyn. Aidith joined us, despite the birth of our baby being almost due. We walked together with Cuthwine, also in his best tunic, marching between us.

"Are you sure you want to do this?" I asked her. "It's a fair walk down to the river and a steep one back again."

"I will be fine Cerdic. I have had one child already remember. I know what I am doing."

Lilla joined us as we walked on down the path through

woodland dotted with daffodils and snowdrops. "So then, what you said about this all working out as you had expected," I said to him. "You were behind all of it weren't you? Am I right that it was Taliesen who suggested that the Bishops try that little trick of letting Augustine enter first? Did he really dream it up or was it your idea all along?" I asked him.

"I may have had something to do with it, Cerdic," he replied nonchalantly, keeping a straight face.

"I bet you did. Then this business of baptism: what is really going on here? Does Edwin really believe in it all or is he just being shrewd. Is this all your advice again perhaps?"

"He is young, Cerdic, and open to new ideas. Our old gods are often lazy and dormant and do little to bear witness to their power. Acts and marvels… and miracles seem almost a daily occurrence with this Christ – if you believe the stories."

"Like the 'miracle' of the cart perhaps?" I said dryly.

"Well that one certainly made it easier for Edwin to be convinced of the power of Eidyn's and Rhun's God – didn't it?" Lilla said. "Or at least it gave him a good excuse to claim that he's convinced."

"But don't you think the gods, our gods, will disapprove of what Edwin is doing."

"Not all of them necessarily."

"You are talking about Loki aren't you?"

Lilla winked, "I might be. And there are yet more miracles to come this day, Cerdic, you mark my words. At least one," he added. Then he glanced at Aidith and smiled, "In fact I predict two." With that he stalked away leaving me pondering what he meant.

So, Edwin was baptised on Easter Sunday - according to the Welsh calculation of it, naturally. At the head of the procession

Prince Cadfan took Edwin's hand and led him into the river then passed him on to Rhun, who stood there waiting. Rather him than me - the bishop's feet and legs must have been blue with the cold! Our prince allowed himself to be tilted backwards into the river then Rhun lifted him up out of the water and turned to us all.

"Witness that Prince Edwin is born again. He is renewed and all his sins are washed away. Amen."

Wading back to the riverbank, Edwin actually looked quite pleased with himself. As he stepped out onto the rocky shore Prince Cadfan took him by the hand once again and presented him to the whole company. "There are many among us who doubted the wisdom of allowing these men to stay with us and shelter in our kingdom. Well, these Angles have fought bravely against the Irish, saved me and helped us regain part of our homeland. Were it not for Prince Edwin here neither my father nor my son would be alive this day." He looked around at the assembled crowd as though daring anyone to contradict.

I looked too and could see that some of the Welsh lords were shifting about and glancing darkly at each other. Whatever Cadfan might say and despite Eidyn's and Rhun's change of heart, it seemed that many retained private doubts. In some cases dissent was not so private and muttered openly, but with our one-time most vociferous critics and opponents – Eidyn, Taliesen and Rhun – if not now our close friends at least no longer bitter enemies, the dissenters had no focus around which to form. No – that's not quite true: there was one individual who might provide a rallying point for our opponents. Prince Cadwallon would not speak out against his father, but I could see him scowling as Cadfan sang Edwin's praises. Was it just irritation at the attention given to a youth not much older than he? That certainly, but was there something else besides? Edwin was merely a vagabond prince whilst Cadwallon was the son of the heir to Gwynedd – a boy destined one day to be king. Watching his sulky face I recalled the boar hunt and how he had sought the glory of being the centre of attention, openly resentful when that attention diverted to Edwin. He turned away now and was the first to start back up the path to Deganwy and the king's hall.

It was a steep climb and with Cuthwine running on ahead, Aidith and I took it slowly, walking together near the back of the procession. As we entered Iago's fortress she groaned. "What is it, love?" I asked, concerned. "Was the climb too much for you?"

"The baby…" she answered and stopped walking abruptly.

I took one look at her face and saw it screw up in a grimace of pain. "What, now?"

A nod was the only reply. I shouted for Millie and trying not to panic helped Aidith out of the courtyard and back across to the old hall. Millie and Gwen came running, shooed me away and sent for a midwife. Glad to leave my wife in their capable hands I found a spot in the corner of a nearby workshop – empty on this festival day – and for want of something to do picked up a discarded offcut of leather and started to mend a hole in one of my boots.

Cuthwine came looking for me a short while later and found me staring at the sole and swearing at the mess I had made of it. "Dada?"

I looked up at him, "Merciful Woden, but it's a good thing I am a decent warrior, son. I would never make a craftsman!"

"Dada?" he asked again.

"Yes son?" I replied, tugging the boot onto my foot and leading my boy back outside. The Easter sun was well up in the sky now, the day becoming pleasantly warm.

"Aunty Millie said I had to stay outside. What is wrong with Ma?"

"Nothing's wrong, Cuthwine, she is just having her baby. Soon you will have a brother or sister."

"Oh," he nodded solemnly and then fell silent as he pondered each possibility for a moment. "You know, Father, I think I'd sooner have a brother. Girls are silly."

"You won't always think that," I laughed. "But I agree, having a brother can be great," I said, thinking of his namesake, my older brother Cuthwine whom I had loved so dearly. As I was speaking a group of riders clattered in through the gates and began dismounting outside the stables. Their horses were flecked with sweat and had obviously been ridden hard. As one of the men turned towards me I saw that it was none other than Hussa, my other brother! I grimaced and ruffling my son's hair, added, "But then again, some of them are not so great. Go now and play with your friends." I pointed to a group of children on the other side of the courtyard. They were playing Tafl, much as Cuthbert, Eduard and I used to do at their age. "Off you go now."

"Yes Dada," he said and scampered away. I smiled to see him so full of energy, living each moment as it came and oblivious to the dangers all around. With those dangers in mind I glanced back towards the stables and saw that Hussa had spotted me and was on his way across the courtyard to speak to me.

"Who was that?" he asked, looking after Cuthwine.

"None of your concern," I replied, tight-lipped.

Hussa smiled, "He looks a lot like you, brother. Could it be my nephew perchance?"

Did I imagine the look of sadness that flitted across his face, as if he were considering the life he might have led? Hussa had betrayed both his family and his country, not once but twice.

Had he not done so, he might even now be holding Cuthwine on his lap or playing games of Tafl with him. Thinking about that possibility I shivered. "He is no nephew of yours, Hussa, just as I am no brother," I replied curtly. "I assume you want to see Iago?" Saying no more I started off towards the king's hall.

He followed, "Yes, indeed. Winter has come and gone and with spring I have returned as I promised I would. Are you packed and ready to leave for Northumbria, dear brother?" he emphasized the word and sneered at me.

I looked back at him, "I would not be so sure of yourself Hussa, we have allies here now you know. It has been a very busy winter."

He considered me for a moment and nodded appreciatively. "I assumed you would not be lazy - would not just wait for fate to come knocking. That would not be the Cerdic I know and love so much," he taunted. When I simply glared at him without reply he sneered, "Ah, I see the feeling is mutual. But all that said, I wonder if Iago is fully aware of what will happen if he refuses to hand you Deirans over to me."

"Do I have to keep reminding you that you're a Deiran too?" I retorted. Then I shrugged, what was the point? This man had no concept of loyalty. "I have found that threats do not work well with the Welsh," I told him. "Iago and his men are brave and most certainly stubborn."

"I don't doubt it, *brother*, but even stubborn bravery will not last long against reality."

"What do you mean?"

"Simply this: if Iago will not hand you over then Aethelfrith has sworn to come here and burn Deganwy to the ground!"

I stared at him, not sure if he was bluffing or serious.

He cleared his throat. "Well now, let us see what this Welsh king is made of shall we?" So saying, he strode past me and led the way towards Iago's hall with me wondering along in his wake, wishing with all my heart that this bastard's mother had never caught my father's eye!

Chapter Twenty-Five
Adopted Homeland

Hussa stomped into Iago's court, drawing up short the moment he caught sight of Prince Edwin, his hair and gown still sopping wet, standing beside Cadfan. Both were deep in conversation with Iago and all three were smiling. Looking up, Iago saw me, nodded and waved me forward.

"King Aethelfrith's envoy has returned, Sire," I reported and then moved to join Lilla and Sabert who, along with Aneirin, were sitting on benches not far away. Hussa walked forward to stand near Edwin. He seemed confident enough, but I could see that he was bemused, looking firstly at Edwin and then at Cadfan, clearly wondering what was going on.

"Lord Hussa isn't it? What news from Bernicia?" Iago asked. His voice was neutral, almost disinterested, as though he was just being polite.

"As I promised I would, I have returned, King Iago. When I was last here, I asked that you release to me Princes Edwin and Hereric and their companions. I have come to make arrangements for their journey to an audience with my king, who sends you his greetings."

"Then I am afraid you have come on a wasted errand, Lord Hussa. Give King Aethelfrith my greetings on your return, if you will, and assure him of my peaceful intent, but it is quite impossible for the princes to come with you today."

My brother frowned at Iago and in a tense voice snapped, "Why is that, your Majesty?"

Iago pursed his lips as though considering the answer, making Hussa wait. I could see my brother tapping his fingers on his thigh, but he contained his impatience.

At length the king spoke, "Well, for one thing Prince Hereric is no longer a guest at my court. By now he will be in Kent with King Aethelberht."

Hussa gaped at him. "Kent?"

"Indeed."

"I see. How did that come to pass?"

Iago snorted. "Lord Hussa, you might be high in the circle of the King of Bernicia, but I do not have to explain to you the considerations of this court, nor defend the decision of a prince to visit the Bretwalda. And furthermore, you will accord me my royal title when you address me!"

Hussa flushed and gritted his teeth. I could tell he was getting angry, but to be fair to him he controlled his temper. He was better at that than I and much better than our father had been. "I apologise, Lord King. What then of Prince Edwin here? My king is particularly keen to… renew his acquaintance. They are, after all, brothers through Queen Acha."

Iago nodded. "I can fully understand that familial bonds are strong – and it is for that very reason that I must refuse you."

Hussa looked puzzled. He was not the only one. I could not understand what Iago was saying either. "My son will explain," Iago said and nodded at Cadfan, who cleared his throat and glanced at me before looking squarely at Hussa.

"As our Holy Father in heaven this day has received Prince Edwin as a new son, so too do I receive him. Today I stood sponsor for this man in his baptism to a new life," Cadfan announced in ringing tones. Raising his gaze to his rapt audience he continued, "Let all of you bear witness that I will be his earthly godfather. Cadwallon is my heir, but I will aid and guide Edwin as if he were a second son. As long as I live he will have my protection." Then, holding out both hands to the prince, he said, "Come forward Prince Edwin."

There was a collective gasp among the company, not least from me.

"*What!*" Hussa blustered and then gawped in astonishment as Edwin, bowing deeply to Cadfan, kissed the outstretched hands.

Arms locked, Cadfan led him to Iago and the two of them stood before the king. "Father, I present to you my godson, Edwin of Deira."

Iago smiled, "Edwin of Deira I welcome you. I bestow upon you also the protection of the Kingdom of Gwynedd as long as it is mine to grant."

Hussa scowled at Edwin and then at me. There was nothing he could do but stand in sullen silence watching the ceremony. I heard Lilla chuckling close by my side and saw him reach across to shake Aneirin's hand. Both bards looked exceptionally pleased with themselves.

"You old rogue," I muttered to Lilla. "Is this another of your miracles?"

He shrugged. "Cadfan was desperate to help Edwin in return for saving the lives of his father and his son, so I asked Aneirin for advice."

The Welsh bard grinned. "I merely suggested that Iago could hardly turn his own son's godson over to Aethelfrith could he?"

"It only remained for me to pass this suggestion on to Cadfan," Lilla said. "It's the obvious solution when you think about it."

The two of them made quite a double act! I shook my head. "You bards are incorrigible and as for you, Lilla, you really are

Loki's mouthpiece!"

"If you mean there is something divine about me... well I will not argue," he smiled. "Your brother does not look happy though."

He was right: Hussa's face was bright red and he looked fit to burst as he prowled back and forth in front of the happy throng of Iago, Cadfan and Edwin, his hands curled tightly into fists at his sides. Suddenly he halted and gave a bark of laughter, "I see that reason has departed this court and madness has descended in its place. It's all very funny, I am sure. But if I can now have your attention, I have to tell you that this changes nothing. King Aethelfrith wants this man," Hussa pointed at Edwin, "and to deny him would be... inadvisable."

The entire court fell silent as Iago now stood. "Are you threatening us, Lord Hussa?"

Hussa nodded. "Not I, Sire, but my king. I am merely the messenger. I am sorry. I must have been insufficiently clear in what I said. So now I will be blunt: hand over Edwin and his whole party or my king will destroy you!"

"Enough!" Iago roared, "You have said enough. Go back to your king and tell him that we are not easily defeated. We will not hand Prince Edwin over to you. We have offered him a home and our protection for as long as he wishes. Now leave us." He pointed towards the door.

"So be it. It is clear that you are determined Edwin should remain with you, King Iago. Mark this moment though, for this is the moment when you decided your own doom and that of Gwynedd. My master is coming. Not yet, maybe not for years. But he is coming... he *will* come!" With these doom-laden words and without even a bow to Iago, Hussa spun on his heel and strode down the hall. As he passed me he faltered, one eyebrow raised. I shrugged and said, "I told you we had a very busy winter, did I not, brother."

"Obviously," he snapped. On his way out he brushed past Cadwallon, who stood alone in the shadows near the door watching his father and his new brother embrace once more. The young prince did not look at all happy.

"Ah, Cadwallon, come and greet your new brother," Cadfan said, spotting him and beckoning him out of the shadows.

Cadwallon went forward. He glanced at Edwin but ignored him. "I hope, Father, that this decision of yours is a good one. You have risked the enmity of a powerful king. One day we may live to regret this action you have taken."

Cadfan said nothing, but Iago looked thoughtfully at his grandson. "Then we must prepare for that day. We must gather allies."

"Sire," Edwin said, "I have a suggestion in that regard, if I may speak?"

Iago, again sitting on his throne, nodded at Edwin to go on.

"It concerns Mercia – a land you fight and strive with along your borders to the east. It was not by chance we came here, Sire, as you know. Ceorl of that land sent us to you. He is a man who may one day be King of Mercia. Pybba is weak and ill; his heir, Penda, a young child. When King Pybba dies, as he must soon do, Ceorl will almost certainly rule in his place. He hopes that an agreement can be found – an accommodation – between Gwynedd and Mercia. He also hopes that peace with Powys can be similarly reached. Think how much more powerful Gwynedd would be were there peace between you, the three kingdoms in alliance. It may be that in this regard I can help you."

Cadwallon snorted. "You may be able to help us with Mercia, but peace with Powys will be hard to win."

297

"That does not mean we should not try, Grandson," Iago replied. Then he smiled, "But come, it is Easter and we have much to celebrate. These matters are not for discussion today." He clapped his hands and called, "Bring out the ale!"

There was cheering at that news and soon a musician had struck up a jolly tune and several warriors were banging their tables calling for beer. Unnoticed by all save Lilla, Sabert and I, Prince Cadwallon gave every one in the hall a disapproving glare then made his way to the door and slipped outside.

"Trouble for the future, I feel," Sabert said thoughtfully looking after him and for a moment I felt gloom descending on the three of us.

"Or perhaps merely a sulking youth," Lilla commented.

"A sulking youth who is a prince and heir to a throne can still be trouble," the old earl countered.

"Maybe... but not today," I said. "Cadfan will keep him in line. For today our troubles are in the past," but as I spoke, I unobtrusively fingered my Loki pendant.

Sabert laughed and the gloom was gone. "Yes, thanks to Edwin we have an adopted homeland; we have shelter and are in the service of the mighty King of Gwynedd. We can rest and think. Gods but I feel so tired. Rest will be good. I am feeling my age," the old earl groaned.

"Beer would be good too," I commented as I watched Iago's servants roll out casks of ale and prepare to serve it.

I was filling my drinking horn and anticipating savouring the contents when Millie appeared at my shoulder. "Cerdic, come with me," she said.

A sudden panic gripped me. In all the tense affairs of the court I had momentarily forgotten I was about to become a father for the second time. "Aidith is she—"

298

"Aidith is fine. She wants you to see your daughter."

My heart leapt inside me. "Daughter?"

Millie nodded, "She is beautiful. Come and greet her."

A while later I was holding my scrap of a daughter in my arms. She was looking up at me out of two tiny, unfocussed dark eyes and was bald save for a wisp of hair curled up on her reddened brow. I thought 'beautiful' was stretching it, but I loved her instantly. Cuthwine was sitting to one side of me staring with puzzlement at his new sister. We were both near Aidith's bed and I had just told her about Edwin and Cadfan, as well as Iago's rebuttal of Hussa.

"Then we are safe?" she asked, her voice tired but relieved.

I shrugged, "For now, though who knows what the gods have in store for us? But meantime we have a home and a lord and... yes my love, we are safe."

"Just as you promised," she said softly, laying a hand on my arm.

"Just as I promised," I echoed, recalling what had seemed a foolish commitment at the time. Aidith smiled at me and I felt again that pang of guilt. She trusted me because we were safe now, but how much had I really influenced things for the better? How much credit could I take for our safety? If little, then that raised another question: how much control did I have over what was yet to come? I pushed that thought to one side. In the end all a man can do is be true to himself, trust in his wyrd and put faith in the gods... and perhaps a good sword as well. I smiled back at Aidith and kissed her.

"Well then, there is just one more thing to decide, and Cerdic," she said solemnly, "it's the most important thing of all."

"What is that?" I asked, unsure what she meant.

"What name shall we give our daughter?"

I laughed and held up the tiny form so all three of us could look at her. "I was about to tell you that on my way through the hall I asked Aedann if there was a Welsh girl's name that means *'miracle.'* It seemed to me that after all the bloody battles we have endured and the miracles that brought us through them safely, such a name would be a good one for this little scrap. Aedann said the closest he could think of was a name that means *'gift from God'*. I am not sure from which god, but after everything that has happened it feels as if our baby girl is a gift indeed."

"So then what did Aedann say? What is the Welsh for *'gift from God'*, Cerdic? What is our daughter's name?"

I smiled, "Sian," I said.

The End

Historical Notes

At times I have referred to the years in which the *Northern Crown Series* is set as the *'darkest years of the dark ages'* not just because they are dangerous times but really meaning that so little is known about what went on due to a paucity of documented evidence. The time period of the exile of Prince Edwin and Hereric occupies the very heart of this period and in trying to write a story about what happened to them a writer has to turn to tradition and fable in an attempt to shed light on what little knowledge there is.

From the point that the Princes cross over the border into Mercia until the end of the exile period virtually nothing reliable is recorded at all. Indeed, due to much confusion that exists around the histories of Deira and of Bernicia (principally to do with mixing up Aethelric of Deira who died around 603 or 604 probably during the annexation of Deira by Aethelfrith, and Aethelric of Bernicia - Aethelfrith's father -who died around 588) that some writers and historians have concluded that the invasion of Deira and this exile started as early as 588 when Edwin would have been about 3! This, however, is nowadays recognised as confusion caused by merging of two people into one. Today we believe that the exile began around 603 or 604. Edwin would have been about 17 and Hereric a couple of years younger.

What then happened? All we know for certain is that the exile was prolonged and that Edwin and Hereric spent years wandering from court to court. Certainly some of that time was in

Mercia, probably when Ceorl became king. We also know of Edwin visiting East Anglia and Hereric travelling to Elmet. But all of that is a tale for a later book. This book focuses on the very beginning of this exile and in truth we KNOW almost nothing. That said there is the role of tradition and fable. There is a myth in Welsh traditions that Edwin at least spent sometime in the court of the Kings of Gwynedd. This tale speaks of him being adopted in some fashion by Cadfan as well as being baptised by Rhun.

The myth is recorded in a very unreliable source, Geoffrey of Monmouth's '*The History of the Kings of Britain*'. Monmouth was really a historical fiction author rather than a historian, his goal being perhaps to entertain rather than to inform and educate. His version of history is almost completely fiction and the reader that consults him must take what he says with not so much a pinch as a bucket of salt. But this tale – of Edwin spending his exile in Gwynedd, being baptised by Rhun and adopted by Cadfan (both real people) and eventually gaining the enmity or rivalry of Cadwallon is embedded in many a work of history so as to have become accepted by many. Other historians pour scorn upon it but given the complete lack of reliable knowledge on this period I took the view that it was better to take a myth than nothing.

What about the Irish raid? Well it seems that before the Romans came to Britain an Irish presence existed in North Wales. Tribes from Leinster travelled across the Irish sea in the 1st century BC and settled in Ynys Mon (Anglesey) and along the north coast as far as the Llyn (or Lleyn) peninsular. Ancestors of the Welsh known as the Ordovices may also have lived in the area. The Romans, who arrived in the vicinity in the 70s AD, called the region *Venedotia* in Latin.

Venedotia remained under Roman control until around 380 when the Roman legions withdrew from the region. Nennius, a 9th century monk, recorded that after this time the region was defenceless and became victim to increasing raids from Ireland.

So, soon after the Romans left, the Northwest of Wales was in effect an Irish province. The expanding Irish domains in South and North Wales along with the Picts raiding down the East coast and the Saxons along the East and South created a crisis that required action. In the Mid-5th Century a certain 'Cunedda' led his sons and their followers in a migration from Manau Goddodin (around Edinburgh) to the North Welsh coast. It is possible that this was at the instigation or suggestion of Vortigern who also (according to tradition) invited the Saxons Hengest and Horsa to settle in Kent. The suggestion is that Vortigern was High King of the British and was responding to Irish raids in the Gwynedd area as well as Pictish raids down the East coast.

Cunnedda was married to the daughter of Coel Hen the powerful King of the whole of the North - the man immortalised by the children's rhyme 'Old King Cole'. Cunneda's sons would rule not just Gwynedd but also huge chunks of the North and West of Britain. The same monk, Nennius, records how Cunedda fought the Irish in North Wales. He then established the kingdom of Gwynedd. It would take successive generations of kings to finish the task of clearing the Irish out and in the mid-6th Century, King Maelgwn completed the task. He probably was the King who built or at least rebuilt Deganwy.

What is left of Deganwy castle are the twin peaks and various bits and pieces of what are mostly a later castle destroyed in the wars between much later Welsh Kings and Kings of England. Yet there are parts of what may be the original ramparts in existence.

The 7th Century rulers of Gwynedd: Iago, Cadfan and Cadwallon existed and held court at Degwany as well as other locations, including possibly Abberfawr in Anglesey. Their descendants will rule Gwynedd for hundreds of years to come.

However, over the years, the Irish certainly raided the coast of Wales and whilst the specific details of the raid in this book are fiction it is by no means far-fetched.

Tre'r Ceiri is a real location in the Llyn Peninsular and is considered one of the most impressive Iron Age hill forts. It was certainly used by the Romans and pottery and other evidence suggests occupation certainly into the 5th or 6th Centuries. It sits, as I have described, on the top of a steep sided hill, which is a challenge to climb. The village of *Clynnogg Fawr*, tucked between the mountains and the sea exists today and there is a church on the spot of an abbey which was founded just shortly after the period of this book.

The first Archbishop of Canterbury, St Augustine arrived in Kent in 597 and converted the Bretwalda, King Aethelberht. He certainly invited the Welsh bishops to a conference around 603 AD and the subjects I mention, including the Welsh hairstyles, were discussed. There was a follow up meeting some months later. Where did the meeting take place? A number of locations have been suggested: Aust Cleeve, Martin Hussingtree, Alfric, Rock, and at the Mitre Oak, Hartlebury all in and around the Severn valley. Rock is considered to have the superior claim, for in Saxon days the village was called Ther Ac (The Oak) and in Domesday is rendered Halac (Holy Oak). Wherever the location, the Welsh solution was indeed to get Augustine to arrive first and then point out that his failure to stand when they arrived after him showed his contempt for them. It would take until the Council of Whitby in the 660s to resolve the divide with the Celtic Church. A wise old man or hermit was supposed to have suggested this tactic.

What then of this wise old man – was that Taliesen? Well, I may be stretching matters here but certainly Taliesen and Aneirin were both powerful and respected 6th to 7th century bards and poets who held a lot of influence over the hearts and minds of the Welsh people and kings, and their poems are not only masterpieces but also, in many ways, the only evidence for much of what went on in these *darkest years of the dark ages'*.

So then, Edwin has his sponsor and Cerdic his growing family and a home. What will happen next? Can they build a power-base to challenge Aethelfrith? There are other mighty Kingdoms like Powys to contend with – will they be able to overcome all the obstacles and find a way home? And what will Hussa be up to during this time?

The story will continue in Book Four of the Northern Crown Series, *The White Chariot.*

The Northern Crown Series

Book One - The Amber Treasure
ISBN: 97809568103-1-1
"I will take care of the body of my lord and you can carry the sword, story teller. For all good stories are about a sword."

6th Century Northumbria: Cerdic, the nephew of the great warrior Cynric, grows up dreaming of glory in battle and writing his name in the sagas.

When war comes for real though, his sister is kidnapped, his family betrayed and his uncle's legendary sword stolen. It falls to Cerdic to avenge his families' loss, rescue his sister and return home with the sword.

Winner of a B.R.A.G. Medallion

Book Two - Child of Loki
ISBN: 97809568103-2-8
A divided land ... a divided family.

The Battle of Catraeth has been won and Cerdic's homeland is safe ... but for how long?

The Northern British were crushed but yet more enemies have risen to replace them.

Soon Cerdic and his friends must go to war again - against the Scots and Picts north of Hadrian's wall. He goes to help his country's allies - the Bernicians - under their great warlord, Aethelfrith.

But what is Aethelfrith's true design? How ambitious is he and how far will he go to fulfil his dreams? And what is Cerdic's treacherous half brother, Hussa up to in these fierce wild lands?

The Hourglass Insitute Series

Book One - Tomorrow's Guardian
Time Travel Sounds like fun until you try it.

Tom Oakley experiences disturbing episodes of déjà-vu and believes he is going mad. Then, he discovers that he's a "Walker"
- someone who can transport himself to other times and places.

Tom dreams about other "Walkers" in moments of mortal
danger: Edward Dyson killed in a battle in 1879; Mary Brown
who perished in the Great Fire of London; and Charlie Hawker,
a sailor who drowned on a U-boat in 1943. Agreeing to travel
back in time and rescue them, Tom has three dangerous adven-
tures, before returning to the present day.

But Tom's troubles have only just begun. He finds that he's
drawn the attention of evil individuals who seek to bend history
to their will. Soon, Tom's family are obliterated from existence
and Tom must make a choice between saving them and saving
his entire world. Tomorrow's Guardian is a Young Adult Fantasy Novel.

Book Two - Yesterday's Treasures
ISBN: 97809564835-8-4
Former Friends make the deadliest of foes.

'Yesterday's Treasures' can mean the destruction of tomorrow.

The Praesidium Series

Book One - The Last Seal
ISBN: 9780956810397
Gunpowder and sorcery in 1666...

17th century London - two rival secret societies are caught in a battle that threatens to destroy the city and beyond. When a truant schoolboy, Ben, finds a scroll revealing the location of magical seals that binds a powerful demon beneath the city, he is thrown into the centre of a dangerous plot that leads to the Great Fire of 1666.

"an awesome array of characters which definitely included the good, the bad and the ugly, and an amazing plot!"
" This young adult historical fantasy had me totally engrossed and I would recommend it to anyway who loves historical fantasy/fiction (especially British) whether you're a teen or an adult. "
FIVE STARS
The Slowest Bookworm

"Denning has a real thirst for historical knowledge and this certainly shines through in his books, with his descriptions of London in 1666 making you feel as if you were in the middle of the raging fire."
YA Yeah Yeah

Winner of a B.R.A.G. Medallion

The Nine Worlds Series

Book One - Shield Maiden
ISBN: 9780956810373

This is the world as it might have been if the stories been true…

Shield Maiden is a Historical Fantasy Adventure For Children of Ages 9+

Anna is a 12 year old girl growing up in a Saxon village in 7th century Mercia. Her life changes when she finds a golden horn in the ruins of a Roman Villa. Soon an ugly dwarf, a beautiful sorceress and even her own people are after her.

What powers does the horn have and why does everyone want it?

And why is Anna the only one who can get a note out of it?

About Shield Maiden

Shield Maiden is the first book in The Nine Worlds series in which the historical world of Anglo-Saxon England meets the mysterious world of myths and legends, gods and monsters our ancestors believed in.

This is the world as it might have been had those stories been true…

Won a Silver Children's Literary Classics Award in 2012.

Lightning Source UK Ltd.
Milton Keynes UK
UKHW010629210820
368607UK00001B/353